THE
PEKING CONNECTION

Peter Hain

For Mike & Annebritt,

Thank you for your hospitality
& help

Kampala, Uganda. 10-12 October 1995

[signature]

LAWRENCE & WISHART LTD
London

Lawrence & Wishart
144a Old South Lambeth Road
London SW8 1XX

First published 1995 by Lawrence & Wishart
Copyright © Peter Hain, 1995

The Peking Connection is a work of fiction. The
characters in it have been invented by the author. Any
resemblance to people living or dead is purely
coincidental.

ISBN 0 85315 823 1

British Library Cataloguing in Publication Data.
A catalogue record for this book is available from the
British Library.

Typeset by Jan Brown Designs
Printed and bound in Great Britain by
Redwood Books, Trowbridge

For Howard and Elaine Davies,
simply the best

ACKNOWLEDGEMENTS

Grateful thanks to my Pat, Sam and Jake for putting up with
yet another project; to my parents and Roger Williams for their
help; to Vicky Grut for her excellent editing and frank advice;
and for her support to Tessa Sayle, good friend and literary
agent whose memory remains with us.

PROLOGUE

Outside, dawn had broken and the sun was shooting out fingers of gold. But inside the prisoner had lost all sense of night and day. The bright light burning constantly had seen to that. Whichever way the prisoner turned or however tightly closed the eyes, light pierced through, blurring consciousness into semi-consciousness. 'We'll leave it on to keep you company. So you don't get lonely.' The thick accent made the sneer more biting, the mirthless laughter more sinister.

They had gone with a promise to 'come and talk again'. The door banged shut and was locked, leaving utter loneliness, and numbing fear. Fear of being forced again to stand at an angle to the wall, feet a yard from it, fingers resting against its whitewashed surface taking bodyweight; simple, yet devastating. Any slump, and a strategic kick sent the prisoner back into position. At first complete concentration was needed simply to stop screaming. Later, senses so deadened, the prisoner could barely produce a grunt in answer to the endless questions – eventually sliding down the wall, collapsing on the concrete floor, too exhausted even to groan.

Now, as their voices died away, the prisoner tried to get a grip. The room was bare, save for some old sacks in a corner. Staggering over, aware for the first time of the bitter cold. Disorientating, that. Surely this was a warm country? Well, not now. Not at night anyway. Not here in this remote building. Sharp memories returned: being kept groggy on the car's backseat, being lifted out into a helicopter, half conscious and aware only of the deafening noise. Minutes later, bundled out again in the dusk and deliberately allowed to glimpse the total isolation: no help to call upon.

Ever since the abrupt detention, trying to question them. What did they want? Where were they going? Who *were* they? But they just fired more questions of their own. The prisoner could only keep repeating: 'You are making a terrible mistake. I don't know what you are talking about. I don't know anything. Anything. Anything.' Even now, hours later, denials bouncing round an aching head, seeming to echo away into the freezing cold – only to be thrown back by the dazzle of the light. Eyes closed, thinking: I just can't believe this is really happening to me. Then, silence broken only by the call of a dove, a sudden, even more bewildering thought. They wouldn't go to all this trouble for nothing. Perhaps I am guilty after all? If only they would tell me what I am supposed to have done.

CHAPTER ONE

Bound for the Great Wall, the minibus assigned to the Noted Persons Delegation pulled out of the Hotel and threaded through the bicycles into East Chang'an Avenue. Jim Evans was fascinated by the dexterity of the cyclists weaving about the road, dodging each other, avoiding buses and cars and ringing their bells incessantly to warn wayward pedestrians. The din was increased by continuous announcements from loudspeakers on the trolley buses giving advice to passengers. Even louder were the constant exhortations erupting from speakers on patrolling vans. At first Evans thought he was hearing political propaganda: in fact the purpose was to control traffic.

The 30 mile journey northward to the tourist section of the Wall at Bedalung took longer than expected. Although cars were conspicuously rare, the roads were filled with packed buses, lorries, handcarts and bullock carts, some piled high with produce or live chickens in bamboo baskets. There were still more cyclists and families walking along leading goats or driving pigs or cows.

Vast fields stretched into the distance framed by trees lining the roads. Despite the great sense of space the countryside was too full of life to be desolate. There were clusters of commune buildings and everywhere peasants grouped in their Production Brigades tended fields of grain and vegetables.

'What's that?' Jenny Stuart pointed along the edge of the road where winnowed grain was spread thinly in bands several feet wide.

'They lay it out by the roadside to dry,' Evans explained. 'It's the only free hard land available.'

He knew already from his preparatory reading that only one-tenth of China's land was cultivable. Other statistics almost defied comprehension, like the 35 million people employed simply to spread sewage for manure on their fields. For at least 4,000 years it had been the law that all excreta should be used as fertiliser and collectors called daily at every house with their barrows.

The driver revved his engine impatiently as they slowed up behind a long queue of traffic in the foothills. Wang Bi Nan, the interpreter assigned to them for the day looked embarrassed.

'I am sorry for the delay. Unfortunately we have chosen to visit our Great Wall on the same day as many local Chinese have a holiday.'

Wang, a slight, thin man, balding with horn-rimmed glasses, had joined the minibus just as it departed, taking the place of the official interpreter who had been with the delegation since their arrival.

The minibus was grinding its way up a steep hill beside a sparkling stream which disappeared between neatly cultivated terraces towards the fields below. Then, through a break in the trees, Evans caught his first sight of the Wall. He could barely contain his excitement. He had read all the blurb: built of great stone slabs, 2,000 years ago when China was divided into warring kingdoms, it stretched 2,800 miles from the eastern seaboard to the north west and was the only humanly created landmark visible from outer-space. It dominated the scene, perched high up, straddling hill tops, a splendid structure winding its way through mountains misty in the distance.

Wang singled out Evans as the bus slipped into the crowded parking area. 'Let me take a photo of you with your camera. For your friends back home. You can tell them President Nixon was photographed on the same spot during his historic visit in 1972.'

'Will your reputation survive that?' Jenny Stuart's sarcasm was ignored by Wang as he took Evans by the arm and led him firmly up the wide steps onto the Wall itself.

About ten metres wide and anything up to a 40 metres high in some places, the pedestrian section on top was paved and had parapet walls on either side where sightseers could lean. Further along the two men climbed shallow steps the width of the wall, taking them on to the next paved section.

Like any good guide, Wang indicated landmarks and trotted out historical facts and figures. Then, pointing to the south-west, he said sharply,

'Twenty miles down there; that is where you were yesterday at the Atomic Energy Authority Institute. Did you enjoy your visit?' Without waiting for a reply, he swung round suddenly, 'I hear you were rude to one of our scientists.' His smile was belied by hard, watchful eyes.

Evans was at a loss for words: what could this suddenly rather intimidating interpreter be getting at? Sensing his uncertainty, Wang continued, 'The scientist you sat next to at lunch. He was most insulted. He told us he had met many Western visitors, but none had questioned his professional integrity before.'

'What? I don't know what you are on about.'

But Wang brushed aside his response, 'As you know he is one of our leading researchers in nuclear energy. That is why we agreed to your request to visit the Institute. We know of your interest in the subject. But our team of scientists there are dedicated to peace. They are most upset that you might think otherwise.'

'I don't think otherwise.' Evans' initial confusion turned to anger. He disliked Wang's manner. But, collecting himself, he said stiffly, 'There has obviously been a misunderstanding. I must apologise to my hosts. Please do so for me.' Better to just make a straight apology. He didn't see the point in arguing that his brief reference to his interest in the technology of conversion from nuclear energy to weaponry had clearly been misinterpreted.

'Have you been photographed for posterity yet?' Jenny called as the rest of the group began to join them, pulling on the handrail set in the sidewall to assist the climb up the sharp rise.

'Oh, well I might as well do it,' she said as Evans shook his head, his mind still churning. He felt rather uncomfortable posing while the rest of the group watched. They all smiled and called out joking comments, causing him to hunch his tall frame as was his habit when embarrassed.

'Damn it. I'll have to take another shot. Wang walked behind you that time blocking the view. Smile please.'

They all took pictures of each other and, when Wang firmly refused to pose with them, persuaded him to take snaps of the whole group with each of their cameras in turn. The lighthearted banter of the occasion lifted Evans' unease. But, watching as Wang struggled awkwardly with the different cameras in marked contrast to the friendly proficiency of the official interpreter, Evans wondered again why she had been replaced for the day.

A group of Chinese teenagers passed by chattering excitedly. One, wearing a digital watch, posed by the side of the wall as another took his photo. Then he passed the watch round so each of them could have their picture taken, sleeve rolled up ostentatiously, the watch prominently displayed. Another sign of creeping consumerism Evans thought, recalling the car parked outside the main gate of the ancient Forbidden City which they had visited on their first day. An enterprising photographer had a queue of Chinese waiting to have their pictures taken standing by the car's open door, hand resting nonchalantly on the steering wheel feigning ownership.

'I shall pass on your apologies as you asked.' Wang came up quietly, making Evans jump and jerk his gaze back from the sheer drop to the rocks below. 'I trust that will be the end of the matter. If you want invitations to meet scientists during the rest of your stay you must avoid insults.' With that, Wang nodded stiffly and strode back to the mini-bus where he sat silently beside the driver, brooding during the return journey.

Evans pulled out his notebook. At 33, he was one of the youngest professors in his field of nuclear radiation. He had made copious notes the previous day while visiting Institute. The place had intrigued him. It wasn't just the old equipment, left by the Russians when they had suddenly withdrawn their technicians in 1960 after the Sino-Soviet split. Nor the rudimentary safety measures on the main reactor which had appalled him. Nor their hosts who had been more friendly and hospitable than he had expected. (He couldn't imagine the canteen at Aldermaston turning out a twelve course lunch of such delicacy.) No, it had been their guide, a scientist in green overalls who had spouted out facts in a machine-like monologue, an impressive feat of memory, since his English was otherwise poor. But some of the spouted information didn't add up and Evans had put a series of question marks in the margin of his notes. He flicked idly through the pages and then stopped, shaken: the relevant notes were missing. It appeared that a page had been neatly removed.

❖

Captain Maritz Swanepoel was sweating profusely. It was cold at this time of the year and there was no heating in the room, but his shirt was damp. He couldn't stop it. Every time he had to set the mechanism, the tension got to him. His colleagues said he sweated because he was unfit and pot bellied. His wife maintained it was because his diet was so bad his kidneys didn't function properly anymore. He had a more simple explanation: fear – an odd emotion for a man whose trade was terror.

Earlier in his career he had been a member of the notorious Z-squad in BOSS, the South African Bureau for State Security. The squad had given itself the final letter in the alphabet because it specialised in final solutions: assassination of apartheid's enemies. Swanepoel had become expert in making up and sending parcel bombs.

His first victim was Dr Eduardo Mondlane, the President of the Mozambiquan liberation movement, FRELIMO, who was killed in Tanzania in 1969 when a letter bomb exploded as he opened it on his desk. Another was Abraham Tiro, a leading figure in the radical black South African Students' Organisation, killed instantly in exile when he opened a parcel sent to a Roman Catholic Mission near Gaborone, Botswana, in February 1974.

When BOSS officially ceased to exist in August 1978, Swanepoel transferred to its successor, DONS, the Department of National Security. Later he joined South Africa's National Intelligence Service, the NIS. His expertise was still in demand as letter bombs were directed all over Africa at organisers of the South African resistance movement, the African National Congress. In 1982, Swanepoel made and sent by post the device which killed writer and ANC activist Ruth First in her study at the Eduardo Mondlane University in Maputo.

His latest assignment was as an undercover agent based in Harare, capital of Zimbabwe, where he rented a house in the suburb of Avondale. In an area of the city formerly populated only by whites and now beginning to become racially mixed, he was still inconspicuous and able to pass comfortably as a retired member of the old Rhodesian civil service.

Over 160,000 whites – about two-thirds of the total white population – had emigrated to South Africa then. But within years, some had returned, realising that their skills were still required and finding that life was not as bad as they had feared. They could still live in their own world of big farms, swimming pools and servants. Swanepoel assumed the identity of one of these returning emigre's, Paul Herson, a former civil servant who had died shortly after moving to Johannesburg. Having been fixed up with the necessary documents by the NIS, Swanepoel was sent to Harare where he co-ordinated activity against ANC leaders based in the city.

Now he crouched below a spotlight, making final adjustments to the device clamped to his bench. The mechanism was built into balsa wood, with metal cylinders and wires protruding. It was 26 cms long, 17 cms wide and 6 cms deep – slim enough to slip into a light brown, A4 jiffy bag and pass as a book. The trickiest bit was to set the gap in the contacts exactly right. It exploded when the device was pulled by out the unsuspecting recipient, leaving behind a small plastic disc which was attached to the envelope inside and positioned between the contacts. If they were set too close, the disc could not be inserted. If they were set too far apart, it didn't go off.

This one was destined for Robert Temba, a Harare-based ANC member. South African intelligence believed that he was training black resistance fighters in sabotage techniques and infiltrating them into the country. They suspected Temba's hand in recent bombings of South African defence installations.

Swanepoel gingerly fitted the disc between the contacts, tested it to his satisfaction and ran a final check on the bomb. Then he carefully inserted the device into a large envelope he had acquired from the Grassroots Bookshop. Its label would not invite suspicion.

Exhausted, he reached for a new bottle of his favourite South African brandy, KWV. Now he could relax. Tomorrow he would drop his package into a letter box in the city centre during lunchtime when he would not be remembered in the crowds. Two days later it should reach its destination.

❖

When the first limpet mine went off Dick Sewell was thrown half-asleep from his bunk bed at the stern of the *Rainbow Warrior*. He hardly heard the shouts and screams of the eleven other members of the crew. The shock of the explosion battered his eardrums almost senseless. He dragged himself off the floor and made for the deck, not even conscious that an ugly gash had appeared on his left leg and his back was bruised. Seconds later the converted 40 metre fishing vessel, belonging to the international environmentalist organisation, Greenpeace, started to list.

Numb and disorientated, Sewell caught a glimpse of of the Greenpeace flag fluttering in the breeze in Auckland harbour. Then a second limpet mine tore through the hull and the boat started to sink. Quick, get into the dinghy tied alongside. Move. Where are the others? Ah – some already climbing in, some jumping into the water. Shouts – checking – are we all all right? Where's Fernando?

Sewell struggled back down to the bunk in the bows where the photographer had been sleeping. The water was pouring in by now. The darkness below was black with menace. He thrust his way forward, desperately calling. Fernando must be there. Come on, come on, where are you? The mess was terrible. All their documents, bedding, food and personal possessions seemed to have been thrust into the compartment. There was a smell of oil. Through the gloom he spotted the photographer's bunk. Or what was left of it. Then the body, torn by the explosion, starting to sink in the rising water. He shook it frantically, uselessly. Oh, Christ, no.

'Dick, what the hell are you doing? Get out! It's going under!' came the shout from the deck.

Sewell woke up with a start, his heart pounding, his mind racing as he experienced it all again, his own special nightmare. It had recurred virtually at quarterly intervals ever since July 10, 1985. Now he was on another anti-nuclear mission. He stretched out, arms folded, cradling his head. It was only 3 a.m. but he knew he wouldn't get back to sleep again for a few hours at least. He never did.

Dick Sewell was haunted by that night in New Zealand. They had anchored in Auckland the previous week and were preparing to sail on an anti-nuclear cruise through the South Pacific. Their target was a French overseas territory, French Polynesia, where they were planning to protest against French Government nuclear tests at Mururoa atoll.

Sewell had volunteered to sail with the Rainbow Warrior. He knew of the extreme danger of entering a nuclear test area and he knew that President Mitterrand's uncompromising instructions to the French navy meant they were likely to be intercepted, as they had been in the past. But although the crew were on continuous security alert, nobody anticipated a terrorist attack. It had been carried out by two members of the Action Division of the French external secret service, their action officially sanctioned at a high level.

The experience hardened Sewell. He gave up his job as a physical education instructor in a London comprehensive school and worked fulltime for Greenpeace. He had never been so content in a job. It became akin to a life mission – a privilege to be able to work fulltime for something you really believed in, he told friends.

He became a member of Greenpeace's non-violent direct action group. They were known as the 'Rainbow Warriors' in honour of the sunken vessel. He participated in direct action protests against the hunting of seals in Canada and the dumping at sea of nuclear waste. He volunteered for an expedition to disrupt the annual killing of thousands of pilot whales in the Faroe islands. Sewell detested the carnage most because the numbers killed far exceeded any food needs of those involved; it was conducted as a sport.

As he dozed, he was conscious of the snores and grunts of others in his compartment, and of the train wheels rumbling over the track with monotonous regularity. Out there, waiting for dawn to break, was another country to list on his travels. He always felt the same way about a new challenge in a strange place: a mixture of excitement and fear. This one could be his most dangerous yet. Normally, Greenpeace operated openly. This time his instructions were to contact a dissident group in a nation known for its intolerance towards dissidents. Peking was still eight hours away on the long journey from Shanghai where he had flown in the previous day. His stomach tightened as he wondered what lay ahead.

Chung-kuo, the name the Chinese give to their country means, literally translated, 'central country' – the centre of world civilisation, containing one-sixth of the human race. Jenny Stuart remembered this as the mini-bus drove through the gates of the English Language Institute, five miles from their hotel. She had been asked to give a current affairs lecture to its students.

'I have no idea how much English they'll understand, so it's difficult to know at what level to pitch it,' she had confided to Evans on the journey back from the Great Wall.

'I'll come along to keep you company. Should be worth it – an English socialist lecturing the Chinese on socialism!' he teased.

They were joined by their official interpreter, Shu Li Ping, who was delighted to be going back to the Institute where she had studied English herself. Unusually, she had been to Britain for two years study. She wore western style skirts and blouses, and quizzed Jenny keenly on the latest London fashions and pop groups. But she was evasive when Evans asked about her absence during the day at the Great Wall.

'I was needed for other duties,' she said, and quickly changed the subject.

The chatter in the packed lecture hall subsided as they arrived. Evans took a seat at the back while Jenny walked to the platform, watched curiously by the 200, mostly male, students. He empathised with her, knowing only too well that nagging moment of nervous tension each time you rose to lecture to a strange audience.

Jenny looked tense, partly he supposed because of what she had said on the way up: 'I don't like it when people get up and speak in a self-indulgent way, as if it is just for themselves or they haven't thought properly about it. It is important to make the effort to relate to people. You won't communicate anything of value unless you do. That's something we try to stress in the women's movement. So many politicians get up and talk endlessly without seeming to have any idea, or concern, for their audience.'

But when she rose to speak, she immediately took on an air of confidence: 'I know I have blonde hair but I am not Margaret Thatcher.'

The students burst out laughing, as she had hoped, having been told of the impact the British Prime Minister had made during a visit to China. Jenny relaxed – and so did Evans. He realised suddenly how anxious he had been on her behalf. He found himself studying her closely.

Just 25, she was a South London social worker and had been active in student politics whilst studying for a history degree at Sussex University. Her tutor had been on the Committee of the Society for Anglo-Chinese Understanding which was how her name had been put forward for the delegation. Attractive and slim, she had an enthusiastic manner and was good company – though her penchant for straight talking did sometimes cause offence.

Now she was arguing forcefully about her membership of the Campaign for Nuclear Disarmament, her opposition to China's possession of nuclear weapons and its reluctance over the years to criticise America's escalation of the arms race equally with Russia's. She was also critical of China's foreign policy, particularly its indirect suppport for extreme right wing movements and regimes like the Chilean junta.

'It is wrong to adopt a certain stance simply because it is the opposite of Russian policy towards a particular country. In South Africa, how can China possibly justify its refusal to back Nelson Mandela's ANC, just because it received Soviet aid? Apartheid is an evil. Our two nations, China and Britain, should give a lead together and adopt a principled foreign policy not aligned to either of the super-powers.'

Jenny assumed an authority, almost a power, when speaking which Evans always found intriguing in people who were not at all pushy on an individual level. She also looked good. Evans found himself noting the way that the swirling white skirt and dark close-fitting jumper which she had substituted for her usual jeans and shirt, provocatively accentuated her figure. He felt faintly guilty. In the circles in which he moved it was frowned upon to see women in sexual terms.

She sat down to an enthusiastic ovation. He wasn't surprised. You always knew a speech was going down well when the audience laughed naturally at your jokes; sometimes, exactly the same jokes went down like a lead balloon. Nevertheless he was struck by how well the students had responded to her humour which had expressed itself in a mild form of irony. And they had obviously followed her arguments closely because they were now vying with each other to fire questions, mostly about foreign policy and disarmament.

'Don't you understand,' one addressed her earnestly, 'the Soviets have been aggressors throughout our history; they even failed to support us against the fascists at a critical time in the 1930s. Now their missiles are pointing at us all along our border. Remember Czechoslovakia. Remember Afghanistan.

Never mind Gorbachev, the Soviets are expansionary imperialists.'

Jenny responded to each point carefully and patiently, impressing Evans with her calmness and the way she treated every questioner with respect. The students were lively and articulate. They made their points openly, often disagreeing amongst themselves. There was none of the rigidity or uniformity he had anticipated. Nor was there any taboo subject. They applauded again at the end, and a small group gathered round her, chatting excitedly, asking more questions.

She beckoned him over.

'Some of them want to talk to us back in their hostel. We can't fit them in tonight because of the banquet. What about tomorrow night?'

Evans nodded in agreement, surprised. He had heard so much about wariness of foreigners and intolerance of free discussion in China. Yet these arrangements were being made easily and spontaneously.

'You will be coming too?' A bespectacled youth with an intense expression addressed him anxiously. 'She told us you are an expert in nuclear technology. Please give her this.' He pressed a piece of paper furtively into Evan's hand, and slipped away.

'A lively bunch.' The familiar voice of Harold Williams startled him.

'They certainly are,' Evans instinctively pushed the paper into his pocket. 'I didn't realise you had come too. Are the rest of the Delegation with you? Did you arrive by bus?'

'Well, I was a little late. Thought I'd come and listen to Jenny. A polished performer, isn't she?' Williams avoided giving a direct answer. A solid figure, with a heavily jowled face, he had the slightly superior, pompous air of a government official, which in fact was what he had been. Attached to the Foreign Office until his retirement the previous year, Evans couldn't recall exactly what he'd said his responsibilities were.

Shu shepherded them outside. 'This time we go by car.'

Evans noted the blue-grey Shanghai Sedan which was based on a 1950s Mercedes design. Their group obviously rated only the most common kind of official transport. He knew that there were different sizes and colours of cars allocated strictly according to rank: blue-grey for the lower orders, and large, shiny black ones for senior Party cadres. Status was still alive and well and living in China. As with all official cars, the rear window of theirs was curtained off: for reasons of privacy Shu said; so that ordinary people couldn't see who was being chauffered about, was Jenny's sceptical reaction.

The chauffeur banged his horn incessantly. A different style of driving, Evans thought. They hoot to announce their impending presence, not to give a specific warning.

Back at the hotel, he drew Jenny aside as they walked with Harold Williams to call a lift. 'Could you come to my room? I've got something to show you.'

Once inside, he pulled the scruffy bit of paper out a trifle sheepishly. 'I thought I should wait until we were alone. One of the students asked me to give this to you.'

She stared at the note, perplexed. It was written in awkward capitals: 'CHINA FOREIGN POLICY SINCE 1978. DISCUSS IN DETAIL'. 'What is that supposed to mean?'

'I have no idea. It's rather like an essay title. We'll have to ask him tomorrow when we meet again at the hostel.'

As she closed the door, he looked again at the scrap of paper in his hand. Another strange incident. Should he tell her about the notebook, and the odd exchange with Wang? Or was it all too trivial?

❖

The newsflash interrupted a music programme on Swanepoel's car radio. 'There was an explosion an hour ago at the Harare home of African National Congress organiser, Robert Temba. Several people are feared dead, but no further details are available.'

Swanepoel let out a whoop of delight and accelerated, hurrying home to contact his 'handler'. He began almost immediately to think ahead to the next stage of their plan codenamed NOSLEN – the first name of the ANC leader Nelson Mandela, in reverse.

His letter bomb had been delivered as scheduled. It was scanned in a pile of mail by the security team who guarded Robert Temba's home 24-hours a day, then passed to his 12-year old daughter, Nomsa.

'Can I open it Dad?' she asked. 'It's a package from Grassroots Books. Looks exciting.'

Temba had a lot on his mind that morning: he was in what his three children fondly called a 'Dad's daze' – a state of mind where he registered ordinary family life around him, but did not engage properly with it. The problems of co-ordinating ANC internal resistance activities were all he could seriously concentrate upon much of the time. The pressure had been intensifying remorselessly. Withdrawal of 10,000 ANC guerrillas from their training camps in Angola following the move towards a Namibia settlement had been a major blow. With Mozambique barring ANC cadres as part of Maputo's Nkomati agreement with Pretoria, their bases had been pushed out of all the front line states. The organisation had been forced to concentrate upon fermenting military action in the townships, and Temba was a key strategist in this task.

He glanced at the package, vaguely registering the bookshop label, and nodded to his daughter. Then he took the rest of the mail to the room where he worked in the rear of the bungalow.

He never reached it. There was a deafening roar as if the whole world was blowing up. He turned desperately, knowing instantly the enormity of his error. Then he was knocked over by a piece of falling masonry and buried under a pile of rubble.

There would be nothing left to identify Nomsa. There was no corpse. The bomb had literally torn her apart. Pathetic lumps of flesh and pieces of bone were scattered through the pile of bricks, sand and wood which had once been the family living room. Some patches of dust were darker and damper than others, and redder too. A foot, torn hideously from the bottom of her leg stuck incongruously out of a shoe. It lay, scraped but still shining, on what had been the windowsill.

The front of the house seemingly on top of him, the ANC security guard was trapped under a collapsed door arch, peering, half conscious and unbelieving, at the gaping hole in his stomach. He closed his eyes in horror. They would never reopen. A grim silence descended, broken only by water gushing from broken pipes.

The Shanghai express pulled slowly into Peking station as Dick Sewell leaned out of the window for his first view of the city. He had never seen so many people on a station concourse. They seemed to fill every available space. There were even scores of little wooden cots for babies; some were sleeping inside, others playing, a few whimpering: an incongruous sight amongst the old, belching steam engines, Sewell thought.

The overnight journey had been comfortable enough. His Greenpeace colleagues had decided that he should go incognito, so he had booked with a regular tour party of holiday makers. The group had travelled 'soft class' and he had been in a compartment with four berths, thick mattresses and lace curtains signifying the section for foreigners, senior officials or army officers. The locals, he had noticed, were travelling 'hard class', jammed together in wooden triple-decker bunk beds with no mattresses and open to the smoke filled corridors.

From the station they were led out by a guide toward a coach that would take them to their hotel. Sewell was weary after the long trip and the hours of sleep lost after his nightmare. It was early evening and he was looking forward to a cool shower. Then maybe a cold beer and a walk round to identify the bar where he was due to collect a package from an unknown contact the following evening. Despite the city's humidity and the close atmosphere of the long train journey, he caught himself shivering with apprehension.

❖

The buzzer sounded on Major Keith Makuyana's desk at 9.16 am and he picked up his internal phone almost immediately. Listening intently, he wrote down a few details, asked several questions and then thanked his caller for his trouble. It was an old friend on the duty desk at Harare police headquarters. Both had been active in ZANU, the Zimbabwe African National Union, whose successful liberation struggle had propelled Robert Mugabe to power in 1980. They had an understanding that whenever there was any incident of a sensitive or political nature reported to the duty officer, Makuyana would be the first to hear of it in his office in security headquarters. This often enabled him to short-circuit the rivalry and jealousy between the police service and the Central Intelligence Organisation in which he was a senior officer.

Makuyana's brief was to maintain links with the South African resistance. He also monitored activity by the apartheid government to disrupt the resistance or interfere in Zimbabwean politics. A tall, lean man, he always wore dark prescription glasses. They gave him an air of menace, though his staff worshipped him for his loyalty and kindness. Now he was on the phone to them, issuing precise, clipped instructions. Exactly two minutes later, an unmarked Nissan estate car was waiting for him in the underground car park as he strode out of the lift and climbed in with two of his officers. Immediately behind was a grey Volkswagen Transporter, also unmarked. It looked somewhat neglected. Nobody would have known that it was armour plated and contained a folding bed, medical equipment, a range of arms and sophisticated electronic gadgetary.

Makuyana reached his destination just ten minutes after his buzzer had sounded. Police and soldiers were milling about, cordoning off the small crowd standing shocked on the pavement outside what had been Robert Temba's house. The VW van pulled up a hundred yards beforehand and parked discreetly as Makuyana's car arrived and he took control, flashing his card with a word of explanation.

His colleagues had sealed off the house and were already searching when Makuyana joined them, restraining himself from a feverish urge to tear into the rubble in case there was still some life. He was close to the Temba family and had enjoyed many hours of hospitality in the bungalow which was now unrecognisable. He forced himself to search methodically. It was obvious the explosion had occurred in the front; the dead ANC security man apart, there couldn't be much left of anyone in that part of the house. He moved to the rear. A shout from his sergeant indicated two bodies had been found, then another: two of the children and their mother, all dead, crushed under the building and covered in dust. The younger girl was clutching a doll, the head of which had been severed and was lying beside her.

He turned, the darkness of his glasses hiding the pain from his subordinates. Where was Robert? Had his old friend been out of the house? A glimmer of hope surged through him. Then he stumbled over another body. The ANC organiser was lying flat on the floor, holding some brown envelopes, head down in a pool of blood. He stooped to turn the body over for confirmation of inevitable death. But, as he did so, he sensed something else: years of experience had taught him dead bodies normally felt different. He reached for Temba's pulse. There seemed to be a few flickering signs of life. God, let it be so, he screamed inside himself, willing desperately as he called his two aides over.

One of the reasons why Keith Makuyana had a high standing in the service was his coolness and professionalism under pressure. He had a facility for making decisions quickly. Sometimes it got him into trouble in internal office politics, but he was not really a desk man. Out in the field he came into his own. Now he was fighting to overcome the emotions of close friendship as he thought through the options. The ambulance would be here soon. So would the other emergency services and police reinforcements. He called his officers over.

'Cover this one up. I don't want anything showing. But treat him very gently. He may be alive. Then get the other bodies and lay them out on the front garden. Leave a mark where you found them.'

He pulled out a handset and spoke urgently to his colleagues listening in the grey VW van. It was 9.36 am – barely four minutes after he had arrived on the scene. Apparently a fire had broken out at the National Sports Stadium over the hill and along the Bulawayo Road, and there was still no ambulance, which gave him the opening he wanted. He went over to the police guarding the crowd.

'There are six dead, the whole family and one security: no survivors. Get those bodies on the lawn covered. I want them out quickly. There is going to be a major political row about this and we can do without the ghouls peering in and getting in the way while we investigate. One body is in a particularly bad state. My men have covered it up. We can't wait for an ambulance. They will take it straight off. Then the forensic boys can come in and get a clear look at the house. They must leave no stone unturned. I want a full report. We must get to the bottom of this – and quickly.'

As he was talking, the grey VW slipped down the drive. Its sliding side door was opened out of sight of the spectators and Temba's battered body was lifted gingerly onto the bed which had been unfolded inside the vehicle. As it eased out into the road, Makuyana climbed in the front and the driver radioed ahead. Not to the main hospital, but to special premises whose existence was known by only a chosen few. On the way the VW passed an ambulance, tearing towards the scene, siren blaring, while Makuyana's remaining officers continued to perform a rapid, systematic search, gathering up any documents still legible. They had almost finished when the local police superintendent arrived to take charge.

❖

It was dark when they were dropped outside the large, imposing gates of the hostel where eight young men awaited them expectantly. They looked like any group of students, thought Evans, except for their shiny dark hair in neat, crew-cuts, their open-necked shirts and cotton trousers in contrast to the jeans and sweat shirts of their British counter-parts.

'We were not sure you would turn up,' said a gangling youth as he led the way courteously towards one of a number of rather drab, rendered block buildings.

There was no lift and they had to climb the stairs to the fifth floor. The meeting took place in a room about ten feet square – typical, they were told, of the rest of the hostel. There were bunk beds either side and a desk at the end: lodgings for six students. Evans smiled inwardly, thinking of the comparative privileges of students back home, wondering how he would have coped with the obvious lack of privacy in such an intensely communal life. The Chinese seemed to have a different attitude to such cramped conditions. Their culture appeared gregarious by comparison with the West, groups being the focus for living, with little scope for individual privacy. In fact, there was no equivalent for the word 'privacy' in the entire Chinese language. At the hotel he noticed that room service rarely knocked before entering and, on a visit to a health clinic, he had watched patients being diagnosed and even treated while others looked on and listened.

The students crowded into the small room, some to sit on the floor, others on the bunk beds and even the desk; their visitors were given the only two available chairs.

As they were about to begin someone else arrived – Hu Shao Ping, the student who had passed the note the previous day. Short and slightly built, Hu looked older than the others. Anxious eyes behind round thin-rimmed spectacles, he seemed to carry a heavy burden on his slim shoulders. Apologising for his lateness, he said he had been delayed at home: unlike the others he lived with his parents.

Soon a lively discussion developed about China's foreign policy, as tea was handed round in an ill-matched assortment of China cups with their characteristic lids. The students argued, explained, cracked jokes and told stories. Each in turn expressed open cynicism with the Communist Party, blaming it for betraying the revolution's ideals

'Are you all members of the Party?'

Jenny was surprised at the sour reaction to her question. Only one youth embarrassedly admitted to membership, drawing ribbing from his colleagues. Several volunteered that they had been demonstrating recently against Party authoritarianism and the lack of democracy in China. Others explained that although the Party was all-powerful and seemed huge with its 42 million members, this figure was under four per cent of the population.

'What do you remember of the Cultural Revolution?' Jenny had read of the tumultuous ten years after 1966 when Chairman Mao's young 'Red Guards' had acted as vanguards of revolutionary purity, fighting for political and social renewal. 'You would have been small children then of course. Could we have had this sort of meeting?'

'Never! We would have denounced you as foreign imperialists and chanted at you with our little red books!' They all burst out laughing and thrust up a hand clutching imaginary booklets, punching the air in imitation of the Red Guards. All, that is, except Hu Shao Ping, who had barely participated. He merely listened studiously, studying the two foreigners.

Evans, remembering Hu's request the day before, tried to draw him in. 'What do you think? Are they correct?'

'My father was very badly treated at the time,' he answered carefully.

A silence descended on the room as the laughter ceased and the others turned to him respectfully.

Evans sensed his diffidence, 'What happened? Can you tell us about it?'

Gradually, almost painfully, encouraged by his comrades when he faltered, Hu told his story in the clear, clipped English they had all mastered.

'My father is a scientist – a nuclear physicist,' he bowed to Evans acknowledging a shared interest. 'He studied first in America, but after Liberation in 1949 he came back. He wanted to build a new China. By the time Mao launched his cultural revolution with his famous swim in the yellow river in 1966, my father was a respected member of his profession. Then some local Red Guards found out he had been a student in the USA. They denounced him as a "rightist" and an "imperialist", even though he had always been a communist. He was taken away one night by a mob and beaten. They imprisoned him in a basement room at his work for several months before he was dispatched to a remote village in the mountains.'

Tears welled up in his eyes, and were impatiently blinked away. 'My father had so much knowledge and skill to give. But they made him work all day with a pick axe in a quarry. We were all labelled "rightists" and denounced as a family. My mother is a nurse – she was immediately transferred from her job and made to clean floors and toilets of the hospital ward which she had previously supervised. My older brother and sister were both expelled from their junior high school and assigned to street cleaning. I was still an infant, but we all suffered by being children of a "reactionary". They simply broke up our family.'

'What a waste.' Jenny murmured sadly.

'The Cultural Revolution was a terrible waste. Over a hundred million people were politically persecuted,' he sighed. 'The tragedy is that it all had a noble aim. Mao started the Cultural Revolution to rid the country of complacency, corruption and fossilised bureaucracy. He wanted to recreate the sense of a socialist crusade which followed Liberation. But it became a nightmare. Only after Mao's death and the overthrow of the Gang of Four – which had been running the country in his name – did things begin to improve. My father was brought back to work again as a scientist, though at a lower grade. My mother also got her job back and we children tried to make up for lost years. But my father never fully recovered his health. He is now retired.'

He paused, looking intently at Jenny, 'I told my father about your lecture. He wants to meet you both. You could come to my home.' As they looked doubtfully at each other, he added quickly, 'Please do not refuse. I will come with you on the bus afterwards and we can talk about it further.'

The discussion then broadened out until it was time to go and the students gave them an escort *en masse* to the hostel gates.

'I think I have learned more tonight than from all the briefings we have been given,' Evans said shaking hands with each one.

As they walked with Hu round the corner to the bus-stop on the main road, he noticed how badly lit the streets were. At the same time he felt safe – quite different from at home in London where he felt increasingly insecure when out at night.

'By the way,' Evans remembered to ask as they reached the bus stop, 'what did that message mean: on the paper you gave me?'

'My father will explain. It is something important that he found when he worked at the Atomic Energy Institute; as I said he retired only two months ago.'

'You mean the Institute at Nankow?'

'Yes.'

'I visited it earlier this week.'

'You did? Even better,' Hu smiled properly for the first time that evening. 'When I told him of Miss Stuart's lecture and of her criticisms of China's foreign policy, and that you are a nuclear physicist, he decided immediately he wanted to see you. Now he will be even more certain. You will come, won't you?'

The trolley bus arrived and they climbed aboard. 'Can't you tell us more?'

Jenny asked.

The bus pulled away, its doors swishing closed, and then stopped almost immediately to let on a tardy passenger. The man brushed past them, panting, to a seat at the back and the bus jerked off again.

'I am sorry, I do not know all the details. My father was most insistent on talking to you personally. He is worried about China's nuclear programme and its foreign policy. He also supports your strong opposition to the South African regime. '

'South Africa? What's that got to do with it?' Jenny asked.

Hu shrugged. He didn't know.

'I suppose we could squeeze in a visit tomorrow afternoon, perhaps about five o'clock,' she said, consulting their itinerary and checking with Evans who nodded, his interest kindled at the mention of the Institute and its reminder of the unexplained missing page of his notebook.

'Thank you,' Hu smiled again. 'I will come myself to collect you. Your hotel is not very far from my home. A short bus ride only. In fact this bus goes right past the street where I live.'

'What is your home like?' Jenny asked.

'It is a *hutong* – a small courtyard house with four rooms in the old part of the city. We share a toilet and kitchen with neighbours. It used to belong to my grandparents.'

He glanced out of the window, 'I get off soon. Look down the next street. If it is light enough you will see our house jutting out into the first alleyway on the left. I will meet you tomorrow at five, on the pavement outside the hotel gates.'

'Why not wait in reception, in case we're late?'

Hu laughed, shaking his head, 'As an ordinary Chinese, I may not enter the hotel without special permission.'

Then he pointed, getting up, 'Ah, there is my home now. The one with the chimney sticking above the street wall.'

The bus stopped and, shaking hands politely, he climbed down and waited formally by the kerbside until the doors closed and the bus was moving again. His slight figure had disappeared into the darkness when there was a shout from the rear of the bus. The driver answered, obviously angry, the passenger shouted back and the bus screeched to a halt once more. The back doors opened, a man got out, then the doors banged closed impatiently and the bus shot off.

❖

The lead story on Voice of Zimbabwe's news programme was quite specific. ANC official Robert Temba and his entire family were dead after an explosion at his house. There was a brief obituary mentioning Temba's commitment to the 'heroic struggle for liberation'. An ANC spokesman angrily denounced 'South African terrorism'. In the safe house near the city centre, Keith Makuyana switched off the radio, relieved. So far so good. The first stage of his operation had worked. He had some loose ends to tidy up, such as the records at the mortuary, but his officers were sorting those out. His immediate anxiety was whether Temba would pull through.

The ANC man was lying unconscious in a purpose built medical centre to the rear of the building. The place had been acquired several years before under a personal directive from the Prime Minister, Robert Mugabe. Few in the security services knew of its existence. From the front, it looked like an old-style Rhodesian family home sandwiched somewhat incongruously between rows of office blocks – a relic of a colonial age in an area which had since been extensively redeveloped. But, attached to the rear, occupying what had once been a spacious lawn with a back gate leading out to the next road, was another building. Large garage doors filled the back wall running along the pavement. Inside, through a video-camera controlled security system, the grey VW van now stood with several other vehicles. Beyond, was a central corridor with rooms on either side. A flight of stairs led down to a basement with another security door, and beyond that was a central control room with computerised communication links to every part of the country, and the medical centre.

The building had a skeleton staff who maintained its facilities all year round and monitored events 24-hours a day. Now they had been joined by others, replacing the usual air of quiet efficiency with one purposefully busy.

'Still no leads?' Makuyana was getting impatient. His officers recognised the mood only too well, exchanging glances behind his back as he paced round the panel of monitors, receivers, push-button telephones and printers.

During their search of the ruins, they had uncovered no important evidence to trace the source of the bomb. All they had to go on was that the time of the explosion coincided with the mail delivery. An interview with Post Office staff hadn't been much help. The postman had remembered a bulky package in amongst the pile of mail for the Tembas – the only household on his round

– 21 –

where there were special delivery arrangements. The package wasn't large enough to have been delivered separately as a parcel, but he hadn't noticed anything special about it. The atmosphere in the sorting office was tense after the interviews, the usual chat and gossip of the staff dampened. They were taking considerable care in handling large envelopes. Letter bombs were their nightmare: rough handling or a small fault and they could go off at any stage of their passage through the postal network.

'Run another check on suspected South African agents in the country,' Makuyana instructed his staff. 'Oh, and ask for a priority monitor on any irregular communications since this morning: phone calls, radio signals, the lot. Whoever was responsible must have had to report back.'

He knew this was a very long shot, that his staff could spend hours fruitlessly combing the surveillance records and double-checking intelligence reports, but the truth was there was nothing else they could do. It was important to maintain the momentum of the investigation. He stepped abruptly out and through to the medical unit to peer anxiously at the screen recording Temba's erratic heart beat and listen to his comrade's fitful breathing.

'Will he pull through?' He had stopped himself asking before, but it was now mid-afternoon and he needed to know. Perhaps the ANC man would remember something important.

'There's an outside chance,' the young doctor replied. She turned, understanding the officer's anxiety. 'He's important – yes?'

'Very.'

A worried frown creased her soft black skin. He hadn't pressured her because he hadn't needed to. She knew – and she sympathised. 'I may be able to bring him round so you can have a few words. The problem is the strain could finish him off. He shouldn't really be brought prematurely into consciousness. There is no doubt what my professional advice should be. But...?' She shrugged her shoulders, her attitude friendly, her eyes questioning rather than reproaching.

He looked away, knowing he couldn't hold her stare. 'Bring him round as soon as you can.' He turned and slipped quickly through the door as the words jerked out. They seemed to ricochet harshly back at him off the stone floor.

CHAPTER TWO

Evans had most of the day on his own; time to meet more scientists and to be briefed by officials in the Energy Ministry, time also to think and make more notes. He had slept badly, his mind racing throughout the night: the confusion over the notebook, Wang's menace, the coming visit to meet Hu's father.

With a half-hour's gap in his programme, he forced himself to relax and sat down on the steps of the Great Hall of the People, a short walk from his hotel. He tried to imagine what it must have felt like during one of Mao's famous addresses from the top of the steps to the cheering masses assembled below. Tiananmen Square stretched out before him, the towering Martyrs Memorial honouring revolutionary heroes on one side, a vast area which had held over a million in its time. Now it was calm in the afternoon sun, people making their way across, some pausing to stare at him. As a white foreigner he was still an object of curiosity, though their stares were almost respectful, not at all intrusive. Several times, as he had paused during the walk, he had been surrounded by scores of Chinese, silently examining him in a manner which, though rather disconcerting, was not oppressive.

He realised he was becoming emotionally pulled towards China. There was something compelling about the country. He checked himself because he had watched with some scepticism British visitors 'falling in love' with Third World countries. That seemed to him merely a modern version of the paternalism which had dominated the colonial age. But he couldn't help being captivated by the straightforward dignity of the Chinese people, and the way their courtesy and old-fashioned formality contrasted with the informality of their attire; even on official visits, open-necked shirts and slacks were the norm and he had been happy to jettison his own tie and suit for casual clothes.

He reflected ruefully on the paradox facing him: the more he found out about China, the more questions raised themselves and the less he seemed to understand how exactly the society functioned, how power was exercised, how ordinary people lived and thought. The country was full of surprises. He had not anticipated the scale of the Japanese commercial presence, for example. The minibus assigned to the group was a Mitsubishi, and the first thing he had noticed as they were driven out of Peking's futuristic new airport was a giant billboard advertising that firm. The Coca-Cola signs at the tourist attractions also confirmed the impact of western capitalism in recent years.

Evans was in two minds about this. He admired the way the Chinese had rebuilt their country after liberation in 1949. Gone were the days when carts went round the streets of cities like Shanghai every morning at dawn, picking up scores of bodies of homeless paupers who had died in the night. Gone were the days when landowners used private armies to control peasants and maintain them in a state of near-starvation. But these achievements were based on an acceptance of austerity for all; the new western consumerism could benefit only a handful. He had a sudden image of the journey back from the Great Wall. Their bus had slowed to pass a line of women pulling handcarts piled high with surplus produce from their communes which they were taking to sell privately in street markets. He remembered their faces now: prematurely aged and lined with fatigue. Then the hourly chime sounded on his digital watch. It was time to get back to the hotel, have a shower and freshen up before the sticky humidity of the evening and his important appointment.

When he returned to his room he found a note to say Jenny had been delayed and he was to meet the student Hu and his father alone. Showering quickly, he wished the time of the appointment could have been altered. He would have felt more secure accompanied by Jenny. After all, she was the political one; he was just a scientist.

He walked over to the table and poured himself a cup of jasmine tea from the thermos flask which seemed always to be topped up. Every room had its own thermos and cups with elegant lids. Sipping the tea, he checked that his notebook was in his jacket pocket and looked out of the window. It was ten minutes before Hu was due. But the young man was already there. Evans could see him standing unobtrusively several yards from the gates, apparently studying traffic on the road, almost as if he didn't want to be seen associating with the hotel, Evans thought, setting down his empty cup.

Then he froze. It all happened so quickly. One minute Hu was standing there, the next he was surrounded by three men, taken firmly towards a black saloon in the hotel car park and bundled in. Evans caught a last glimpse of his face, creased and suddenly hollow as he struggled to turn towards the hotel, searching and straining in vain. His expression of utter defeat was blotted out behind the window curtains as the door was slammed. The car revved up, pulled out into the road and roared away.

Evans stood in front of the open window torn by conflicting emotions.

Despite the sunshine outside and the warmth of his recent shower he realised he was shivering. Hu had been snatched before his very eyes with a clinical efficiency which was almost indecent. Nobody seemed to notice: not the cyclists, not the pedestrians, not the tourists hanging around the front of the hotel. Only he seemed to understand what had taken place. And he was completely helpless. He remembered Hu's haunted sense of tension and secrecy as they had made the arrangements to meet his father. It was no use seeking help from an official: who could he trust?

A sense of disbelief gripped him – the way he'd felt over the notebook incident and the later confrontation with Wang. Then came resentment: why was this happening to *him*? All he wanted was to visit the bloody country. It wasn't his style to be involved. He was by temperament an observer not an activist. It wasn't that he didn't care. Of course he did. But he preferred to get on with things he was good at.

He sat down and poured another cup of tea, nervously spilling it onto the table. An image of the man jumping belatedly on and off the bus the previous night flashed through his mind. Had somebody been watching Hu?

❖

Temba's eyes took an age to inch open. When they did, he stared dully and unfocused at the two figures bending over him, one clad in white, the other wearing dark glasses. He didn't really want to wake up. He had no motivation to do anything. Nothing mattered anymore. He was content just to lie there. But the dark glasses triggered a reaction which seemed a long way away, deep down in the back of his numbed mind. The glasses were calling him, signalling … what was it? He couldn't get his thoughts together and his body told him he didn't want to. How much nicer simply to close his eyes and rest again. But the glasses kept shining, recognising him. Or was he recognising them?

Then a voice, also far away. 'Robert – can you hear me? It's me – Keith.' He tried to wrap his mind around the voice, to bring it nearer, to get hold of it; but it kept slipping away. He closed his eyes. Sheer bliss. I don't want to open them again. Just leave me alone.

'Robert! Please wake up! It's important.' The voice was still there, annoying him, disturbing his rest. He opened his eyes once more to tell it to go away. There were the glasses again. He *knew* them. Why? He felt confused.

Then, suddenly, it all came tumbling back. The face behind the glasses – he knew it too. And the familiar voice: 'Robert. How are you?'

Everything hit him at once. The instant he recognised his old friend Keith Makuyana he remembered the searing, terrible roar of the explosion, and the pain came flooding back.

'My fault.' The words stuttered out of his dry, caked lips.

'What was?' The voice, gentle now, encouraging, consoling.

'The bomb. Should have checked. Must have been the Grassroots envelope.'

'Grassroots? Are you sure.' The voice was disbelieving, probing.

'Yes. Sure. Could have killed myself.' He didn't notice the irony.

'What did it look like?'

He felt there was a machine inside him speaking now. 'Large. Brown envelope. Grassroots label. My daughter was excited. My daughter ... Oh no ... Nomsa ... My fault.' It was all flooding back now. He couldn't cope, didn't want to.

'Leave me alone,' he said exhausted, his eyes shutting. He didn't want them to open again – ever.

The doctor motioned Makuyana away and tucked up the blanket. She took Temba's pulse and temperature, her face grim, hardly noticing the security chief as he walked to the door.

Makuyana hadn't felt this way for years. Not since the time of the guerrilla war, when the notorious Selous Scouts – the official killer force in the Rhodesian army – had raided his base camp, burning it to the ground and taking no prisoners. He had had to discipline himself then, to control his thirst for vengeance. He stopped in the corridor, clenching his fists, breathing deeply, fighting the conflicting emotions of anger and guilt. Slowly, they were replaced by the ruthless determination he needed.

He went directly to the control room. His officers turned expectantly as he barked instructions for them to check out the Grassroots shop.

'It was a local job. The bastard could be based here in Harare. I want every bit of intelligence on the situation in the city. We don't know what we are looking for. Everything could be relevant.'

Just as Makuyana's staff were beginning to comb intelligence reports in Harare, Swanepoel was gazing at the main nightly ZTV news bulletin. It led on his handiwork. Watching shots of the remains of the family home and the bodies being taken away in canvas bags, even he had to admit it wasn't a pretty sight. The reports highlighted the children's deaths. They would, wouldn't they, he sneered inwardly. He felt no sympathy: although he had grandchildren himself, *blacks* weren't the same.

Responsibility was attributed to 'South African backed terrorists'. That didn't surprise or worry him. He judged that the security forces would be looking for an outside group and be watching the border.

He went out to his car and drove to a hotel where he had an arrangement to pay for phone calls. Although he felt somewhat exposed talking on an extension in the foyer, there was little alternative – public call boxes were virtually non-existent in the city. First he called the mortuary, pretending to be a friend and sought the confirmation he wanted that the entire family had died. Next he tried his handler – a businessman based in the city centre – but the man was unavailable that night, so he had no alternative but to make direct contact with Pretoria. With direct dialling between Harare and the South African capital he judged that it should be safe enough, though once he had identified himself with the codename NOSLEN, he was careful as always, to keep the conversation apparently about family matters. It was always possible that the Zimbabweans monitored calls to the cities such as Pretoria and Johannesburg; direct dialling to the Transvaal area went through a satellite link, and the technology was available to listen in on particular conversations. He had been warned that computerised eavesdropping systems could be programmed to identify key words and phrases. They 'sucked' individual phone calls out of the jumble of routine ones being made at any time, and recorded them.

After buying some hamburgers and beer, Swanepoel returned home to eat and relax. He missed the comfy reassurance of the state controlled South African Broadcasting Corporation and tried to avoid local television as much as he could, preferring Afrikaner folk songs on his cassette player.

Reaching for a fresh bottle of KWV brandy, he sniffed eagerly over his favourite shaped glass, the aroma drifting up to his nostrils. People said KWV wasn't up to fine European brandies, but he didn't agree; there was no better companion to fend off the loneliness of an alienated agent in the field. These days he felt the need for consolation; the job was no longer what it had been.

At times like this his thoughts turned with longing to the certainty, the discipline, the sense of a crusade of his youth. The crisp brown shorts, with neat turn-ups, the toe-capped shoes, always polished by the servants at home, and the summer evenings spent with his friends. The burning pride of Afrikaner nationalism which had aroused a generation sick of the arrogance and paternalism of the English speaking whites – contemptuous of their complacency too, as if the British Empire would always be nanny.

How good it had been to join the clandestine Afrikaner nationalist group, *Ossewa Brandwag* (Ox-wagon Brigade). What a proud moment to be recruited to the elite *Stormjaers* (stormtroopers) inside *Ossewa Brandwag*, which supported the Nazis and carried out sabotage against the Allies. His first experience of explosives had been when he planted dynamite on a railway line, damaging a train carrying British troops. One man who was later to become South Africa's Prime Minister, Balthazar Johannes Vorster, was a senior colleague. Those were the days, he smiled. A man really felt like a man, fighting for the cause. The cause had become stale now, and everybody was getting soft, including himself. He was halfway through the KWV when the phone rang.

'I have a long distance call from South Africa,' the bored operator said mechanically. 'Hold for a call'.

It was his wife Sarie, crackling down the line from their daughter's home in the small town of Port Alfred on the Eastern Cape coast. For security reasons, it was most unusual for her to call. 'Is that you? Have you been drinking again?'

'Only a bit,' he slurred.

'We have another grandchild. Isn't that marvellous! Can you take some time off and join us here. The others are coming down next weekend to inspect the new arrival. The family would love to see you.'

He thought for a moment. He would have to lie low for a while after the letter bomb anyway. It would be a good time to return for a holiday. 'Yes – I am due a break. I will try to make arrangements.' He bade her farewell and settled down to finish off the bottle, falling asleep an hour later, his glass spilling from his hand, unaware of the significance his wife's call.

'Still nothing, sir.' Makuyana's deputy, Ed Tombe, was strained and apprehensive as he faced his boss. It was dawn, the day after the bombing and his staff had been working non-stop. There were no unusual movements on the frontier. Extra vigilance at official border posts like Beitbridge hadn't turned up anything. Security reports on the city were also unhelpful. The Grassroots shop was closed until the morning.

'All right, send them home for some sleep. I want everyone back in five hours. Will you stay here? We can get some rest on the camp beds. I don't want to lose the initiative. I have a feeling there is something out there waiting to be spotted.'

Tombe left to carry out the instructions and was back a few minutes later. He felt like a whisky, but his boss never touched spirits. He was offered fresh orange juice instead.

'Unless the bomb was brought into the city to post, the equipment to make it must still be here. They wouldn't ship that about and risk getting caught in transit. Let's assume they are in the city. Why else post it locally? Put yourself in their position, Ed. If you had sent that bomb,' – Tombe noticed the slight pause as his eyes clouded momentarily – 'you would have made contact afterwards with your superiors, wouldn't you? They couldn't rely on the news alone. That communication must have been by phone – yes?'

Tombe nodded. Radio contact would have been too risky.

'Right. Talk to our people at Telecom headquarters. See if their eavesdropping system has picked up anything, and ask for a print-out on every operator call made between Harare and South Africa in the last 24 hours. Outgoing and incoming. It's a long shot, I know. But until we talk to the Grassroots staff, we have nothing else to go on.'

He motioned Tombe away. 'That's all for now. Get some sleep. I will see you shortly. I am going to check on Robert.'

He walked along the stone-tiled corridor, the fluorescent lighting and white paint giving it a sanitised atmosphere. A nurse was at Temba's bedside checking on his heartbeat and adjusting his drip. He was asleep. She looked up without any enthusiasm.

'He is not recovering. He may not last to the morning.'

Makuyana looked at the still figure of his friend. Somehow he knew it was all over, just as he had sensed there was still life left in the battered body in the rubble of the bombed home nearly twenty hours ago. He didn't know why but he found himself reaching for Temba's hand, stretched out on top of the sheet and holding it. He forced their palms together and turned them upwards in the traditional handshake of the African National Congress.

'*Amandla*,' he said quietly.

'*Awethu*,' the nurse behind him replied.

He turned in surprise, half embarrassed, half pleased: 'He is special. Look after him for me would you.'

❖

Dick Sewell had been booked into the Dragon Springs Hotel with his party. Although tired after his train journey, he had asked for guidance from their interpreter and then walked out with a map of the city to find the bar where he was due to rendezvous. It was just five minutes walk from the Great Hall of the People.

Now he was heading back there, having ducked out of a visit to a concert which was on the party's itinerary for that evening. As he approached the bar, he realised he would be the only non-Chinese. It was full of young people, tables and chairs spilling out onto the pavement in the warmth of the evening. The bar itself had no counter in the conventional sense – more like a little platform across which beer and a thin fruit juice were served.

'Do you speak English?' A girl in a grey tunic and grey trousers stopped politely in front of him.

'Yes,' he replied rather hesitantly.

'We are students studying English,' she pointed to a group watching them from a nearby table. 'Can we practice on you?'

Sewell was taken aback. Surely this wasn't the contact? He looked at his watch: 8.20 – he was ten minutes early. He had been told that English-speaking tourists could be politely accosted in this way. Nevertheless, the directness of the approach was unexpected.

'Yes, why not,' he smiled. 'But first could you tell me how I ask for a beer?'

'Of course,' the girl giggled, walking with him to the bar and making the order. She helped him give the necessary yuan. They returned to her friends.

'Are you married?' she asked?

What is this? A pick-up? Sewell wondered, bridling at the intrusion, but his professionalism overcame his instinctive aversion to discussing personal things.

'No – I used to be married. But I was always too busy with work. We drifted apart. How about you?' A characteristic change of tack: always ask a question to fend off having to talk about yourself.

She smiled. 'I am too young. We have a marriage bar of 28 for men and 25 for women. But some of my friends live together in their parents' home. We call it *zhu-li*, or "living-in". The Government don't like this, but still it happens.'

'Can I buy everyone another drink?' Noting that it was 8.40 already, he looked about. Perhaps I should have remained on my own, he thought, worried. Although the subject of mild curiosity, nobody else seemed to be taking a close interest in him.

The girl in grey came along to help him order again. 'When you return to your chair you will see a large brown envelope up against its legs,' she said quietly while the drinks were being put on the counter. 'Please pick it up when you go as if you brought it with you. It is very important. And good luck.'

The conversation continued for a while and then Sewell said his farewells, leaving them chatting as he collected the envelope and tucked it under his arm. He wanted to return to the hotel before his expedition was noticed.

An hour later, the students left and went their separate ways. One of them, a bespectacled youth, lingered behind. He checked that he was alone and then headed towards an anonymous building occupied by the Ministry of State Security. At reception he asked for a Mr Wang Bi Nan. The two had an animated conversation, during which Wang reprimanded his informer for not discovering the identity of the Englishman.

An hour after Hu had been snatched Evans was still in turmoil. Christ, if only Jenny had been there. He'd gone looking for her without success. What would she have done? Although he knew the answer just as soon as he'd posed the question, he didn't want to accept it. But he was feeling increasingly guilty. How self-indulgent to become pre-occupied with your own emotions, he thought, pull yourself together! He had better force himself to go round to Hu's house to find his father.

He grabbed his coat, scribbled a quick note and pushed it under Jenny's door on his way down. Although he remembered the number from the night before, it took him some time to work out the correct bus stop. In fact it was right outside the hotel gates and a trolley bus came almost immediately. He climbed on, feeling lonely and apprehensive.

Hu's house was only a mile away and he recognised the road leading to it.

As the bus pulled up and he waited for the doors to open, he was conscious of being scrutinised by the rest of the passengers. Most foreigners went about in cars or coaches. Were they just curious at the unusual sight of one using a public bus? Or was one of them watching him as somebody had obviously watched Hu?

He climbed off and stood deliberately still, apparently consulting his street map. The passengers who had got off at the same stop all hurried away. He waited, checking that none had lingered behind, and then crossed the road as a gap appeared in the stream of cyclists. Nobody seemed to be taking any real interest in him. Not, he supposed, that he would necessarily have spotted anybody. They were professionals, he a mere amateur stumbling around. But then who were *they*, he wondered, feeling incongruous and very exposed as he surveyed the scene before him.

Hu's house was easy to spot a hundred metres away. He could see it clearly where last night it had been something of a blur. It was one of a series of *hutongs*, small courtyard homes that were positioned in winding quarters leading off the road. It wasn't always clear where the boundaries of one home stopped and another began. The walls were mostly made of bricks and large stones set on each other without any mortar. Piles of rubble seemed to merge into the buildings.

The road was quiet, contrasting with the noise of the main street. Evans was conscious of a stillness under the evening sunshine, heightening the sense of unreality which he could not shake off. Yet there was nothing obviously unusual. There was nobody else about. Perhaps Hu would be there after all? He dismissed the thought as instantly as it had appeared.

Instinctively, he decided to walk on past the house, and then check to see whether he had been followed. He found himself near an alley and turned quickly into it, his heart pounding. The minute he waited seemed to take an hour. He was embarrassed at himself, hoping none of the residents would notice this strange behaviour of a foreigner. Then he peered carefully back down towards the main street. Still nobody in sight. He didn't feel embarrassed any longer, just ridiculous – as if he was engaging in an adult version of cops and robbers. He had a sudden vision of crouching behind a rubbish bin as a ten-year old, hiding from his friends on the way back from school, and then jumping out to surprise them. He slipped through an arch into the courtyard surrounding Hu's home, knocked on a battered old door, and waited. The knocks echoed in the quietness. He knocked again. Still no response.

He hadn't known what to expect. His decision to come had been taken against his better judgement. He hadn't thought of what he would do if nobody was at home. He began to consider the alternatives. He could leave a note and return with Jenny later, but perhaps it would be unwise to identify himself. He could wait, but for how long?

'Psst!' He swung round, startled, to see a young woman at the doorway of a house across the courtyard motioning urgently to him.

He walked tentatively over. 'What is it?'

The woman looked to be in her early twenties and was clearly nervous. That makes two of us Evans thought glumly. He had an overwhelming desire to draw back, but maybe he had knocked at the wrong house by mistake?

He followed the woman into the house and found himself in a small room, clearly the living quarters. A table and chairs stood in the middle, and at the rear a large bed which doubled as a settee and had built into its base a fireplace so that the bed could be kept warm in the bitter winter nights. The ceiling was so low that he had to stoop.

Now that he was inside, the woman looked terrified. 'Go!' she hissed, 'Hu's family gone. Nobody lives there anymore. Empty! Empty! Go!'

Her terror frightened him even more, and after a brief hesitation, he turned on his heel and did as she asked. Longing for the security of his hotel, he walked swiftly down a dark alley, catching smells of cooking mixed in with sewage coming from the surrounding homes. Soon he could see the main road again, and the bus stop for the return journey came into view. The sun was disappearing over buildings silhouetted black on orange. A group of students walked by on the pavement, chattering. A mother pushed a pram made of wicker-basket. Life was going on as if nothing untoward had happened. He had a sudden urge to shout out to them, to tell the truth – but what was the truth in all this?

On his return to the hotel, he went straight to Jenny's room and knocked.

'Who is it? I'm in the shower?' Her voice was muffled.

'It's me, Jim. I need to talk, urgently'

'Oh – come in then. I'll be out in a minute.'

As is customary in Chinese hotels, the door was not locked. He pushed it open and walked in. A minute later Jenny emerged from the bathroom wrapped in a towel, her blonde hair dark from the shower, water dripping off her bare legs.

'Sorry to disturb you,' he said.

She brushed aside his obvious embarrassment, noticing that he looked pale and drawn. 'What happened? Are you all right?'

Staring at him intently, she seemed unaware of how disturbingly attractive she was. Evans forced himself to concentrate on the story he needed to tell. When he had finished, she pulled the towel closer, staring at the floor. He might not have been there.

'Shouldn't we inform our Delegation leader?' he suggested after a minute.

Jenny shook her head, 'I don't think we should involve anybody else. We are official guests. They would feel obliged to notify the authorities, and who knows whether the authorities aren't behind all this. In any case, what would we actually report? A missing page from a notebook? A student's story? An empty house? We have no alternative except to sit tight for the moment Jim.'

❖

Wang Bi Nan thanked his young informer courteously, if a little contemptuously. Reaching for his phone, he dialled a number and asked for an immediate appointment with the Old Man.

Twenty minutes later he knocked and entered a room at the end of a long corridor on the tenth floor of the state building. The Old Man was on his own, Wang was relieved to note. Normally, someone at his relatively low level in the Ministry would never get to see such an important Government Minister. Their contact had always to be outside usual channels.

The Old Man looked up from the pile of documents on his desk. 'Any progress?'

Wang stood almost to attention. He felt in such awe, he had to restrain himself from saluting. These encounters were often tense. The Old Man did not suffer fools gladly. Wang spoke in clipped, formal terms, summarising as precisely as he could.

'So – you intercepted the student Hu and his father before they could get to the English visitors. That was efficient.'

A flush slipped across Wang's sallow complexion. 'Yes, sir. The son was devastated, the father even more so. He suspected the purpose of our project. He obviously wanted to communicate his suspicions to Evans. But we got to him first.'

The Old Man cut in sharply. 'We still have another problem, do we not.'

Wang pursed his lips. 'Yes, sir. My student informer insists the Englishman took away an envelope with him. Although he did not actually see it passed over, he is sure he arrived without it. He could not confirm the Englishman's name, but I think we must assume it is our friend Evans again.'

'I am surprised that this Evans was not vetted more closely before being accepted onto the Noted Persons Delegation.' The Old Man drummed his fingers on the desk in exasperation, swinging his chair around with his back to Wang.

There was silence for a moment. Wang stared at the giant revolutionary paintings on the wall, all products of the 1950s and the Russian influence. The bold simplicity of the figures expressed a confidence in the triumph of communism. The peasants were all strong and handsome, striding into the future, the workers at their side. Wang longed for the return of that confidence, that certainty. This was his mission. This was why he worshipped the Old Man who alone remained uncorrupted whilst lesser leaders dodged and trimmed towards the market economy and the capitalist West.

Although the one-party state seemed monolithic, Wang knew that internally there were many divisions, jealousies and conflicts, some based upon disagreements over ideology or policy, others upon personality. Periodically, prominent leaders fell from power and found themselves almost overnight 'disgraced': one day the fount of all wisdom, the next all along secret 'revisionists' or even 'counter-revolutionaries'. Their rise and fall was symbolic of the factional battles teeming underneath the surface of the state edifice.

Wang's eyes swivelled to fix on the frail shoulders sunk in the back of the deep padding on the leather chair, and waited.

The Old Man turned abruptly. 'The Englishman presents us with a dilemma. We must be careful. We cannot afford to arouse the suspicions of our colleagues in the Public Security Bureau or create a diplomatic incident. He must meet with an accident. And keep an eye on the girl. Find out if she knows anything. You must also try to recover the envelope handed over by the students at the bar. And the students themselves,' – he paused, hesitating – 'no, leave them for now. They can be dealt with in due course.'

❖

Makuyana woke with a start as his assistant Tombe shook him hard. He blinked his eyes open and glanced at his watch. 'God – ten a.m.! Why the hell did you let me sleep so long?'

'Bad news, I am afraid.'

Tombe's face told him everything. No clarification was necessary. Robert Temba had not made it through the night, dying while Makuyana slept. He pulled on his trousers, had a quick wash and finished dressing.

Then he went down to the medical centre. The doctor wouldn't look him in the eye, nor the nurse. Just as well. He doubted that he could have held their stares. There was a hint of reproach in the way they went busily about laying out the body, though it was more resigned than antagonistic.

'Thank you for all you have done,' he said quietly, as arrangements were made for his friend to be taken to the mortuary.

'We have some other news,' said Tombe, following him out to the control room. 'There are 211 phone numbers logged by the operator involving calls to and from South Africa in the period you specified. We are going through them systematically. It could take days if not weeks for a complete check. But we may have a lead from Grassroots. One of the staff there said a man came to the shop three days ago. He bought a solidarity poster and some cards. He asked for a large jiffy bag to post it to relatives. She remembers him because he had a heavy accent and she wondered whether he might be South African.'

Makuyana didn't respond. His mind was elsewhere.

'We now have a description. Balding, overweight man. Elderly – probably in his sixties. I am having a photofit made up and we will copy it for the staff checking the phone numbers. Mind you, identification evidence is notoriously unreliable, as you know.' Tombe paused. He had never seen his boss so distant, so apparently disinterested in such important information.

But Makuyana had heard – and absorbed – though his thoughts were focused on an incident in the bush, over ten years before. He and Robert Temba had been tracking a group of South Africans who were on a sabotage raid deep into independent Mozambique, and the pair had walked into a trap. Temba had got them out of it. Makuyana could see him now behind a boulder in the gulley, firing from his Russian AK-47 fixed on automatic, following up with three RGD-5 fragmentation grenades. The four South Africans had been wiped out within two minutes, their ambush turned first into a retreat, then a rout. They couldn't have known they were taking on perhaps the ANC's finest field combatant. No wonder Pretoria had targeted him. Makuyana focussed his eyes back from his image of Temba checking the enemy were all dead in the burning sun. So. They had got their revenge – but not the last word: he was determined upon that.

'Get the ANC. I must talk to them soon,' he said softly.

❖

It was late at night before Sewell was able to study the contents of the students' envelope. His fellow tourists in the hotel had interrupted him in his room soon after he had returned and insisted on a drink. They were all high on the wonders of the concert they had attended. Now they had turned in.

There were photocopies of official documents. Also a couple of maps and several sheets with writing in English, meticulously neat and almost childlike. One map detailed the Gobi desert and there was a spot marked about a hundred miles north of the town of Hongor. The second had a spot marked at a point in the Gulf of Chihli above the Yellow Sea, near the small islands of Tachin, midway between Penglai and Lushun. As the documentation on the accompanying sheets made clear, these were secret Chinese dumping sites for nuclear waste. It was unprocessed and stored in sealed containers, for burial under the desert or lowering onto the seabed.

Greenpeace had long suspected that in order to boost much needed foreign exchange earnings, China had also been accepting foreign nuclear waste for storage; and the papers confirmed this. But the most alarming evidence they contained was that there had been leakages from both the sand and sea sites. These leakages had been covered up by the authorities who now claimed to have re-sealed the containers.

The details on the sheets were familiar to Sewell. The waste was 'high level' and extremely dangerous, containing unused enriched uranium and fission products such as plutonium. It was vital to alert the international community before a major disaster struck. He stuffed the material carefully back into the envelope and inserted it into a special compartment built into the bottom of his suitcase.

There was nothing further he could do until he got home. So far all had gone smoothly. Now he had to concentrate on acting like a normal tourist, enjoying the rest of the two-week holiday with the others. Already he was looking forward to his week in Peking and then the planned trip on a steamer down the Yangtse river.

CHAPTER THREE

Evans wondered whether being an agent living a double life in enemy territory felt like this. Perhaps not, he concluded. Agents were trained for the role, trained to exist under the constant threat of exposure whilst living a life intended to look as normal as possible. Some married and had families – neither their wives nor their children having any idea of their real identity. They had active social lives, followed football teams and had favourite TV programmes. But underneath it all they were other people, driven by a deeper mission, dedicated by an ideal that made them despise the values and the lifestyles of their 'friends', even their 'loved ones'.

Presumably you had to be disciplined to a fault to lead such a double life successfully. Turning emotions on and off, expressing enthusiasm when you didn't really feel it, arguing fiercely for things you didn't believe in. Did living such a life make you doubt your own integrity and roots, make it hard to distinguish between right and wrong, between reality and unreality?

He was finding it difficult enough coping with his own much more nebulous, predicament. The world he had stumbled into seemed so far away from the wonder of China. He felt constantly preoccupied, as if he was looking over his shoulder all the time, yet unsure what he was supposed to be looking for. Even here in the tranquillity of the Summer Palace on Peking's north-western outskirts, he felt claustrophobic in the humidity of the afternoon, as if there was a cloud hanging over him. He shuddered involuntarily.

'Are you all right?' Jenny looked at him quizzically. There had been hardly a moment to be together since their discussion after Hu's abduction; even now they were in a crowd.

'Oh – yes,' He smiled apologetically. For a split second he doubted whether the events of the previous evening had happened. They seemed unbelievable set against the serenity of the scene before him.

Now a public park, the Summer Palace had belonged to the last of the Manchu Empresses. Its splendour epitomised the tourist's image of an imperial retreat. A covered walk way linked one set of pagodas to another, its ceiling decorated with extraordinarily intricate scenes of colour and shade; according to Chinese legend, if a pair of lovers passed through here, their futures would be entwined forever after. Ornamental bridges passed among water lilies. Temples towered on Longevity Hill over Kunming Lake and permanently moored to the quay was a paddle-steamer, built of marble. The

Empress had built the palace from funds earmarked for the Chinese navy and the outlandish marble steamer was a defiant gesture at the navy commanders who had protested at her decadence.

As Evans turned to look at the lake, boats drifting languidly across in the late afternoon, something seemed to stir in the shadow of the marble steamer. He peered closer. Reflected in the water were two pairs of staring eyes protruding from pale, haggard faces: Hu and his father, grotesquely bunched together. Christ! They were haunting him! He narrowed his eyes against the sun hanging low across the water. The vision passed. What was true and what was false? He looked sheepishly around, relieved that nobody had spotted his behaviour. Although his trade was certainty, he was beginning to doubt himself. It was a distinctly uncomfortable experience.

❖

Keith Makuyana's appointment with the ANC was fixed in a safe house in the suburbs of Harare. The house was discreetly guarded, and Makuyana and Tombe were searched before they were let in to meet Selby Mngadi, a top man in the ANC's military wing, Umkhonto we Sizwe. In his late-forties, he was a veteran of Umkhonto's first abortive attempt in 1967 to infiltrate guerrillas into South Africa through Rhodesia. High on South African security's wanted list, he had survived a number of assassination attempts and travelled frequently to other parts of Africa. A slight, wiry figure with a small beard, he had a ready laugh and an easy manner which contrasted with the Zimbabwean's rather stiff reserve.

Makuyana was all too aware that relations between the chief South African liberation force and the ruling Zimbabwe African National Union had been tense prior to independence in 1980, and there had been rocky moments since. During the liberation struggle, the ANC had worked closely with the rival Zimbabwe African Peoples Union; both had enjoyed the patronage of the Soviets and had been courted by the West. ZANU had a much lower international profile, its chief supporter being China.

Makuyana decided to lay all his cards on the table. 'As you may know I was close to Robert Temba. We had an understanding which overcame problems between our organisations. We worked well together. Our mutual trust was based on years of friendship. Such trust cannot be built up easily. But I want to try. It is essential for both our interests that I have a direct link through you to the ANC.'

Mngadi did not seem that impressed. He was wary of Zimbabwe security. Too often they seemed to obstruct the ANC just when Mngadi and his comrades most needed assistance.

Continuing, Makuyana said, 'We know there have been a spate of attacks on ANC people recently in Zimbabwe.' He paused, weighing his next words carefully. 'I gather you suspect Pretoria has infiltrated the ANC at a high level. Their information on targets has been too precise.'

Mngadi looked irritated but did not respond. The Zimbabwean pressed on. 'Robert's killing convinces me South African intelligence have a cell based here in Harare. I cannot tell you why, but we suspect the letter bomb was local.'

'Really?' The ANC man leaned forward, alert where he had previously been non-committal.

'All my instincts tell me if we can crack this cell, it could be very important. Not only in neutralising their activity here, but in getting to the source of their infiltration of your organisation. The trouble is, we have come to a halt with our investigations.' He didn't mention that, three days after the event, his staff were still patiently combing through the telephone operator list, visiting the homes of those whose phones had been used, as yet without any positive leads. But he had the ANC man's close attention. Now was the time to ask.

'So I have come for some help.'

Mngadi leaned back in his chair and stared at the ceiling for a moment. Help, huh? Why wasn't it more forthcoming when the boot was on the other foot? He felt like blurting out the question.

Instead, he turned to a colleague, lounging bored at the sitting room doorway. 'Could you leave us alone for a minute please?' The man looked startled, but turned without comment and closed the door. Tombe, taking the hint, excused himself and left too.

'You probably did not know the full extent to which Robert kept me posted on contacts between the two of you,' Mngadi said. 'I want you to keep in close touch with me from now on. But, please, no intermediaries, on either side. Just the two of us. And whatever we tell each other goes no further without joint agreement. OK?'

'Sounds fine to me.'

'This information is for you alone. We have just had a break. Our people lifted an Inspector in the security services in Pretoria. You will have seen the news?'

Makuyana nodded. Images of news reports flashed through his mind: white officials running around like headless chickens trying to trace the Inspector who had disappeared from his house in the old Afrikaner capital, Pretoria. It was still causing a minor panic in the comfortable white suburbs. The war was coming home.

'Well, he talked – like nobody's business. About infiltration and disruption of the ANC. We were also told there definitely is a cell based here in Harare. Apparently Pretoria thinks it is now too risky to launch assassinations from home. It has to be organised locally. We didn't get any names, unfortunately. Our source claimed he wasn't running individuals, just involved in overall strategy. But we got the codename for the operation: NOSLEN.'

'How do you spell that? ' Makuyana made a note. 'You didn't ask him about Robert's death by any chance?'

'No, we lifted him the day afterwards – too soon to brief our people. Communications with the comrades inside are difficult, as you know. They could be easier if we had more help from our friends.'

Makuyana ignored this sting in the tale. His staff were used to the way even the most biting remark washed off him. Instead he bade his farewell and they exchanged direct line phone numbers.

As he drove off with his assistant Tombe, the ANC man who had been excluded from the conversation took down their car registration number and then went back inside to talk to Mngadi. 'Any joy?' he asked.

'What? That lot? Only the usual fishing expedition. That's all we get from the Government these days. I sometimes wonder whether Harare would like a truce with Pretoria. We seem to be an embarrassment to them.'

The ANC man looked away from Mngadi to hide his disappointment. He didn't believe a word his chief had just said. He knew that meant that the car number could be more important than he had first imagined.

❖

'Purpose of journey Mr Herson?' The young border guard glared suspiciously at Swanepoel.

'A holiday – to see my grandchildren in the Cape,' he replied easily. He wasn't going to be bothered by someone the age of his children, and a black to boot.

'How long?'

'Two weeks, maybe three. I am retired now. I don't have to rush back.'

The guard disappeared inside an office to run a computer check on his name. Swanepoel still wasn't bothered. His cover was watertight. It had never failed him before. He stared down into the muddy waters of the Limpopo swirling a hundred feet below, and thought back to the days when he used to bring his kids in the other direction across Beitbridge to holiday in what was then Rhodesia. There was never any delay. The white customs and passport officers had been friendly in those days, waving them through with only a cursory glance at their documentation.

'You can go now Mr Herson.' He looked up as the guard handed him back his passport, feeling contemptuous. This young upstart didn't know anything, couldn't know he was on his way to security headquarters in Pretoria where he would stay overnight with a colleague before travelling on southward to the Cape by plane.

But almost as he drove off, heading into the hinterland of Northern Transvaal, Ed Tombe was knocking on his front door. Makuyana's staff man had about him the air of someone going through the motions. The name Paul Herson was number 194 on the long list supplied by Zimbabwe telecommunications and he had no reason to suppose it would be any more informative than the previous 193 he and his colleagues had been wading through.

There was no answer. He knocked again. Still no reply. He walked round the bungalow. It looked deserted. Nobody was about. The back garden was unkempt. Perhaps the owner had been away some time? He turned to walk to his car, almost running into a small boy on a BMX bike.

'Uncle has gone away on holiday,' said the boy.

'Uncle? Is he your uncle?'

'No – just call him that. Don't know his name.'

'Nice bike you've got there. I bet you can race fast on it,' Tombe smiled, ruffling the boy's hair, 'When did Uncle go?'

'Early this morning. I was out on my bike before breakfast. He told me.' The boy smiled confidentially, as if he was the recipient of treasured information.

'What does uncle look like?'

The boy shrugged his shoulders. 'A bit fat. Old. Got a moustache too.'

'Anything else?'

'He gave me some sweets once. Who are you?' The boy's eyes narrowed pointedly.

Tombe smiled again. 'Friend of a friend. I must go now. Look after that bike.'

He marked a routine tick on the telephone operator list against Herson's name, and scribbled 'Gone on holiday today. Old, fat.' Then he paused. Old? The description from the Grassroots assistant had mentioned being elderly. On holiday? Just a coincidence so soon after the bomb? Where on holiday? On an impulse, he decided to call for a check on people crossing the border to South Africa that day. Maybe a waste of time. But then the whole laborious exercise seemed a waste of time; there were still no leads. He drove off to check the next address.

❖

Across the other side of the world, another old man was also on the mind of someone younger. Wang was troubled about his mentor. The Chinese Communist Party Congress had just ended. At its closing session 90 retirements from the 209 strong Central Committee had been read out. They included most of the older champions of Marxist orthodoxy, veterans of the Long March. A smaller committee with younger faces was to take over. Nine members of the 20 strong Politburo were also missing. Deng Xiaoping's modernisers had made virtually a complete sweep of pushing out the old guard.

Although Wang's mentor had survived, this was only because he had deliberately kept his head low and gone along with the changes. Wang's hatred of the new revisionists bubbled up as he watched the Congress adopt, one after the other, economic reform policies, policies he believed were betraying the revolution and taking China down the capitalist road.

Now everything depended upon the Old Man. Although he was 85, his mind was as sharp as ever and he was in good health. He was a survivor. He had joined a peasant uprising in 1927, was a captain in the Long March, joined the Politburo in 1956 and remained a member through the shifting alliances of the next thirty years. His colleagues saw him as a pragmatist, perhaps a little weak, but an efficient Minister who got on with the job whatever the Party line at any given time. They never realised how fiercely the anger welled inside him as he saw all around him a crumbling of the ideals behind the Chinese road to communism.

'They are corrupt. All corrupt, these modernisers,' he had ranted at Wang during a moment when his usual cold control had snapped so uncharacteristically.

The reformist circle never imagined that the Old Man had the backing of leading officials in the State Security Ministry and that he still had considerable support within the People's Liberation Army. The PLA had 13 per cent of the delegates at the Party Congress. But, when the time came, it could exert a power much greater than that. That time could be sooner than we all predicted, Wang thought to himself. He stared through the tall window out of his characterless grey office, hardly noticing dusk closing in, nor the dancing shadows on the road outside as the cyclists, silhouetted against the red sky, hurried home.

He had an immediate task: to arrange for the nuisance Evans to be dealt with. It could be tricky because he had to do it through unofficial channels. Any mistake and he could find himself under investigation from China's ubiquitous security services. He sighed in disgust. That a revolutionary patriot like himself could become the target of his own Party's apparatus showed just how deep the rot had set in.

Makuyana was buried in a pile of paper on his desk. Days of inquiries and he had got nowhere on the Temba case. His staff were exhausted and he could tell they were losing their commitment and drive. There had been no breaks and now there were mutterings from his superiors about wasted hours. They were clamouring for action in the wake of another raid across the border.

The South African helicopters had come in at dawn, flying low to avoid radar, skimming across the bare landscape, blending into the blue-grey sky. They had hardly arrived before they were gone, leaving a wreckage of terror and devastation. Almost nothing was left of the village they'd hit. The first choppers had come in slowly, confident there were no defences, dropping scores of metal eggs. They burst upon impact, filling the atmosphere with a silver, shining sheet which drifted over the village. It seemed innocuous. The sleepy villagers alerted by the crashing sound of the engines stared up bewildered as the damp, clammy, mist enveloped them. They cowered as one of the choppers turned back and hovered briefly. But it did nothing – except drop a small burning object before banking away sharply.

Suddenly the mist ignited and the napalm ate the villagers alive. Screaming children ran out of their beds with their skin on fire, only to fall, writhing in agony until they became terribly still. Their parents were unable to heed their desperate cries because they too were being burnt, tormented by the shocking violence of an attack which had been so quiet: no machine guns, no bombs – just the deadly rain of napalm, getting in everywhere.

Makuyana had read the news agency reports from Pretoria where the Minister expressed 'regret' at the need to take retaliatory action against the ANC by hitting one of its bases in Zimbabwe. The fact that the village was not a base didn't bother the South Africans. Putting the frighteners on Zimbabwe was what mattered.

He looked up from his desk as his number two knocked on the door. Ed Tombe sat down wearily, speaking mechanically.

'We may have something at last. Paul Johann Herson. Retired civil servant, aged 67 years. I went to his home on a routine check earlier today. Seems to fit the description of the man who visited the Grassroots shop. Found he had just left to go on holiday. So I checked with the border. He went across into South Africa at midday. Said he was visiting relatives on holiday. Nothing suspicious, and he was let through without a search. I contacted the pensions department and they confirmed he worked in agriculture for 20 years before retiring. No blemishes: a solid if unspectacular career.'

'So? An old man who goes on holiday?'

Tombe looked sheepish at his boss' scepticism. 'I know it's not much, but its more than we have got with all the other names. They have produced bugger all.'

'OK. Put on a special alert so we hear when he returns.' Makuyana did not sound very enthusiastic. 'Now, a complete change of direction. I want you to check our dossiers on every senior ANC person in the country. Our team needs a rest, I know. But afterwards. This is a priority. An urgent one.'

Tombe nodded woodenly. His shoulders seemed to sag around him. All that effort after the Temba killing and now switched to another job, just like that, but loyalty stopped him protesting. He said nothing, making quickly for the door.

'Ed,' Makuyana called after him, 'I'm sorry. I know you have put everything into the investigations over Robert. I appreciate that. But I am not taking you off the inquiry. This is simply another part of it. Sit down and let me explain.'

The two men remained closeted for an hour, before Tombe got up again to leave, this time with more of a spring in his step.

❖

More than three million people lived in the city of Chengtu. But to Evans it had a small-town atmosphere which contrasted with the industrial bustle of Peking. It felt older, too, as if from a generation further back in time. The people were evidently less used to encountering foreigners and congregated to stare at members of the delegation whenever they ventured forth from the imposing Jinjiang hotel situated alongside a muddy river. The vegetation surrounding the city was a great deal richer and the climate in the province of Sichuan much wetter and more humid than in the east of the country.

Half the city seemed to be a sprawling series of gaunt factories and blocks of flats, the other half made up of traditional brick homes with courtyards lurking off twisting side streets. Huge free markets sprawled along the roadsides, make-shift trestle tables groaning under the weight of fruit and vegetables.

Their hotel was again a concrete block, the grounds of which were full of vegetable patches. Inside, each room had an Hitachi air conditioner. It was early in the morning as one of the guests, in a room on the third floor with a view out onto the main entrance, picked up the handset of the old-fashioned black phone and asked the operator downstairs for a number. Thirty seconds later the phone rang at the other end. Wang picked it up immediately.

'He is leaving now,' the Noted Person in the hotel said.

A middle aged woman sat hunched over a stream of water snaking its way alongside one of the main roads through Chengtu. She was brushing her teeth, Evans noticed as he jogged past, slowing to watch in astonishment as she cleared her throat and spat.

'Come on! You are slacking!' His fellow 'Noted Person', Simon Jeffries, called to him.

The two men ran on, passing at regular intervals small groups of people doing their early morning exercises out in the open. The old women were the most incongruous as they shadow boxed in a world of their own, not noticing the foreigners running past.

Evans was unfit. He hadn't responded with much enthusiasm when Jeffries cajoled him into running over drinks the previous night. He felt grateful that the surroundings were so interesting. Even a fifteen minute jog could seem like an hour if you had nothing else to think about. When he ran every weekday morning through the park near his home it was invariably with a friend and the time slipped by as they talked continuously. Now he was intrigued by the fitness fanatics around him performing a cross between yoga and a sort of static dance out in the open, quite oblivious to his stares.

He was starting to sweat and the traffic in the road alongside was becoming heavier. 'That shower when we return can't come soon enough,' he muttered to Jeffries. 'I have become pretty sluggish during this trip, all this eating and sitting around.'

'Watch out!' Jeffries' scream was dulled as Evans, half stumbling, saw a car veering onto the pavement towards him. He barely had time to turn slightly to avoid its front bumper before it brushed him sideways on, flinging his body away. He caught a glimpse of the familiar curtain drawn across the back window before he hit the ground and passed out.

❖

Swanepoel whistled to himself down the long, straight road to Pretoria. It was a crisp, bright, cloudless winter's day, though he knew that when the sun went down, the cold and the dark would sweep in swiftly and envelope the countryside of his beloved Northern Transvaal. This was his country. He took in the wide expanse of the veld on either side, bounded by rolling hills. The flatness of the terrain and the seemingly endless stretch of road ahead to the horizon was monotonous to others, but not to him. The sense of space gave him a feeling of power and destiny.

When he stopped briefly for petrol, he bought some biltong to chew and to help pass the time away. He loved the salty taste of the dried venison.

Swanepoel had mixed feelings about taking a holiday. His job was his whole life. He was a workaholic, without much time for family matters. The thought of retirement had filled him with fear, so much so that he had pleaded with his superiors to keep him on after his 65th birthday. Most agents were happy to accept their pension and relax after the years of pressure and disruption of their personal lives. Swanepoel was different. In his darkest moments, alone with his bottle of KWV and after rather too many refills of his perfectly shaped brandy glass, he would contemplate the utter emptiness of his future when they finally gave him the push and put him out to grass.

Although his Nissan saloon cruised comfortably at 140 kilometres per hour, it was late before he reached the outskirts of Pretoria and then headed down Arcadia Street for the small hotel near security headquarters where he intended to spend the night. The following day he would pay a visit to the office, then drive to Jan Smuts Airport and catch a plane for the Cape and his family. He had a quick steak, washed down with a bottle of wine, before turning in for the night, exhausted after the day-long drive. It was great being home again.

That night, as he lay in his hotel bed, he woke briefly in the early hours of the morning, half conscious of a roaring noise. It passed and he slipped back into a deep sleep. But the next morning's news bulletins confirmed that he had not been dreaming. A powerful bomb planted under a truck had exploded next to the military barracks in central Pretoria, killing five soldiers and injuring 67 other people, the majority of them whites. It was the biggest attack on a military installation in over a year since a car bomb had killed 19 people near Air Force headquarters in Pretoria. The blast gouged a crater in the road and shattered windows in offices for several blocks around. Wreckage was hurled more than a hundred yards. The glass front of the accident and emergency ward of the hospital nearby was blown in, adding to the chaos as the wounded had to be rushed elsewhere.

The previous day, a black police constable had been killed in a hand-grenade attack in the township of Mamelodi to the east of the city. The day before that a car bomb killed four white policemen outside the city magistrates' courts and a mine had exploded in a hotel frequented by foreign businessmen.

These events weighed heavily on Swanepoel's mind as he strolled to the office, spoiling his enjoyment of the familiar sounds and sights of the streets he knew so well from many years of life in Pretoria. He had always thought of it as *the* capital city of South Africa. Why they had conceded to co-capital status with Cape Town just to satisfy the English-speaking whites in the south of the country, he could never comprehend. What a ridiculous business, shifting all the paraphernalia of government between the two cities every six months. Afrikanerdom had been in total control for four decades now, there was no need to pander to the English speakers anymore.

Still, his beloved Pretoria seemed much the same, though there were unfamiliar signs of tension, and he noticed that the black pedestrians had shed some of their obedient deference. Why, a black youth had just bumped into him without even the usual grovelling apology!

Swanepoel was pondering all this as he turned the corner towards the precinct of security headquarters. Then he pulled up in shock. The imposing modern building was still the same. But the ground floor was surrounded by sandbags. A barbed wire 'corridor' stretched from the entrance down to the pavement where a temporary construction had been erected to act as a security check and a surveillance point to guard the building. From a platform on top, machine guns poked out of slits in the fortifications and two pairs of eyes scrutinised him carefully as he walked up to a heavily guarded wooden hut.

After showing his identification he was taken up by lift to the tenth floor to meet his chief, General K.J. van der Walt, known as 'KJ' to colleagues in the trade. Over six foot tall, balding with grey hair, and a paunch, he had dominated the security services since the military moved in to push aside the old leadership of BOSS in the late 1970s.

'Ah, Maritz, good to see you. Are you well?'

'I was until I saw all the changes around here.'

'You mean the extra protection? Don't worry about that, man,' KJ waved his hand airily. 'The ANC are getting cheekier, that's all. We don't want to take any chances.'

The General was never much one for chit-chat and he got straight to the point.

'I want a favour of you, Maritz. I know you are here to see your family. I know you haven't had a break for over a year. But my men are being stretched all ways. There have been lots of retirements recently. Too many of our officers are too young. There is a special operation coming up and we need your experience. Will you stay on here for a while to take charge?'

Swanepoel paused and looked out of the armour plated window. He had never understood why they bothered to armour plate this high up. He did not want to give the impression of being too enthusiastic; never let them guess they were doing *him* a favour by involving him in real action when he would only have been bored lounging about with his family and drinking too much.

'What do you want me to do?' he said, as non-committally as he could.

❖

Jenny was worried. Evans had insisted to the group, and to the Chinese officials who had bustled in to assist with a medical check, that it had all been an accident: his fault for running too near the road. But when she pressed Simon Jeffries, he had been equally insistent that they had been jogging well inside the boundary of the wide pavement. Although he remained confused because it had happened so suddenly, the car appeared to veer directly towards Evans.

She was less concerned now about his physical health. He had pulled out of the day's events to rest, badly bruised and shaken. But, remarkably, nothing was broken. Although he wouldn't be able to jog for a while, he was still able to walk slowly.

Jenny mechanically noted details of the commune they were visiting. The facts came pouring out of the Chair of the Management Committee like a burst pipe: 7,000 households, 27,500 people, 800 of whom were Party members. At times the sheer quantity of information seemed like an alternative to explanation. The rest of the Delegation waited tolerantly for Jenny's by now ritual question: what was the proportion of Party members on the Commune's Management Committee and other key committees controlling the factories and the Production Brigades? About 80 per cent, was the answer.

Jenny pulled out her pocket calculator: 'So, Party members form just four per cent of the population, but hold 80 per cent of the key positions?'

'If you say so.' The Management Committee Chair, a middle-aged mother of two, did not smile.

Jenny found it ironic that, though the most left-wing person in their group, she invariably found herself asking the most critical questions about China's political structure. But her mind was elsewhere, and she asked to be excused from the remaining day's programme.

Back at the hotel, she knocked on Evans' door. There was no reply. For the first time on the visit she was grateful that no hotel doors were locked. She eased the door open. He was breathing fitfully, tossing and turning in his bed.

She sat down next to him and held his hand gently: 'How are you?'

Evans jerked bolt upright, eyes blinking wide-open. 'You frightened me.'

'I am sorry.'

He looked awful, she thought. In place of his normal easy manner there was a tension which gave him a haunted appearance.

'I can't sleep. I feel drained, but I can't relax. My mind keeps racing round. I'm glad you came.' He smiled weakly for the first time, gripping her hand. 'My room was searched during the jog.'

'Are you sure?'

'Yes. I don't think anything was taken, but I need to double-check. Someone turned over my files and searched my luggage, someone who knew that I was going jogging, otherwise they could have searched during one of our visits.'

'Perhaps they wanted to search in case you did not come back. Was it really an accident, Jim?'

'No. I told them it was because I can't prove otherwise. But the pavement was very wide at that point. There were people all over doing their early exercises. We were running well away from the road. They are trying to kill me, Jenny. What are we going to do?'

He slumped back. The sudden impact of the car flashed back through his mind, like an action replay on a television sports programme. He could see himself being hit and thrown over. The same sense of disorientated panic gripped him again as he remembered coming to in the street surrounded by Chinese faces. They seemed friendly, even sympathetic, behind their impassive expressions. But he felt claustrophobic. Out there, behind them, one of their number had tried to injure him, maybe even to kill him.

'The first thing is to get you into a decent state.' She handed him his vest and underpants which were draped untidily over a chair, rather to his embarrassment. 'Get these on and lie down on the floor. I'll try relaxing you using the Alexander technique.'

She told him to lie on his back, then propped his head up on a couple of books, pulling his neck firmly so that it stretched as she massaged it. Then she eased his shoulders, loosening them while she tugged his arms outwards, and folded his hands across his stomach. Finally she stood astride his legs, lifting them from underneath his knees as she stretched the length of his body again. She left his knees bent and his legs raised up in a vee-shape, with his feet pulled back.

He felt absolutely placid. She was massaging his temples now and he could feel the tension evaporating, conscious only of her soothing hands and her disciplined coolness as she had progressed methodically through the different stages specified under the technique. She didn't say anything. She hardly seemed aware of him as he lay there feeling perfectly spoiled, and a little alive again.

When she had finished, he was almost asleep. She went out and came back a few minutes later with a plastic jar of tablets.

'Right. I want you to lie there for twenty minutes without moving. You must not sit straight up, that would undo the relaxation process. Roll over sideways before getting up. Then I want you to take some of these Calcium Pantothenate capsules. Your blood sugar levels will be very low after the accident. The capsules will help.'

He dozed for half an hour before rolling over, climbing into bed and falling asleep instantly. It was dark when he awoke to find Jenny reading under a lampshade, a shadow falling across her hair. She came and sat on his bed.

'How are you?'

'Much better. Just stiff, that's all.'

'Good'. She leaned over to kiss him lightly on the cheek and she held his hand as if he were her patient. Then she frowned. 'I've been thinking. If they tried to kill you once, they will try again. It must be very important to them. So, don't be caught alone outside the hotel. We ought to stick together, and if I am not around, stay with the others.'

Evans didn't need persuading. 'I don't feel comfortable with Harold Williams, though. The guy gives me the creeps.'

'Me too. Remember his sudden appearance at my lecture. He appeared out of nowhere, just when Hu passed that surreptitious note.' She paused. 'What interests me is that the authorities haven't detained you or warned you formally. Perhaps we are dealing with an unofficial group – maybe one of the factions in the ruling elite. In which case they will have to be careful about how they move against you. Protection in numbers may be more effective than it seems.'

'There is something else Jim,' Jenny paused, 'Shu is being withdrawn as our interpreter again. She is flying back to Peking in the morning. Some special assignment, they said. Her replacement is a friend of your's – Wang Bi Nan.'

❖

Makuyana crouched in the shadow of a hedge alongside the driveway of the house tucked discreetly back from the road. He was grateful for the power cut which had knocked out the northern part of Harare an hour before. It was pitch black.

His knees were aching. It was some time since he had been on active surveillance; his responsibilities generally kept him at arms length from his field agents. He had been in the same position for two hours now and the waiting brought back memories. He hated vigils like this. It might come to something. On the other hand it might not. He was by temperament an impatient person, one who had to be doing something all the time or he got frustrated. Like now.

'Where are you, you bastards,' he muttered to himself.

Across the road, he knew Ed Tombe would be hiding and watching too. The others were on call when their target appeared, ready to follow him in relays, so that nobody stayed long enough to be recognised as a tail.

Selby Mngadi had tipped them off about an unofficial ANC gathering in the house which he insisted they should be monitoring. The meeting had already started. Could someone get up there right away and find out who was attending?

After hastily briefing his team, Makuyana had been driven up in Tombe's car which they had left down the road. Two similarly unmarked vehicles had followed them. He hoped they would be sufficient for the task.

Makuyana wondered who was inside and what lay behind Mngadi's concern. He didn't like untidy missions like this. Mngadi had sounded so urgent, so insistent, but Makuyana did not know what he was really after here. The targets might be on foot or emerge from the driveway in a car. He assumed there was more than one person, but he didn't even know that. Not for the first time during his lonely sojourn, he felt distinctly uneasy.

Then he tensed. A light shone out of the side of the house as a door opened. Two figures moved swiftly out and into a garage nearby. He spoke fiercely into his walkie-talkie: 'Ed, get to your car. They are coming out.'

As he finished speaking the car started up and roared down past him almost in one movement, its lights out. It veered leftwards into the road. Seconds later, he heard the familiar sound of Tombe's engine starting up. It was lucky, Makuyana thought, that Tombe and his other colleagues were wearing special night glasses, which meant that they wouldn't need car lights either.

In the next instant the whole road seemed to explode. The darkness turned first white, then orange, almost blinding him with its ferocity. One split-second Tombe's car was accelerating past, the next it had been engulfed in an inferno, pieces of metal shooting everywhere. The heat swept past Makuyana, singeing his eyebrows. Pellets of glass dug into his face. He fell back into the bush as another lightless car swept past him down the drive and roared off.

For the second time in little over a week Makuyana needed to steel himself and use every bit of his willpower to push his professionalism to the fore and push his emotions back as he was confronted with investigating the death of a close comrade.

There was virtually nothing left of Tombe in all of the wreckage. The eighteen pound bomb had been attached under the rear wheelarch, next to the boot of his Nissan saloon, and activated by radio signal.

Makuyana remembered reading a recent brief on the war in the north of Ireland describing how the IRA and British army electronic engineers had been battling for supremacy over the use of remote, radio-controlled bombs. Mistakes had been made: some British landmines had been triggered by their own army scanning high frequencies, and the same practice had jammed or neutralised other British devices. Republicans claimed that the British had also accidentally activated several IRA bombs. But there had been no accident this time. This bomb had exploded with clinical efficiency, sending parts of the car into nearby trees and front gardens. Neighbours had poured out of their homes to see Makuyana transfixed before the smoking remains.

After some time the car pursuing the target vehicles returned. The bombers had got away. Makayana and his team made a search of the house, but found nothing. One room had been used – there was warm cigarette ash left – but the furniture and been completely wiped. They had left no leads inside, and the owners were oblivious, away on business in Europe.

These were no amateurs, Makuyana reflected. The bomb was highly sophisticated. Because it was radio-controlled, it could be attached very easily: no need to link it to the engine, or another moving part. It could be placed quickly – ideal for the job in question. The selection and use of the house also showed a professional hand. Who were they? It all led back to Selby Mngadi. The ANC man had sent them to the house on a pretty vague brief. And something else was troubling Makuyana: was it merely a coincidence that the saboteurs had attacked Tombe's car?

❖

Evans stared at the butcher. The man's small moustache twitched as he talked flat-out and shook the carcass of the pig as it dangled across the pavement. Then he let it go and abruptly grabbed another carcass, turning to cajole a customer into making a purchase. There were several others in the shop, a dark recess with a series of hinged panels opening upwards and sideways onto the pavement. The sight of the meat hanging out in the open shocked Evans.

There weren't any flies – he hadn't seen any flies since he arrived in China – but that didn't placate him. The scene brought back the sense that life and living was very much in the raw here in Chengtu.

He and Jenny strolled on through the backstreets of the city. Though still a little unsteady, stiff and bruised, he was relieved to be out in the open. There were shops on all sides, their shutters opening directly onto the streets with no pavement between. Fronting the narrow streets there were also small workshops with groups of people crouched over ancient machines. Cyclists dodged amongst market stalls covered with produce.

They slipped into a park, Jenny taking him by the arm. He felt at ease with her leading him around.

'Do you have a partner at home?', he asked.

'No. I was involved with someone until last year – but he couldn't stand the pace!' She smiled, relaxed. 'And you?'

'I've been too busy for relationships these past few years.' He didn't like being asked questions which made him talk about himself like that. Still, he couldn't complain, he had raised the subject.

They stood transfixed before a row of open shelters containing a dozen statues about fifteen feet high, all in bright colours, all enormously fat men with thin handlebar type moustaches and pointed caps. In a London park the figures would have looked ludicrous and garish. Here they were simply part of the scene: monuments to local rulers from past dynasties.

It began to spit with rain. Nothing to worry about, but they were due back at the hotel for an evening meal anyway. A fresh breeze brushed past, as they came closer, seeking in each other a shield. Evans could feel warmth under her thin blouse growing damp and opaque as it clung to her skin. The accident in the morning seemed suddenly very distant: perhaps Chengtu was all right after all.

In another part of the city Wang replaced the telephone receiver in its cradle. His conversation with Peking had been brief but the instructions were perfectly clear: on *no* account must Evans leave the country alive. There must be no more risky attacks in public. He must bide his time.

❖

Swanepoel peered out from the Casspir. It wasn't very comfortable but he felt secure in the Armoured Personnel Carrier. He would be much more exposed when he went back in with a team early the next morning.

Although it was some years since he had been into Mamelodi, the township seemed much the same. He had made a special request to come on a routine patrol. He wanted to soak it all in again. To see the smog that hung like a permanent cloud over the shacks and small square homes with their corrugated asbestos rooves. To listen to the babies with streaming noses who cried continuously. To watch the women washing household goods in bowls under standpipes. To sense the tension around anything that moved. To feel the bitterness of the children as they peered defiantly at the APC.

He didn't like to admit it, but, God, those kids frightened him. He wasn't bothered by the adults: he had seen too many of them bruised and bleeding, cowering under interrogation. They could be broken. All of them could be broken. But their children? They were getting younger all the time. In the Soweto uprising of 1976, when hundreds revolted against being taught in Afrikaans and sparked off a conflict that shook the country, the leaders were in their mid-to-late teens. Now the leaders were eleven, twelve, thirteen. The younger they were, the harder they seemed.

There was something distant about them, Swanepoel thought. They didn't seem to care for themselves as much. They didn't seem to have so much too lose. His apprehension turned to anger. Didn't they realise how lucky they were? Living in the south of Africa when their black brethren in the north were trapped in countries run by communists like Nyerere and Kaunda and Mugabe?

The APC slid round a corner. People were gathering. There were discordant sounds of screams and chants. A young black man burst out of the crowd. Swanepoel had never seen anyone so mortally terrified. The young man ran. The crowd chased, teenagers out in front. They pursued him as he ducked into what was presumably his home. Then they started to batter on the walls and break the windows. Swanepoel could see a mass of axes and hammers swirling in the frenzy. Knives glinted in the sun.

'God, they are going to demolish the house with their bare hands,' Swanepoel exclaimed to the APC driver.

But he was wrong. The young man's relatives pushed him out of the front door. They didn't want their house razed to the ground. He was set upon immediately, knives jabbing, fists flying. He ran round the house. They followed, tearing at him. Swanepoel could see blood spurting from his back, but still he struggled away, as if possessed.

The crowd also seemed possessed, unaware that the APC had crept up upon them. They were hacking at him now. Swanepoel had to admit to himself he had never seen anything so brutal. His violence was always calculated, always cool. This violence was naked, animal-like.

The young man fell to the ground and Swanepoel knew the instant he died. His eyes finally gave up. His body stopped fighting, shuddered and lay terribly still. The crowd drew back, almost ecstatic. Then a stillness descended as they suddenly noticed the APC. It revved up and pulled away quickly; no point in looking for trouble when the blacks were killing themselves.

'Another informer eliminated,' the driver muttered laconically. 'Your sources will be drying up soon.' He didn't seem that bothered. There was little love lost between the soldiers who took all the flak at the frontline and the security officers who manipulated from behind.

❖

It was at times like this that Makuyana wished he had a family to retreat into. His mind flashed back fourteen years, three months, two weeks and four days. His wife, pregnant with their second child, watching as he fooled around with his three-year-old son in the yard of the camouflaged ZANU camp deep in Mozambique. She enjoyed being pregnant and she looked radiant. He thought her bulge was quite sexy. She thought that was ridiculous and teased him: if men had to bear babies they would realise that amidst the joy it was damned uncomfortable and awkward. He had been thrilled to cup his hands over her belly and feel the baby kicking inside her. At night he had spent hours stroking her all over. Just as with the first one, they had made love, gently, as she lay on her side, until the day before her contractions began.

Over the years, he had torn himself away from those memories. He could not afford to wallow in nostalgia; it would have consumed him. Instead, he allowed himself to be consumed by his work. Anyhow, he rationalised, in his profession it was safer not having a family. He felt relieved that Ed Tombe had been single.

Occasionally, however, he would remember the steaming hot day when a Rhodesian army killer squad attacked their camp and destroyed it in minutes: barracks, school, temporary hospital, make-do homes – and people. He had returned in the evening from training a young squad in the bush to find the dismembered remains of his wife and son amongst the ruins. Men who were leaders like him didn't cry outwardly, but for weeks he cried inwardly. No doubt it was wrong to bottle up his emotions. He knew that ever since then, he had often given the impression of being cold and aloof.

He sat in his office, a desk lamp lighting up a file he was studying. Most of his staff had gone home hours before in a state of shock, some of the hardened agents hiding it better than others. The subject of his attention was Selby Mngadi.

There was nothing in the file to suggest that the man was suspect. Makuyana noted that he was a Zulu, but that he had not joined Chief Buthelezi's Inkatha movement, instead opting from his earliest days for the ANC and becoming one of their most trusted officials. His father too had been an ANC man; a leading activist in the Ladysmith area of the Natal province. He had been jailed, placed under house arrest and later murdered after what was reported to be a clash between Inkatha activists and ANC supporters of the United Democratic Front.

Mngadi himself had been responsible for some of the most successful ANC incursions deep inside the country, notably the sabotage raid at Sasolburg – the town in the Transvaal which was so dominated by South Africa's indigenous Sasol oil refinery complex that local car number plates bore the prefix 'OIL'. The raid had stopped production for three weeks, causing a slide on the Johannesburg stock exchange and a devaluation of the Rand.

Makuyana reached for the phone. It was late, but he needed to talk – this time in safety, on *his* patch.

❖

It was nine o' clock in the morning and the informality of the court room was disconcerting. Evans had to remind himself it was a murder trial. He was in the Intermediate People's Court in Chengtu, the defendant a 22-year-old worker charged with stabbing his girlfriend to death.

The accused was led in quietly, walking between the spectators who sat on the same level as the Judge and his two assessors in a small plain hall. There was no pomp or ceremony. It was hard to distinguish the three at the top table from the lawyers or the public, they all had similar, informal dress. Occasionally, the spectators would chatter amongst themselves without reprimand. Some walked in and out during the proceedings. Evans saw two women push past a policeman and the defendant to sit on the front row.

When the young man answered questions he was calm and fluent. His evidence was interspersed with that of witnesses and he was asked to comment on their accounts. After completing their evidence, witnesses were asked to listen to a record of it read out by a short-hand writer. Then a statement was brought across for their signature by the policeman guarding the defendant who was left standing on his own each time. All the witnesses spoke fluently with none of the nervousness and deference so characteristic of British courts. Evans was impressed. Perhaps it was because of the absence of hierarchy and ritualistic tradition.

In the early 1980s it had apparently been the practice of defendants to blame the Gang of Four for 'bad influences' in order to get lower sentences. But it seemed this young man was being made a public example, because the Judge gave a lecture about morality and respect for others. Then, after only two hours, the court was adjourned.

'We have arranged for you to meet the defence and prosecuting lawyers during the adjournment,' Wang told the delegation.

Though hardly acknowledging Evans' presence, he had been a model of courtesy this time. They moved into an empty courtroom next door for their discussion with the lawyers which turned into a fascinating exchange over court procedures. Evans was intrigued to hear that the two assessors were appointed after consultations with the defendant's workplace and the dead girl's technical college.

After half an hour the court resumed and the defendant was brought back, showing emotion for the first time. He was crying. The judge read out a statement and referred the case for final sentence to the President of the Court – the procedure necessary for a capital offence. A trial that would have taken one or two weeks in Britain was over in a morning.

Wang caught Evans' eye for the first time since his return. 'Next week he will probably be sentenced to be shot in the back of the neck – our country's method of execution. I do not suppose you would like to be in his position.'

CHAPTER FOUR

The sweaty smell of tension had always appealed to Swanepoel. He was pleased to be back in action again. They were going in early – at three a.m. – to catch the residents of Mamelodi unawares before they rose at four to get their trains and buses to Pretoria for work in the white city. His wife Sarie had been none too happy when he had phoned to say he would be delayed. He knew she suspected he was quietly delighted at being able to avoid the family again.

The unmarked car crept slowly through the entrance and down the dusty track that passed for the township's main street. He was glad he had taken the trouble to visit with the APC the day before. He didn't feel he was coming in cold.

Things were getting messy in the townships, though. In the old days a mission like this to hit a suspected ANC safe house would have been a piece of cake. Now there were so many different forces at work. The residents were more militant. That was a big enough problem, especially in terms of getting out safely again. But now there were the added complications caused by divisions within the black community – divisions carefully fostered by the white authorities. The trouble was that they could backfire sometimes.

Swanepoel had kept abreast of developments while in Zimbabwe. In an area like Mamelodi there was sharp conflict between the 'comrades' as they were called and the 'vigilantes'. The comrades were young and highly political. They brooked no compromise. Elected black councillors in the townships were treated as quislings, their houses and businesses attacked. The vigilantes were less impatient, more willing to cooperate – especially those secretly being paid by the security forces as informers or *agents provocateur*. The two groups squeezed ordinary people between them mercilessly. When the comrades attacked a 'collaborator', the vigilantes moved in to retaliate.

It was clever, Swanepoel thought, encouraging civil war *within* the black community. But it was risky too. The communal violence had started spilling over into neighbouring white areas.

The Government was also making great efforts to sponsor a black 'middle ground' which could be co-opted politically. The aim was to give the appearance of self-government in the townships which in the mid-1980s had been at the point of ungovernability. At the same time real power was being exercised by a network of joint management committees, under the control of the military and the police, not elected and only barely publicised. A soft outside and a rock hard inside to run the show; Swanepoel liked it.

The local police and army knew he was going in with a team. They were maintaining a discreet distance, but were on immediate call if needed. His information was that the house they were about to hit had been used by those who had lifted the Special Branch Inspector. The bastards. He would teach them a lesson.

They went through both the front and back simultaneously, crashing in the flimsy doors as if they weren't there. There were shrieks from the children and screams from the women who had been lying asleep on mats across the bare floor.

'The men! Where are they?' Swanepoel shouted at one of the women, probably in her early thirties who looked about fifty. He knew it was best to hit them while they were half-asleep to disorientate and frighten. You could achieve more that way sometimes than by physical assault.

She sobbed, terrified, 'They are away. At the mines. Near Johannesburg.'

'Don't lie you bitch.' He shook her, turning to a colleague: 'Take that kid out and stick it in the car.' It always helped to have a go at the children if the parents were proving obstructive.

But it made no difference on this occasion. None of the women had anything to tell them. Swanepoel asked for a computer trawl on the men and his Sergeant scurried out to the car radio. Minutes later he was back.

'They check out, Sir.'

By this time the home had been turned upside down, the few precious possessions it contained thrown outside, blankets trodden on, the small amount of food in the kitchen ground under heel.

Swanepoel bellowed in frustration. All his experience told him this wasn't a safe house after all. They had turned over the wrong place. Without so much as a backward glance he ordered his men out, seemingly unconscious and certainly uncaring of the sobbing chaos behind him.

Across the road two men stared through a small window in the house where the Inspector had spilled the beans and spoken his last words. They looked at each other. A narrow escape. It was time to move on before the information became more accurate.

❖

Noted Persons Delegation? They sounded a right bunch of wallies. Dick Sewell frowned when he heard the news that his party was to join another group, also on a visit from England, at Chungking for the trip down the Yangtse river.

He had made the most of his holiday – his first proper one for years. It was a real treat, particularly since Greenpeace were funding the basic cost of the trip.

He turned on the television set in his room. There was an advertisement for a Japanese hi-fi set. Then came the news and pictures of student uprisings all over the country. In Peking, 100,000 demonstrators gathered amidst the symbols of power – Mao's mausoleum, the Great Hall of the People and the gates of the Forbidden City. In Shanghai, several thousand marched to the Party headquarters demanding democracy and freedom of speech. In other cities, students were joined by workers carrying banners demanding reform.

Sewell couldn't follow the detail, but he knew from the news digests for tourists, translated into English from the daily press, that the unrest was widespread, with unprecedented riots involving not only the young, but peasants, workers and even football fans.

But he didn't feel threatened by the disturbances. They seemed so remote from his presence as a tourist. Only the documents in the false bottom of his suitcase were a reminder of danger. But the way things were going he should be out of the country, flying home safely in just over a week.

❖

'My room was searched again this morning,' Evans said to Jenny in a matter-of-a-fact way. As a piece of information, it seemed almost routine. 'Nothing was taken. God knows what they wanted.'

He passed on this news as their Delegation walked round one of the local schools. In spite of his preoccupation, he noticed how extraordinarily obedient the young children were, sitting in disciplined classroom rows before their teachers. Some teenagers were playing table tennis on concrete tables out in the afternoon sun. Jenny seemed a little remote he thought. He wondered if she was finding him irritating, out of place in her political world. The thought bothered him.

But that night she asked him up to her room for a chat. 'I've been trying to make sense of the last few days. It's all so intangible. But perhaps there's one aspect we could pin down: China's nuclear policy. Do you much know about it?'

It was an odd sensation for him to be the authority in a discussion with her. 'Not much is known. China wouldn't sign the Nuclear Non-Proliferation Treaty nor would it join the International Atomic Energy Agency; that closed another source of information and monitoring. After the Sino-Soviet split in 1960, the Government made a big push to develop an independent capability. I think it was 1964 when its first nuclear device successfully detonated. A major civil nuclear programme came later – in the mid-1980s. '

'But I thought China had a good supply of alternative energy sources,' Jenny interjected.

'That's quite true. It has probably the biggest fossil fuel reserves in the world and huge untapped hydropower resources. My own view is that the official reason for going nuclear for energy is not the whole truth. I think they are obsessed with nuclear energy because it is intimately bound up with developing and sustaining their nuclear weapons programme. That's why I questioned the scientist at the Institute.'

'Ah – the question that caused all the fuss. Is the sensitivity really about nuclear weapons?' She thought for a moment, recalling Hu's comments. 'What about links to other countries?'

Evans tried to recall some research papers he'd read before the trip. 'I remember an article on China's nuclear exports. It involved things like selling unsafeguarded heavy water to Argentina shortly before the Falklands War in 1982. And supplying nuclear fuels to Pakistan. There were also reports that China enriched uranium for South Africa in the early 1980s.'

'South Africa? Didn't Hu say his father had some information on that? But we are not much wiser, are we? All we do know is somebody here is pretty damm sensitive about matters nuclear.' She yawned and glanced at her watch. It was late.

Then there was a slight rustle at the door – and a sound of footsteps receding quickly. As if by instinct Jenny rushed out to the corridor. To her left, she heard a door shut – the door to the central stairway.

Heart pounding, she ran there. Through the door, listening. Down the stairs. One flight. Sound of another door shutting. She followed quickly. Through the second door and into the corridor below. She looked. Nobody to be seen. Just the click of another door closing, quietly this time: a bedroom door. She couldn't tell which – only that someone on the third floor had taken a good deal of trouble to avoid being seen..

Jenny turned to walk back up the stairs, the stillness of the sleeping hotel all around her. Then on impulse she took the lift down to reception and asked who was resident on the third floor. There was only one foreigner: a Mr Harold Williams. A sensation of pins and needles swept up her back and down her arms.

❖

Makuyana was unusual for a ZANU man. Almost without exception his comrades were from the majority Shona people. He was from the minority Ndebele who were concentrated in the South West of the country around Bulawayo. But he was fluent in three languages: SiNdebele, Shona and English.

As he waited for Mngadi, he reflected that he couldn't help liking the man. His Ndebele background gave him a special cultural affinity with the South African. The Ndebele were descendants of the Nguni who formed the majority of blacks in South Africa and culturally, they were close relatives of Mngadi's Zulu people.

Makuyana bitterly resented the way the West, the British especially, referred disparagingly to 'tribalism'. The word 'tribe' had become pejorative – yet what were the Scots, the Welsh, the Cornish, if they weren't 'tribes'? He felt a pride in the cultural traditions of his people, and frustration at the way these traditions were denied or suppressed.

There was a knock on his door and Mngadi was shown in – alone, as he had insisted. The room was bare: no pictures on the walls, no family photos – no give-aways to the personality of the occupant. The atmosphere was thick with tension.

Makuyana wasted no time on formalities. 'You know what happened last night?'

'Yes – I blame myself entirely. Of course you must know that.'

No response from Makuyana.

Mngadi changed tack. 'I need some help.'

'*You* need help! My number two was killed on a wild goose chase you started! I can't get a single sodding lead on the culprits! My department has been thrown into chaos.' Makuyana reigned himself in; he knew he would explode otherwise. It was uncomfortable to find his emotions overcoming him like this. But his outburst seemed to break the ice.

'I do apologise,' Mngadi said, 'I should have made myself clearer. It's just that I feel so guilty. To help you find those responsible, I need some help.'

He sat back in his chair, choosing his words carefully. 'At the moment I am not certain who I can trust in my own organisation. I told you when we first met that I suspected infiltration. This was confirmed when we lifted that security agent in Pretoria. When I was tipped off about the meeting in that house I asked you to go there because I thought that would be the most secure and effective method of surveillance. You see, I was informed there were ANC men in that house. Now we know it was a set-up.'

'Where did the tip-off come from?'

'A phone call. Anonymous. The caller sounded frightened. But when I asked him for some corroboration that he was genuine he gave several facts which could only be known by someone deep inside the ANC's Harare network. Of course he also knew where to reach me: that was significant in itself.'

'Why should I trust you?' It was a good question to ask, Makuyana had learnt from his years of experience as an interrogator. It put them on the spot. A professional might be able to dodge around it, but most of the genuine ones reacted in one of three ways: either fatalistic, resigned to being misunderstood; or hurt at their integrity being challenged; or angry.

Mngadi got angry, his fine white teeth flashing. 'Why should you trust me? Yes – a bloody good question. Have you any idea what it's like to be plagued with doubts about your closest comrades? How it feels when you cannot risk telling them things and yet you know you have to in order to get anything done? Do you know what it does to your spirit when you can sense the cancer of corruption and betrayal in a movement for which people are willing to sacrifice everything: their home comforts, their careers, their families, their lives?' His clenched fist smashed down on the desk.

There was a slight knock on the door. 'Coffee for two, sir.' A teenage boy entered, put two cups down on the desk, then retreated swiftly from the unpromising atmosphere.

The coffee relaxed them. Makuyana liked his black and had a habit of drinking it straight down, however hot. He peered upwards at the bare light bulb hanging from the bare ceiling. All his human instincts, all his professional know-how told him that this man was to be trusted. He had reached a senior level in Zimbabwe security because he could take decisions quickly. He took one now.

'OK Selby, what help do you need? Where do we begin?'

Makuyana leant forward, making notes as Mngadi talked. 'It pains me to admit it, but the ANC is seriously penetrated. I have already told you about the information coughed up by the Special Branch Inspector when we lifted him in Pretoria. And about operation NOSLEN. We think there may be a problem in London. In Harare there certainly is. It was made worse by the Soweto uprising in 1976. Afterwards, a whole generation of militants fled the country and went into exile to escape persecution. Many of them are now among our finest combatants and officials. But hundreds came out all at once. It was impossible to vet them all. We had a major organisational problem simply to place and disperse them. It would have been quite easy to place some sleepers or agents at that time.'

Makuyana pushed his chair back and stood up to stretch his legs. 'So. What do we do about it? How can we help?'

'I want you to come and work directly with us.' Mngadi paused, plucking at his beard as was his habit. 'It is hard to give concrete reasons, but I believe we are entering a crucial time. Something important must be on the boil. Otherwise they would not take so many chances: killing Tombe, for example, that was very risky. We have to get to them before the cancer spreads. We have to expose and smash operation NOSLEN before it smashes us.'

❖

When Swanepoel reached the scene he immediately spotted the tell tale signs of a professional job. They were getting better all the time, these terrorists; he had to admit it.

The assassination had been clinical. No hiccups. No clues left behind. Yes – a clean job, the only mess being the flesh, bone and blood that had once been the Minister's head.

He had been hit on his temple by two rounds from a heavy calibre pistol. The force had been enough to throw him backwards over six feet. The gunman must have been quite close: perhaps ten yards, Swanepoel surmised.

He stared down at the body of Chris Kruger, the man who had been tipped as a future Prime Minister. He found it difficult to focus his memory of the charismatic politician who could captivate smalltown audiences in the Orange Free State just as he could charm television viewers abroad. The perfect all-rounder: a Doctorate of Philosophy obtained from Oxford University and a Springbok cap as fly-half who would have been internationally famous amongst rugby followers had South Africa not been stopped from playing abroad. A man who, two hours ago, had been in his prime, whose rugged, handsome features and blonde hair had led the local press to dub him the 'Afrikaner Robert Redford'. Swanepoel smashed his fist against the palm of his other hand. Would these bloody politicians never learn? Why did each one always think he would be the exception and never get caught having an affair?

Kruger's personal assistant was in a state of deep shock. A sophisticated young woman with dark hair falling over her bronzed skin, she confirmed they had come to this spot in the hills overlooking Pretoria many times. It was their spot, she sobbed. Somewhere they could be together in the sun during weekends, when he had an hour or two to spare from his family or his duties.

She didn't remember anything significant about the assassin. She had been lying face down in the sun on a blanket, sipping a glass of cold wine, when Kruger had muttered something and got up. He didn't seem particularly bothered; she hadn't realised there was anything amiss until the double roar of the gun had hurled him, dead and bleeding, on top of her.

She couldn't believe that bullets had enough power to throw a twelve stone man like that. She had been too hysterical to concentrate on anything except the mess of his body draped grotesquely over her. She had just the vague memory of running footsteps and a car screeching away.

First the Inspector and now Kruger. A week apart. There was a precision about both jobs which someone in the trade like Swanepoel had to admire. They *were* getting good, he thought again. Too fucking good. There was no point in chasing around after them, hoping they would make a mistake or leave a calling card. Let the police do that. His team had more important priorities.

Again, the key strategic importance of Operation NOSLEN came home to him. Outnumbered six to one, the whites couldn't survive forever by force of arms. They had to destablise the black majority. Balkanise the country and create conflict and division amongst the blacks through forcing them into the tribal 'homelands' most had never seen. Nurture a black middle class. Sponsor black businesses. Co-opt some of their politicians. Finance rival political groups, rival trade unions, rival community networks, to the main opposition forces. Put Zulu up against Xhosa. Sponsor Buthelezi as a rival to Mandela.

Encourage the Inkatha Zulus to knock the hell out of the United Democratic Front in their increasingly bloody clashes. Set comrade up against vigilante in the townships. Invade hostile neighbouring states if necessary. Above all, through NOSLEN, penetrate the resistance movements, break them from within. A total strategy: it was beautiful, as beautiful as the hillside around him. What a pity it had been temporarily disfigured by this ugly stain.

❖

In his room on the fifth floor of the Chengtu Hotel, Wang was on the phone to Peking again, filing another report. He had more information for the Old Man, and he knew it was important enough to risk talking on an open line.

'Evans may be onto more than we think. He was overheard talking to the the girl last night.'

'What? Another one? Is the whole Delegation full of subversives?' The Old Man sounded highly irritated.

Wang summarised the over-heard conversation. There was a long pause. Wang knew that the Old Man was thinking. He would sometimes stay silent for a full minute during a telephone conversation as he considered one option after another.

'Keep your ear to the ground – and find those documents. But don't get him in Chengtu. The rumours going around security circles here are bad enough already. We don't want another incident or Sichuan police will start getting even more suspicious. Get him as soon as possible afterwards.'

The Old Man put the phone down, wondering whether his protégé in the field was up to the job. He sighed. In the old days he could have moved someone fresh in. Still, Wang was conscientious and loyal. That counted for a great deal, especially in this dark period.

He settled back to digest the brief on his desk. The Party Leader was postponing major reforms for two years because of the economic crisis. Good. Another sign of the way things were falling apart. He turned to a second memo. There was an acute aluminium shortage, and a Government edict would shortly be issued forbidding anyone to use aluminium window frames. What a joke, the Old Man mused. He shook his head. They really were in trouble.

❖

The Noted Persons were well into the second half of their trip now. Chengtu was one hundred miles distant as Evans pulled the sheet and blanket more closely around him and listened to the regular beat of the carriage wheels on the track underneath. They would be in Chungking by early morning.

If you really want to see China, the best way is to travel by train, he had been told. He tried to visualise what the countryside might be like as it flashed by anonymously in the darkness outside. He wasn't certain whether he would fall fully asleep again. It was quite likely he would drift through to the morning half awake, his mind alive and, at the end, not quite sure whether he had slept or not. Eventually, the train pulled in – spot on 6.50 a.m. Chinese trains had a reputation for punctuality.

During the Second World War, Chungking had been the capital of the Nationalist government headed by Chiang Kai-shek's Kuomintang Party. Today it was a heaving industrial city perched spectacularly on cliffs and hillsides with the Yangtse and Kialing rivers converging around it. The population of six million seemed to be all out, teeming through the streets as Evans watched from the minibus which had picked them up from the station. It pulled up outside the most extraordinary hotel he had ever seen, standing in spacious gardens, almost palace-like, with domes and spires, reflecting a kind of tatty decadence which contrasted sharply with the toiling women pulling their handcarts along the hilly streets outside.

Time passed quickly. They visited the hot spring parks, the University, the Working People's Palace of Culture, but the highlight was Red Crag village. It had been the Communist base in the city during the Second World War when Mao's Party were in an uneasy alliance with the nationalists against the Japanese. Evans paused for a while in the bedroom where Mao had slept when he came to negotiate personally with the Kuomintang in the autumn of 1945. He felt the desk where the great man had written thousands of his famous words. A guerrilla for all those long years, then finally the triumph of liberation in 1949. A hero of the peasant masses and yet a womaniser and an autocrat. What sort of a person was he really?

A touch on the shoulder interrupted his day-dream. It was Jenny. She looked around to make sure they were alone.

'I've been asking around the Delegation about Harold Williams' background. He's just taken early retirement from the Foreign Office. But apparently he's very evasive when you ask him about his old job. My guess is he was in British Intelligence.'

Before Evans could react, the room filled. They both stared out at the control post which stood across the small valley, some two hundred yards from the buildings now called the Red Crag Revolutionary Commemoration Centre. Empty and almost innocuous now, the control post was positioned perfectly for the supervisory role assigned to the Kuomintang soldiers who had kept watch, night and day, over the comrades' comings and goings. Not exactly the relationship of trusted partners in a united war front, Evans mused. He wondered how easily the comrades had slept at night or gone about their business by day with the guns and the binoculars from the control post permanently trained upon them. They must have been aware that the united front might fracture at any time and the order could come from above to open fire. They must have lived in a constant state of suspended tension, Evans thought – rather the way he was feeling now.

❖

Callous wasn't a description Swanepoel would have applied to himself. Ruthless, yes. Cold, maybe. Hard, of course; you had to be in his job. These were his watchwords. In his book the terrorists were the callous ones – vile specimens out to destroy Afrikanerdom, the ones who would stoop at nothing to kill a top politician like Chris Kruger in the sunshine and leave his body in a bloody pool beside an hysterical girl.

Revenge was another of his watchwords. Not blind, lashing-out revenge born in a moment of temper. No, calculating revenge with an iron law that specified retaliation whenever your side was hit. Never let them get away with anything. Always strike back. Teach them that they couldn't mess about.

He had been summoned from Pretoria to John Vorster Square, the dreaded security headquarters at the centre of the sprawling city of Johannesburg. With its bright blue panels and plate glass windows, John Vorster Square was the building where scores of detainees went in never to come out: they 'fell in the showers', 'slipped on the stairs', 'hanged themselves'. Those who didn't die were left in terror of the interrogation rooms deep inside.

His brief was simple, even if the logistics needed the care and attention of a professional, take out an ANC leader in London and a top black trade unionist based in Jo'burg. He accepted his orders without question. To

Captain Maritz Swanepoel both targets were legitimate. He despised the South African exiles living comfortably in the big cities of the world, was disgusted at the way they were courted diplomatically and politically, their leaders familiar on the embassy cocktail circuits. They were vermin who wrought havoc by pressing buttons and pulling levers from safety thousands of miles away. Black trade unionists, he feared more than despised. He knew that the growing industrial power of the black workforce was perhaps the most serious threat to continued white dominance. He relished the opportunity to strike a blow against their unions.

Swanepoel prepared methodically for the two operations. He rang the registry and asked for the file on Dulcie September, the 45-year old ANC representative in Paris who'd been killed by South African National Intelligence Service agents, hit by five bullets fired at close range. It was a neat job, he thought. Two NIS Z-squad agents had flown in several days before, their arrival being noted by the French internal secret service, the DST, according to a report in *Le Monde* contained in the file. Only weeks before the assassination, the French had refused Mrs September's request for police protection. The killers had got away unscathed and had gone to ground until the fuss over the incident had died down. He detected a clean feel of professionalism in the cryptic notes on file. He liked that. They could be activated again. London wouldn't be a problem. MI5 and MI6 would turn a blind eye in practice, even if political pressure forced them to go through the motions of an investigation.

Next he turned to the file on Thabo Kumalo, who had become internationally known for his astute handling of the last major strike in the gold mines. The file on the 41-year old miners' leader was thick with detail. He would have merited security service attention because of his position alone. He was a key figure at the top of the two and a half million strong, black trade union movement, which was still growing and now accounted for a third of the economically active black population. In the previous year nine million days had been lost because of strikes by black workers. The year before it had been one million. The militancy was rising.

But there was another reason for targeting Kumalo. He was suspected of helping to organise community-based street committees in Alexandra township, and plotting to make the township ungovernable. His hand was said to be behind successful consumer boycotts. He was also believed to be instrumental in campaigns against black collaborators, especially black policemen, who were disparagingly referred to as 'green beans' after the colour of their uniforms. Township comrades had forced scores of 'green beans' to move out of their homes in Alexandra into tents erected in the neighbouring white suburb of Kew. But no hard evidence could be pinned on Kumalo.

Swanepoel sat back and stretched in his chair, noting for the first time how late it was, well after midnight. The hours had rushed by since he had first opened the files. Although he felt like a drink, he knew it would be difficult to get one this late. He decided to go out to the late night cafe off Commissioner Street and get a hamburger and coffee. He was tired, but content; content that the old adrenalin was pumping through him. This was hard work, but much better than socialising with the wife and relatives. After a sleep in his hotel he would start work early in the morning on the operational details of taking out the two targets.

❖

Dick Sewell's tourist group and the Noted Persons Delegation found themselves aboard the same steamer on the Yangtse river from Chungking to Wuhan. Both parties had been booked into first class cabins. Sewell couldn't help feeling uncomfortable, noticing the scores of people sleeping rough in the gangways outside, or staring through the restaurant windows as he and his companions ate in relative luxury inside.

He had been determined to keep his distance from the Noted Persons. He didn't go much on the idea of people on freebies, and the fatuous title of the delegation was the final straw for him. But the only spare space at lunch was at a table occupied by Evans and Jenny. He sat down reluctantly. As they introduced themselves he made up his mind about them: she seemed quite a girl, he a bit of a wimp.

The three of them grappled with their chopsticks as the muddy brown water of the Yangtse spread around their steamer. It swept passed villages and towns on the banks, its waves gently rocking continuous lines of small boats. There were signs of the devastation left by fierce spring hail storms. Hailstones, some the size of eggs, had been driven by winds of up to force 11. Eight river barges had been sunk and hundreds of nearby factories stopped production. Houses collapsed and crops were badly damaged.

Jenny broke the awkward silence. 'Since you men usually introduce yourselves via your jobs, I'm a social worker, Jim's a nuclear physicist. What about you?'

Her directness was engaging.

'Bits and pieces. Used to be in physical education,' he replied. 'Nuclear physics, hey? A practical man or an academic?' Sewell's tone wasn't hostile, but each syllable of a-ca-de-mi-c seemed to hang out, as if waiting to be shot down.

'A professor, actually,' Evans said evenly.

'But almost normal despite that,' Jenny interjected brightly. They all laughed. 'What exactly is your job now?'

'As I said, bits and pieces. Whatever I can do. Odd jobs here and there.' Sewell affected a relaxed air of nonchalance, lounging back. The steamer's horn gave out one of its periodic blares as it passed a large village. A Chinese junk drifted lazily in the afternoon sun.

'I don't think I have had the pleasure of meeting your friend.' The heavy, jowelled face of Harold Williams appeared at their table smiling.

'Sewell. Dick Sewell. I'm with the other party on holiday.' He stood up, politely.

They shook hands. 'Old friends, are you?'

'No. We've just met for the first time.'

'Ah. Don't let me interrupt any further. See you all later, perhaps.'

'Then again, maybe not,' Jenny muttered as Williams departed. Catching Sewell's puzzled glance, she explained: 'He's not exactly a bosom buddy.'

❖

Venter and Coetzee checked through Heathrow without difficulty. They had arrived overnight on a South African Airways jumbo, with an open return which allowed them to spend as much time in England as their holiday money would allow. They were in their late twenties, squash rackets under their arms, typical bronzed South African males. The man at the passport desk let them through with only perfunctory queries about their holiday. He might have probed further had he known they had only hand luggage, but nobody noticed or cared that they walked straight out through customs without collecting any suitcases.

From Terminal Three they caught the Piccadilly line tube and headed for an address off Earls Court Road where a self-catering flat had been booked for them, a week paid in advance, by a middle-aged secretary in the Embassy who wanted accommodation for her nephews. Nobody noticed them arrive and nobody noticed them leave after a sleep and a shower five hours later.

The man from the Embassy was waiting for them in the pizza house off Oxford Street when they arrived punctually as arranged at three p.m. They spent a pleasant hour talking about sport and each consumed several glasses of imported German lager before their host paid the bill and they all left. Nobody noticed that Venter was carrying the sports hold-all left underneath the table by the man from the Embassy who had retrieved it from the diplomatic bags in from Pretoria the previous day.

When they returned to their flat, Venter and Coetzee checked through the contents of the hold-all. Two air tickets via Gatwick to Berlin for the following day. Details of the hotel off the Kurfürstendamm where they had been booked to stay for a week. A new set of passports in different names. A couple of Walther pistols with optional silencers and several rounds of ammunition. Everything else they needed was in their heads: the name of the target, the face from pictures studied in John Vorster Square, images of the video recordings showing the target going to and from his home, the family details, the daily routines, the address, the route memorised as if they had followed it all their lives.

Venter and Coetzee had been chosen as much for their discipline as their ability. A couple of unattached young men could have a good time in London, but if Venter and Coetzee were tempted, they didn't show it. There would be enough time to enjoy themselves in Berlin. They spent the evening watching TV, popping out only to bring in a snack, some orange juice and food for a good breakfast bought from one of the late-opening stores in Earls Court Road. Nobody noticed the lights in their flat going out at 10 p.m. as they turned in for the night. Nobody noticed the lights come on at 5 a.m. the next morning and nobody noticed the two leaving an hour later for the local tube station where they caught a Wimbledon bound train on the District Line.

❖

Looking beyond the retreating figure of Harold Williams, Evans noticed again that the banks of the Yangtse were extensively cultivated in terraces which disappeared in the mist, hardly a square metre wasted.

'Do you know how much plutonium Britain exports?' Dick Sewell's question pulled him back to their conversation.

'Quite a bit. About four tons of pre-1969 plutonium produced from the civil nuclear programme were exported, mainly to America. Between 1969 and 1985 the figure was three tons. All of it has been for the express purpose of making nuclear weapons, as the Americans at least have publicly admitted.'

In response to Jenny's quizzical glance Evans elaborated: 'Nuclear energy and weapons are Siamese twins. In fact Britain's nuclear energy capacity largely grew out of our weapons programme. Our military reactors at Calder Hall, Sellafield and Chapel Cross all produce weapons grade plutonium for the Ministry of Defence. In the early history of the nuclear industry, enrichment plants were developed as part of the weapons programme. Only later were they adapted for civilian purposes.'

Sewell nodded. 'Our civil nuclear plants have virtually become bomb factories for the Americans.'

'That's an overstatement, I think,' Evans replied cautiously.

'Come on!' Sewell's sarcasm was clear.

'Okay. The relationship is more complex than that, but I suppose you are broadly correct,' Evans frowned. 'You seem well informed.'

'I know a bit about the issue. I'm a member of Greenpeace.' Sewell looked embarrassed, adding hurriedly. 'But I'd be grateful if you could keep that to yourselves. I prefer my political views to remain private. In a country like China you never know who is listening.'

Their security had been pathetic, Venter thought to himself, smiling to relieve the tension. It had begun with the wait in the garden of the large house in a leafy road in the South West London suburb of Putney. The house was divided into flats, one of which was occupied by George Kasinga, his wife and two teenage sons. For such an important person in the ANC, Kasinga had hardly been protected at all. Just one security man in the car which had come to collect him. It had been a piece of cake.

Like a television action replay, the events of the morning flashed in front of Venter. Everything had gone to plan. Even now he was carrying out instructions as he pretended to read a copy of the Guardian on the 8.38 from Clapham Junction, due in at Gatwick at 9.05.

It had all happened so fast. The security guard rang the bell and spoke into the entry-phone, then Coetzee jumped him, breaking his neck textbook style, grabbing his keys and climbing into the driver's seat. The front door opened and Kasinga walked out unconcerned. The heavy calibre bullets tore into his head and through his heart as Venter pumped out six shots to make sure. Then into the car, Coetzee pulling away, and dropping him near Putney station where he caught the next train to Clapham Junction, five minutes away.

Coetzee would now be amongst the rush hour commuters from Putney Bridge station to Victoria, having abandoned the car in a quiet side street in Fulham. In a Victoria Station locker he would leave the guns and their old passports in the hold-all for the man from the Embassy to collect, before catching the next train to Gatwick.

Soon they would be flying out over the well manicured fields of Sussex as the world's press descended on what had been such a nice quiet road in such a nice quiet part of London.

❖

It was during the rush hour that Thabo Kumalo simply disappeared. The bearded union leader was on his way from his home near Soweto to his office in a building owned by the local council of churches.

Nobody seemed to spot an unmarked car pulling up alongside him as he walked down the pavement in downtown Johannesburg's Plein Street. If anyone had seen the incident, it would have been the last public view of the man who had stirred up such bitterness and hatred in government circles.

Exactly what happened to him was never confirmed. He joined a long list of black radicals who had disappeared or been mysteriously murdered since 1978. The Government law and order Minister officially denied any police involvement. He also poured scorn on the notion of a right wing death squad.

But a leading black theologian warned that Kumalo's disappearance coming on top of all the others was causing a crisis for the church over its attitude to violence. 'It is becoming more and more difficult for us in the church to criticise people who use violence to defend themselves against the violence of the apartheid regime,' he said.

Reading this statement in the morning newspapers, Swanepoel grimaced and entered the churchman's name in the cross-referenced notebook he kept for himself.

'If you want a war to the death, Kaffir, we'll give it to you,' he muttered.

CHAPTER FIVE

The Old Man sat back in his padded swivel chair behind his large wooden desk, sipping tepid tea and gazing down at the rooftops of Peking as they stretched away in the distance.

His office was high up and the view always used to excite him; now he found it depressing. All he seemed to notice these days was the smog hanging heavily in the atmosphere. An official memo in his in-tray confirmed that things were getting worse. Peking had become one of the world's most polluted capitals, with air 35 times dirtier than London's and 16 times more contaminated even than crowded Tokyo's.

Another sign of decay. He longed for the past – for the fresh clean air of the mountains and the beauty of the valleys which they had conquered in his youth, 60 years before during the Long March. Over 6,000 miles covered by foot during a year's marching to escape Chiang Kai-shek's pursuing Kuomintang forces and join their comrades in Yenan. Crossing mountains, glaciers and rivers, marching through swamps and snow; raising the consciousness of the marchers and their revolutionary spirit; educating the peasants along the way; spreading optimism. Of the 90,000 who started, only 7,000 finished. Some dropped out, others died from wounds, hunger, disease or cold. But through such an extraordinary feat of willpower and imagination they had demonstrated a vision that could one day emancipate the long-suffering people of China.

He had never since experienced quite that degree of continuous exhilaration. Liberation had been exciting in its own way; so too had the years of progress afterwards. But now it was all going sour. Even the massive Revolutionary Museum at Yenan, where millions had once flocked each year like pilgrims to Mecca, was now almost deserted, the hotels empty. There was no belief anymore. The principles of the communist revolution were being abandoned as competition, market forces and localised decision making were encouraged. Only he could change the present destructive course of events. It was all down to him: one of the last surviving veterans from Mao's closest circle still holding office.

He was in good health, the product of a careful diet and regular exercise. There weren't many like him in their late eighties who could retain the authority of leadership and stay the pace in the punishing cycle of ministerial responsibilities. He was unique. He had to fulfil his destiny – to perform one last task for the masses.

❖

It was breathtaking. Evans leant over the railing and inhaled the sharpness of the night. They had first entered the Gorges five hours ago when it was still light. Then came a spectacular sunset of orange and red shrouded in the mist from the cliffs. Now, high above him, the mist hung in the dark, while the swirling currents of the Yangtse stirred viciously below, powerful waters, capable of the colossal destruction.

He felt like taking some exercise after another delicious meal and decided to walk around the steamer, picking his way carefully between the bodies of the passengers resting on the deck, hoping that he wasn't disturbing anyone. Periodically, eyes would open and a face would stare up blankly before tucking back into the protection of an overcoat. Now, feeling the coolness of air, he turned to reach for the heavy steel door and climb over the ridge into the warmth of the corridor inside.

He never knew much about what happened next. Something hard hit him on the head. He reeled back, stunned. Two pairs of hands grabbed him. In the confusion of the moment he thought help was on hand. Then he felt himself heaved up and over the railing. No, surely not. No. No. No.

He tried to shout. But his voice wouldn't come out of the terror shooting through his semi-consciousness. His legs scraped awkwardly, scratching his knees and shins. Then he was falling clumsily. The tip of his shoe caught on something jutting out from the side. He fell, half crouching, for what seemed like ages, before his head hit the icy cold river. For a split second he was shocked at how rock hard the water felt upon impact. Then he was under, twisting as the current pulled him down.

❖

Officially, Keith Makuyana was covered. He had obtained clearance at the highest political level. Enquirers were told he was on special leave. His room was occupied by his new deputy, Florence Sithole. Operationally, only she and two of his most trusted staff knew the truth.

His cover with the ANC was as a 'Political Liaison Officer' to improve communications with the Government. Most ANC cadres accepted this without question. Since the merger of the ruling ZANU party with its rival ZAPU, it made sense for the ANC and the new ZANU-Patriotic Front to cement relations and work to overcome past misunderstandings over the close ANC-ZAPU link. The Political Liaison Officer role also gave Makuyana the perfect excuse to set up meetings and visits throughout the ANC network, not just in Zimbabwe but in Zambia and Tanzania too.

It brought back memories. The limbo life of the exile in the big city; the tension of relationships with even sympathetic governments; the problems of security for a group engaged in both clandestine armed struggle and open political campaigning; the desperate vulnerability of the guerrilla camps stationed in the bush; the methodical de-briefings of young guerrillas unwinding after a mission deep into enemy territory. But beyond remembering, Makuyana watched and listened. Somewhere in the undergrowth of his talks and travels, of his questions and answers, were the clues he needed. He was by nature an impatient person. But this time, he told himself, patience was of the essence. Patience and perseverance.

Now he was waiting for her. He had an instinctive confidence in Deputy Florence Sithole. The first woman to occupy the job, her appointment had raised a few eyebrows. She wasn't as experienced as Ed Tombe had been, but she was a cool customer who did her work without any fuss.

He was reminded of a conversation at a party with a young English woman who was visiting Harare to help set up a research consultancy. She was Managing Director of her own small firm back in London and had talked eloquently about the way women were more successful than men at running their own businesses. She had put it down to the fact that women were more interested in doing the job effectively, rather than being obsessed with status, perks or the latest flashy equipment. Florence Sithole was of the same mould: determined and efficient, a good sense of humour, but hard too. You had to be in their trade.

Makuyana was parked in a layby on the main road south, about fifteen minutes from Harare. As he leant out of the window to take in some fresh air, heat leapt up at him from the dry, dusty brown earth. There was a buzz of flies. It was still hot for autumn. One of the Department's dark blue Toyotas pulled up behind him. He could see her at the wheel in his driving mirror. They each sat still for several minutes, listening and watching: standard routine for a meet like this. A couple of lorries drove past, then a Volkswagen Golf. But the drivers took no notice of the two parked vehicles.

Makuyana started his engine and drove back along the way they had both come, eyes alert for any waiting pursuers. There were none. Still, they weren't taking any chances. Not after Ed Tombe's death. The next time someone died in this affair, Makuyana had vowed, it wouldn't be a member of *his* department.

Shortly afterwards Florence Sithole joined Makuyana in the passenger seat of his car, their vehicles having pulled off the main road a mile down from their rendezvous.

'Ciao!' she greeted him with an impish grin. 'How's the holiday going then?'

He couldn't help grinning back. Here they were for a serious meeting to discuss mutual progress, but she had done it again, eased the tension by poking fun at him.

'Not too bad. Lots of travel. But no time for boozing or socialising, I'm afraid.'

'Ah – what a shame.' She stared at her boss. He could be good company when he relaxed, but she couldn't imagine him boozing. He was too self-contained, too disciplined to let himself go like that.

'Any happenings in the Department?'

'Not much. Mostly routine. Still no lead on the Temba bomb. As far as we know that suspect hasn't come back into the country. Just one major item. I was called in to the President's office. Apparently we are to be visited by a high-level delegation from China next month.'

'Oh yes?' Makuyana sounded indifferent.

'Of course we will provide the usual security. But the President's man was concerned about something else. As you know we have traditionally had good relations with the Chinese, dating from their support for ZANU in our liberation struggle. This time the President has picked up something he wants us to keep an eye on. The briefing wasn't very specific. All hush-hush and rather vague. The gist of it is that Peking is worried about Pretoria for some reason.'

The crunch of the impact and the freezing wetness jerked Evans into consciousness again. It felt as though he was in a whirlpool. He had a momentary vision of looking down at himself in the brown water, twisting and turning, a multitude of eddies on the surface as the river thrust its way down though the Gorges to the Yellow Sea over a thousand miles away.

He was swallowing the stuff. He couldn't help it. His arms felt heavy and useless as he fought against the power thrusting at him seemingly from every direction. It was crushing him from without and suffocating him within. He couldn't do anything. Not even breathe.

Time seemed to be hanging still, waiting for him to die. A series of unconnected thoughts cascaded through his mind. Guilt. Regrets. He wished he had posted that card to his parents before getting on the boat, rather than leaving it in his jacket. He wished he had told Jenny how he felt about her. He wished he had left clearer guidelines on the course of his latest research project. All those years of research would be wasted now. He wished he had made a will, as he had always promised himself he would.

Then the regret turned to rage. Why him? He had too much still to do with his life. Why pick on him? All the time he knew he was drowning.

As he started to hallucinate, he felt as if something was lifting up and out of him, separating from the body wallowing uselessly beneath him. The coming sense of a release from the pain and struggle was seductive. There was a long tunnel before him. It was attractive, full of colour, beckoning him on. Now he wanted to die.

❖

Dick Sewell heard a scuffle somewhere ahead of him in the darkness. He caught a glimpse of a body falling over the side of the boat. Almost instinctively he knew who it was. Evans had left their table ten minutes earlier and he had followed him out for some fresh air. He ran forward, conscious of a door slamming shut at his side.

He saw the body in the water, the fast flowing current carrying it along, in the same direction as the boat. Sewell didn't panic. He was trained not to do so. He scanned the deck hurriedly, lifebelts were hanging alongside the cabin walls. Grabbing some rope, he tied them together. Every second was precious. His own experience told him that no one could survive in those currents for very long.

As he tore off his jacket and shoes, he banged on the restaurant windows and held up two lifebelts, gesticulating back at the river, a wild figure startling the diners. He hoped to Christ someone would realise that it was deadly serious. Then he ran to the stern, clambering up on the rail and looking desperately at the water. He thought he could see the body bobbing behind as the waves of the steamer spread out. Clutching the lifebelts, he jumped, vaguely aware of shouts behind him.

He hit the surface of the Yangtse feet first, clinging onto the lifebelts as his arms almost jerked out of their sockets.

Wavelets broke over him, the current dragging him fast. It was bitterly cold. He couldn't see properly. He tried to paddle back, straining against the tide. He wasn't making much progress, but he figured that even if he was halting the speed at which he was being dragged back, the body stood a chance of catching him up. The body. Christ! It wasn't a body, it was Evans, he thought.

If it hadn't been for a slight movement on the surface, the moonlight glancing off a sodden white shirt, Sewell might never have spotted his target. Paddling across furiously, he reached out to grab the still form. It was Evans all right, drifting lifelessly. The fight had gone out of him, his body was sinking.

Sewell would never have believed an ordinary, slightly built man could be so heavy. He had been trained to save drowning people. He knew all the tricks. But training didn't cover real life – or real death. He tugged in frustration, heaving Evans onto the spare lifebelt, managing at least to get his head out of the water, catching a sight of his eyes staring blankly. He couldn't tell whether the man was still breathing, but at least he had him. Now what? He hadn't planned the next stage. Suddenly he felt helpless.

The steamer's horn sounded and hope came surging back. Their lifebelts were catching it up now, swept along in the current. Was that a boat being lowered down over the side? Perhaps. No, he must be mistaken. Yes! The boat splashed in and rocked crazily as the steamer swung away. Sewell screamed out desperately. At last the boat was alongside amidst a jabbering of Chinese voices.

Seeing Evans' crumpled figure lying prone in the bottom of the boat, his face a ghostly grey-blue under the boat's lamp, it all seemed hopeless again. Sewell grabbed both legs, gesticulating for help. Somehow he managed to communicate with the boatmen and they rolled Evans onto his back, head resting on the bottom, water dribbling out of his mouth.

The seconds ticked away, each one striking another piece off Evans' life. They had to get all the water out of his stomach. Sewell pushed his shoulders up. Nothing. Then they turned him round again and Sewell pushed hard on his back repeating the pressure until at last water and vomit gushed out of his mouth.But there was still no sign of breathing. Quick. Push on his chest. Then the kiss of life next. Shivering with tension and cold, he knelt over Evans. Nothing in his life had ever seemed so vital. Deep breath. Then out. Lips cupped over Evans' mouth. Pumping the chest. It was impossible! Four times. Five times. Six. Seven. It wasn't working. It had to! He mustn't fail now.

Sewell was in a frenzy, driving his exhausted frame along. There was still no heartbeat! He slapped Evans' face, pinching his arms and roughly massaging his sternum. Evans' face contorted. With renewed vigour Sewell rolled back, picking up Evans' legs under the knees and firmly folded his thighs over onto his stomach. Again and again. Then the kiss of life.

Evans stirred, gave a splutter, seemed to half breathe. Sewell tried again. This time the breathing was sustained but fitful. It grew steadier, though it still seemed terribly precarious. Sewell knelt beside him, willing the breathing on, aware that the boat had bumped into the side of the steamer. He caught a sight of Jenny staring down from the steamer, her eyes a terrified glaze.

'Get a stomach pump. And some oxygen. Quick.'

The long tunnel was being pulled away from Evans, the walls rushing past all around him as if he was an object hurtling backwards inside. He opened his eyes, aware of a confused blur of faces around him. He was hooked up to an intravenous drip and a cardiac monitor. He closed them again. What had happened? He was naked underneath the blanket. Where were his clothes? He felt so cold and numb and battered, as if he didn't fit properly into his body anymore.

Then, slowly, he began to remember. Suddenly, he felt frightened. Start fighting, he told himself, stop accepting and start fighting. He forced his eyes open again.

Sewell started to cry. There was nothing he could do to stop himself. He felt incurably embarrassed. It wasn't the way a man behaved. He had never before cried in public as an adult. But then he had never before helped pull anyone back from the dead.

Swanepoel was reminiscing. He loved a captive audience. They were in a secluded cubicle in a restaurant in Johannesburg's Houghton district, a venue he had chosen deliberately. It appealed to his sense of humour to celebrate the success of his two missions in the rich, English-speaking suburb which had elected the renowned opposition MP, Helen Suzman, for so many years. The three young security service agents sharing the table were happy to let him talk of the old times as the wine flowed.

'The early sixties were good years. There was less bureaucracy in those days. You could just *do* things. Sometimes there was an outcry, but – what the hell. Nobody could touch us. They still can't, I suppose, but there's more red tape today, more desk men pushing forms around.

'Things were more clearcut then.' He chuckled. 'We had some real coups. We caught Mandela's ANC cronies at Rivonia in 1963. Their Umkhonto we Sizwe group was planning a campaign of sabotage. But they had become too casual with security and we tumbled them.

'Then there was the John Harris business. He was a young teacher, a member of the old Alan Paton Liberal Party – one of a number of young turks who couldn't accept the party's non-violence. Harris joined a group called ARM – African Resistance Movement. They were *amateurs*!' He spat the word out, pausing only to order another bottle of wine.

'We had the ARM sussed almost from the beginning. I remember when the call came through – July 1964, I think – that there was a bomb in a suitcase on the concourse of Jo'burg railway station. It was due to go off in fifteen minutes. The caller said he was ARM. He said something like: "This is a symbolic protest against apartheid. Nobody must get hurt. Please clear the concourse. Do not try to defuse the bomb. The suitcase is triggered to explode if it is opened." He wanted to have his cake and eat it. To make an impact without hurting anyone.'

Swanepoel paused, enjoying the moment, holding his audience expectant as he savoured the wine. 'Now what would *you* have done in a situation like that?'

'Let it go off,' the blonde young sergeant spoke quietly. He had a reputation for toughness in the interrogation room. The others looked shocked.

'Exactly!' Swanepoel gave the young man an approving glance. 'They did us a big favour. Things were awkward at the time. There was a lot of trouble, a lot of resistance. But after that – 22 innocent people injured and an old woman killed – we had a free hand. We launched a massive operation, picking up hundreds of activists. No messing – we beat the hell out of everyone. Those who had something to say talked. The others we just let go. It took us seven hours to get to John Harris. One of my colleagues interrogated him. Harris' jaw got broken. Don't know how!' Swanepoel enjoyed his joke and laughter broke out around the table.

'He was hanged the following year: the first white to be executed for a political crime. I always remember the date, 1 April 1965 – April fool's day.'

❖

Makuyana was huddled together with Selby Mngadi, a list of names before them. Some they crossed off, satisfied. Others they left on. There were still questions to pursue. Three of the names particularly interested the man from Zimbabwe security. They had all been present when he and Ed Tombe had met Mngadi the first time after Temba's murder. He made a mental note to get to know them.

Makuyana folded up the list and put it in his pocket. 'Can you also get me a list of the people who would have known your confidential number – the one they phoned with the tip-off about the house we put under surveillance where Ed was killed?'

Mngadi nodded, getting up. 'I'm thirsty. A beer?'

'Yes, please.' He waited for the other man to return with two glasses and a couple of bottles of cold lager. 'There is another matter. Why do you think the Chinese Government would be worried about South Africa?'

Mngadi's lips tightened, as did the permanent creases on his forehead. He thought for a minute, pensively sipping his beer, then shrugged.

'No idea, I'm afraid.'

'Let me know if you have any thoughts on it,' Makuyana said. 'I have the feeling it's important somehow – call it an instinct.'

❖

The Gorges were behind them now and the banks of the Yangtse resumed their muddy appearance. The steamer had stopped for half a day while Evans was rushed to hospital. To the relief of the Group he had pulled through remarkably well, but he was still in a deep sleep in his cabin when Wang called the Delegation together. The interpreter looked worried, even a little haggard, Jenny noted. She felt rather that way herself.

'I must ask you to be extra careful for the remainder of the journey. I will have to report the accident to my superiors in the Peoples Friendship Association in Peking. They were most concerned when Mr Evans was nearly run over by the car in Chengtu. We cannot allow anything to happen to our foreign guests. This latest accident puts in jeopardy future invitations for delegations like yours,' he said.

'Accident? A grown man falling over the side? He was pushed, wasn't he?' Jenny's outburst was spontaneous. She hadn't had a chance to talk to either Evans or Sewell.

'No. It was an *accident*,' Wang dwelt on the word pointedly. 'Now I must phone Peking.'

From the radio telephone situated in a cabin behind the bridge, Wang phoned not one but two Peking numbers. The unofficial call was to the Old Man – a cryptic, awkward conversation, reporting another failure and asking for further guidance.

A little later Harold Williams stood in the same cabin waiting to be connected to a London number. His call came through to a small bare office in Curzon Street belonging to F7, the section within MI5's Directorate for domestic subversion, for radical groups including feminists, pacifists, nuclear disarmers and ecologists.

'Gerald? Good to hear your voice. It's Harold here. Sorry about the line. An open one from the middle of the Yangtse.'

He paused at the exclamation on the other end.

'I need a hand old boy. A lead on a name. Sewell. Dick Sewell. Probably about thirty. Nothing else known. If you have anything on him, could you call me? Not back on this boat. Communications have improved fantastically out here, but not to that degree. I should be booked in a hotel in Wuhan in thirty-six hours time.' He gave the hotel number. 'Oh – and another name, too, please. Dr Jim Evans, nuclear physicist.'

Evans jerked awake from another desperate dream, heart pounding, eyes slowly focusing on two figures near to him. What had happened? Where was he? He became conscious of a tension in the room. Jenny was sitting nearby. Wang was hovering alongside.

'How are you feeling?' Jenny tucked the blanket more comfortably around him.

'I'm not sure.' He looked over toward Wang.

'Mr Evans. I must apologise for speaking so bluntly. But this is the second time in a few days you have come close to death. It is causing us a great worry. I must ask that you be more careful. No more accidents please.'

Evans closed his eyes, trying to arrange the jumbled thoughts racing through his mind, trying to collect himself. Falling over the side. Water. Drowning. Death. Yet he wasn't dead anymore. And now there was Wang. Always Wang. Reprimanding, threatening.

'Please leave me alone,' he muttered weakly, reaching out for Jenny's hand. Then, as if escaping, he felt himself slipping back to sleep.

He awoke with a caked dry mouth, knotted stomach, splitting head and aching limbs. He had no idea how much time had gone by. Again there were two figures, talking quietly in the corner of the cabin. He relaxed when he realised that this time it was Sewell with Jenny and not Wang.

He began to remember more clearly now, the horror of it all coming back. The sensation of drowning and dying was stark in his mind. He could recall his emotions, the bizarre sense in which he felt he was leaving his body. But the ending wasn't right. He shouldn't be here. What had happened?

Over the next two hours the three pieced together the story. Evans was at a loss for words. Sewell had saved his life. Simply to say thanks seemed inadequate. He would have to repay the debt one day.

Sewell had already moved to the more urgent concerns. 'There are people on board who tried to kill you Jim,' he looked thoughtful. 'But why?'

There was an awkward silence. 'It's time we levelled with each other,' Jenny startled them both. 'If Dick is putting his life on the line for you, he should know all the facts.'

After they had put Sewell in the picture, he looked grim. He paused, thinking about his own position. If he became more involved in this business would he be seen simply as a gallant rescuer? Or would he too come under suspicion? When he had jumped in after Evans, he had no idea of the complexity of the situation. The irony of his dilemma was sharp. His own mission could be compromised by his inadvertent involvement in this strange affair. The two seemed entirely separate – or were they? The nuclear link at least was common. He sat forward suddenly, his broad shoulders filling his shirt. He had come to a decision.

Evans felt envious of the other man's physical prowess. There wasn't a spare ounce of fat on him.

But he seemed indifferent to his own good looks, treating his body almost casually. A quiet man, quietly confident.

'There is something I have to tell you,' Sewell said. 'But I have to insist on your absolute confidence. You must promise me not to tell anybody about this, certainly no one inside China.'

The other two nodded, Evans pulling himself upwards against his pillow. As Sewell began to talk, they both grew silent, and even more afraid: 'For good or ill, we are now in this together,' Sewell said.

'And now, if you don't mind Jim, I think I'll join you here in the spare bunk. They may try again whoever they are. We have another fourteen hours before we disembark at Ichang. Jenny, could you guard him while I get my things and make the necessary arrangements?'

When Sewell had gone, Jenny locked the door. Then she sat on the edge of the bunk and kissed Evans on the cheek, her eyes suddenly moist. She didn't have to say anything, didn't have to confess she thought she had lost him. He didn't have to tell her how, in those last deathly moments in the river, he had wanted to shout out how much he cared for her. No words were needed. They both knew. Her soft lips found his, dry and cracked. Their tongues explored each other lightly, gently. He was beginning to feel like living again.

❖

Selby Mngadi was in something of a dilemma. The ANC man was acting on Keith Makuyana's request to make discreet enquiries about a possible Peking-Pretoria connection. To pursue the matter it would be necessary to go through intermediaries to Dar es Salaam, Lusaka – maybe even the London office. That meant breaching the security which the two men believed was absolutely essential to their task. Still he had no choice.

He called in his three closest aides, suddenly aware as they joined him of his embarrassment that Makuyana had singled them out for further investigation. They were all very different. Amir Bhajee was thin and small, the son of a veteran of the banned Indian National Congress of South Africa who had been driven into exile. George Peterson was a Cape Coloured, curly haired and a little overweight. Moses Msimang was tall and broody, the deep blackness of his skin giving him an ebony like quality. The three were a good team, Mngadi reflected. Where Bhajee was intense and serious, Peterson was always in high spirits and Msimang provided the drive. Could one of his most trusted comrades be a traitor? It was hard to accept.

They listened to his briefing in silence, all three showing the sort of scepticism Mngadi had to admit he felt himself.

'Check it out for me, would you. But I don't want to set any hares running. Be discreet.'

'A Peking connection with apartheid? It's hard to believe. What's the source?' Bhajee asked.

'I can't say, I'm afraid. Let's call it privileged information.'

The answer didn't surprise any of them or give offence. They were used to that sort of briefing. Mngadi worked strictly on a need-to-know basis. Although they sometimes found this frustrating, Mngadi insisted the less people knew the less they could give away.

But one of them suspected who the source might be. And one of them was distinctly perturbed about the information.

❖

Swanepoel had been called in by his chief, General K.J. van der Walt. This time the appointment was at John Vorster Square.

On his way there he was acutely aware of the abnormal stillness in the city centre. Nearly two million black workers had stayed at home that morning at the start of a three-day protest against government restrictions on trade unions and fresh bans on anti-apartheid groups. Early trains coming in from the townships, normally packed to the gunnels, were virtually empty. It was the biggest strike in the country's history.

The recent disappearance of Thabo Kumalo had only inflamed the situation. Protesters in Soweto carried posters with his name and picture. Two limpet mines went off on the main railway line to Pretoria, knocking it out for the rest of the day. There were petrol bomb attacks on buses. Patrolling armoured vehicles were pelted with stones. Two black policemen were stoned to death.

Still, life went on as normal, Swanepoel reflected. They won't humiliate us. His wife had given up trying to persuade him to join the family. She wasn't really missing him anyway. There was no physical bond between them. For years they had slept in separate beds, growing apart as he had spent more and more time away from home on various operations. They had very little in common anymore except for their children and grandchildren. As long as she could busy herself looking after them, she was almost happier without him.

Swanepoel waited outside the General's office, making small talk to a secretary about the grandchildren whose names he hardly remembered. One had to keep up appearances, though, so he was quite happy to keep chatting. The door opened and the tall figure of KJ beckoned him in. There were two other men in the room: business types, Swanepoel thought. Smart suits, coloured handkerchiefs protruding from their top pockets, expensive leather briefcases and a superior air about them.

'Captain Swanepoel, gentleman.'

The three shook hands as KJ paused. 'Maritz, you won't mind if I don't introduce our two friends, they prefer to remain as anonymous as possible.'

Swanepoel shrugged. It didn't bother him who these two jumped-up yuppies were.

'Good. Now, a whisky for everyone?'

KJ's timely offer broke the tension. As he poured the drinks, he started to talk. 'Maritz,' he began, again the first name terms deliberately signalling familiarity and trust, 'we have a problem. Potentially very serious. Our friends are experts in – let us say – nuclear matters.'

He paused, gulping at his whisky, the sun shining through the plate glass window highlighting his features which Swanepoel noticed seemed suddenly haggard. So, the boss was worried?

'For some years now we have been extending relationships with foreign elements to assist with the development and expansion of our independent nuclear capacity. It is a project crucial to our survival. We need assistance to improve our technical know-how and we need to import reprocessed material, and modern equipment – launchers, that sort of thing. Fortunately other countries need these sort of exchanges and co-operation for their own development too. You scratch my back, I'll scratch yours. So we have found friends in unlikely places. Israel for example – that should appeal to your sense of historic irony, Maritz!'

KJ chuckled at his own joke, the others smiled weakly. Then his eyes narrowed. 'All this is Section 4 classified.' He turned to the two visitors, 'That means top secret. Which is why I need a trusted colleague like Maritz to help.'

He's building me up the whole time, putting on a show. Why? Swanepoel was perplexed. The others were silent.

'There's been a leak. We've had a message from Harare. The ANC have been tipped off about the Peking connection.'

'Peking connection?' Swanepoel's surprised exclamation seemed to relax the other two as they exchanged significant glances.

One of them spoke. 'We have had secret contacts with friendly elements in China. They have been of considerable assistance. Unless that assistance continues, we may not be able to achieve our objective of becoming the dominant nuclear power in the whole of Africa.'

KJ leant forward. 'We need to discover the source of the leak, to assess its importance, to find out how we can plug it.'

'Can you rubbish it as a rumour?' The younger of the two leant forward, his forehead furrowed.

A streak of annoyance passed across KJ's face. The others might not have noticed, but Swanepoel did. He recognised too the irritable tapping of his fingernails on the side of the whisky glass.

'Many things are possible. Leave that to us. Is there anything more we need to know? Any names? Any other leads on potential sources of the leak from your end?'

'Not that we know of.' The two seemed deflated, even depressed. Swanepoel was pleased.

KJ poured out another whisky, beckoning Swanepoel to remain. As his two visitors left, he gestured towards the door closing behind them.

'Smartarses. Makes you wonder why we are still fighting Maritz. Protecting our country for a future under creeps like that. They couldn't fight their way out of a paper bag. Our people have become soft, Maritz, damned soft. One day they'll find this out to their cost.'

Swanepoel nodded in sympathy. The two men were kindred spirits. He supposed that's why he was kept on for special missions. The general didn't relate well to his younger staff anymore, the generation gap was growing wider.

KJ handed him a refilled glass, grimacing as he paced about the room. 'That's all we're breeding these days. People who don't know how hard it can be. Don't know what real struggle is. Not like us, eh, Maritz. Not like us. Did you know that the psychiatric failure rate of our young soldiers on the border is three times that of the Rhodesian Army in the sixties and seventies? Three times! The Rhodesians were tough, man, tough! They were reared in the bush. Ours are urban disco-goers. Soft as butter. Cheers!'

He sat down, breathing heavily. And looking old, Swanepoel thought. Christ, he *is* old. And so am I.

'Anyway, Maritz. Down to business. That leak about the nuclear connection. I want you to follow it up. Go back to our ANC source. The one on your patch in Harare. Lie low. Remember there's been lots of bother up there recently. Most of it created by us. So don't attract attention. Just fish about. See what you catch. OK?'

Swanepoel nodded. 'No problem.' If he didn't sound enthusiastic it was because he didn't feel enthusiastic. He had enjoyed his spell of action in the old country and it was lonely across the border.

'There's a second matter. The military are getting restless. All those years bogged down in Angola and Namibia, chases into Mozambique, and all the time the bloody ANC slipping through the fokkin net. The chiefs are fed up. The boys are trying to dodge the draft, the parents are getting worried they'll come back home in wooden boxes.'

Swanepoel nodded, remembering the way America's Vietnam War effort had suddenly collapsed in the late 1960s. His whisky glass was empty again. KJ topped it up.

'The word is the military want to teach everyone a lesson. A big lesson. They have developed a new battlefield nuclear weapon: the warhead is inside a special shell launched from our new Olifants 2B tank – you know, the tank we converted from the British-made Centurion. They might just try it out in Zimbabwe. That'll frighten off the ANC, stop them coming across the Limpopo! The only problem is the range is too short to prevent our own troops being harmed, if not from the explosion itself then by fall-out. We are ready to use it, but we are trying to get another battlefield weapon with a longer range. Something like NATO's Lance missile in Western Europe. That has a range of 75 miles. It sits astride a trailer-type truck which is pretty mobile. But to develop a comparable weapon we need know-how from the Chinese. It has reached a critical stage. Time is pressing. We may even have to import the warheads from our friends in Peking.'

He hunched over his desk, glass empty again. 'So there you have it Maritz. Real, grade A info. If it doesn't scare the shit out of you, it sure does me. Be careful, Maritz. Bloody careful. This one is big. Very big.'

❖

The Old Man asked his chauffeur to pull in so that he could get a better view. The students were milling about, filling Tiananmen Square which had been closed off by police. Patrol cars drove up and down to try and clear the crowds. The road to Peking University was also closed. Police with Japanese hand-held video cameras filmed demonstrators as they sat on the steps of the Museum of Revolution in the Square. The students were protesting about lack of democracy, their demands coinciding with simmering public discontent over rising food prices and public corruption.

The Old Man didn't like the anarchy in front of him. It offended his sense of discipline and order. Nevertheless he was smiling. Student protests across the country in the winter of 1986-87 had led to the resignation of Hu Yaobang, the Communist Party's General Secretary. There had been other outbreaks since. Perhaps this latest wave of protest might trigger a further round of destabilisation and torpedo the reform programme instituted by the placemen of Deng Xiaoping. If so, the position of the Party Leader could well become untenable. And if that happened, the Old Man could move.

Even the People's Liberation Army was growing restive. Morale was sagging, the defence budget had been cut again, pay and status were low. There was a shortage of good quality recruits. The army had been instructed to become more self-financing, selling arms abroad and transforming its supply factories into commercial enterprises. Deals with foreigners were no longer enmeshed in suffocating bureaucracy. The Old Man knew these opportunities could be, and probably were, exploited by the unscrupulous for corrupt personal gain, which offended his puritanical character. But he had to reflect on the irony that this capitalist road had presented him with the opening he needed to regroup and acquire the technology and military strength he needed to succeed.

The Old Man hated the Leader, hated his western airs and graces, hated the way his beautiful wife walked the international stage alongside him, flaunting her expensive silk dresses and acting as a world celebrity. He supposed he would have to be on his best behaviour when he accompanied them on the official visit to Africa in two months time: Kenya, Tanzania and Zimbabwe. He would be a model of courtesy and deference – at least in public.

'We always aim at military or police targets. Never innocent bystanders,' Amir Bhajee gave a standard ANC reply to Makuyana's question: how do you draw the boundaries between legitimate and illegitimate targets inside South Africa?

Like his two colleagues, each a close aide of Mngadi, he looked bored. They didn't really know why they were here in a bare room at the back of an empty community hall in one of Harare's townships. Except that they had been invited – instructed would have been more accurate – to discuss the political situation with Makuyana.

'But who is innocent? Surely *every* White benefits from apartheid? Even the most liberal ones are doing nicely out of the system,' Makuyana pressed.

'Of course, but we cannot afford to be equated with terrorist groups like the IRA or the Red Brigade,' Moses Msimang sounded irritated.

'So it's just tactical?'

'It's a matter of principle. Our quarrel is not with the ordinary white people. Our fight is against the system of apartheid and the police-military power which props it up.' Bhajee was engaged by the argument now. 'We will have to – we want to – live peacefully with Whites after we have secured liberation. We will need their skills to help run the country. We don't deny their right to live as equals. We always try to avoid violence against civilians.'

'But sometimes you can't.'

'I accept that. There will always be a risk of casualties amongst the innocent. That is a fact of war. There were millions of innocent people killed in the war against the Nazis. People who weren't in uniform. Sometimes people who got caught in the crossfire during the resistance in places like France and Yugoslavia. I would compare our struggle with those of the French resistance or Tito's Partisans. *Guerrilla* struggle – not *terrorism*.'

'What's the difference?'

George Peterson interjected. 'You should know. You were part of ZANU's liberation struggle. Was it all clean? Was it all neat and tidy?'

'No. But our roots were much more firmly based within the country. The ANC's armed action is largely organised from outside. You have to rely more than we did on hit-and-run tactics, rather than a continuous war of attrition.'

Bhajee continued, 'One of the key differences between terrorist and guerrilla groups is that terrorism is indiscriminate. It is deliberately aimed at innocent by-standers: hi-jacking aircraft, putting a bomb in a crowded shopping centre. Guerrilla action may provoke casualties but that is not the purpose. The objective is to damage the state.'

'Why are you raising this question?' Moses Msimang spoke quietly. He hadn't said much. He never did.

'I am just interested in how the ANC sees things,' Makuyana replied evenly. 'What if the casualties are black? The fact is that most ANC action to date has resulted in more black than white casualties. What if your own relatives, your own friends were killed, not deliberately, but as a consequence of some armed action?'

Msimang exploded. 'The trouble with you ZANU people is that you are running the country now. Stability is suddenly important for you. Your jobs, your lifestyles, become the priority. You want everything nice and orderly. You've forgotten what it's really like. My family are Zulus. At home in Natal they are targets for Buthelezi's Inkatha forces because they back the ANC and the United Democratic Front. We can have pretty little conversations all night. But for me it's life and death.'

He got up and left the room.

Bhajee was soothing. 'Never mind about Moses, he has a short fuse. Also he recently lost his father and two brothers. Murdered. He thinks it was Inkatha, though it may have been the security services.'

'What about your own families?' Makuyana looked at Bhajee and Peterson.

Bhajee answered first. 'My sister served two long periods in detention without trial. Then she was banned. The family is regularly harassed by the Special Branch.'

'My people have always kept their heads low, got on with their daily lives. It's a bit easier to do that if you are a Coloured. Because we are mixed race we can even pass for whites sometimes!' Peterson chuckled at the thought.

'The life of an exile is not easy, is it?' Makuyana said sympathetically. 'Everyone needs a home. You are marooned up here. I know what it is like. Then you have the worry about your relatives or family left behind. Does the Government ever try to get at you through intimidating or harassing those closest to you?'

'Yes, that's always a worry.' Bhajee nodded.

'I don't think that's a serious problem,' Peterson said quickly.

'Really?' Bhajee looked at him in surprise, like a someone who discovers something about a friend for the first time.

Makuyana had raised the issue almost casually, trying to switch the conversation to a more relaxed level after his probing about the ethics of guerrilla warfare. But he had succeeded in provoking reactions from two of the three. When their families were mentioned, Msimang had stormed out and Peterson had given an odd answer.

Why? Makuyana wondered whether he had stumbled onto something. What would turn an ANC cadre into a traitor? Money? Possibly – but where could you spend it without attracting suspicion? Pressure on the family? Now that's interesting, he thought.

❖

Evans was slowly getting his strength back. Jenny had given him some dietary supplements: zinc and other trace minerals to rebuild his strength, calcium Pantothenate and choline inositol to help raise his blood sugar levels. She herself followed a very strict diet: no milk products, no wheat, virtually no meat and certainly no sugar or salt. Coffee and tea with caffeine were out. It had been the subject of much teasing from him earlier in the trip. Now he was grateful for any help he could get in recovering.

The last five days of the trip were going very quickly. Evans hadn't seen much more of the Yangtse. Nor had Sewell who stayed with him in the cabin until they had docked at Ichang. Afterwards the Group were driven to a special entrance at the side of the main station. There they waited in a room with plush rugs and deep sofas reserved for 'soft class' passengers, before boarding the overnight train to Wuhan. The two parties which had travelled separately before were now together for the final leg of the tour.

Sewell stuck close to Evans and had switched accommodation to be in the same twin-bedded room in their hotel in Wuhan.

In the same hotel, the phone rang in Harold Williams' room. It was the man from Curzon Street, choosing his words carefully on the open line.

'Hullo – Harold?'

'Yes.'

'Gerald here. Got some playback for you. Nothing on the Professor. He seems clean. A good professional record. No sign of extra-mural interests.'

'That's a surprise.' In the context 'extra-mural' meant 'political'.

'But the other laddie, he's quite a goer. Seen lots of action. An eco-freak. Was on the Rainbow Warrior when the frogs sunk it. His file is pretty bulky.

Of the two, he's the one to keep an eye on, I would have thought.'

❖

When Swanepoel drove up to the Beitbridge border post, his mind was on other things. He was thinking about the arrangements he had made for his most recent assignment. The car bomb would probably be activated about now, he thought, looking at his watch. The target was a fifty year old lawyer, Hugh Goldberg, who was working in the Ministry of Justice for the Mozambique Government. The bomb was planned to explode as he turned the key to the door of his Honda car, parked outside a block of flats where he lived in Maputo.

An ANC member, Goldberg had been detained without trial under the 90-day law for his anti-apartheid activities in Cape Town in the 1960s. Although he was no direct threat to Pretoria – his work drafting legislation for the Mozambiquean Government was too time-consuming for him to remain active – he had been deliberately selected by Swanepoel. A few years before General Magnus Malan, South Africa's Minister of Defence, had pledged in a public statement: 'Wherever the ANC is we will eliminate it.' Now, not just ANC activists, but all known ANC supporters would live in fear of their lives.

'Good holiday was it?' The border guard looked idly at his papers.

'Fine, thanks. Saw too much of the grandchildren though. It was tiring. I'm pleased to be going home.'

'Just need to run you through the computer. I won't be long.'

The guard went into his kiosk. Swanepoel wasn't worried. It was normal routine on a return journey. He was thinking of the bomb going off, the shattering of a life, another blow struck against the enemy.

'Excuse me Mr Herson. Could you step inside for a minute? We need this filled out.' He handed Swanepoel a long form, shrugging his shoulders with an apologetic explanation. 'This is a random check. A new procedure. When we aren't too busy' – he gestured at the empty road to the south – 'we have to get additional particulars. Also I must search your car. Please step inside.'

Swanepoel felt like grumbling and protesting, but he was anxious to seem co-operative. 'Ah, well, us pensioners, we've got all the time in the world!'

He was shown to a bare desk in the kiosk. It was chilly. Winter was setting in. Outside, two men were making a perfunctory search of the car. If Swanepoel had been watching closely, he would have noticed how uninterested they were in the car's contents. He might even have noticed the special attention one of them was paying to the offside rear wheel arch of his Nissan saloon. Being a professional, Swanepoel would almost certainly have spotted that a small transmitter was being fixed at the top of the arch. But he was too busy filling in the form. All bureaucratic details which they probably knew anyway. Inwardly he cursed officialdom. Outwardly he remained polite.

The man in the cubicle behind the glass partition accepted the form and gave it a cursory glance. 'All questions completed?'

Swanepoel nodded, imagining the buzzer positioned discreetly above the official's right knee. The buzzer which, if pressed, would produce a lot of hassle he could do without.

'OK. That seems in order. Here's your passport.'

After paying a visit to the gents, Swanepoel returned to his car, standing on its own at the side of the road. Another car was being inspected. He looked around to check whether he needed clearance to depart. But nobody seemed to be taking any notice of him.

God, he could do with a slug of brandy. The delay at the border had rattled him. Perhaps he was getting too long in the tooth for the tension of action in the field. Still, not to worry, he was on his way now. He would stop in Harare and collect some booze and a bite to eat. Then he would go home and relax.

As Swanepoel's car pulled away, Florence Sithole's phone rang and a voice spoke urgently. She had to strain to hear clearly on the long distance line.

'Beitbridge here. The Temba subject has just crossed the border. We've fixed on the transmitter as instructed. You should pick up the signal when he gets near to Harare.'

'Any bother?' she asked.

'No. All routine. The old bugger was a little put out, but co-operative. We swept the car. Clean. No electronic gadgets, no contraband.'

'Thanks.'

'Pleasure. Any time.' The border official tried to visualise the person to match the voice at the other end, wondering whether she was as stunning as she sounded.

Florence Sithole looked up the Temba file. She spent an hour reading it thoroughly, spotting the record of Ed Tombe's instructions to Beitbridge and his scribbled comments on the subject, a Mr Paul Herson. She noted the tenuous basis of Tombe's decision to target him, but then she had every confidence in her former colleague. Experienced at intelligence work, he had been nothing if not thorough. Also, there was no other lead. Nothing else had come of the days of inquiries which followed Temba's death. Days of wasted effort. She could remember trudging round the city herself on pointless visits to innocuous people.

Details of Herson's background were on a separate sheet, together with a print-out from the vehicle licensing centre giving his car registration number, type and colour. She decided quickly on the next step. She would drive out on the main Harare road and spot him on the way in. The transmitter was a godsend. She could tail at a distance, have a look at the guy, see what he was up to.

❖

When Hugh Goldberg opened his car door, there was a deafening explosion which threw him across the road. A child playing nearby and a passing motorist were badly injured. The blast reduced his Honda to a pile of tangled metal. It shattered windows in his block of flats which adjoined the Portuguese Embassy, though it did not damage the Maputo office of the South African Trade Mission across the road.

Miraculously, Goldberg was still conscious after the explosion. His right arm shattered and his body drenched in blood, he struggled into a sitting position and asked for an ambulance. Soon he would be struggling for his life in intensive care.

The previous year a white Angolan paratrooper with a South African passport had been arrested in Maputo with a suitcase bomb in his possession. This time KJ had insisted there must be no trace of the agent. Swanepoel, always to be relied upon, had ensured that.

❖

Wang Bi Nan was pondering his next step. The information from London was disorientating. Evans in the clear and Sewell suspect? It didn't make sense. There was no question that Evans was onto them. Perhaps he had stumbled in by accident, perhaps he had been sent in, there was no way of knowing, but why did the British not have something on him? He was not innocent, of that Wang was sure. But Sewell? The only vaguely relevant factor that Wang could locate was his presence in Peking at the time when Evans had picked up the information from the students.

Maybe that was it. Maybe he was doing errands for Evans. Maybe he had collected the documents. After all, his informer had not been able to follow the Englishman back. He smacked the table in frustration. He should have got his man to identify the culprit. If Sewell had been the collector, it would naturally explain why they had never found the documents when searching Evans' room and belongings. It was also possible that Evans had nothing to do with receiving the documents. Wang's mind raced, assessing the situation and the options before him. Now he had not one, but two, targets. He would have to brief his team on this latest complication.

❖

Evans wondered if he was having some sort of breakdown. He had felt secure recuperating on the boat with his friends and then he had slept throughout the train journey. But now in the hotel in Wuhan he felt vulnerable again. His concentration had gone. He couldn't follow the morning briefing at the city's university and had asked to be excused from the rest of the day's itinerary. As he tried to relax in his room, he couldn't read or sleep. He was living on his nerves.

The rat-a-tat-tat of knocking on his door jerked him bolt upright. Sewell was out with his own party for the day. Evans was on his own. And the door wasn't even locked! He cursed the local custom of leaving hotel rooms accessible.

'Who is it?' his voice had a note of desperation in it.

'Security officers.'

Hell, not more bloody officials. He had answered enough questions already, first on the boat, then waiting for the train at Ichang while the others visited the giant hydro-electric complex which fed off the mighty waters of the Yangtse. He opened the door tentatively. Three Chinese; their stiff formality made him shiver uncontrollably. He felt embarrassed.

'Come in please,' he said in the best professorial voice he could muster.

'Professor Evans,' the senior of the three began, 'we work for the Public

Security Bureau. We have had reports. First the collision with the car, then near-drowning. One version says these were accidents.' He let the word hang in the air for a moment. 'Accidents? Is that what they were Professor Evans?'

Evans felt he was being put on the spot. 'I can't be sure.'

'But you are doubtful – yes?'

'Yes.'

'So, who would want to harm you, Professor Evans?'

'I have no idea. I haven't done anything wrong, have I?'

'Not that we know of.' The security man wasn't building any bridges. His manner was distinctly cold. 'But we cannot afford to risk anything else happening to you. It would not be good for our reputation. If you agree, from now on you will be placed under official surveillance and protection. You will not go anywhere without informing one of my staff.' He pointed at the other two.

'My men will keep your hotel room under observation and they will follow you wherever you go. Until you cross the border into Hong Kong, you will stay within their sight please. Is that acceptable?'

The question was rhetorical and Evans knew it. 'Thank you,' he heard himself stuttering.

CHAPTER SIX

Florence Sithole was parked in an empty yard alongside a petrol station on the outskirts of the city. Her car was fitted with a receiver which would pick up the transmitter on Swanepoel's to a distance of about thirty miles. The signal would be displayed on a small screen fixed to the dashboard and tilted towards the driving seat.

She had arrived early, partly to avoid the rush hour traffic which was beginning to build up and partly to give her time to read a report which her office had prepared. It documented a series of attacks on Government and ANC personnel, going back to 1981, including the assassination of the ANC representative in Zimbabwe, Joe Gqabi.

Early in 1988, a ring of six men, five whites and one black, had been arrested following a bomb attack on an ANC house in Bulawayo. They were later convicted of murder and conspiracy. The whites were all ex-soldiers in the old white Rhodesian army and evidence in court proved that the ring was being run from Pretoria. In August 1981 they had organised the bombing of the Inkomo army barracks armoury outside Harare, destroying £20 million worth of armaments. Early in 1982 ZANU's Harare headquarters was ripped apart by a bomb and in July one-quarter of the country's air force was destroyed in an attack on Thornhill air base outside Gweru. In 1987 two ANC houses were damaged, one by explosives in a television set, the other by mortar fire. Recently a series of car bomb and other attacks had begun again, this time even more deadly and explicitly targeted at ANC officials. With the exception of the Temba incident where his whole family had died, only the targets had been killed. The intelligence in possession of the saboteurs seemed uncannily accurate.

She stared out of the window, not noticing the rush of cars, unaware of the cold creeping in as the sun went down. Her mind was elsewhere, a sombre expression on her finely shaped features. How much danger was Makuyana in? Any traitors in the ANC would quickly suspect the purpose of his investigations. They had tried to eliminate him once already – and had killed her predecessor, Ed Tombe, instead. She pushed her fingers through her hair, plaited, dreadlock-style, troubled thoughts racing through her mind.

The first faint sound from the monitor startled her: the car signal. Now, what was in the second file again? She flicked through it, noting Mr Paul Herson's background; all unexceptional. Then the reasons for surveillance:

rather tenuous.

The blip on the monitor was getting stronger now, the sound a little sharper. She waited, fingers thrusting through her hair.

Swanepoel was making good time and would soon be on the perimeter of the city. He had some American country music playing on his car cassette radio; Willy Nelson was his favourite and helped pass the time on a long drive. The petrol gauge was showing low. He must top up. A filling station came into view and he pulled in, unconscious that he was now under close surveillance from an attractive young woman parked twenty yards away.

If he had been expecting a tail he might have noticed her pull out after him. On the other hand, he might not. She was following at a distance, at least several cars behind. He didn't notice that she stopped when he stopped, first to do some shopping and then at a liquor store. He didn't notice her drive past his house when he reached it.

She got a very good look at him. Was he an old gent, arriving home to a musty house with some alcohol to keep him happy? Or was he part of an assassin's ring? What she saw made her feel instinctively that they were onto something. It was not a wild goose chase. The description from the Grassroots bookshop fitted him perfectly.

She decided to put a tap on his phone and order permanent surveillance by two of her subordinates. Also, she would report to her boss the next time he made contact.

❖

Evans sat waiting in the bar for Jenny and Sewell, his Chinese minder sitting ten yards away reading a paper. His spirit had picked up. The visit from Chinese security, initially startling, had made him feel less nervy. The omnipresence of the men deputed to watch him, odd at first, was now re-assuring.

'Can I buy you a drink?' Harold Williams was at his shoulder, smiling for a change.

'That's kind of you. But I'm afraid I was waiting for someone else.'

'Never mind. I'll buy them one too.' Williams wasn't taking no for an answer and was already at the bar, ordering.

Where were the other two? Evans felt exposed.

'We don't know each other that well, I thought it was time I introduced myself properly.'

What's coming next? Evans wondered.

'You've had a rough time on this trip.'

'I suppose so.' Evans smiled sheepishly.' What's he up to?

'It occurred to me,' Williams paused as if searching for the correct words, 'that once is coincidence, twice is conspiracy.'

Evans shrugged, sipping his beer. 'Perhaps I've been unlucky. Could have happened to anyone.'

'It's a strange country and I thought I'd mention that I could possibly be of some help.'

'Oh?' Evans was caught by surprise.

'You see, I have intelligence connections.'

'Oh – really? This time Evans had to make himself sound surprised. 'I though you were a retired civil servant.'

'I am – but I used to work for both MI5 and MI6. I could be of assistance if you need any.'

'That's very good of you. But I really don't think it's necessary. I'll be fine.'

Williams made as if he hadn't heard. 'Is there any reason why you might be in danger? Can I give any advice? If you need any help, I need to know if there are any grounds for anxiety. You haven't got into some sort of trouble, have you?'

'Not that I know of!' Evans felt in control now. The initial reaction of surprise had passed.

Williams looked sceptical and perhaps a little disappointed. 'Well, if there is anything I can do, please tell me. We don't want any harm to come to you, do we?'

'Thanks for your concern. If anything occurs to me I will let you know,' Evans found himself lying almost without thinking.

'Jim!' Jenny's voice called him from the other side of the bar.

'More attractive company I suppose?' Williams was almost leering. 'Anyway, remember, you can always call on me if you change your mind.'

Like hell, Evans muttered to himself, like hell.

'What was he after?' Jenny asked.

After buying a round of drinks, Evans explained.

'That's interesting,' she said, 'they must be in a fix. He was obviously trying to pump you for information. Maybe because they can't get to you so easily with Chinese security around.'

'Maybe because they are onto *me*,' Sewell interjected. 'Someone searched my room today. Very professionally. I might not have noticed, except that I had taken precautions to detect any tampering with my things.'

They sat down, Evans felt deflated again, 'What are we up against? Something really big?'

'It seems so,' Sewell replied, 'but what I can't understand is Williams' role.'

Jenny sipped at her mango juice. 'I am beginning to think it could be quite significant. He has now confirmed he worked for British Intelligence.' She turned to Sewell. 'Remember the evidence of that right wing faction in MI5.'

He nodded. 'Peter Wright revealed it in *Spycatcher*, didn't he? The MI5 faction had plotted against the 1974-76 Labour Government. Colin Wallace, that British intelligence officer who'd served in Northern Ireland gave much the same account.'

Evans felt rather excluded. 'I vaguely recall all that stuff. But nothing much came of it, surely?'

'No,' Jenny replied, squeezing him on the knee as if she sensed his insecurity, 'there was a cover-up. By the mid-1970s key sections in the British establishment were extremely worried: about Northern Ireland, about the succession of defeats inflicted on the Conservative government by the trade unions, and so on. Remember the three-day week? Many on the right believed they really were faced with the end of civilisation in Britain as they had known and controlled it.'

'I remember a senior Conservative warning about the country being plunged into a state of chaos. The way they were going on you'd have thought they were preparing for a minor nuclear attack,' said Sewell.

Jenny smiled wryly. There was even talk in senior circles about an army coup, and there were reports of private 'citizens armies' being recruited by retired military figures. Right wing British intelligence was involved in all this. MI5 also had close links with right wing pressure groups and the South African security agency, BOSS.'

'What's all this got to do with Harold Williams and our current predicament?' Evans sounded irritated. Jenny and Dick seemed to have retreated into an intense political world of their own.

'Be patient!' Jenny said affectionately. 'The point is that many of the same right wing officers active in the F4 and F6 branches of MI5 at the time are still around, some in higher positions. My guess is Harold Williams was one of them.'

Makuyana was not a man who allowed himself the luxury of nostalgia. When his comrades started to talk about their guerrilla days in the bush, he invariably stayed silent or made an excuse and left. Wallowing in nostalgia was a sign of weakness; he dismissed it as a self-indulgent emotion, always coming back to the present, to the situation confronting him.

Never go back was his motto. George Orwell's *Coming up for Air* had made a big impact upon him when he read it as a student. He retained in his mind the image of Orwell's character who escaped briefly from his middle-aged, middle-class lifestyle to travel back to a spot where he had fished as a boy. The man had vivid memories of happy hours spent in the sun catching huge fish by the side of an idyllic stream. When he returned, the fish had gone, the stream was polluted, the spot had been built around and the neighbouring area urbanised.

Still, Makuyana had to admit to pangs of nostalgia at the feel of the countryside. The ground was hard, the grass brown and baked dry. There were sprinklings of thorn bushes here and there. Nearby the terrain was flat. In the distance a series of small hills or *kopjes* framed the horizon. There was no sign of life anywhere.

Then, under the shade of a msasa tree as he drove past, he noticed an elderly man with tatty clothes and a stubby grey beard sheltering from the midday sun. A typical African image. The man was curled up on the ground, a battered hat tipped over his eyes, asleep. Or was he? Makuyana craned his neck to look and then switched to his rear view mirror. But the dust was billowing up behind the car, obscuring his vision. He couldn't see the elderly man roll over and reach for a portable handset, speaking into it briefly. A mile up the dusty track was the farmhouse where Makuyana would rendezvous with the man from Lusaka; the man who could have something important to tell him.

It was a remote spot, fifty miles north of Harare, and Makuyana had come prepared. He wasn't taking any chances in this second meeting set up by the ANC – not after the Tombe affair. A Kalashnikov automatic rifle lay on the passenger seat. Inside his slim briefcase there were three grenades and plenty of spare ammunition. Under his jacket he had a shoulder pistol. His eyes scanned the scene before him, concentrating, looking for anything unusual. All his instincts, all the training and skills from his days fighting the old

Rhodesian Army would be invaluable now.

You are worried, he thought to himself. He dismissed the thought the moment it surfaced, comforted by the knowledge that Florence Sithole and her team were approaching from the other side of the farmhouse. By the time he arrived, they should be in position immediately to its rear. His briefcase also contained a console so that he could be in radio contact with her if necessary, though they had maintained strict silence during the approach to the farmhouse.

She was never one to shirk action, he mused. At the same time she was not one for heroics. She simply did her job quietly and with total dedication. If she drew attention to herself within Zimbabwe security circles it was not because she was immodest or pushy, but because she was admired for her tenacity and willingness to court danger when it was unavoidable. A number of the younger male officers had made advances, but they were rebuffed politely. She was her own woman, secure within herself, with plenty of friends but none close enough to threaten her fierce independence.

As the farmhouse came into view he slowed down, searching the layout of the buildings, assessing where any attack might come from. The farm was modern, white-washed walls standing out from the brown of the surrounding land. Flecks of sand stained the base of the whiteness, swept up by rain. A series of outhouses and barns stood in a U-shape behind it. There were several cars parked between the house and the other buildings.

If he parked there too, he would be surrounded by buildings. Or trapped as the case may be. Gunmen could be hiding in any one of them, cutting off an escape back the way he had come. He decided to pull off the approach road and park in front of the house, alongside the low fence made of wooden slats. Hard luck if the owners weren't happy with that.

The car rolled to a halt on the bumpy ground, skidding a little as he avoided several large stones and turned to face back the way he had come. He switched off the engine deliberately, aware that with each action he was taking an irrevocable step from which there might be no return. He waited, eyes scanning the front door and windows. No movement, no sound. He couldn't see the buildings behind the house. Then he picked up the Kalash and the briefcase, climbed out, and opened the front gate. The silence around him was total.

As he walked up the short path to the farmhouse, the door swung open and a short, stocky man stepped out.

'Comrade Makuyana? Welcome – I have been expecting you.' He spread his arms out. 'Come in. Can I get you a glass of water? There's not much else here, I'm afraid.'

Makuyana nodded, eyes adjusting to the gloom inside, sweeping round what appeared to be the main living room, a large fireplace set in stone at one end. Besides his host, there were two men standing up at the end of the room, both armed with AK47s.

'My name is Oliver Khama. I am sorry about the venue. It must be inconvenient for you. But we can't be too careful. Harare is such a hothouse, nobody can move without being seen or whisper without being heard.' He waved Makuyana to an armchair, ushering his men outside so that they were alone.

Makuyana listened impassively, forcing the other man to do all the talking, assessing him, thinking about logistics: the size of the room, its position in the house, the distance from his car. Some of what Khama was saying was going over his head. He pulled his attention back to the man from Lusaka.

'Over the past year or so we have had persistent reports of political contacts between Pretoria and Peking,' Khama was saying. 'And unexplained business visits – comings and goings which don't add up. But nothing you could get your teeth into. We have the impression the pace of activity is stepping up, but we don't know why.'

'What do you think is behind it?' Makuyana averted his gaze to his car, just visible through the front window. The two men with the AK47s were standing idly by the low fence.

'You could help us find out.'

'Me?'

'Yes,' Khama leant forward, his white pupils prominent in his dark brown eyes, 'we want you to go inside.'

Makuyana shook his head immediately. 'No way. My people would never sanction it. Not worth the risk of jeopardising diplomatic relations with Pretoria. Use a team of your own.'

Khama was almost whispering now. 'This one must be done down the legside. Total security. No leaks. No danger of betrayals. I had one of my most trusted men deputed to try and make sense of the Peking connection. The week after I briefed him, he was shot. The Zambian police said it was a random murder, the sort that is unfortunately all too frequent in Lusaka these days. I don't doubt their good faith. But I don't doubt either that they were wrong. The killing was too coincidental. It also took place at a spot where my man would not have had any reason to be. It was outside a nightclub, in the early hours. My man was teetotal, a strict disciplinarian. He wouldn't have been seen dead at a place like that.' He paused, 'except of course that he was.'

Makuyana ignored the irony. 'You are certain it wasn't an accident? Absolutely certain?'

'Yes. I wouldn't have travelled all this way if it wasn't serious. All my vibes tell me something big is happening. But I don't know what. We need you to find out.'

'But the risk…'

'The risk! For Chrissake. Don't you think its risky sending a team over the border? Many of them never come back.' He thumped the small wicker table between them in frustration. It almost collapsed under the shock. 'I'm sorry,' he muttered, 'this thing has been getting to me.' He suddenly looked desperate, cornered as if he had been hunted down like an animal.

Makuyana didn't respond. He just stared. There was a moment of stillness in the room. Khama started to feel resentful at the man's coolness. Didn't these ZANU people realise what the score was anymore, now they were desk-bound?

More silence.

'Look,' Khama said awkwardly, feeling the need to say something, 'can I make a suggestion?'

Makuyana shrugged his shoulders. 'I'm listening.'

'How about going in legit? As a diplomat or something. That way there would be less risk – and you would be more in control. We can get you out if needs be. '

'I'm still listening.'

They talked for another hour. Then Makuyana asked for the toilet and was directed to the rear of the house. He needed a pee, but he also needed to have a quick look outside the back. It was quiet in the courtyard. There were a couple of tractors but no sign of movement. The large double door to the barn was open, but the blackness inside made it impossible to see anything from where he was, on his toes, peering through the toilet window. He hoped Florence and her team had closed in by now.

Khama was pacing about the room when Makuyana returned. 'Well?'

'Okay. I'll examine the feasibility. When must it be and whom do I contact inside?'

Khama passed him a piece of paper, with a name, address, phone number and date. 'Memorise this now and destroy it before you leave please.'

Makuyana recognised the name. He was surprised. It was a prominent white lawyer. The date startled him. 'That soon?'

Khama nodded. The men outside had started to get restless. They were leaning up against Makuyana's car.

'Time to go. I will leave first. Give me ten minutes. There's only one way out.'

'Which way are you travelling when you reach the main road?'

'South. Why?' Khama looked surprised.

Makuyana thought for a moment. 'There's a petrol station a few miles along in that direction. A few houses and a cafe, too, I think. You take my car. I'll take yours. We'll meet there and swop.'

'Why?' Khama asked again, suspicious now. 'Who set up this meet?'

'Mngadi's men.'

'Which ones?'

'I don't know. The message came through from one of his aides.'

'Well, that's even more reason for us to be careful. I trust him, but I am worried about his aides. Send your men round the back to collect your car. Then we'll swop. The three of you will stand a better chance if anyone tries to attack.'

'Attack?' Khama frowned.

'I am taking no chances. The last time Mngadi's office sent me to meet someone, my number two was murdered.'

'I heard about that. All right, I will tell my men.' He went outside.

Makuyana opened his briefcase and switched on his console so that Florence could contact him if need be. He memorised the name, the address and the phone, then he burnt the paper.

The two minders appeared round the front of the house, driving a Volkswagen Passat, looking moody and irritable. They got out and climbed into Makuyana's car, one in the front passenger seat the other in the back, their AK47s cradled on their laps. Khama jumped in behind the wheel. 'See you later.'

❖

As the Nissan saloon pulled away, a cloud of dust rising up behind it, Makuyana ran through to the kitchen at the rear, dragging his Kalash and his briefcase with him. He was just in time to see a jeep roar out of the barn, its tyres clinging desperately to the loose surface as it twisted through the courtyard. A man was hunched in the front alongside the driver, something balanced on his shoulder, protruding across the windscreen. Christ, it was a hand-held anti-tank missile, Makuyana couldn't quite see what type. He rushed round to the front of the living room. The jeep screeched to a halt. The man in the front steadied himself instantly, then fired.

Makuyana watched, helpless, as if the scene had been captured on screen and frozen. The missile closed in rapidly on the dusty image of his car. It seemed to dip down, exploding just underneath the boot, blowing a huge crater in the track. The car was thrown sideways, juddering to a halt. The jeep's engine screamed, its tyres spinning in the dust as it took off towards the stricken Nissan.

Then there was a crash at the rear of the house. Makuyana spun around, pulling out his pistol as a man came through the connecting door, firing. Makuyana shot him between the eyes. He fell, an expression of total astonishment fixed on what remained of his face, his gun clattering to the floor. He was white, the men in the jeep were black. Makuyana picked up the gun: it was the familiar South African-made RI assault rifle. Makuyana heard a distant shout from the courtyard and he was vaguely aware of the familiar sound of AK47s firing from a distance in the front. So, Khama's boys were not dead?

He grabbed one of the RG-42 high explosive grenades out of his briefcase and crept into the kitchen. A round of bullets shattered the window and another poured through the open door. The noise in the confined space was deafening. They are panicking, he thought, spreading himself across the floor.

The missile must have been aimed at him and so he had to assume that the attackers believed three men were still in the house – Khama and his two associates. If there were enough of them, they would probably have encircled the house by now. He pulled back and along the corridor to the toilet next door. There was no sound.

Makuyana stood up carefully by the toilet window and peered out, just catching a glimpse of two men creeping along the wall towards the back door, guns at the ready. Nobody else was in view, but there could be others round the front. He reached for the grenade and pulled the pin out, steeling himself to wait as the seconds ticked away. Then he stuck his hand out of the window, lobbing the grenade sideways.

The two didn't stand a chance. They were blown apart, along with most of the kitchen wall, leaving an ugly mess of blood, flesh and bones stuck onto the rumble. There was dust everywhere. Makuyana reached for his console and tugged out the aerial, pointing it through the window.

'Florence, can you hear me?'

There was a crackling sound, then her voice came through faintly. 'We can hear shots. Are you okay?'

'All in one piece in the house. But in a fix. I have taken some out but I think there are others round the front. Also there's a jeep nearby with a nasty missile. Maybe some gunmen too.'

'Right, we're coming in. Give us a couple of minutes.'

That might be too long, he thought, sliding along the corridor towards the living room. He waited. Then he looked around, noticing an empty cardboard box behind him. Putting down his guns and his briefcase, he picked up the box and then, as if throwing a discus, he swung it around through the doorway into the living room. A fusillade of bullets ripped into it. So, they were waiting. His way out to the front was blocked. The house was a trap. He had to get out to the rear. He pulled up short at the roar of the jeep returning. It seemed to be coming up to the front. Christ, if they started loosing off missiles, the house wouldn't last long. Nor would he.

There was a wooshing sound, then a massive explosion rocked the whole structure, tearing down the far end of the corridor in which he was crouching. They had fired directly into the living room. He pulled his equipment towards what remained of the kitchen, catching the sound of the jeep starting off again. It roared into the courtyard.

Makuyana knew he was cornered now. The tempo was accelerating. He moved around and fired a burst from his Kalash at the jeep, hoping to catch the man with the missile. The bullets broke through the windscreen, screams from the driver suggesting a hit.

He was suddenly aware of movement behind him. They must be coming in through the front of the house. The bazooka-like weapon was swinging round towards the house. It was steadying, pointing right at him. This is it, he thought, ducking sideways back along the corridor. There's no escaping a bastard like that aimed at a confined space in which you are trapped. He was backing into what looked like a bedroom at the end of the corridor when a face and a gun appeared through the living room door. He fired immediately and both were pulled out of sight. They must know he was on his own now. There was another explosion and the kitchen seemed to fall into the corridor, water gushing through the debris.

Again the jeep's engine screamed. It came into view through the bedroom window. He didn't need to check what they were up to. It was plain bloody obvious. They were going to blow in each wall until they finally got him.

It was as if he was paralysed, watching another missile being loaded. The ugly cylinder was heaved up and swung slowly, relentlessly in the direction of the bedroom. Then – yes! – the front of the weapon suddenly heaved upwards as its operator was thrown bodily out of the jeep by the impact of automatic fire ripping into his chest.

Florence ... thank Christ, Florence. Figures flitted across the window. Bullets seemed to crash everywhere. He swung round as someone lurched into the corridor, obviously wounded, half raising a gun in his direction. Makuyana shot him in the knee, a hideous scream of agony drowning the noise outside. Then, save for the moaning of the man in the corridor, a sort of silence descended. Makuyana stayed still, listening. The sound of freedom crackled through his radio.

'Are you receiving me?' Florence's voice quivered, as if expecting no answer.

'I'm here. You took your time didn't you?'

'Cheeky bugger!' Her relief was obvious. 'We've shot them all out here. Is it clear to come in.'

He thought how ludicrous it was to talk of 'coming in' to what was little more than a pile of rubble. 'Yes. Got an enemy in here, but he's in a bad way.'

Her team surveyed the scene in disbelief. Makuyana took command.

'Take the Passat and drive up the track to my car. It was attacked. Check if there are any survivors. The ANC team were using it.'

He went over to the man curled up in agony on the floor, shaking his shoulder aggressively. 'Talk you bastard. Talk. Or else you'll get another one.' He pointed his pistol at the other knee.

'Don't!' The man screeched in terror.

'Who are you? Who sent you here?' Makuyana felt no pity. As he pressured the man, he thought of Ed Tombe, saw his car exploding. A good image to stop your humanity thwarting the job in hand.

Florence Sithole watched her boss. She didn't like to see him so brutal and brutalised, but she couldn't see any alternative.

The man's eyes glazed. He was in a bad way. 'Renamo,' he muttered, 'Renamo.'

Makuyana looked at Florence, raising his eyebrows. Renamo, the South African backed Mozambique National Resistance, had been set up by the Rhodesians in 1970 to spy on guerrilla groups then based in Mozambique. In 1980, on Zimbabwe's independence, South Africa had taken over stewardship. From that time, Renamo had become increasingly hostile to the new Harare Government, particularly as it was dragged into the war in Mozambique, partly to defend the Frelimo Government there and partly to protect the Beira corridor, a road, railway and oil pipeline carrying vital imports and exports from Zimbabwe to the coast.

'Who sent you?' Makuyana shook the Renamo man once more, banging his pistol on the the mess of his knee.

He screamed again, sobbing in terror. 'Pretoria,' he shouted, 'Pretoria. One of them came with us.'

The white he had shot. A pity dead bodies don't talk. 'Yes, I know *that*,' Makuyana replied sarcastically, 'But who told you where to come?'

Through his pain the man seemed almost to be smiling mirthlessly. 'Your people.'

'Which one? Which one?' Makuyana barked out the questions. He had to keep him on the run, had to keep him terrified.

'Don't know his name. Honest. Don't know his name.'

Florence spoke quietly, 'Khama's two bodyguards are dead, but he is still alive. Just. We must rush him to hospital.'

'Okay. The other two can drive him in the Passat. We will follow later.' He paused as if a thought had struck him. 'Do you want to go to hospital now too?' The wounded man nodded, hope springing up in his eyes. 'Can you identify the man who told you we would be here?'

The man nodded, 'Yes.'

At last ... Makuyana felt he was getting somewhere.

❖

Swanepoel hadn't done very much since his return to Harare: pottered about, slept and drunk a lot. The morning after his return, he had made a phone call from a kiosk in the local shopping arcade, reporting in to a businessman in the city centre; he was connected back into the network again.

As KJ had insisted, he was lying low for a while and it was pretty boring. The only consolation, had he been aware of it, was that the people from Zimbabwe security watching him were bored too. As they reported in regularly to Florence Sithole, she began to doubt the wisdom of allocating hard-pressed resources to the task. She would keep the watchers on for few another day and then, if nothing happened, rely on long distance surveillance by tracking his movements through the transmitter on his car, by tapping his phone, by intercepting his mail.

Swanepoel was beginning to realise just how much he had enjoyed his visit down South. The adrenaline of action gave him a kick. He also felt he was having more of an effect, hitting the opposition directly at home. His role in Harare was like that of a surrogate: although he knew of its strategic value, it was frustrating. Particularly when he read reports like the one on the front page of the *The Herald*. Ten people had been killed in a lunch-hour explosion at an amusement centre in Johannesburg, the blast from a limpet mine destroying the inside of the centre and a fire breaking out seconds later. All those dead were whites.

Swanepoel resented the restrained glee with which *The Herald* also carried a story about the 'End Conscription Campaign' (ECC), a small but active group which campaigned to persuade the estimated 64,000 young whites who face conscription to resist the 'unjust war against apartheid'. Amongst the ECC's leaders were former soldiers who told how they had shot women and children in cold blood, how they had exposed themselves to women to degrade and intimidate, how they had driven army vehicles over flimsy huts, and how they had collected ears and fingers as souvenirs. In spite of violent intimidation their members faced, the group's influence was growing as the number of draft dodgers rose steadily.

He threw down the paper. What were the young coming to? His own *volk* bottling out. It was disgusting.

❖

Makuyana had sent the wounded Oliver Khama straight to hospital. But the Renamo man was despatched in secret to the medical centre where Robert Temba had been treated. Nobody was to know he had survived. He was in a bad way, a bullet in his stomach as well as the shattered knee-cap. Makuyana was taking no chances. He could be important in identifying the ANC traitor.

Next, he called Mngadi and his three aides into security headquarters and briefed them on the events at the farm, telling them that only Khama had survived.

'Another set-up!' Makuyana did not hide his contempt.

As Mngadi started to apologise, Makuyana brushed him aside, 'I will be reporting straight to the President. We may decide to close down your Harare operations.'

He was determined to maintain pressure on Mngadi. The greater the pressure the greater the chance that somebody would crack or that someone would spot a discrepancy in a colleague's behaviour.

As the ANC men sheepishly left the room, he called Mngadi back and closed the door. Another deliberate bit of pressure. 'I want full details on the family backgrounds of Msimang and Peterson. There was something not quite right about their reactions when I probed them the other day.'

Mngadi looked even more troubled. 'That won't be easy. Nor will it be quick. We will have to contact our people in Natal and the Cape. That could take several days. Then allow a week or two for the necessary checks and replies.'

'It must be done, however difficult it is. But make sure the two don't know they are under investigation.'

❖

Wuhan's airport had a small-town feel. The terminal was modest, the air traffic light. It had a sense of openness which surprised Evans. He would have expected it to be crawling with security. Even the military planes parked in rows over to the side were exposed to all eyes. There was an air of informality about the way the pilots clambered into the old Mig fighters, pulled on their helmets and took straight off.

By contrast, Canton's airport was much more modern, as befitted a city on the border with Hong Kong, China's gateway to the West. The five hundred mile flight had gone smoothly, the old twin-prop Tupolev flying low so that they had a spectacular view of the scenery.

The Group stayed in Canton's prestigious 28-storey White Swan hotel. With a marble lobby containing birds in a gilded cage and an artificial three-storey waterfall, it offered a panoramic view of the Pearl river which crawled with wooden junks. The couple of days spent in the city passed without incident, but Evans was feeling increasingly claustrophobic with his friends and his Chinese minders keeping a constant eye on him. His anxiousness to get back home saddened him, souring the end to a trip which had promised so much.

The hundred mile train journey to Hong Kong was like being in a tightly sealed capsule. They had been ushered on after their papers were checked and their passports stamped. During the three-hour journey, young girls in uniform acted as both guards and hostesses, standing at the end of each carriage and keeping a wary eye on the passengers. The train didn't stop. It reminded Evans of his trip a couple of years before through East Germany to Berlin. As they swept across the border, past the high security fencing which separated the mainland from the Hong Kong Territories, Evans wondered what it would be like to be back in the old British colony after three weeks virtually sealed off from the West.

The first cultural shock wave hit Evans almost immediately he stepped off the train. Hong Kong's main station was teeming with humanity, a hubbub of voices, shouting, greeting, cajoling, directing.

The din was incredible. So was the hustle and bustle as travellers hailed down porters and people poured through the throng. Evans felt disorientated, longing suddenly for the orderly dignity of the mainland Chinese and beginning already to feel resentful of their pushy cousins in the West. As they made their way to the chartered bus bathed in sunshine in the road outside, he saw his first beggar for three weeks, scuttling through the crowd. Dozens of trinket-sellers hassled for trade. It was a relief to slip out of the rabble into his cool seat on the air-conditioned bus. While the soft beauty of the countryside on the way in had surprised him, he found the rampant materialism of the main city was almost obscene. A collage of neon lights, garish signs and dwarfing concrete, the place lacked a sense of proportion, a human touch.

Two hotel rooms had been reserved for the group to use as a base and leave their luggage, with about ten hours for a sight-seeing tour before catching the overnight flight to London. Time to shop. Time to relax. Time to enjoy the company of the group before it broke up. Evans put aside the curious sense of loss he felt at leaving China and decided to make the most of the day sightseeing. He was free – free of minders, of harassers, of the tension of the past few weeks. Perhaps the West wasn't too bad after all.

Jenny left the party while they wandered through the maze of tourist shops, with a specific task. She had Sewell's documents quickly photocopied in an instant print shop, bought a large brown envelope, some stamps, and addressed the copy to her aunt who lived in a Dorset seaside village. Inside she scribbled a brief note asking for it to be locked away until she got in touch.

Her aunt would understand the need for secrecy. Ruth Brown was a veteran campaigner against nuclear weapons. She had been one of the early CND marchers to Aldermaston in the late 1950s, and had been arrested at Trafalgar Square during a famous sit-down demonstration led by Bertrand Russell in 1961. At the age of 63, she had joined the women's peace camp established outside the cruise missile base at Greenham Common in the early 1980s. For nearly a year she had lived in the mud and cold, her tent torn down ten times and her possessions scattered as the authorities made persistent attempts to clear the campers.

Jenny felt almost embarrassed at her own subterfuge, playing silly games when surely they were safely back in the West again, out of reach of the unseen forces which had dogged them in China? Nevertheless, she felt relief when she was finally able to slip the envelope into a letter box. She found herself turning abruptly on her heel to check if anybody was watching. If they were, she couldn't see them. She pushed the original into her shoulder bag, walked back to the hotel, let herself into the room where their luggage was stored and slipped it into the false compartment in his suitcase.

Some hours later, Wang sat studying the documents in his hands: dynamite, pure dynamite.

He had come across the border on the same train, but in a different carriage, having previously bid the Group farewell at Canton's station. Arranging for their luggage to be searched in the empty hotel room hadn't been difficult. He had enough of his own people and his own resources in Hong Kong for almost any undercover operation. The irony was he could operate with greater freedom here than he could inside China.

So Harold Williams' MI5 tip-off had been corroborated. The culprit was Sewell after all. The incontrovertible evidence of the scruffy Chinese envelope recovered from the Englishman's suitcase placed him in a dilemma. Had they been after the wrong target? Was Evans an innocent who had stumbled across some peripheral information by accident? Or were Sewell and Evans acting together? What was his priority? To stop the evidence in the documents from leaking out verbally? Or risk going for both men in the few hours before they flew out of his easy reach?

He weighed up the matrix of factors and the odds of success. Then he made *his* decision. It had to be his decision. The Old Man could not be contacted in time for guidance. He was on his own.

❖

Florence Sithole spoke softly as the doctor bent over her unconscious patient, 'How is he doing?'

The Doctor shrugged her shoulders. 'So-so. The operation on his chest went smoothly. We extracted the bullets. His knee-cap? Well, we have patched him up. But his knee will never work properly again. He'll be crippled for life. A very deliberate place to shoot someone, a knee-cap. A coincidence, I suppose?'

The question was rhetorical, a hint of reproach in the doctor's eyes. No response was expected, none was given.

'How soon can I talk to him?'

'Tomorrow perhaps. Is it very important?'

'Very. He is a Renamo man. He must talk. Otherwise he is dispensable.'

A neat word, 'dispensable'; almost clinical. The Doctor thought this young woman might be a kindred spirit, might be more caring than her boss. But they were all similar, these security people. She worked for them, so she couldn't help understanding. Underneath, they probably did care. She didn't feel contempt, only sadness.

❖

Hong Kong's Kaitak airport seemed absurdly cramped to cope with the 74,000 flights which came in and out of the territory every year. The main runway thrust out from the land like a giant seaside pier, squatting flat in the water. During the 1980s the number of passengers flying into the territory with its population of five and a half million was almost exactly the same in total as those flying into China with a population over two hundred times the size.

Evans' initial relief at leaving the unknown hazards of the big country had given way to a realisation that anything was possible in the hustle and bustle of congested Hong Kong. Although the day's sight-seeing had been enjoyable, the tension had returned as the hours passed. He didn't need to discuss his nervousness with Jenny and Sewell. Each knew what the other was going through.

Evans made sure he wasn't standing near the edge of any of the vantage points they visited, and he tried to avoid being alone at any time: laughable precautions, when you came to think of it, he knew that. A sniper could be anywhere and could disappear into the frenetic swirl of the traffic and the crowds.

But at last it was nightfall and they were at the airport. The air was uncomfortably humid despite the late hour, but everyone checked in smoothly, without last-minute hitches. The Cathay Pacific jumbo was being prepared, glistening against the darkness of the mountain towering behind Kaitak. Soon their flight would be called. Evans could feel his muscles beginning to ease as he made polite conversation.

There it was, the chime followed by the call of their flight to Heathrow, departing 22.00 hours. He collected his hand luggage, catching a quick smile from Jenny, checked that his boarding card was to hand and headed with her into the queue. They were booked into seats next to each other. Sewell had been allocated one farther back in the plane with his own party, but the three had arranged to have a celebratory drink once the flight was well under way. The engines whined now as the jumbo filled and the stewardesses walked up and down the gangways checking that seatbelts were fastened and luggage safely stowed away.

Evans always found himself marvelling at the way these great birds flew in, were serviced, and then flew back out often not much more than an hour or two later. They were engaged in almost perpetual motion, with working lives lasting over twenty years, covering over twenty thousand flights and millions of miles. It was extraordinary that mishaps were so relatively few and far between.

Mishaps? Squeezing Jenny's hand as the jumbo pulled back out of the loading bay, he looked over his shoulder to check on Sewell. Seat 61C was it? He couldn't see him amidst the rows of faces growing tense as they waited for take-off.

❖

As he had queued, waiting for the final stub to be torn off his boarding card, Sewell had caught a sight of Evans walking down the gangway behind Jenny.

'Ah, Mr Sewell, there's a message for you.' The slim clerk in the green and white Cathay Pacific hat beckoned him from the desk. 'Please step this way.' She took him to a door set in the side of the boarding lounge, knocked, then let him into what looked like a staff restroom. Empty paper cups littered the low table. A corridor led off to the rear. She gestured towards it.

'They will be coming. Don't worry, there is enough time, I will return to collect you in a minute.'

As the door clicked shut, a smart man – probably European, Sewell thought – walked in from the corridor.

'Sorry to have kept you old boy,' he said in a voice that might have come straight from Eton. 'There's a little problem with your suitcase. It split open while loading. We just want you to check everything's still there before we strap it up. Had lots of thefts recently. Can't take too many precautions. This way please.'

Sewell stepped into the corridor, irritated. Then he felt the beginnings of anxiety. Was something wrong? Had his documents been discovered?

He had no time to speculate further. In the next instant he was hit on the head and everything went dead. The Englishman bundled him into a metal skip sitting on a trolley and pushed it out and across the tarmac passing almost underneath the jumbo as the chocks on its fat rubber tyres were pulled away.

Ten minutes later, the aircraft took off and climbed steeply, banking away from the mountain side and the teeming city below. Everything was normal on board. The cabin staff had been informed of a very late cancellation. But down below, the man who should have been sitting in seat 61C was disappearing into the night.

❖

Selby Mngadi was waiting for him in a bar of the Monomatapa hotel. Makuyana often arranged meets there because it was central and he enjoyed the view of Harare's beautiful park. It was a good venue because the high turnover of international guests using its five star facilities provided cover for a chat over a drink – though he was aware bars in the area were known haunts of security people.

Their conversation was to the point. All three of Mngadi's close aides had known of the rendezvous on the farm with Oliver Khama. It had been unavoidable. But none had made any obvious move which could have set up the ambush.

Makuyana told him that Khama was in hospital, emphasising that the man from Lusaka knew nothing about the source of the attack.

'Make sure you mention that to your people. I don't want any heavies descending on his hospital room.' But still he made no mention of the Renamo survivor, the man who could possibly point the finger at the traitor.

They downed the last of their beers, the froth curling up inside the empty glasses. Makuyana left, Mngadi making his move five minutes later.

Their separate departures didn't fool the driver of the mini-cab parked across the road who didn't seem keen on taking a fare. He watched, wondering what the meeting had been about.

❖

When Sewell came to, he had a splitting headache. His neck was numb; it felt permanently cricked. It was dark. He appeared to be in a cellar of some sort. He pressed the light on his digital watch. Well past midnight. He began to panic. The plane would have taken off. Then the realisation broke: they had got him.

A sudden click and a light, blinding him. Several men crowded round, two of them familiar: the Englishman from the restroom, the Chinese interpreter, Wang. Jim and Jenny's suspicions had been correct.

Wang spoke first, sneering, confident, arrogant – a contrast with his apparent deference as an interpreter.

'We have the documents. Don't waste time with denials. They were found in your suitcase.'

Sewell nodded. Everything was blown. All the planning, all the effort, all the courage of the student contacts. He felt very old. He was finished. There was no way back. He sensed that from the faces surrounding him.

Then, a faint spark of hope. Jenny had a copy and she'd got away with Jim. He was sure he had seen them walking down through the boarding tunnel to the plane. He had to protect them. That was the only chance of rescuing the mission from complete failure.

'You collected the documents from the students at the bar in Peking?' It was an assertion rather than a question.

'Yes.'

'Good,' Wang looked satisfied. 'Don't waste my time with lies. We had an informer amongst the students. He reported to me the same night after your meeting.'

But why then had they not acted earlier against him? Why had Evans been the target? Sewell was confused.

'Who planned it?'

'I did.'

'Don't lie!' As Wang screamed the Englishmen smashed his fist into Sewell's jaw, dislocating some teeth. Blood spurted into his mouth. The shock bounced through his brain.

'We know all about you. You weren't acting alone, were you?'

Sewell tried to stick to his strategy. To reveal just enough to satisfy, but not sufficient to inform. Even as he wrestled with the pain in his jaw and the horror of being at the mercy of these thugs, he knew instinctively how treacherous it could be to volunteer only partial information. He didn't know how much they knew and how much was informed speculation. But he had to steer them away from his two friends.

'Okay. It was planned by my colleagues in Greenpeace. I was sent in to make contact and collect the documents. Now it has failed.' He didn't need to try too hard to sound utterly dispirited and deflated.

'Tell us all about it.' Wang sounded almost conciliatory now.

So Sewell told them. How Greenpeace had been contacted by radical sources within China concerned about the dangers of nuclear pollution. How he had been selected as the courier. About the arrangements to make contact.

Wang exchanged significant – perhaps satisfied? – glances with his colleagues. Then his manner changed abruptly. 'What about your two friends?'

'What about them?'

'Don't be insolent! I want the truth! Otherwise you will suffer. Do you want me to turn my colleagues loose on you?'

They moved closer. Sewell's jaw was shot through with pain. The warm taste of blood swam in his mouth.

'They knew nothing. I swear it.'

This time the blow was to his groin, a searing shock. The pain was excruciating. He doubled up, an incongruous flash of memory reminding him of the adolescent taunts of schoolfriends when he had been hit in the groin by a cricket ball: 'Be careful or it'll ruin your future!' He had no future now.

Of that he was certain.

'Stop hurting yourself. You can't protect them. We can check with them if we need to. Save yourself.' Wang sounded almost sympathetic.

It would have been easier simply to spill all the beans. But Sewell was determined to keep fighting. Otherwise his mission, indeed his own life — everything — would have been futile.

'Look,' he pleaded, 'I know Evans had some story about the nuclear energy programme he had picked up in Peking. To be honest, it was all too confusing to follow. I don't know if he could make sense of it himself. But I had never met him before the Yangtse trip.'

'You saved his life.'

'Yes but I would have done the same for anybody. I was trained in that sort of thing. We only got to be friends afterwards.'

'Exactly.' Wang smirked, knowingly.

Sewell found himself exploding in frustration. 'He is an *amateur*. He spat the word out. 'So is the girl. I am a *professional*. My whole mission was based upon the tightest security. Do you think I would risk that by involving strangers? They knew nothing.'

Then, as if an afterthought, he added: 'Why did you search Evans's room? Why did you try to kill him?'

Wang's reply was involuntary. 'We thought it was Evans who had made contact with the students.'

For a moment it was almost as if Sewell was engaged in a discussion, not an interrogation. 'So you only got onto me after I had saved Evans' life? How ironic. If I had let him drown, you would never have spotted me.'

Wang was unsettled by this twist in their exchange. Sewell's replies made a certain kind of sense. Evans and the girl *were* amateurs. He despised the way they had stumbled about. They would have to be watched back in Britain — and eliminated if necessary. It had been his decision to let them go on the plane. If all three had been taken out together, there might have been reverberations throughout the security world which could have rebounded on him.

He was reassured by Sewell's replies. Reassured that his decision had been justified. He *wanted* to believe Sewell. Otherwise he would have to answer for his own misjudgement.

There was a trap-door leading from the cellar. Sewell could see it in the gloom.

They had left him after some further routine questions, locking the door at the top of the narrow concrete steps. He hadn't a clue where he was. He could hardly think straight for the pain and the tension. More tired than he remembered feeling in his entire life, he collapsed and slept fitfully. When he awoke, he felt dreadful.

A sliver of light framed the trapdoor. It was heavy. He couldn't shift it. Then he noticed a large bolt. Although it was rusty, he managed to slide it back, the effort provoking near-nausea and a pounding pressure on his injuries.

Standing on a packing case, he eased the door up. It moved freely. He peered out into an alley. It seemed deserted. An area in Hong Kong deserted? That was unlikely. He waited for a couple of minutes, looking. The moon was bright. A street light shone almost overhead: the source, presumably, of the pencilled light he had spotted in the cellar. His watch showed just after 5 a.m. Still nobody about. He pushed the door back carefully and hauled himself out.

The alley led out to a narrow road running down to the waterfront. He walked quickly, his body aching, aware of a growing sound of voices which turned out to be those of fishermen clustered around their junks silhouetted against the moon.

He made his way toward them, drawn to the security of the crowd. He must be on the outskirts of the main city, in one of the poor areas where street markets thrived. Little children ran about barefoot and the junks lined up scruffily along the shore, water lapping against their hulls.

Just back from the shoreline, market traders were beginning to set up their stalls. He mingled with them. Nobody took any notice. He was exhilarated. He had escaped. He could begin to plan ahead, to think how he could get out of the colony unnoticed.

'Coffee?' A man stood in front of him, smiling, with a steaming paper cup. Sewell nodded. He was desperate for the boost of caffeine. He felt in his pocket for some coins. The man pressed the cup forward, tipping it. Sewell reached out with a steadying hand. Then he glanced up, noticing the man's eyes staring over his shoulder. They weren't smiling anymore. As Sewell turned to follow his gaze a hand thrust itself against his back and the glint of a knife flashed. He felt the blade cut deep into his larynx. Then he understood at last.

They had let him escape on purpose. The anonymity of the crowd was much safer for them than murder on premises to which they could be traced. But even as he fell, he felt high with elation. They had him, but they had not won. A copy of the documents still existed. He had passed the baton to Jim and Jenny; they wouldn't let him down.

When the local police arrived at the scene, they shook their heads in astonishment at the grotesque contrast between the grisly murder and the corpse's smiling face.

CHAPTER SEVEN

Makuyana made all the arrangements himself: a false identity complete with passport, plane tickets, a tailor-made story. These things could not be left to a subordinate. He didn't seek official clearance, because he knew he wouldn't have got it. He was going off duty and he knew he was taking a big risk. Only Florence Sithole had been informed. He knew the responsibility lay with him. It was a deniable operation. If his cover was blown he would be on his own.

Why was he doing it? He wasn't really sure he could give a logical answer to the question. Instinct, he supposed. Instinct that it could be vital. But there was another factor as well: he had something to prove. Nobody was going to get the better of him. Just because he had his own office and secretary, didn't mean he had gone soft. There was nothing like the buzz you got from action in the field. He had not experienced it since his guerrilla days. Perhaps the void could be filled by the mission into South Africa.

He felt more uncomfortable about the suit he had bought as part of his new identity than anything else. In truth, he was looking forward to the mission with a mixture of anticipation and curiosity. Anticipation at the prize to be found there. Curiosity at what South Africa would feel like from the inside.

❖

Johannesburg's Jan Smuts airport was named after the old wartime Leader unexpectedly defeated by Malan's Afrikaner Nationalists in 1948.

Makuyana considered General Smuts' reputation with little enthusiasm. Ostensibly more liberal than the Nats, in practice he was just as dedicated to apartheid. A racist with a human face, more than that, a puppet of British imperialism – Makuyana smiled as he allowed himself to sloganise in a manner he so despised in others. He detested the rhetorical baggage that seemed to accompany some types of socialist politics. He liked cool rationality and clear language; he saw no reason why socialism should be defaced by repetitive one-liners.

The airport was no more attractive to him than the man after whom it had been named. He was conscious of security everywhere: of men in cubicles, watching and checking. It reminded him of Moscow: cold, calculating bureaucracy and steely suspicion. Would his passport and new identity clear the system? He queued up, waiting, the tension growing.

'Sydney K. Nkala,' the official grunted the name as he paged through the passport, looking up to stare at Makuyana. 'Your visa's stamped for a trade visit. Who will you be visiting, Mr Nkala?' He spat the name out carefully, as if distancing himself from the black before him.

Makuyana rattled off institutions and places. The man wasn't that interested. By now he was used to blacks in sharp suits carrying filofaxes and talking business. It all fitted in with his Government's policy of pulling the rest of Africa into economic ties which would make it more difficult for the North to turn on the fortress in the South. Mind you, he didn't like them any the better for it: kaffirs were kaffirs, whether they were smart or not.

As they talked, the man waited for a signal on his screen from the Special Branch terminal sectioned off twenty yards away. Up came the clearance sign.

Although he was waved through, Makuyana knew that he had only passed the easy stage. From now onwards, the slightest slip and he would be finished. The ubiquitous eyes and ears of the police state were all around him. He was a target simply because he was not white. Would he be returning through here in two days time as planned? Or would they rumble him?

Carrying only hand luggage — fresh shirts and underwear pressed into his briefcase — he headed out through the bustle of passengers and into the unknown.

❖

Florence Sithole made her decision. There didn't seem much to watch, just an old man passing the time of day, pretending to be busy. What was it many retired people said? They'd never been so busy in their lives. It seemed a curious kind of busyness: lots of little routines; down to the shops, back; a walk round the garden, back inside; a cup of coffee in the morning, back into the garden; reading the paper; a drink before lunch; a bite to eat; an afternoon nap; doing a crossword; a walk to the local park; a late afternoon aperitif; an evening meal; falling asleep in front of the TV. What was there to watch? She had her fallback: the car bleeper, the telephone tap, the mail intercept. And the watchers could be put back on very quickly. She called them off.

Another matter was troubling her. The Renamo man was still in a coma down in the medical centre. She was under pressure from the doctor responsible to move him into hospital where there were superior facilities. But she had refused. After the events of the last few weeks, no chances could be taken. You had to assume the eyes of the opposition were everywhere, especially with such a potentially serious threat to their security.

❖

Swanepoel hated the period of dormancy which his masters had insisted upon when he returned to Harare. Filling in time was like vegetating. He had enjoyed his period of action back home, he even enjoyed the tension of living a double life. But he couldn't cope with doing nothing.

At the same time he knew that frustration was dangerous. It could eat at your concentration, corrode your defences, expose you for the briefest moment – that was all they needed to blow your cover. He swilled the KWV in his glass and sniffed the aroma wafting upward. The clear brown liquid shone gold in the setting sun. Soon the warmth that had drenched the verandah would be gone. With a shiver Swanepoel anticipated the chill that would follow if he stayed out too long. It was getting colder by the day.

He looked across at the small garden to the rear of his bungalow. It butted up against a fence behind which was the wide sweep of lawn and bougainvillaea belonging to the sprawling mansion on the other side of the block. His own garden was in a tatty state, grass growing unkempt against the fence, creeping haphazardly across the path and even starting to crawl up onto the verandah. He hated gardening – women's work, if you couldn't get a reliable servant to do it for you. They had given him instructions to keep his garden in good order, to play out the role of a retiree to perfection. Bugger them. They didn't know what it was like, wasting away in the field. They didn't know it was the pits doing nothing, cut off from your roots, your drinking partners, the men with whom you could swop stories and talk of old times.

How long would they keep him dangling here? It could be days, weeks, perhaps even months. Apart from the brandy, there was one consolation: he hadn't been rumbled after the letter bomb. That was his trickiest mission yet in Harare, because he was the activator rather than the co-ordinator as usual. There were none of the tell-tale signs that he had been spotted. Life in his little suburban street continued as usual: kids playing in gardens; people going to and from work; cars driving past; music from teenage ghetto-blasters occasionally disturbing the peace. It was all boringly normal.

He stood up, a little unsteadily, and pulled his chair inside the back door.

Time for a bite to eat. Then the phone rang. Startled, he almost knocked it over. Nobody ever phoned him here, except his wife Sarie, unless it was important.

'Mr Herson?'

'Yes.' He recognised the voice.

'Sorry I didn't phone earlier. We've finally got the part for your camera and repaired it. Could you pick it up tomorrow morning? About ten if you want to catch me. Otherwise my assistant will be there.'

The instruction was clear. Be there at ten. On the dot. No messing.

❖

The young man in the monitoring centre at security headquarters in Harare was finding it difficult to concentrate. Nothing much had been happening since he came on the late afternoon shift. He flicked through the text on the VDU in front of him. Not much activity was being logged by the surveillance system.

Suddenly the cursor was flashing, claiming his attention. A phone call had just been received by a target, the first since monitoring had started. He prompted the menu to dive into another part of the computer system and check it out.

The name came up, HERSON, PAUL. The address, a house in Avondale. Lucky guy, he thought, a nice area of the city. He noted the code number, switched back into monitoring mode and checked nothing else was happening. Then he moved across to the other side of the room and opened a door leading into the taping unit.

'Could you play this back for me, please?' He gave the code number to the middle-aged woman sitting in front of the console.

'Sure.' She smiled easily, handing him a pair of earphones. He could always get a favour from her any time. She was like a mother to him.

She watched him listening, noticing a frown of disappointment as he took off the earphones.

'Nothing?'

'Just some message about collecting a camera which has been repaired. Still, could you check out the number of the caller for me? I'll log it into the memory.' He went back to his screen, hoping for another flashing cursor.

Five minutes later there was a tap on his shoulder. She was frowning as he turned. 'Rather odd, this number of yours. It's a home, not a shop.'

'Now why would that be?' He looked puzzled. 'Perhaps he forgot to make the call in the day and telephoned from home?'

'Perhaps.' She sounded sceptical.

She wasn't going to say anything, but he could feel her inwardly urging him on. She was so bloody conscientious. So pernickety. Everything was important to her. No loose ends when she was around.

'What the hell. I'll do a little report and stick it in Mr Makuyana's mailbox. See what he makes of it.'

She smiled. Good boy. He was coming along nicely – with a little mothering help.

❖

The Old Man looked at his itinerary. A decade or two ago he would have been excited by the thought of a foreign visit. New places to see, maybe new heights to conquer. Now he viewed the whole idea with resigned wariness.

First Nairobi, in the grip of the capitalist West. Then down past Kilimanjaro, over Arusha and into Dar es Salaam – at least he had some friends there from the days when his technicians had helped build Tanzania's rudimentary infrastructure. Then, across the plains, across the deep waters of Lake Nyasa and over the giant Cabora Bassa Dam project.

The magic of Africa held no interest for him, but the last leg of the journey did. They were due to land in Harare at nightfall and the next five days were packed with receptions, visits and meetings, some superficial, others very important. He had all the times, the venues, the procedure, neatly arranged on his printed schedule, with the security procedures attached. The visit had been organised with customary efficiency and attention to detail.

He scanned the sheets before him. There was nothing unexpected. The list of his aides was also attached. Good – they had accepted all his nominees. His handpicked nominees, *his* people: Wang, the others – their loyalty and dedication could not be faulted. They were all true believers. The only slight hiccup had been when the Party Secretary's office had queried the unusually large number of aides. But he had insisted he would need each of them.

Wang and a colleague would go on ahead to Zimbabwe, missing out Dar es Salaam. They would be waiting, preparing for the operation when the Delegation arrived. He compared the official itinerary for Harare with the unofficial one. Yes: they fitted together perfectly.

When his secretary knocked and entered she was surprised to find him smiling. That hadn't happened for years, she thought.

❖

Florence Sithole strained to hear what the Renamo man was saying. His speech was slurred and intermittent; he responded only occasionally to her questions. All the time she was conscious of the doctor's disapproval behind her.

'Why did you go to the farm?'

'Eliminate.'

'Eliminate who?'

'Makuyana ... bastard ... shot me.'

'How did you know he was going to be there.'

'Information.'

'Where did you get the information from?'

He shook his head, 'Don't know.'

'Crap. Don't piss me about!' She stood up angrily, turning to the doctor. 'He's no use to us. You can move him to the main hospital.'

There was a screech from the Renamo man. 'No! They'll kill me!'

'Who will kill you?' She sneered at him, deliberately disbelieving.

'ANC.'

'Why should they kill you? You're more use to them alive.'

'No. Inside the ANC. Inside.'

'Who inside?'

'Don't know,' he slumped back, mumbling, 'don't know.'

She pounced. 'Don't know? Don't know? What do you mean you don't know?'

'Don't know the name. Only the face.'

The doctor intervened. 'I think you should leave him to rest now. Otherwise, he might not survive.'

❖

Swanepoel was early for his appointment. Having combed the concrete car park, checking and re-checking for anything unusual, any surveillance, he sat

– 132 –

in his car and waited. Right on time a familiar figure appeared and climbed into the passenger seat. After the usual exchange of passwords, the man gave Swanepoel his instructions.

He was to re-activate his Harare network and keep it on hold. Two new operatives were being shipped in to give assistance – specialists in assassination who would make direct contact themselves. The target was a VIP. At the appropriate time Swanepoel would be given the target's name and the details of the plan. He was to expect an approach from a foreigner who would give the necessary passwords.

Meanwhile there was another matter. Something equally delicate. His controller paused and coughed. Swanepoel caught his face outlined in the gloom. The face of a wealthy entrepreneur who had thrown his lot in with black nationalism from the moment he had seen the writing on the wall for white minority rule in the old Rhodesia of Ian Smith. Publicly loyal to the Zimbabwean Government, privately he was playing both ends off against the middle to protect his investments and the ever-rising profits they generated on both sides of the Limpopo.

'KJ briefed you on the foreign connection and the nukes. We think it is time to rattle a few cages. The attacks on Makuyana's mob have not yet achieved their objective. He seems to have gone to ground. We think he may be getting a bit too close for comfort. Find out from our friends what the score is. Also, they have one of our field combatants...'

'One of ours?' Swanepoel was surprised he hadn't heard directly from his own sources.

'A deniable combatant. Badly injured, we think. Reports from the scene were confused. We think they are spreading disinformation. Find him for us and eliminate.'

❖

Florence Sithole flicked idly through the messages in the mail box on Makuyana's PC, only half concentrating. What should she do with the Renamo man? Confront him with Mngadi's three aides, the ones Makuyana had been trying to check out? The logistics of that would be risky to say the least.

The message from the monitoring centre flicked up on the screen.

How could she organise a confrontation so that they had no prior warning?

The message was staring at her but she didn't notice it.

It was frustrating with Makuyana being away. She enjoyed the responsibility, but she needed his experience to advise her now.

Still the message hung on the screen.

She picked up the phone and dialled the doctor in the medical centre.

The message was out of her line of vision now.

The doctor's response was cool. 'He cannot be moved for at least a day – probably longer.'

'But I need him in the main hospital.'

'You need him alive, presumably?' The question was rhetorical, gently sarcastic.

'Of course,' Florence snapped, then she recovered herself. 'Look, I am sorry. It's not easy you know.'

'I know,' the doctor softened a little. 'I'll be as helpful as possible. As soon as he can be moved I will book a bed and contact you immediately.'

Florence put the phone down. Something was nagging at the back of her head; the mail box. She scanned the messages again quickly. Now she saw it. She snatched a glance at her watch. No! It was an hour after the pick-up and a full sixteen hours after the message had been sent. Perhaps it was as innocent as it sounded but she couldn't afford to assume that.

She sat down at the keyboard and tapped in the commands to send a message back to the monitoring centre. She couldn't spare any watchers but she wanted a priority given to monitoring Mr Herson's line and any car movements bleeped in. She was to be contacted immediately there was anything to report.

The newspapers ran the story, but it didn't make the front pages. An English tourist murdered in Hong Kong, no apparent motive, no trace of the killer. There was a brief mention of Sewell's background as a physical education teacher, but no reference to his activist life. In the London office of Greenpeace there was gloom at the news, but no acknowledgement of his role.

Jenny bought all the papers and read each report, searching for a different angle. She felt empty. All she could think about was the waste – the desperate waste – of Sewell's life. And when she met Evans for a drink that evening, she could hardly communicate. He hugged her warmly, but she seemed stiff and remote, like an acquaintance rather than a close friend. For a moment he was consumed by jealousy. Had she cared so much for Sewell? More than she did about him? Instantly, Evans was ashamed and he dismissed such thoughts.

Jenny spoke. 'We must take extra care with our security once I have got the copied documentation back from my Aunt. If it was worth killing for once, it'll be worth it again. So – no open chats on the phone, no careless behaviour.'

Then, as if she was reading his mind, she looked directly at Evans for the first time that evening, touching him lightly. 'I'm sorry, Jim. I've got no emotional space in me at the moment. I just want to do justice by Dick.'

Evans nodded, putting aside his own selfish feelings. He did understand. Sewell's memory continued to haunt him too. The last thing he felt like at the moment was another foreign trip. But the powers that be had decided he must attend the conference and present a paper. He showed Jenny the letter: they'd given him only a few weeks notice. He was to represent his research team at an international conference in Zimbabwe

❖

The next morning Jenny stopped off at a callbox on her way to work.

'Jenny! How nice to hear from you,' her aunt exclaimed.

When the phone rang Ruth Brown had been catching some of the early morning sun on the patio of her rambling little cottage on the main road through the Dorset coastal village of Burton Bradstock.

The two women had been close ever since Jenny's teenage years when Jenny had chosen to spend weekends and the odd holiday with her aunt. They would discuss politics well into the night, continuing during long walks over the hillsides and seaside cliff paths in nearby Hardy country. Much of Jenny's basic political education had been gained from her aunt.

'Can I pop down for a visit? It seems ages since we saw each other. I got back from China a week ago and there's so much to talk about.'

'That would be lovely. I was hoping you'd call. There is a special present waiting for you down here.'

Jenny smiled in relief at the news and at her aunt's prudence over the open line. 'Could I come this weekend? There's a train to Dorchester which gets in about eight o'clock on Friday evening.'

'Fine, I'll pick you up there.'

Makuyana bought an evening paper from the kiosk outside the hotel. The law had been altered to allow visitors like him to stay in hotels if the owners agreed – 'honorary whites' they were called by sceptical local blacks.

The front page of the Johannesburg *Star* was entirely taken up with a screaming headline and a sensational story. The audacity of the attack had sent shockwaves through the normally imperturbable layers of Afrikaner government. An ANC team had infiltrated the cleaning force at the Koeberg pressurised water reactor near Cape Town and planted explosives which had torn a gaping hole in the nuclear power station during the night.

The bombs had been carefully placed to avoid damaging the reactor, but had deliberately wrecked the attached electricity generator. White residents in nearby Cape Town were numb with horror at the implications of the attack. The black suburb of Atlantis, right on the reactor's doorstep, was torn between applause for the ANC's success and relief that the danger of a nuclear catastrophe had been avoided.

Makuyana read the accounts with growing elation boosted by a sense of defiance that he was actually in the country lifting two fingers to the system as he lived and breathed apartheid. The next day he would travel to Pretoria, to the address that Oliver Khama had given him. The address that might bring him vital new information – or might be a trap. If it was the latter he knew that, in the capital of Afrikanerdom, there would be no way out.

❖

The Leader stood erect on the podium surveying the million-strong mass before him. They filled Peking's Square of Heavenly Peace where Chairman Mao had proclaimed the birth of the people's republic over forty years before.

There was a hush of expectancy in the crowd. He knew he had to rise to the occasion. Months of work and planning had preceded the event, assembling majorities in the Party for the next great leap forward, orchestrating news stories to prepare the public and the world for the new line. As he had sat in his special seat, waiting for the moment when he would be called – *his* moment – the Leader wondered what Mao would have made of things today. Not far from the Great Helmsman's mausoleum at the other end of the Square, now obscured behind a sea of faces, stood a symbol of the changes: a

Kentucky Fried Chicken restaurant, surrounded by crowds wearing fashionable bright clothes instead of the sombre blue or grey uniforms that used to fill the Square in Mao's day.

The Leader knew that Mao's dictums still commanded loyalty among the old guard on the Central Committee. He knew that they would not hesitate to pounce and consign him to the role of a non-person should his reforms falter. And he knew throughout his country, were rumblings of unease which could turn into mighty waves of discontent if he did not get a hold on the current economic crisis.

He spoke for a long time – over two hours – but if the masses below felt restless they did not show it. There was no disrespectful coughing or shuffling of feet, no talking; just studied concentration, the posture of self-control ingrained in the people.

The Leader spoke of how he would be taking action to tackle inflation. Falls in living standards would be reversed by giving managers greater independence and by allowing inefficient companies to close. Enterprise would be encouraged. Egalitarianism would be 'eliminated' so that underpaid professionals – particularly doctors, teachers, scientists – could be given special pay rises. The crowd broke into cheers and respectful clapping.

The Leader also reminded them about his achievements: that industrial growth had reached a record 18 per cent over the past year; that nearly a third of Chinese households now had a colour television and one in eight a washing machine. Then he turned to the most sensitive part of his speech: corruption. One survey had found 63 per cent of Party cadres were involved in corrupt practices. The Party would have to be cleansed. Inefficiency was pervasive. Serious crime was rising – 36 per cent up on the previous year. Prostitution and VD, both stamped out in the Mao era, had returned to cities like Shanghai and Canton. Malnutrition which had gradually disappeared since Liberation was resurfacing.

The masses were now hushed, attentive. But these problems were the problems of change, the Leader insisted. They were like the flies that entered a room when a window was opened.

'We can put up with the flies, but we cannot do without fresh air.'

As the Old Man listened to the speech on the podium and clapped politely at the correct moments, he had real reasons for contentment. First the elimination of the English dissident, now the report that Wang's contacts in British intelligence were being helpful in monitoring Evans and the girl. Nothing too serious, just discreet surveillance of contacts and communications – a little precaution in case the chapter had not been closed with Sewell's death.

The Leader finished with a ringing oration and the Old Man reflected on the speech. It had been carefully constructed. Yes, even skilfully, he had to admit. There was a certain courage in admitting openly to the reform programme's failures. A calculated risk.

At the reception for the Party bigwigs later, the Old Man circulated smoothly, testing his closest, most trusted supporters, making sure he spent special time with the Generals. What had they felt about the speech? There was general agreement. The Leader might have pulled it off for the moment, but he was still in deep trouble.

The time was approaching, thought the Old Man, when he would have to reveal his hand.

❖

Aunt Ruth drove Jenny from the station out through the centre of Dorchester, past the courthouse where the Tolpuddle Martyrs had been tried and sentenced in 1834. The journey along the Bridport road and then left to Burton Bradstock would take about half an hour. It was a bright summer's evening, traffic was light and signposts to passing villages flashed by. Toller Porcorum, Toller Fratrum, Puncknowle, Littlebredy: the quaint charm of these Dorset names had always appealed to Jenny.

She told her story, having been given a pledge of strict confidence. They talked animatedly, hardly pausing as they stopped off at a favourite pub before moving on to enjoy a meal Ruth had cooked with a bottle of red wine that Jenny had brought. It was past midnight before they turned in. Jenny felt more relaxed than she had for weeks. She enjoyed the atmosphere. Although an urbanite, she loved the way the pressure seemed to lift as London receded and the gentle pace of village life absorbed all her tensions and spirited them away.

She had another reason to be elated. The copies of Sewell's documents had arrived safely and were now tucked underneath her mattress. The next morning she would get some additional photocopies done in Bridport, one to be left with her aunt, and then she would be free to enjoy the rest of the weekend. Once back in London, Sewell's death would be avenged as they broke the story in the media.

Ruth's advice as a veteran campaigner had been helpful on that too. But as she kissed Jenny goodbye on the Sunday evening, she was worried: 'Be careful. Above all, keep your names out of the press.'

❖

The Renamo man was recovering slowly. He could soon be moved to the hospital, the Doctor had told Florence Sithole. Now came the tricky bit. If she calculated wrongly, the whole thing could blow up in her face. But she had to try the confrontation. The Renamo man was too weak to be taken to a spot where he could covertly watch Mngadi's three ANC aides. They would have to come to him. It was virtually an invitation to murder, she knew that, but time was pressing. The traitor had to be exposed. It was the only option left to her. She hoped Makuyana would have agreed.

Leaning back in his chair, she ran her fingers through her hair – a habit of hers when she was under stress. She had noticed a couple of spots on her face. On her last visit home her mother had complained, 'You are not looking after yourself properly. Too much work. Always eating on the move. Not enough decent food.' Her mother was right of course, but there was no time for her to take extra care of her body.

What was the best way to proceed? She was in such deep thought, she hardly noticed a secretary had come in with a cup of coffee. They were all rooting for her, the junior staff in the unit, especially the women. She had made it, she could lead the way for other women. None of them doubted her ability to succeed.

Oliver Khama, the ANC man from Lusaka, had recovered. He was being discharged later in the day. That was a relief. She didn't want too many potential targets in the hospital.

She called in an assistant and gave him instructions. She was keeping well out of the picture; the other side were not to know that Makuyana was offstage or that she was in charge. The more confused they were the better. She would contact Selby Mngadi and arrange a meeting with the three aides, Peterson, Bhajee and Msimang. They would be told the Renamo man had survived.

Nothing more. Then they would each be monitored to see what reaction if any followed. Depending upon this, he would be moved into Harare hospital and they would be invited to interrogate him.

❖

Swanepoel was doing his duty in his garden – the minimum necessary to keep up appearances – when he noticed a young woman with a youngster walking along the pavement towards him. As she drew level, she spoke firmly, as if she was talking to her child. 'NOSLEN is threatened. Please follow me discreetly so we can talk.'

Anybody watching the house would not have noticed that the two had communicated. But nobody was watching. Nobody saw Swanepoel stretch up from his weeding, walk inside his house and then re-emerge several minutes later, carefully surveying the road. Satisfied, he headed off after the woman still visible on the pavement three hundred yards ahead.

He found her playing with her little boy on a piece of waste land where the road left the rows of houses with their wide gardens. The child was tottering about, crying out with laughter as he followed a brightly coloured rubber ball around. It rolled over towards Swanepoel. He stooped, grabbed it and then knelt down, smiling, as the boy ran over, gibbering enthusiastically.

'Come on, Kevin,' the mother called, for all the world embarrassed that a stranger should have been troubled by her carelessness in letting the ball run free.

But as she walked over, her eyes were not those of a blushing Mum. They darted around, checking who might be watching. Then she started to talk quickly in Afrikaans, her remarks clearly addressed to Swanepoel though apparently directed at the child.

'They have a Renamo man. We don't know where. In the main hospital maybe, injured badly, we think. A survivor from the operation at the farm who could identify our NOSLEN source in the ANC. It's too risky for that source to act, though he might need to if there is no alternative. We want your people to deal with the Renamo man before any identification. You haven't got much time.'

She bent down with an affectionate grin, slipping back into English. 'Come on tootsie. Time we went home.' Retrieving the ball with a thank you, she beckoned to the boy and made off back down the way she had come.

Swanepoel walked on, away from her. He knew what he had to do: phone a number on a direct line into a businessman's plush office in the centre of the city.

❖

Jonathan Fletcher sat waiting in Greenpeace's headquarters off Islington Green in North London. He had initially been sceptical when Jenny rang the day before. In the constant flow of calls they received, there was always the odd one from a nutter or a well-intentioned obsessive. Some refused to give their names, but complained their mail was intercepted or they were being followed. Most wanted to talk urgently, but rarely turned up for appointments. When they did – like the crumpled Glaswegian in his fifties who claimed that the state was sending messages direct into his brain by electronic pulses – there was little he could do except listen.

But Fletcher was a patient man. He dealt with public information and enquiries, filtering communications to the organisation's hard-pressed and under-resourced campaign organisers. He saw it as his job to be co-operative, to give Greenpeace a friendly face. A veteran radical who had himself experienced Special Branch surveillance and come up against unsympathetic policing of demonstrations, he was not intrinsically sceptical of tales of harassment or pleas for secrecy. And there was something about this caller that rang true. She had talked only briefly about having important material on nuclear waste, saying that she needed to meet him in person, and it had to be soon.

His phone rang. It was reception. Jenny Stuart was on her way up to his sparse but computerised office. He went to meet her at the top of the stairs. There was no bureaucratic formality or status role-playing in the office – no women secretaries pampering senior men; everyone mucked in together. He shook hands, noting a young blonde woman, attractive, if somewhat uncaring of her appearance, a sense of busyness about her. She was also tense he noticed.

'Thanks for seeing me at such short notice.'

'No problem,' his voice was cool, but not hostile, putting the onus back on her.

'Look,' she paused as if embarrassed, 'I hope you don't mind. But I would prefer to talk somewhere else. Can we go to a pub?'

If Fletcher was irritated, he hid it well. Actually he was curious. 'If you like,' he kept his tone neutral. 'There's one just round the corner. It should be empty this time of the day.'

When they stepped out onto the pavement, away from the threat of bugging, Jenny wasted no time with small talk. Her opening remark took him completely by surprise.

'Remember Dick Sewell?'

'What about him?'

'I was with him in China.'

'Oh yes?' The tone was still reserved. What was this? A girlfriend Dick hadn't mentioned?

'We were both on visits and our paths crossed.'

They reached the pub, a rather scruffy one geared very much to the locals. Jenny was definite about buying the drinks. She strode purposefully up to the bar through the gaggle of men who stopped their conversations to stare at her while she ordered two glasses of orange juice.

Fletcher had chosen a table on its own in a corner of the pub, well out of earshot. A tired sounding jukebox was playing *Yesterday*. Jenny put the drinks down, pulled up a chair, and told him the full story. He listened without interruption. When she had finished he was silent.

He hadn't expected anything like this. The Sewell affair was a taboo subject in the office. Although nobody believed his death was accidental, they couldn't compromise the organisation by revealing the real nature of his mission. They had tried to put him out of their minds. But for some of his close friends, Fletcher included, that was extremely difficult. And here was this woman, quite out of the blue, telling him what the few in the know had feared ever since the impersonal little death report had appeared in the press one morning.

'What happened to the documents, then?' He almost didn't dare ask.

For the first time since they had met, she smiled. A burden was being lifted off her shoulders, a debt repaid, recognition given to a brave man.

'I have copies with me. I'll give them to you back in your office. But there are some conditions. I imagine – I hope – you will wish to call a press conference or something. That's fine. But please don't bring my name or that of Jim Evans into it. There have already been two attempts on his life. As far as I am concerned nobody else in Greenpeace needs to know exactly how the documents got out of China. Nobody in the media must know. Can you give me that assurance?'

Fletcher sipped at his juice, thinking aloud, 'This is too big for me to handle on my own. Greenpeace's credibility is at stake. My senior colleagues will want convincing. I'll have to tell some people in the office. But they needn't know your names. As for the press, that shouldn't be too much of a problem.'

If the press believe us, he thought to himself, *if* they believe us. If they didn't, he might have to break his pledge to Jenny. But the cause was bigger than the individual, even for one normally as scrupulously honest as he.

❖

Just two stops on the bus from the Forbidden City and the busy Peking shopping street of Wangfujing, red walls surround Zhongnanhai, the area where the Chinese leaders live. In one of the pavilions situated in the shade amidst trees and shrubs, the Old Man was saying goodbye to a small group of confidantes. He felt satisfied. It had been a productive gathering. A little risky for him to convene it so openly perhaps, but necessary all the same.

The first stage of his plan was well underway. Operation 'Touch the Tiger' was already bringing rewards. 'Touch the Tiger' was a Chinese way of describing an attack on the relative of an influential official; this one touched the bottom of the largest tiger in the land: the Party Leader himself.

His son, the Old Man's network had discovered, had been trading illicitly on the black market, using a respectable front company to obtain scarce consumer durables from abroad and then selling them at mark-up prices through unofficial channels. The Leader had responded to the public outcry by announcing a general campaign against corruption. He had even established the first nationwide 'corruption hotline', staffed 24-hours from a cramped third floor room in a Peking office block, where people could report official bribery, extortion or general corruption.

But the Leader was up against formidable odds. Nepotism and *guanxi wang* (networks of connections) were at the heart of Chinese public life. Since feudal times business had been conducted in that way. There had been times when children of nobles were given honorary posts and salaries even before they could walk. The traditional Chinese saying – 'when you get to the top, even your chickens and dogs go to heaven' – still applied.

The Old Man knew that the campaign was up against such entrenched interests that it would not succeed. But he also knew that his own effort in exposing the misdeeds of Leader's son was already feeding into the web of rising popular dissatisfaction with the reform programme.

❖

Wang Bi Nan moved smoothly amongst the defence attachés and procurement agents at the Asiandex arms fair in a modern complex of halls in Peking. It was being staged for the first time in China, reflecting the country's growing role as an arms merchant.

The fair impressed even the old hands. English- and Arab- language interpreters guided visitors through a variety of Chinese-made missiles, tanks and armaments. The Silkworm missile was prominently displayed amidst a range of brightly coloured projectiles in the main hall. The C802 anti-ship weapon was creating a buzz of interest. It was Peking's answer to the Exocet, the scourge of British frigates in the Falklands war. In the parking lot outside, a mobile launcher whined through a simulated exercise, aiming a missile skywards. Gossip at the fair suggested that Arab countries were interested in the M-9, a medium range missile capable of hitting targets at 375 miles.

Although some of the weapons were outdated, China's ability to produce cheap systems had turned it into the world's fifth-biggest arms exporter, after the US, Soviet Union, France and Britain. Some 70 per cent of its sales in the mid-1980s went on the Iran-Iraq war. The official brochure for the fair proudly proclaimed expanding sales in Africa as well as far-eastern countries such as Thailand and Pakistan. It also confirmed development of a new generation of fighter planes and offered the sale of old Russian aircraft modernised with Western electronics at prices which representatives of Third World governments would find especially attractive.

Wang used the opportunity to cultivate contacts. He also had a specific task to fulfil: a deal had to be finalised. It was a vital missing piece in the Old Man's jigsaw.

❖

Venter and Coetzee were angry. They had cut short their holiday in Germany and flown into Harare with Balkan Airways as instructed. Apart from a bumpy flight accompanied by the sound of dreadful Bulgarian folk songs, everything had gone smoothly and they had checked through customs without a hitch.

The plan was they would pose as archeology students. They would lie low for several weeks, playing as much tennis as they could in between field trips to some of Zimbabwe's archaeological sites. The studies themselves didn't appeal, but they needed the cover. There would also be plenty of time for sport and a few beers. With a bit of luck they could suss out some of the local talent as well.

All this time they would be preparing for the big one, the operation that had to go like clockwork if they were to succeed in taking out their target and get away safely. They had to be mentally prepared: no nerves, no doubts, just a single, steely purpose of mind. They also had to be anonymous. They were the wild card, the assassins who would come from nowhere and deliver the *coup de grâce*.

But now all this was threatened. Not because another operation as big had come up: there was no operation as big as this one. No, because some berk had been caught and held by the opposition. He had to be eliminated before he spilled the beans, and they had to do the eliminating. A quick job, hardly any time to plan and prepare – just in and out and hope to hell nothing would go wrong.

They had argued somebody else should do it, so they could be saved, nice and fresh, for the big one. But their controller had been insistent, and he was not a man to cross. Captain Maritz Swanepoel was emphatic that they were the only people for the job: outsiders who couldn't be whispered about after the deed had been done.

❖

Makuyana sat reading as he waited to see Jimmy Wessels, just another client wanting to squeeze in to see the advocate before the end of the day. The normally sympathetic receptionist reproached him for not making an appointment, but Makuyana's quiet persistence and authority persuaded her to direct him to the waiting room. He had left his car in the underground car park as instructed. He looked up as the receptionist popped her head round the door. The air of reproach was gone.

'Mr Sizani,' – she used the name he had given as instructed – 'Mr Wessels will see you now.'

The advocate's room was lined with books. There was a small table in the corner where an assistant might sit in on client conferences and take notes, in the middle a large desk behind which Jimmy Wessels now stood, a broad welcoming smile on his face.

Wessels was a large, chubby man of Afrikaner-Jewish stock. He had an infectious laugh, more of a guffaw, and was known as one of the most tenacious lawyers in the country, a man who would take on a political trial and fight regardless of threats to his family and attacks on his professional integrity. There was an air of purposeful untidiness about his desk.

'Mr Sizani, welcome. I am sorry to have kept you waiting.' He pointed to a chair. 'Make yourself comfortable.'

Then his genial manner changed. 'Now, this problem of yours. The relatives are proving troublesome, I gather. I am not surprised. Badly drafted wills have a habit of creating more problems than they solve.'

He leant forward suddenly, pushing across a piece of paper, continuing to talk and pointing around the room.

Makuyana read the hastily scrawled note: 'Not safe here. We must talk as client-lawyer. Then you become my chauffeur and drive to where we can talk. Give me the keys of your car so it can be brought to you.'

Wessel's voice rattled on, covering the intricacies of property rights, while Makuyana responded with an occasional 'Yes' or 'No'. All the time he was thinking about Nelson Mandela and the way the ANC leader had eluded the authorities for months with a similar ruse. He had acted as a chauffeur to a sympathetic white family while on the run for nearly a year in the early 1960s, during which time he managed to pop up at clandestine press conferences, appear at meetings, meet his wife Winnie and organise the ANC underground movement, Umkhonto we Sizwe.

The conversation lasted about twenty minutes, after which Wessels formally bade his 'client' goodbye and led him to the door, putting his finger to his lips to indicate silence. He opened and closed the door, as if Makuyana was departing. Then he checked to see that all his staff had gone home for the night, packed his briefcase and motioned Makuyana to follow, switching off the lights and locking the door.

Handing him a chauffeur's cap and car keys, he pointed to a lift which led down to an underground car park. Wessels's car was a two litre Audi, its body aerodynamically designed and shaped to exert minimum wind resistance. Makuyana, who had always had a soft spot for a luxury car, thrilled to the prospect of driving it.

They pulled away from the city centre, now throbbing quietly after the day's workers had departed, and Makuyana accelerated up along Church Street, heading East. The car, unfamiliar at first, began to respond to his touch, it was almost driving itself. As the suburbs swished by, they reached more open country, the lights dimming behind them.

Wessels tapped him on the shoulder. 'Bugger it! A puncture. Stop over there.' He pointed to a lay-by. Makuyana, initially confused, pulled in. They jacked the car up and rolled the spare round, Makuyana squatting down with Wessels appearing to direct operations.

'Sorry about this charade,' the lawyer whispered, his grin showing up in the headlights. 'My office is definitely bugged. And I've never been absolutely certain about the car. I had it swept, but last week it was impounded by traffic wardens. Said it was illegally parked; they had it lifted from a parking meter.'

Makuyana pretended to fiddle with the wheel brace while Wessels quietly briefed him.

'We have a Deep Throat in the Military Intelligence Service. Our man doesn't come up with the goods very often, but when he does it can be pure gold. Basically, his message is this. The South Africans have been developing battlefield nuclear weapons – shells for tanks or ground attack aircraft, that sort of thing – and not just for defensive purposes. They are contemplating taking out suspected ANC bases in Namibia, Angola and Zimbabwe.'

'But none of these countries – certainly not ourselves – allow official ANC bases,' Makuyana retorted, looking up from the wheel.

'I know. But the fact is that you and I both know that the ANC infiltrate through all the frontline states and Pretoria is getting so frustrated it wants to teach everyone a big lesson.'

Makuyana frowned. 'I didn't realise they had the capability to produce specialist nuclear hardware like that.'

'Here we come to the other side of the information. Apparently they are collaborating with China.'

Wessels considered him quizzically, 'You don't seem shocked? I certainly was. Pretoria and Peking? Doesn't that strike you as an unlikely alliance?'

Makuyana shook his head. 'We had a sniff of some sort of link there, although only a sniff.'

Wessels shrugged his shoulders. 'There is something else. I am to direct you to another contact who may have the information you need about ANC officials in Harare. I don't know what it's about.'

He stopped as another car pulled up in front of them. Makuyana tensed.

Then he realised it was his own hire car. A man got out and slipped into the Audi's driving seat. Wessels took the chauffeur's cap and switched it, smiling mischievously.

'All in a day's work. Now, drive to the next lay-by. Your contact will be waiting. Good luck. And be careful. You are on your own now. One slip and they'll have you.'

They shook hands and then the Audi disappeared into the night, leaving Makuyana apprehensive and alone.

❖

Florence Sithole wondered where they would strike first. They must know by now, nearly a day after she had leaked the news of the Renamo man's survival. For the moment he was safe in the medical centre and she was fairly certain that they didn't know of its existence.

So where would they aim? Deep in thought, she walked down the bleak corridor towards Makuyana's office, oblivious of the buzz of conversation and the sounds of typing seeping out of the surrounding doorways. Where would they strike first? Where would *she* strike first in their position? At the security centre, probably, they didn't have much alternative. The full implications of her thought suddenly struck her. Christ! Yes! Here. Makuyana would be the target; they wouldn't know he was away.

Two white men passed her carrying briefcases, nodding politely. She grunted in response. White men. Strange men that she had never seen before. Who were they? As she turned, she remembered she wasn't armed and they might be. She must phone through to have them intercepted. She rushed around the corner to the office door. Makuyana! Of course. They would want to strike back at the top man, create maximum confusion and panic. Then it hit her. *She* was Makuyana now. She was doing his job, occupying his office. *His* office. The men in the corridor, were walking away from the office ...

Her instinct pulled her up short. What if they'd been in here? What would they have done? She looked around, eyes searching the desk and the steel filing cabinet, passing over the dirty cup, noting the dried patches where she had spilt her coffee that morning. What would they be expecting him to do in the office?

She shook herself. Stop wasting time. Get them intercepted. Phone through. She reached out. Then she froze in horror. *Phone* through. That could be it. A familiar South African technique. A signal activated by lifting the receiver away from a small transmitter placed inside. The bomb would be elsewhere in the room. It would only take minutes to set up. She dashed out and into the neighbouring office, phoning immediately to have the two stopped, calling for assistance.

Venter and Coetzee knew they were in trouble as soon as the alarm started ringing, the noise bouncing harshly off the bare walls.

Their briefing had been meticulously accurate. They had entered the security centre through the underground car port used by the field agents, but now they were going out through the main entrance. The plate glass reception area loomed ahead and the man in the reinforced cubicle who scrutinised all ingress and egress was getting to his feet and reaching for something.

They both went into action almost unconsciously, pulling on masks from their briefcases as Venter threw a CS gas canister at the cubicle and Coetzee swept the area with his 9mm Z88 hand pistol, South African-made to beat the international arms boycott. He fired off shots at people running down the corridors converging on the reception area.

Then they made their escape, leaving the security man to writhe in agony on the floor, coughing and scratching frantically at his eyes as the gas bit into the soft tissue. Their driver, alerted by the alarm, was already beginning to pull away as they bundled into the back of the old Ford transit.

They had made it again. But at what cost? Their cover might be blown. So bloody stupid. Venter smashed his fist on the floor of the van in frustration. Coetzee didn't have to ask why.

A little over an hour later the explosives experts on the team had safely defused the bomb in Makuyana's office. It had been hidden under the desk and – as Florence Sithole had suspected – would have been activated by lifting the phone.

Twice in the last fortnight she had smelt death: first on the farm, now in Makuyana's office. They were getting closer, and they were certainly well informed. Makuyana's instinct had been correct. There was something big in the air. Now she knew it too.

❖

The car was, as Makuyana had been told, a Nissan Bluebird, its parking lights on, standing in the lay-by half a mile down the road from where he had left

Wessels.

On the other side of the road, the ground sloped gently up to a series of *kopjes*, shadowy in the darkness. Alongside the lay-by fields fell away to clumps of trees, probably firs, Makuyana thought.

There wasn't much cover for the two cars, but at least there was the advantage that nobody could get near them without being spotted. Although the meet with Wessels had gone smoothly, Makuyana had been discomforted by the lawyer's final warning to be careful. He had a sensation of pins and needles sweeping down his back as he pulled up and waited, leaving his engine running and flashing his lights three times as instructed.

The driver of the vehicle in front got out and walked back in long, loping strides, apparently carefree, a beret pulled at an angle over his head. He was white, perhaps in his early twenties, casually dressed. He stopped at the door and they exchanged greetings. There had been no time to arrange passwords. His name was Janie Craven. It reminded Makuyana incongrously of the Mr Rugby of white South Africa, Danie Craven.

'I haven't got much time,' he seemed agitated now, looking repeatedly around him and speaking in a thick Afrikaner accent. 'We checked out Bhajee, Peterson and Msimang as instructed. Nothing in their backgrounds stands out as a problem, but one line might be worth following up. George Peterson's family were not very chatty. Our people said they seemed scared. The other thing is that they seemed to be much better off than their neighbours. The wife had a new car. It's not unheard of in the district but still, it's unusual.'

'Thank you my friend.'

'I must go. You turn round and head straight back for Jo'burg. Take the main road left to by-pass the city centre. Good luck.'

They shook hands.

Then two shots broke the silence of the night, bullets hitting the offside tyres of the Nissan in quick succession. Craven turned, thunderstruck, looking over to the trees. Makuyana was already backing his Fiat, thanking his lucky stars he had kept the engine running.

Another shot rang out, this time glancing off one of Makuyana's hub caps. Christ, this is for real, he thought. Craven was running towards him, gesticulating as he hurled himself into the car.

'Put your foot down!' he screamed.

Makuyana spun the car round and screeched off, back the way he'd come, his mind racing at the implications. Two more shots sounded, this time missing the Fiat altogether.

'Shit! We're in dead trouble man,' Craven sounded bitter. He was holding a pistol, staring behind at his own car, now a spot in the distance.

'Can they trace the Nissan to you?' Makuyana was sorting out the angles on their predicament, desperate to find a way out.

'No, I stole it in the city an hour ago. I'm more worried about whether they have others up ahead of us. Keep your eyes peeled. And don't drive too fast. We don't want to be picked up for speeding.'

Makuyana slowed obediently. They might have got the Fiat's number. If the attackers were the security services, it would be merely a matter of time before they traced him. If that was the case, he should head straight for the airport and catch the first flight north.

Chapter Eight

It was the lead front page story in Monday's edition of the *Guardian*. Above the headline NUCLEAR WASTE LEAK IN CHINA, there was a strapline 'Exclusive: Greenpeace exposes radiation crisis'. The prominence given to the story was partly due to the exclusivity and partly that Sunday was a weak news day and so there was a better chance of a decent spread the next morning.

The piece was sympathetically written, and made no reference to the way the documents were obtained, simply stating they had been 'smuggled out' to Greenpeace. It detailed the waste leakages and described the environmental threat. The Chinese Embassy refused to comment, but the paper's Sino expert confirmed that the documents were genuine from his own independent sources.

Inside the paper there was an editorial calling for international action to tackle such incidents. It reminded readers that there were also 48 known nuclear warheads and nuclear reactors lying on the ocean floor. 'Chernobyl made us understand that ecological catastrophe recognises no frontiers. These incidents are potentially just as lethal: simply because we cannot observe the effects as easily as radioactive fallout, we should not imagine that poisoning our waters is less serious.'

❖

In Greenpeace's office the telephones rang ceaselessly as the rest of the media chased up the story. Jonathan Fletcher fielded most of the calls and did a number of interviews for both the press and broadcasting organisations. As he had anticipated, many reporters wanted photocopies of the documents which he was happy to agree to.

There was a generally supportive tone about the enquiries. Most of the press were alive to the news value of green issues, even if their own proprietors were engaged in business ventures which showed scant regard for the environmental impact.

Despite the pressure – he didn't even have time to go to the toilet – Fletcher began to relax. Greenpeace had come up trumps again. He was on a high.

❖

Six miles across the city, in a medium sized flat in Ashley Gardens behind Victoria Street, Harold Williams was in a more sober mood. The *Guardian* wasn't his paper – he preferred the *Telegraph* – and had gone out specially for a copy after listening to the BBC's morning *Today* programme.

Having read the Greenpeace story, he thought for several minutes, then picked up his phone. The number he dialled was unlisted and the intelligence officer who answered would have been inaccessible to all but a few. Their conversation lasted nearly fifteen minutes.

Williams then phoned the home number of a Conservative MP widely known for his keen interest in security matters. He followed this up with a call to a journalist on the *Daily Express*, again a home number – the man rarely went into the office. A well known author with a penchant for books on intelligence matters that breached the official secrets laws without ever incurring official wrath, the journalist had recently been given a knighthood and could get an important story into the *Express* whenever he chose. These two conversations also lasted about fifteen minutes.

The next call was brief almost to the point of curtness. Williams arranged to see a man at place where they had often met before, one that he was careful not to mention over the open line.

❖

In the early afternoon the tone of the callers on Jonathan Fletcher's extension started to change perceptibly.

A young reporter from the *Express* news desk wanted to know more about the source of the documents and he was persistent to the point of being aggressive. The Foreign Office was playing down the significance of the *Guardian* report, he said. A billion pound contract was near to being concluded for the supply of British telecommunications equipment to Peking and London was anxious not to jeopardise this boost to British trade. Furthermore, a backbench Tory MP had let it be known in a statement to the Press Association news agency that he had grave doubts about the authenticity of the documents and he accused Greenpeace of attempting to hoodwink the public with over-dramatic allegations.

'Unless you are willing to tell us how you got the documents, we will have no alternative but to question the credibility of the story,' the reporter threatened.

Fletcher was in a quandry. He was aware that late afternoon deadlines for the morning's first editions were approaching and follow-up calls from other journalists were starting to reflect the *Express* line. The story was taking on a new shape. Radio news items began carrying the MP's rubbishing statement and reporting the FO's caution. He had given Jenny Stuart a promise, but he also knew that there was no way of keeping Dick Sewell out of the story if they decided to reveal the process by which the documents were obtained. His colleagues were unanimous: Greenpeace's credibility was at stake and the source and, if necessary, even the couriers would need to be made known.

Fletcher put a call through to Jenny at her work, an area office of Southwark Council's social services department. She was out on home visits they said; they didn't know when she would be back. He left a message for her. He also left one on her ansaphone at home.

As the afternoon wore on, he began to feel more and more dispirited. Things were starting to drift steadily away from the agenda set by Greenpeace, partly because of political pressures and partly because the media's insatiable thirst for a 'new' angle encouraged coverage of the attacks rather than the story itself.

By 5 pm, Jenny had still not called. He checked again with her office and repeated the message, this time giving his direct line and home numbers too. Then he decided to act. He and an assistant called every journalist who had made enquiries to say that Greenpeace was holding a press conference at 10 am the next morning with 'important new information' on the story. Many pressed for clarification, but he would say only that their source was rock solid and the media would be able to confirm that for themselves at the press conference.

He worked into the night to prepare detailed hand-outs on Dick Sewell, on his personal background and the nature of his mission. He hoped to God he could keep the woman and her colleague out of it.

❖

The drive with Craven away from the lay-by was quite eerie Makuyana thought. It was all too quiet. There were no signs of pursuit, nor of any interception ahead.

Perhaps the security services had not been behind the shooting? Perhaps he could drive back to his hotel and act as if he was completing his business visit normally; that would be preferable. It was untidy, skipping in a hurry and inevitably drawing attention to the illicit nature of his visit. But could he chance going back? On the other hand, if the security services were not involved, who had been behind the attack? Had the attack been staged to tie Craven to him? Was the man sitting beside him a friend or a foe?

'How did you get involved in all this?' he asked.

Craven had often asked himself the same question, because what he was doing here was so alien to his background and the values which had been pumped into him from birth: at home, at school, at college, in the army. It was also completely against his own self-interest. He had a good standard of living. He could swing along with the rest of his generation, making piles of money, boozing, womanising, holidaying, playing rugby.

'The thing that changed my life happened while I was doing military service in Namibia nine years ago,' he said slowly.

Makuyana nodded, encouraging him to continue.

'I was one of thousands of occupying troops deployed by South Africa to tame the Ovambo and Kavango, and to combat the forces of the South West African People's Organisation, SWAPO. My main job was to liaise with the Namibian police and their counter-insurgency unit, Koevoet, It means "crowbar".'

Makuyana nodded again. He knew their brutal reputation.

'Initially, it seemed like a fairly soft option for a young soldier on the front-line. But the more I had to accompany Koevoet patrols into operational areas the more I saw what they were really about.'

'The unit was an elite group of about 3,000 men, mainly in their early twenties, not much older than me. But they were something else those guys,' Craven shook his head. 'For me the army was a job, a duty. I didn't go in protesting, but I was there to do my time and get back out into real life in one piece. For them, chasing "terrs" was a whole way of life. They were intoxicated by aggression, their adrenalin constantly pumped up whenever they were in combat. They were on a high when they were hunting and killing.

'One evening I went with them into an operational area. The sun was setting, but you could still see the outline of mud rondavels, against the brilliant orange of the sky. Children came out to watch, half curious, half terrified. The Koevoet men piled out and combed through the village, kicking over food cooking on open fires, tearing the clothes off the women.

They pretended to search by poking machine guns between the women's thighs. I was disgusted, but I couldn't help being fascinated at the same time. Here were the finest blonde specimens of white Afrikanerdom displaying such a perverse sexual attraction for these black tribal women.

'Then a couple of guys started shouting "We've found gooks".'

Makuyana flinched; it had become too personal, this story, too close to home.

'I saw them pushing a black man in combat gear out into the open. A white went up to him with a gun. I could see his face, his eyes excited, gripped by something like pleasure. He squeezed out three shots, deliberately missing. Then he fired at both legs. I thought that would be it: disabled and screaming with pain, the man would be taken in and interrogated. But then the gunman started laughing out loud and gesticulating to his mates to gather round. And he fired deliberately into the man's face. It literally exploded. It was just a mess of blood, bone and flesh. I could hear them all laughing and congratulating the gunman while I was being sick.'

There was a silence in the car.

'*That* is what changed me,' Craven said simply.

Makuyana nodded. He began to think hard as he continued driving into the night, the lights of Johannesburg growing bright before him.

❖

Florence Sithole had taken elaborate precautions to protect the Renamo man. He was in a room isolated from the main wards. There were two guards on his door.

The surgeon had operated as soon as he was admitted late the previous night and she was told she must wait for at least thirty-six hours before confronting him with Mngadi's three aides. Now it was nearing midnight and Florence was longing to get to bed, but this was her baby. She had made the decision to admit the man. The buck stopped with her. So she was on her way to do another check on the security arrangements.

The hospital was quiet, glistening fluorescent-like in the dark as she drove up. There was a calm about it never present in the hustle of people coming and going in the daytime. She showed her card at reception and one of the guards was summoned to collect her. As she waited she found herself musing how Msimang, Peterson or Bhajee – whoever the traitor really was – might approach the problem of eliminating the Renamo man.

The guard arrived and they took the lift and walked along a corridor. He chatted away idly, but her mind was still turning over the options for an attack. Ahead, a nurse pushed a trolley of medicine. Two white doctors walked by, talking. They nodded to the guard as she glanced up. The guard barely glanced at them, still chattering on to Florence. White doctors. They were vaguely familiar. Why? Florence turned back to see them step into the lift.

Suddenly she was on full alert. Two white doctors. Not an unusual sight in Harare's main hospital. Two white men. Not unusual either. But *those* two white men? She knew she had seen them before. Jesus! Another corridor, another time. Two vaguely familiar white men. She started running, the guard startled into following her. They reached the room, the other guard also surprised as she rushed past. The Renamo man was asleep, but he was breathing fitfully. The monitor showed a regular heartbeat. Everything seemed in order.

'Who were they?' she barked at the guards, gesticulating down the corridor.

'Doctors, Madam.' They looked confused and just a little sullen.

'Yes – but *which* doctors?'

'Part of the team looking after him. They took over when the shifts changed an hour ago. Just came in for a routine check-up.'

'How did you know they were genuine?'

'We had the usual phone call to say they were coming up beforehand.' The guards exchanged a silent look at each other. Was the woman cracking up? They had heard about the attack on their headquarters and the near-miss in her office; perhaps the stress was too much for her.

'What are their names?'

One of the guards picked up a sheet of paper. 'Doctors David Lewin and John McKay.'

'Right, get them back in here immediately. I want to see them.' Maybe she was over-reacting. The patient seemed comfortable. All the security procedures were being followed. It was just that nagging sense of recognition. She could have sworn the men were the same two she had spotted walking away from Makuyana's office the day before.

One of the guards turned back from the phone. 'They can't locate the doctors at the moment. They are down to be on their rounds, but are not responding to their bleepers.'

'Find out where in the building they are based. And get a nurse and another doctor up here right away. Tell them its an emergency.'

'Three floors down, number 110,' the guard called details of the doctors' room over his shoulder.

Florence pulled a pistol out of her handbag and slipped it into her jacket pocket. She was no longer tired. The adrenalin was pumping round her body. 'You two stay here. I'm going to check their room.'

The corridor leading to room 110 was deserted and still. The room itself also seemed to be quiet as she listened at the door, gun in hand. She opened it carefully and eased herself in. Save for two desk lights burning, it was dark, nobody about. She felt for the main light switch and turned it on, the sudden glare dazzling her. Still nobody, still quiet. A couple of briefcases stood open near the desks, a couple of stethoscopes tossed on top. Everything apparently normal.

Or was it? Stethoscopes? She had a vague image of the two doctors in the corridor each carrying one. Then she noticed two white coats hanging up behind the door. And was there something odd about the aroma of the room? Something different from the clinical, disinfected smell of the rest of the hospital?

She was tense, her stomach taught, her heart thudding. She was onto something. She knew it. If the men she had passed were impostors, the real doctors might still be here somewhere. But where? At the end of the room was a door marked 'bathroom'. She eased it open. The stench of chloroform almost choked her. Holding her nose, she switched on the light. There, in a huddle on the floor were two men in shirt sleeves. White men. But not the same pair she had seen.

She raced for the phone, calling hospital security, alerting her guards. Another doctor and nurse had just reached them and were checking on the Renamo man. But they were too late. The tell-tale syringe mark on his arm told of the poison that was already winding its way through his system. Within minutes he would be dead.

A mixture of emotions engulfed Florence: triumph that her instinct had been proved correct again; despondency that another life had very probably been lost; anger at being outwitted again; frustration that she had come so close to catching them again. And determination: determination that they wouldn't get the better of her again. Next time she would get them first.

Evans knew there was something wrong the moment he walked through the door of his small terraced house in Islington. He had stopped off from work to change into more casual clothes and collect his photographs of China before driving down to the Covent Garden pub where he had arranged to meet Jenny.

The house was a shambles: drawers left open, cupboards emptied, books pulled off shelves. His papers were strewn everywhere. Burglars, he thought bitterly. What timing! Just as he was out on a date. He looked at his watch. Shortly after six. He hadn't much time before leaving to meet Jenny. He hated being late at the best of times and he was anxious not to leave her hanging around for him. He couldn't afford to wait for the police. What would they do anyway?

He did a quick check round the house, starting with the obvious things: the video, TV, hi-fi. None of them had been taken. His passport, driving licence, spare cheque book were all still there. Odd. As he went through the house quickly, he could not find anything valuable missing. Even odder.

Grabbing some clothes from under a pile on the floor, he changed quickly and went to the kitchen to collect his photos. They had been pulled out of their processing wallets and spread all over the table. Weird. He stuffed them back in, grabbed a jacket and locked the door behind him. As he turned the key he realised that, not only had nothing been taken, there was also no sign of forcible entry. He started shivering uncontrollably. The bad vibes he had left behind in China were with him again.

❖

It was all quiet on the main Pretoria-Johannesburg highway, but Makuyana remained on his guard. Craven, his passenger, kept a constant watch on the road, but so far there was nothing untoward.

'I think we should stop and take stock,' Craven muttered, his tension showing too.

Makuyana, nodded, slowing down until he found a suitable place to pull in. It was nearly nine o'clock now. Another hour and he could be in bed at his hotel. Or he could be walking into a trap, possibly even led into one by Craven. He would have to keep his wits about him – and keep his options open too.

He switched off the engine. 'What now?'

'For starters, you had better sit in the back seat and I'll drive. Then we won't attract attention. I could be your *baas*, taking you back to your township.' Craven smiled, a taught little smile, his earlier jaunty air gone. 'I think it's best that we keep heading for Jo'burg. But we must case your hotel carefully.'

Makuyana nodded slowly, weighing up the situation. He might need Craven. He might need him badly. If, that is, the man was genuine.

❖

Jenny had arrived early at the pub, looking for a payphone. She found one near the ladies toilet and dialled the duty officer at work to find out if there were any messages; she hadn't had an opportunity to call before. Few of the people she visited in cramped flats on decaying housing estates had phones.

She called Fletcher on his direct line immediately, reversing the charge as she had run out of change. It was nearly seven o'clock and she wondered whether he would still be in the Greenpeace office, but he picked up his phone after the first ring.

Jenny's spirits drooped as she listened to him explaining his dilemma. The press conference details were relayed to her. Fletcher was apologetic, but firm; there was no other option.

'I hope neither of your names will come out but, to be honest, I can't give any guarantees if the press start digging further. We will have to tell them that a fellow tourist brought the documents out.'

Jenny knew she ought to be angry but, as was so often the case with her, she found herself appreciating the other point of view. Having reacted with irritation at the beginning, by the end of the conversation she was coolly weighing up the situation.

'If you absolutely have to identify your source, please try to leave Jim Evans' name out of it. He has his professional reputation to protect; that is not so much of a problem for me but Jim's situation is different. And he was twice nearly killed out there you know.'

'What!' Fletcher was genuinely astonished.

'It's a long story. But we suspect there are powerful interests determined to keep the lid on the nuclear connection in China. If I were you I'd be pretty careful myself.'

'Perhaps that explains why the story suddenly shifted during the day,' Fletcher remarked, thinking aloud. 'Could there be forces here in Britain wanting to keep the lid on things too?'

'Almost certainly,' Jenny replied, suddenly aware that they were talking on a line that was probably tapped. 'I don't want to say any more at the moment.'

As she put down the phone she saw Evans come into pub and stand looking around until he spotted her. She had been anticipating with pleasure their evening together. She realised, perhaps for the first time, how much she had missed him. But now he seemed uneasy. He looked harassed. They hugged almost absent-mindedly, that same sense of anti-climax again enveloping them both.

Evans found himself staring at each person in the pub, not knowing what he was looking for. Then he forced himself to suppress his paranoia. 'A quick pint before we eat?'

She nodded, making for a free table in the corner while he went to the bar. The pub was full of chat and laughter, crowded with people who had called on the way home from work, people meeting before going to the theatre, teenage girls sipping camparis as they waited for their blokes. Normal people. She felt out of place.

Evans came back with two pints of real ale. 'That should cheer you up.'

'Do I look as if I need cheering up?' she asked rhetorically, smiling weakly, noting again how tense he looked himself.

He shrugged his shoulders. 'Yes you do, actually. What sort of day have you had?'

She told him about the conversation with Fletcher, expecting him to react strongly. But he took it calmly, almost philosophically.

'I am worried about my academic position, Jenny; to do work in this area you have to be trusted by officialdom. But we must ensure Dick didn't die for nothing. That's our duty. Frankly, my main reservation is I don't feel comfortable under the spotlight, particularly if it becomes too public.'

She reached across the table and touched his hand. He took hers, somewhat tentatively, and squeezed gently. 'What about the impact on you?' he asked.

Not for the first time, she noticed how he had a habit of switching the conversation away from himself. It was an engaging trait, though one which could be frustrating for anybody trying to get closer to him.

'I'm not too bothered,' she replied. 'Like you, I feel it has to be done. But I am worried that you might become a target again.'

'Perhaps I already have.'

'What do you mean?'

He told her about the break-in that hadn't really been a 'break-in' and, for the first time since he had returned home, he felt again that sense of not knowing to whom he could turn.

'What do I say to the police? Somebody got in without force and stole nothing? They don't do much with normal burglaries these days. They'd do even less about this, wouldn't they?'

Later, they found a small vegetarian restaurant with a secluded table lit by a soft candle. The meal was good and so was the wine. The evening drew them closer together again. Over coffee Evans produced his photos and they re-lived the best parts of the visit.

When he came across the shots taken on the Great Wall Evans smiled. Wang had taken one of the whole group and Jenny had taken one of him which came out well. *One* of him? Surely there had been another? The one that captured Wang walking past in the background by mistake. Jenny clearly remembered taking it. Evans even remembered seeing it; when he had first glanced at the photos, he had been surprised at how clearly Wang had appeared in the shot.

He looked for the negatives. Normally they were tucked into the wallet in a separate section. But then he realised that, not only was the picture with Wang missing, so too was the relevant sheet of negatives.

❖

Captain Maritz Swanepoel was pleased at the way his boys had performed. They had redeemed themselves after that previous botched job. None of the media had covered the death of the Renamo man. That didn't surprise him. It would have been hushed up.

Now that the boys were safely out of the way on one of their field trips, he could get down to preparing for the main task in hand. Only one thing nagged at him. Where was Makuyana? His sources told him the bomb intended for the security chief nearly took out his deputy, and the man hadn't been seen at the hospital either. Apparently there was some woman in charge now. Sithole – that was her name. A woman! Christ, they must be getting desperate. No way would he take orders from some female sitting in an office back home. Still, he had better have her checked – and he would also file a request for Makuyana's whereabouts to be traced. That bugger had always worried him: a formidable adversary for whom even he had to admit a grudging respect. The man was probably up to no bloody good.

❖

Makuyana agreed to wait in the car, parked round the corner from his Jo'burg hotel while Craven went ahead to check out the lay of the land. Craven had advised him to slump down in the back as if asleep. Although increasing numbers of blacks were now living illegally in the nearby white area of Hillbrow and there were black taxi drivers everywhere, a black sitting in a car late at night when he should probably have been confined to his township might attract too much attention.

They had entered the city smoothly. It was pulsing with nightlife. As agreed, Craven had gone ahead to the hotel to ask for him under his assumed identity. The idea was Craven would hang around in the hotel foyer, waiting to see if his enquiry provoked any reaction. If possible he would also slip upstairs and knock on Makuyana's room door. If anyone was in the room, Craven could feign surprise, and make some excuse that he had the wrong person. If all was clear, Makuyana could move in, with Craven still watching and ready to help him get out should the need arise.

Except that Makuyana did not stay behind in the car. Once Craven was out of sight, Makuyana went round to the service entrance and slipped inside. Although he was taking a chance, it might prove less risky than hanging around – a sitting target in the car. He headed for the black staff quarters which he had taken care to case when he first arrived. There was nobody about. In a cupboard he found some dark grey overalls which he pulled over his suit. Grabbing a trolley, he pushed it to the service lift and headed up to the first floor balcony from where he could survey the foyer.

Craven was hunched over a newspaper on one of the settees. Nobody seemed to be taking any notice of him. After several minutes, Craven got up and headed towards the nearby bar. The man was quite good, Makuyana thought. He moved with confidence, the key attribute in such circumstances: never look out of place. Makuyana saw him turn almost casually and slip unnoticed into a lift; he must be on his way up to the bedroom. Some minutes later, he re-appeared and went up to reception where a woman checked the room keys and then shook her head. Craven returned to the settee and his paper. Still no suspicious movements around him.

Makuyana headed back swiftly to the staff quarters, passing a white waiter carrying drinks on a tray. The man took no notice of him. Fortunately there was still nobody around when he replaced the overalls and the trolley, heading out of the back entrance again. He circled the car until he was satisfied it wasn't being watched, then climbed back in and slumped down.

A little while later Craven returned. 'No apparent sign of trouble,' he reported.

'What does that mean? Was it one of your people and not the Special Branch firing at us?'

'Could be,' Craven shrugged. 'Or it could be that nobody had the chance to get a fix on your car.'

He handed Makuyana a phone number. 'I'll be holed up for the next few days with a friend. Ring me if you have any problems.'

They shook hands, and he was off. Makuyana drove round to the hotel's underground car park. Then he walked back out and found a public call box. He rang the hotel reception desk.

'Ah, Mr Inkala. A friend of your's called to see you, but you weren't in. Didn't leave a name but said he'd return tomorrow.'

'Thank you. I would like to check out now. My business plans have changed and I need to leave right away. Could you please have my things collected from my room immediately and brought to reception for me? I'll be along shortly to settle the bill.'

'Certainly sir. You realise you'll have to pay for tonight as well?'

'Of course.'

Ten minutes later, he walked through the back entrance again and scanned the reception area. Satisfied, he paid his bill and picked up his small suitcase. Then he drove straight out of the city towards Jan Smuts airport where, by a process of elimination, he discovered that the first flight out was to Nairobi, boarding now. It was frustrating that he would be making such a long detour to get home, especially since the information he had was so urgently needed. But he couldn't take any chances. He had to steel himself as he went through passport control, but the official gave him only a cursory glance.

As the plane taxied out and took off, two men in plain clothes arrived at his hotel and asked for him. They seemed taken aback to discover he was no longer resident.

'Dick was one of our most trusted activists.'

Fletcher sat under the glare of the TV lights and detailed the facts coolly. He referred the journalists to the small report of Sewell's death in Hong Kong every paper had carried ten days before. After his opening statement there was a buzz of questions which he was able to field easily. Most sought clarification. Almost all were sympathetic. To his relief, the tone of the questioning had swung back from the hostility of the previous afternoon when the right-wing papers were going strongly on challenges to the credibility of the documents. Their representatives seemed muted in the press conference; none could deny the seriousness of a British citizen's murder.

Then the *Daily Mail* man popped up his hand. 'Who brought out the documents?'

'Sewell gave a copy to a fellow tourist who passed them to us,' replied Fletcher evenly.

'What was his name?'

'*Her* name. Jennifer Stuart. She's not a Greenpeace activist. She knew nothing of Sewell's mission. We are grateful for her co-operation because otherwise the world would not have been alerted to a major environmental threat. But all she did was act as a courier.'

'Where can she be reached?' the *Mail* man persisted.

'She's not available today. She is a social worker with Southwark Council.' Fletcher had suggested that Jenny remain incommunicado during the day so that the media were initially forced to concentrate on Sewell's role rather than hers; she had been happy to agree. 'Any more questions? No? Thank you very much for coming.'

Fletcher did several interviews direct to camera and a number of ones for radio as well. Journalists from the quality papers remained for some more background information, but most of it was in the fact sheets prepared the previous night and issued together with a portrait photograph of Sewell provided to the Press Association for wider distribution.

From midday onwards, Jenny's office was plagued with press enquiries. She had warned her colleagues in advance and explained the circumstances to her Officer in charge. He had alerted the Council's press office and the assistant to the Council Leader. Jenny had another heavy programme of case visits during the day and was happy to escape the calls.

Later she watched the evening TV news bulletins at the house of a fellow social worker. A lump developed in her throat when the picture of Sewell flashed up, emotion welling up in her eyes. There was only a passing reference to her; still, it was an odd feeling hearing herself mentioned in the media. The item was the lead on all the bulletins which reported demands from backbench Labour MPs for a fullscale Government inquiry and a statement to Parliament. At long last, she felt, Sewell was gaining the recognition he deserved. While his role had remained a secret it was as if his bravery had been so pointless.

She called Evans. He too had been excited and emotional watching the news. They arranged to see each other over the weekend.

'By the way,' he added, 'the only other thing stolen was my notebook from the Chinese trip.'

'The one with the page that went missing?'

'Yes,' he said.

Suddenly they were both subdued again.

Harold Williams had been monitoring the news of the Greenpeace exposé, carefully clipping all the morning's press.

When he tuned in to the BBC's lunchtime *World at One* programme, he realised that much of his previous day's work had been undone. Sewell's death was a bombshell and he had to concede that Greenpeace had done well to wrest back the initiative in news management. But the aspect that intrigued him most was the reference to Jenny Stuart who had never really been a suspect during the trip. He recalled, however, the forthrightness with which she had expressed her left wing political views. Impressively articulate at the lecture for English speaking students which he had attended, she was in fact the most politically vocal member of the delegation; Evans had been virtually silent by contrast.

There must be something in her background as an activist which they could uncover. And, she had grown close to Evans during the trip. He had suspected they might even have been lovers. Perhaps the time had come to up the ante again. Once more, he decided to make some phone calls, to his friend in British Intelligence, the backbench Conservative MP and, this time, contacts on the *Sun*, the *Mail* and the *Telegraph* as well as the *Express*.

He also called an official at the Chinese Embassy and arranged a private meeting in a Kensington coffee bar where the man's superiors could not monitor them.

❖

Outwardly, the Old Man took the news stoically. Inwardly he was seething, his mood already dark after the latest overtures from Moscow. Ever since the revisionist Gorbachev had come to power and *glasnost* had started melting thirty years of frozen relations with Peking, the Old Man feared the cementing of an alliance between the modernisers in both countries. They would threaten his bid for power.

Wang's assurances that the Englishman's death and the recovery of the documents had closed the file on the nuclear leaks were clearly worthless. But the Old Man's concern was over the timing of the news as much as the content. It was dangerous to have fresh attention being focused on the nuclear area since it was so important to the success of his own plan now advancing steadily toward a climax.

Everything else was falling into place. One of the country's worst-ever droughts was threatening the wheat crop at a time when the Government had already predicted food shortages. The northern wheat-growing provinces, the Yangtse valley and southwestern areas had had only half the normal amount of rainfall so far in the year. Zheijiang province had received less than a fifth of its usual rainfall and in Sahndong the drought was the worst for over 70 years.

For the fifth year in a row the annual harvest had failed to reach the minimum level needed. Confidential briefings warned that 80 million people were likely to face food shortages and 20 million positive hardship. Grain rations would have to be cut for Peking and other cities, and provincial governments would need to set up roadblocks to prevent grain being smuggled by speculators. A request might have to be made to the World Bank for a further loan to finance grain imports.

He would call Wang in and carpet the man. He had to have people around him who would deliver. No complications, no rebounds. Efficient and ruthless. Those qualities were essential to the historic task of setting China back on the Marxist-Leninist road.

It was after 10 p.m. when Jenny stepped out of her local underground station and set off along the half mile walk to her converted ground floor flat in a Victorian terraced house.

Although there was a constant hum of traffic, the pavements were quiet and deserted. A man walked a dog on the other side of the road. Some teenagers spilled out of a pub on the corner, giggling and larking about. It was dark, the moon hidden behind dense cloud.

She never enjoyed the walk. Rapes and violent attacks on women had been steadily rising in number and intensity over the past few years. She had herself given regular talks to local Labour Parties and trade union branches about the problem. But being an expert on the subject made her no more comfortable coping with it on her own. She kept a wary eye open for any signs of someone lurking in one of the front gardens she was passing, in a dark corner somewhere ahead or behind. It was always with considerable relief that she turned into her own street and saw her own house ahead of her.

But as she reached for her keys she froze. Two men were standing idly on the small path before the front door that she shared with the upstairs flat. They saw her almost at the same time. One straightened up. The other grabbed a camera and – before she realised what was happening – flashlights popped.

'Jenny Stuart?' The man was wearing a light coat, its collar turned up casually. The top button of his shirt was undone and his tie hung loosely.

'Err … Yes.'

'We are from the *Sun*. I wanted a word about your part in the Dick Sewell story.' The photographer was still clicking away.

'What about it? Greenpeace gave you all the details.'

'Is it true you were part of the plot?'

'What plot?'

'To discredit the nuclear power programme?'

She found her temper rising. So *this* was what it was like to be doorstepped. 'Look, I don't know what you are trying to get at. I was simply a tourist on a delegation invited by the Chinese authorities. Dick asked me to ensure a copy of his documents reached Greenpeace. That's all I did.'

'So he was worried he might be killed, was he?'

'No. He was simply being careful. Just as well, as it turned out.'

'What sort of person was he?'

'Very brave. Very dedicated.' She wasn't going to let his memory be besmirched.

'How close were you?'

'We only got to know each other out there.'

'Were you lovers?'

'No! Now piss off! I am not answering any more of your questions. Don't you care that one of your fellow country-men was murdered? Don't you care about the danger of nuclear leakages?' She was angry now.

Thrusting her keys in the lock, she went in and slammed the door shut. Outside she could hear the reporter shout: 'We know all about your political background.'

She was shaking. Her phone was ringing.

'Jenny Stuart?'

'Yes.'

'*Daily Mail*' here. There were a few questions we wanted to ask about your role in the China documents.'

And so the night went on. Her ansaphone was full of messages too. It was midnight before the calls stopped: she had been in the hallway, virtually anchored to the phone for well over an hour.

She walked into her living room and slumped on the sofa, exhausted. It was only then that she realised the papers on her desk were jumbled, the drawers open, books were strewn on the floor, cupboards emptied. Someone had been in and turned the flat right over.

Jenny had hardly slept that night. By 6 a.m. she was up again, listening to the radio and grabbing some breakfast. She was now being quoted in the news bulletins. She decided to re-connect her phone. Almost immediately it started to ring: BBC and independent radio and TV wanted interviews. Then her doorbell went. She peered out of her front window. About a dozen photographers were standing outside. She had read somewhere that they moved around in a pack together, but it was something else to actually see them gathered there, chatting in the early summer sunshine.

She decided not to answer yet, collecting her thoughts first, eating her breakfast and getting changed. There was no way she could avoid them without being trapped in her house all day. She knew that for big stories like the birth of a royal baby they would doorstep for days if necessary. She wasn't that important of course, but she had to get out to go to the office anyway. The doorbell continued to ring at regular intervals.

At about 6.45 a.m. she opened the door to be confronted by a rush of clicking photographers, with several TV cameras and microphones thrust out in the front. Unlike the incident with the *Sun* reporter the previous night, everyone seemed friendly. Some apologised for disturbing her. They were clearly sizing her up, she thought.

She had decided over breakfast that there was no point in being unco-operative. She might as well try to get her side of the story straight and take the opportunity to say something about the main issues which seemed to be disappearing fast under a pile of irrelevancies about her own role. After her initial shock, she had been forced to smile when she heard the early morning review of the papers on radio refer to the *Sun*'s description of her as 'Red Jen'.

For nearly half an hour she answered questions and gave interviews. She was astonished to see outside broadcast vans standing in the street. The interviews were being relayed straight to the studio for use in the breakfast radio and TV programmes. One of the TV stations wanted her to do an interview in the studio itself, so she agreed, provided they arranged to drive her on to the office.

By the time she got to work, she was feeling harassed: too tired to enjoy the novelty of being an instant celebrity.

❖

In the Johannesburg *Star*, which Makuyana bought before departing, there was a feature story describing how South Africa had developed a new generation of weapons with the capability to strike deep into front line states and withdraw swiftly. An airbase close the Zimbabwe's border at Louis Trichardt had been operational for some years, with two squadrons of Cheetah jet fighters based there. South African made and built in co-operation with the makers of Israel's Kfir fighter, their modernised French Snecma engines gave them sufficient range to strike as far north as Dar es Salaam in Tanzania – that meant all the ANC's main guerrilla bases were targets.

Makuyana reflected on these facts and began to turn his mind to the picture of the nuclear connection which he had started to sketch. It was still very hazy, but he began to make notes. He would use the time during his enforced detour to fill in the detail and try to make sense of it all.

When he reached Nairobi, he booked the first available plane to Harare and made two calls. The first was to Florence Sithole, asking her to keep tabs on 'our friend George'. From her guarded response it was clear she recognised the reference to Mngadi's aide, George Peterson. In return, he was startled to learn from her that 'the hostage' had been eliminated, but it was not safe to ask for further details on her direct line.

Makuyana's second call was to the Johannesburg hotel he had just left, asking whether there were any messages for him. There was a pause at the other end, some clicks, and then another voice came on the line.

'Ah, Mr Inkala. It's the manager here. So glad you called. We had some enquiries for you shortly after you had left. Is there anywhere you can be reached?'

Makuyana thought fast. He knew it could take under thirty seconds to trace a call with the correct equipment. 'I am in between appointments in Pretoria at the moment. I'll call back later today for any messages if that's convenient.'

And then, before the manager, could respond, Makuyana hung up.

With several hours to kill before his flight, he made for the Executive Lounge; it would be more comfortable than the shambolic bustle of a typically African airport. Citing his security status, he talked his way into it.

A fresh supply of newspapers had just come in on the flight from London. Makuyana was pleased, they brought back memories of his student days in Britain. The front page of the *Sun* had a picture of an attractive young woman and the headline caught his eye: RED JEN'S CHINESE PUZZLE. The two angles – China and nuclear – intrigued him. He read the reports in the quality papers voraciously. Then, checking nobody was looking, he slipped the *Sun* into his briefcase. People in Executive lounges wouldn't miss a pop paper.

Here it was again – The Peking Connection – so tantalising. It kept coming at him from different angles: the original tip from the President's office, the briefing from Oliver Khama at the farmhouse, the information from Wessels in Pretoria and now this. It was almost as if the issue was dogging him, like one of those heat-seeking missiles in pursuit of an enemy aircraft, he couldn't shake it off.

But what could he do about it? His thoughts turned to his work priorities when he reached Harare. Problem number one was that security problems in Harare remained critical, the killing of the Renamo man another major setback. Clearly, the South Africans had regrouped since their well-connected espionage network in Zimbabwe had been smashed. It was frustrating to have so few leads in this case. There was really only the follow-up to the bomb sent by post to Robert Temba's house. Someone had been pin-pointed for surveillance. Who was it again? He made a note. The pressure had to be increased. So far they had taken all the knocks. It was time they started hitting the enemy.

Problem number two was how to test the accuracy of the information Craven had given him in Pretoria. If the guy was genuine, it pointed the finger directly at Peterson as the traitor amongst Mngadi's inner ANC circle. But, as the events of the night showed, Craven might not have been genuine. It was hard to be sure. Fingering Peterson could be part of a de-stabilising move or it could be the key to breaking Pretoria's new network in Harare.

What else? How could he have forgotten – the security arrangements for that Chinese Government visit. China again. He paused. The visit had been at the bottom of his list of priorities: another foreign delegation – a routine matter which his staff could handle. But, in the circumstances he should perhaps push it higher up on the list.

❖

Wang assured the Old Man everything was being done to undermine the Greenpeace story. It was however not possible to take out the girl. She had to be discredited. To eliminate her would guarantee that the whole story was blown up even further.

It was a tense meeting. Wang had never seen the Old Man so tetchy. The deep wrinkles on his forehead were bulging and he was drumming nervously on the large expanse of his desk. Then he changed the subject abruptly and started to rant in a way Wang had never heard. It was almost as if he was using the younger man as a microphone, for Wang was clearly not expected to respond, only to nod his agreement.

'Have you noticed the appearance of our young recently? The Government is saying that fashion and consumerism is patriotic, part of our duty to society!' He spat the words out. 'There are now nearly a thousand privately owned beauty parlours in Peking alone. In the old days we banned cosmetics – and bras too. We insisted our women wear standard clothes. We insisted that their hair was cut short or plaited into pigtails. Now they look like westerners. They scream and swoon at rock concerts. They hanker after a life of videos, hi-fi and designer clothes. It is disgusting.'

Wang nodded in agreement. He didn't have much choice, though personally he found the Old Man's obsession boring. The gap between young and old was growing, but it was a fact of life. The old continued to dress simply – white collar workers in grey suits or clean white shirts, peasants in cotton jackets and trousers, grannies with dark trousers and loose blue or grey jackets, a few still hobbling painfully along with bound feet. Some women students by contrast wore high heels, denim jeans, and bright blouses and jumpers. Even young men were to be found using moisturizing cream, after-shave, cologne and chapstick for their lips in the cold.

The Old Man had worked himself up into quite a state. Wang wondered briefly whether he was losing his marbles, but he couldn't permit himself such thoughts. Then the Old Man swung his chair round. One of those long silences again. Wang might as well have been on his own; no sound, not even any sight of the Old Man who was hidden from Wang by the high back of the chair.

Minutes passed before the chair swung back equally abruptly, its occupant cool and collected once more.

'Now, about our Zimbabwe visit. We leave for Africa next week. Once we have finished at Nairobi you will be going on ahead to Harare. Everything must be double checked. No hitches.'

'No hitches, sir,' Wang nodded, relieved he was being excused at last to get on with his own preparations. He had managed to carve out sufficient autonomy for himself to perform a free-wheeling role in the bureaucracy which normally stifled any independence and viewed initiative with some suspicion. Because he was so clearly one of the Old Man's protégés he was treated with some deference, even by his immediate superiors. Consequently, there was no problem about making international phone calls on his secure line or maintaining contacts outside the normal channels.

His most recent call to London had given him cause to reflect. It was hard to assess its significance. He had been briefed on events after the Greenpeace press conference and noted with satisfaction the demolition job that the popular press had done on the girl's credibility. He was also given surveillance reports on both her and Evans. Nothing special there – except for one thing. Evans was apparently going to some sort of conference in Zimbabwe at the same time as the Chinese delegation would be out there. Just a coincidence?

No reason to suppose otherwise, his contacts in British intelligence told him. Evans was a bit of a paradox. Ostensibly a political innocent with no record of, or interest in, activism, he had nevertheless been up to no good during his China visit. Moreover, his association with the girl might draw him into new political pastures. They would have to keep an eye on the man: Wang was conscious that he had slipped up before and could not afford to do so again – not this time.

CHAPTER NINE

The hardware was delivered to Swanepoel's house in a van apparently carrying garden furniture. There were two rifles: R1s, manufactured in South Africa, the equivalent of Belgian FNs, with plenty of spare ammunition – as well as stun grenades and tear gas canisters, and two 9 mm Z88 pistols.

He checked it all thoroughly, ensuring everything was in good working order. Then he packed each item away carefully, wrapped in blankets or stuffed into carrier bags: the sort of containers that would excite no interest on the back seat of his car. Having checked the street to see that he was not observed, he carried them to the car.

It was a warm winter's day. He drove around in no particular direction for half an hour, assiduously watching his rear-view mirror: not a sausage. He couldn't help feeling contempt for the opposition's security forces. Satisfied that nobody was following, he headed off towards a suburb to the east of the city and the safe house there.

As he turned right into the main road, a bicycle nearly collided into his offside, and veered off to crash into the pavement. Christ! He pulled up immediately and went over to the man. Although he had been tempted to drive on, it was too great a risk. Somebody might have taken his number. He prayed to God the cyclist was okay. Everything had gone so smoothly – and now this. All he needed was some busy-body policeman poking about.

The cyclist was seething with anger, but unhurt, save for a grazed knee. The bike was scratched and the front mudguard was bent. Swanepoel calmed the man down with an abject apology, and then taking him completely by surprise, reached into his pocket and pulled out sixty Zimbabwe dollars: 'I can't afford another endorsement on my licence. They may take it away,' he explained.

When he reached the safe house, he drove up the spacious front drive and unlocked the garage, parking the car inside and closing the up-and-over door again. Then he unlocked a connecting door into the kitchen and ferried the equipment through, stacking it neatly away. Everything was ready for the Boys once they came back from their trip down south. They would have several more days to prepare, to check and to re-check. He probably wouldn't hear from them until the message came through that they had accomplished their mission.

The Boys. He thought of them wistfully for a moment. He had been like them once: lean and fit, keen as hell. It was comforting to know there were still some youngsters like them who were willing to die for the cause.

❖

The two of them were enjoying the day together. They had driven to Richmond Park and walked amidst the royal deer, majestic in the grass, the young ones prancing about as the senior males paraded their antlers for all the world to see. For a change the weather was warm and sunny, and they sat down to catch their breath on the hill to the south-west of the park overlooking Kingston. The river Thames was just visible as it wound its way back through Richmond.

The right wing press had gone to town on Jenny. They had dredged up all sorts of details about her past role as a student activist, much of it accurate, but placed in such a pejorative context that she was made to sound like an ogre. What surprised her was the extent of the information in some of them. She was not a public figure and had played only a small role in student politics, the women's movement and the Labour Party.

She was particularly angry about the RED JEN story in the *Sun*. By clever insinuation and juxtaposition of her own answers to the the reporter she had been presented as a left-wing firebrand, Sewell's lover and co-conspirator on the mission, a feckless social worker who abandoned her clients to go on foreign jaunts. Worse than this, a backbench Tory MP, known in the trade as 'Rentaquote Rod', had attacked her 'irresponsibility' in allowing her friend to be killed.

But here she felt at last as if the burden of the past week was being lifted away from her. She liked being with this rather shy man. He was diffident and tentative in his approach towards her. She sensed that if their relationship was to deepen physically as well as emotionally – and she wanted that – then she would have to make the running. It was a reversal of traditional roles.

They walked back to the car and drove down to the river side. It was early afternoon now and people were lazing on grass banks above the towpath or spilling out of pubs. They made their way to one of the pubs, set back across the road that ran parallel to the river, and found some spare seats amongst the crowd. She went to order two pints of real ale.

Evans checked out the food. It was difficult to choose a suitable meal for her from the conventional pub bar fare, because her diet was unusual: hardly any meat, no dairy products and a ban on caffeine, though she ate fish, loved salads and vegetables and apparently drank huge quantities of herbal tea at home. He had to concede, however, that she seemed healthy on it. Her only weakness was a willingness to drink a bit of alcohol, which was just as well, he thought, since they seemed to be spending a fair amount of their time together in pubs.

When he returned with the food, she was sitting, head tilted back and eyes closed, soaking up the sun, her hair falling back over the chair. She looked great. Although he felt they were growing closer, he was still pleasurably surprised that she was apparently content to spend so much time with him.

'There you are, some of your funny food,' he joked, handing over a mixture of salad and broccoli. 'I'm afraid there wasn't anything else suitable.'

'That's fine.' She peered at him. 'What rubbish are you eating then?'

'Ham, egg and chips.'

'Don't you realise that's really bad for you?'

He hadn't ever heard her criticise someone else's choice of food before. Throughout the China visit she had made clear her own preferences but never commented on the others'.

As if reading his thoughts, she continued: 'I don't normally like to have a go at other people's diets.'

'Why start now then?'

'Because I care for you,' she said simply, leaning over to kiss him.

There was a quietness between them. As they savoured each other's company, Evans realisied how much he craved it.

The afternoon passed quickly. Evans had never been with anybody with whom he always had something to talk about. There was an animated buzz between them as they discussed their upbringings, their jobs and, inevitably, Jenny's activism.

In the evening they went back to his house, armed with a bottle of wine and some food which she had supervised buying and which they cooked together. Afterwards they sat on the sofa listening to music.

'It's been a lovely day,' Jenny said. 'Thanks for looking after me. For a while I completely forgot about the past week.'

'My pleasure.' He had been determined to give her a proper break. He looked at his watch. 'God, its eleven already. I'd better run you home.'

'Oh,' she looked disappointed, 'can't I stay?'

Across the road outside the house two men eavesdropped on their passion through long range bugging equipment targeted on the bedroom window.

It was some compensation to be a voyeur after a wasted evening listening to nothing which remotely connected to the subject of their investigation.

❖

K.J. van der Walt sat in the garden of his spacious new bungalow which nestled half-way up the *kopje* on the outskirts of the Golden City and overlooked the bush below. It was Sunday afternoon and he was enjoying a whisky after a good lunch. His wife was asleep, now he could relax on his own.

For him, this was what it was all about, what he had fought so hard over so many years to protect. The right to sit in your garden listening to the birds while the *boy* looked after the shrubs, the bushes and the fruit trees. The right to enjoy a winter's afternoon under a clear blue sky in the sun. After he had topped up his glass a few more times, he would cat-nap out there in his chair until he was woken up by the cold creeping in as it did so abruptly when the sun disappeared; a perfect Sunday.

And yet he was worried. His wife had sensed it but she decided not to comment; she would choose her moment carefully to find out what was wrong. The scene before him brought home even more sharply what was at stake: his whole way of life.

These were difficult times. Independence for Namibia had been conceded. The South African army had been defeated in Angola. There was some consolation that the ANC had been forced to close its training camps in Angola. And, Unita, the guerrilla force still at loggerheads with Luanda, was being supported covertly by Pretoria – just as they had continued clandestine backing for the rebel Renamo movement despite the 1984 Nkomati Accord with Mozambique. Nevertheless the stark reality could not be dodged: South Africa was now surrounded by independent countries, and hostile ones at that. In under fifteen years the position of having compliant front-line states had been reversed.

There were other worries too. The economy was not in good shape after a decade of relatively low growth, international pressure and rising government expenditure (particularly on defence and financing home produced substitutes for goods cut off by sanctions). Gold no longer played the pivotal role of old because world prices and demand had fallen. There was a huge problem of international debt. The Rand had depreciated markedly. Interest rates were high. The budget deficit was historically high and still rising.

Inflation was continuing to run away. Not surprisingly, the *volk* were getting restless. Class divisions within the white population had sharpened. For the first time in generations the automatic expectation of rising prosperity was no longer available to all whites. The yuppies – a phenomenon imported from Europe and the USA – were doing nicely thank you, but you couldn't build a strong nation on yuppies; KJ knew that only too well.

That was why so much depended on Operation NOSLEN and on the development of a flexible and effective nuclear capability. The two ran in harness. Nothing must stand in their way. The planned action in Harare over the next fortnight was vital. The disturbing leaks must be sealed, the recipients hunted out and crushed. Security had been breached far too often recently. We may have penetrated them, but we are leaking like a sieve as never before he thought uneasily; his old comrade Maritz would have to be given fresh instructions.

When he dozed off at last in his chair, his black maid came and tucked a small blanket around him. Though she couldn't help having a deferential fondness for the old devil, she had a sudden sense of power as she leant over his sleeping frame. Here was the most feared head of the security forces, so strong and yet, in this moment, so totally vulnerable. She had him in her hands, the man to whom the politicians conceded authority to mastermind the police state and its apparatus of torture, repression and killings. For one wild moment she imagined using the blanket to suffocate him.

Down below the house, where the garden sloped away to a clump of trees, his white security guards patrolled the perimeter fence constantly, only glancing up briefly as they saw her perform the usual Sunday routine. They would never know her thoughts.

❖

Florence Sithole was frustrated and not a little depressed. There was no sign of the two white men she had spotted in the hospital. They had disappeared into thin air. None of her ring of informers had anything to tell her.

She hated having mucked it up while Makuyana was away. She wondered what he really felt about the news of the Renamo man's death. Nevertheless, her spell as his deputy had been exhilarating. She had enjoyed the responsibility of being in charge, of doing the planning and the overall thinking, of being able to get others to do the routine tasks. Still, now she could relax a little, pacify her mother by eating better, and stop thinking about the job all the time.

What had Makuyana been up to? She had been worried stiff about the unofficial status of his mission. If it had gone wrong all hell would break loose. His call from Nairobi had been a relief, but it left her none the wiser. Soon he would be through customs. She wouldn't have to wait long; knowing him, he had probably travelled light.

Mind you, *did* she really know him? It was one thing to work closely with Keith Makuyana, quite another to get close to the man. She admired him. She also fancied him – probably rather more than she cared to admit, even to herself. But she couldn't ever see that coming to anything. He had erected a Berlin Wall around his emotions after his family had been murdered by the South Africans. Yet she sensed that, under that cool, even cold, exterior was a deeply emotional man.

There he was, walking through with the people waiting expectantly for their loved ones or their business contacts. For once, he wasn't wearing his dark glasses, and without the air of menace that they conveyed, she saw a handsome man with gentle eyes in a rather flash suit and tie. He looked so completely different that he might have been in disguise.

She didn't move. Let him spot her. Let him take the lead. She wasn't sure precisely how he wanted to play the home-coming. That was why she had come to the airport just like anybody else waiting for an arrival: no use of the usual security channels available to her, nothing unusual to excite interest in Mr Inkala's return.

He spotted her. Their eyes met and held for an instant, but he stood still and took out a notepad, frowning. She moved off, pausing at the shop to browse across the front page of the *Herald*. Out of the corner of her eye, she noticed him sidle round to stand nearby and appear to be searching the magazine rack.

He seemed to cough, hand covering his mouth.

'I think I'm being watched,' he muttered. 'Leave your car keys somewhere here and catch a taxi to the office. We'll meet there. Did you bring your Nissan?'

She nodded imperceptibly, then moved over to the souvenir shelf which, like any other airport, was full of junk. She picked up a copper mug and slipped her key inside, hoping he had been watching closely, then put the item back and walked off.

From her vantage point at the other end of the shop, she saw him buy the mug and carry it off in a bag. What she couldn't see was the man tailing him in a parallel direction across the building.

Swanepoel's man followed 'Mr Inkala' out to the car park, his driver waiting nearby, ready to move. They had to trace the guy, and find out who he really was. None of their sources had been able to confirm his identity.

The Nissan pulled away from the airport complex and began the fifteen minute journey to the city centre. Swanepoel's man followed at a discreet distance. At the crossroads after the army barracks, instead of taking the usual right-turn into town at Coke Corner, the target shot straight on and the pursuers had to accelerate quickly to veer round the next corner and tail it again. They almost found themselves overshooting as the Nissan stopped unexpectedly at the first line of shops under the railway bridge and 'Inkala' got out and went into a food store, emerging minutes later with a carrier bag.

He drove off again until both pulled up, a car apart, at a set of traffic lights. Almost immediately the Nissan screamed off on a sharp left turn, jumping the lights, its rear tyres spinning furiously, leaving black marks on the tarmac. The pursuers were trapped behind another vehicle, powerless and speechless with frustration.

❖

Sheltering in the FO entrance just around the corner from 10 Downing Street, Evans and Jenny could see that the pickets were wet through, their banner sodden, their leaflets damp and crumpled. But still they kept up their chants, perhaps more to raise their own spirit than to influence the the evening rush-hour pedestrians who hurried by, heads down in the driving rain.

The 24-hour permanent picket had become an institution, so much so that it was mentioned in tourist guides. Organised by the Azania Liberation Committee, it had been running continuously for over three years and they had pledged to continue until the British Government implemented comprehensive mandatory sanctions against South Africa. Normally there was a group of half a dozen pickets, mainly young students. When they began, police had tried to move them on and there were frequent arrests. But they persisted and magistrates seemed reluctant to convict them for obstruction. They attracted widespread admiration for their selfless dedication and tenacity, even from political opponents.

Jenny's contact would not allow himself to be described as a 'leader' of the picket because the group did not recognise any leaders; they were all equals and decisions were taken democratically. But he was clearly one of the driving spirits, walking amongst the others now, chatting to them, keeping the morale high. John Howells was tall and thin, a woolly hat covering his closely cropped hair. Jenny remembered reading somewhere that he had been raised in the South Wales Valleys and now worked part-time as a computer programmer, earning enough money to enable him to be what amounted to a fulltime activist. Her own political involvements seemed puny by comparison.

He caught her eye and walked over.

'Be with you in a minute. How about meeting in the pub over there?' He pointed to the other side of Whitehall, down toward the Houses of Parliament.

They were well into their drinks by the time Howells joined them. After introductions, Jenny briefed him on their China experience. He was a good listener. Periodically he would seek clarification, but mostly he scribbled away in a notebook. Then she paused, looking embarrassed.

'Sewell's reference to South Africa in all this was only in passing but it stuck in my mind. And then there was a young student whose father wanted to talk to Jim about the Atomic Energy Institute of Nankow – except that both of them disappeared before we could meet them – he spoke of links with South Africa too. It's one aspect of this business that I feel we don't properly understand. I hope we're not wasting your time, but ...'

'Not at all. This is very important,' Howells said sombrely. 'You will be discreet, won't you?'

'Of course,' Jenny replied, 'I was going to say the same thing to you. As I mentioned at the beginning, I didn't want to approach the ANC's London office cold because I don't know anybody there personally and the place is probably bugged anyway. That's why I went to a friend who I knew had been active in anti-apartheid work. He said you would know how best to pass the information confidentially to the ANC. You will be very careful, won't you? Jim was nearly killed because of it.'

If Howells was shocked at this, he didn't show it. He merely shrugged. 'Of course I'll be careful,' he said, his expression indicating that he didn't need any lessons from a couple of bourgeois interlopers. 'I would also like your assurance that you won't mention this to anyone else. The ANC high command in Dar es Salaam will want to have the time and space to act on the information before Pretoria knows they have it.'

They were happy to concur.

'Not exactly a bundle of fun, that guy,' Evans muttered as Howells walked out into the rain to rejoin his comrades.

'No,' Jenny said, 'but it's a great relief to get it off my chest.' She was about to add 'At least that's the end of the story for us.' But, she bit her lip; that might be tempting fate rather too much.

❖

Makuyana had shaken off his followers easily enough, but not before he had got a clear sight of the car's registration number. As soon as he got back to the office he had the number traced. It turned out to be a pool car belonging to a company with its headquarters in the city centre. At first, the management couldn't explain the car's presence at the airport. Then a senior manager came on the line to say it must have been stolen overnight, but nobody had realised until now.

Though the explanation seemed straightforward enough, Makuyana asked Florence Sithole to investigate the company and interview the relevant staff more thoroughly. He also asked her to check again on the man Herson, the only name they had some sort of lead on, however tenuous, from the Robert Temba murder the previous month. A lot had happened since then, an awful lot, but it was sometimes worth going back over old ground when you were high and dry like this.

Next on his agenda was the Chinese leadership visit. He asked for the file and called in the staff directly responsible for overseeing security. Two hours later, he made an official request to see one of the President's key advisers. The excuse was to go over details of the visit; in fact, he wanted to report what he had learnt about the Peking connection, however hazy it might seem. Night was falling before he had a chance to reach the next main task he had set himself: the George Peterson problem. He drummed his fingers on the desk. Then he looked up a special number and picked up the phone. It was time to make contact again with Selby Mngadi.

❖

Swanepoel looked at the photographs taken at the airport. They weren't very good. The focus was bad and the light had hardly been favourable, even with a 1000 ASA fast film. About the only features he could confirm with absolute certainty were that the man was tall, smart and clean shaven.

Still, they had enough to go on to allow Pretoria to act officially over 'Mr Inkala'. His behaviour had been very far from that of a man on a normal trade mission. First the involvement with the ANC outside Pretoria, then the sudden flight, and finally the professional way Swanepoel's men were shaken off after leaving Harare Airport.

He rang the businessman in the city centre and asked for a message to be ferried back to KJ. There was no need to spell it out over the open line for they had a conversational routine able to cover what they were really talking about, a series of banal exchanges about the company's commercial life.

Later he was amused to see the story reported in the Zimbabwe media, though in a low-key, matter-of-fact way. He got a vicarious pleasure from seeing the results of his work surface in the public arena, knowing that he'd played a hidden role in making the news. The journalists dealing with the stories never knew what *he* knew. In this case he had to smile at the way the diplomatic protest was handled. The newscaster simply reported that South Africa had complained of a Zimbabwe businessman entering the country under false pretences. There was no more explanation. By the next day the story would have been forgotten.

But back home, Swanepoel knew the papers would be going to town on it. He could visualise the headlines and the lurid hyping-up of espionage and deception. Stories such as these had a deeper purpose than pop-paper sensationalism, however. Swanepoel knew they were part of a constant process of worrying away at the white population, of reminding them to be on their guard against the scheming black forces in the North.

Even he had to admit there was a contradiction here. On the one hand Pretoria was deliberately promoting trade in order to lock the front line states into an economic dependency on the South Africa. Let the African leaders continue to denounce apartheid publicly whilst privately acknowledging that their economic and military vulnerability meant they could do little more than indulge in gestures. On the other hand you couldn't allow your own constituency in the white heartlands to become too soft or complacent about black Africa.

Hence the protest about 'Mr Elliott Inkala' — whoever he was. The disconcerting aspect of the affair for Swanepoel was that he genuinely *didn't* know, though he had an uncomfortable feeling he ought to.

He went and looked at the photos again. There was something vaguely familiar about the face – or, rather, the impression it left you with. He kept thinking of someone strong and threatening. It made him feel uneasy.

❖

Although Evans wouldn't admit it, he got a buzz from writing under pressure: first researching, then organising the material, then pulling it together. Sometimes, he would begin making notes with only the haziest concept or idea in his mind. Gradually he would work out a logical structure. But it was not until he actually started writing that each argument developed into a coherent analysis. Sometimes he sat down at the word processor with only fragments of notes and half-formed ideas, but as he started tapping out the words they took over, almost as if they had an autonomous life, and, before he knew it, pages had been covered.

Nevertheless, the stress on him now had mounted to an almost unbearable pitch. He had been racing to meet his deadline for the paper on plutonium proliferation when one of the London organisers of the Harare conference had phoned to ask a favour. A Scottish expert on radiation had been forced to pull out at the last moment. Could Evans take his place? Given the shortage of time, he wouldn't be expected to deliver a full paper. Just a lecture would do. 'After all, it's your field. You could probably do it half-pissed,' the organiser had joked.

Evans had agreed, though very reluctantly. He didn't like speaking off-the-cuff. It wasn't his style. He always prepared carefully for lectures, perhaps over-carefully; he was sometimes so weighed-down with controversies and counter-arguments that he was accused of missing the wood for the trees.

But in this case he had no alternative but to pull together some of his existing work and talk from headings which he planned to rehearse on the plane going over. The obsession with such advanced availability of papers was a bit ridiculous anyway since most conference delegates didn't read them before the session started. They spent their time gossiping and back-biting about developments in their particular professions – despite their gloss of academic seriousness, that was the real purpose of these conferences, Evans always thought.

His first evening free was when Jenny came round for a meal – their last chance to be together before he left. His mind was still on the subject of his lecture and, for almost the first time since they had met, Evans found himself doing all the explaining. He planned to talk about the constant leakage of radioactivity into the air, water and soil, which, according to his research, the government was attempting to conceal rather than clear up.

'It's in the food too,' Jenny added, opening a second bottle of wine.

Evans smiled at the return to her pet subject. 'Yes, plenty of food you can now buy in supermarkets has been irradiated, mainly for preservation purposes.'

Jenny nodded.

'There are also radioisotopes in food from researchers using them to monitor the progress of pesticides and fertilisers through plants and soils. Radioisotope guages are used to check whether beer cans are filled to the correct levels ...' Evans rocked back in his chair, pleasantly full after the food and the drink. 'I could rattle off facts and figures for hours, but it's late.'

'Time for me to go then is it?' Jenny asked, her impish grin making it clear she intended to do nothing of the sort.

❖

Makuyana briefed Selby Mngadi about his information on George Peterson. It looked more and more likely that he was the traitor in the ANC camp.

The two men sat in a van in a city centre car park. Mngadi was subdued.

'He's been such a good comrade over the years,' he insisted, 'It's very hard to swallow.'

'But you know you are penetrated.' Makuyana didn't want to rub it in.

'What if this is disinformation? What if Pretoria is deliberately drawing attention away from the real culprit? George has a good reputation amongst our younger cadres in particular. You know we have had some problems with them. They are more impatient, more radical, more militant. Many don't want us to follow the more sophisticated political and diplomatic strategy of the past five years. They thirst for action all the time. George understands that. He responds to it. If you move against him, you risk destabilising the organisation, at least in Lusaka and Harare. And that is precisely what Pretoria would want.'

'And if we don't move against him?' Makuyana left the question hanging.

He could see from Mngadi's face that the point had gone home.

❖

After the excitement of the past few weeks in charge, Florence Sithole was back to the routine of investigating, checking and re-checking.

She had never been able to convince her family and friends that her work was not all highly dramatic, secret agent stuff. They would have been disappointed to discover how much of her time was spent doing things which were incredibly boring: waiting for the results of surveillance, sometimes for a whole day with no return; checking lists, checking names. Running data through the computer had cut out some of the drudgery, but there was still an awful lot of it left.

Part of her rapid rise in the service was due to the fact that she was so thorough and conscientious. Nevertheless she had to make a special effort on the two tasks Makuyana had given her. She found out all there was to know publicly about Vitel, the company which owned the car which had tailed Makuyana from the airport. It marketed computer software and telecommunications systems and its Managing Director, Eugene Fraser, had good relations with the Government. He was even known to make donations to Party coffers. She noted that Vitel supplied material to South Africa, but that wasn't unusual.

She had also asked for a print-out on the phone calls made by Mr Paul Herson and for a record of his movements as monitored by the bleeper on his car. The latter showed up as a confusing blur of trips around the city which didn't really tell her anything.

She stared at the list of numbers for incoming and outgoing calls. There weren't many. He didn't seem to have a lot of friends. Then there was a knock on her office door. An assistant brought in a mug of coffee together with a photocopy of the numbers that Herson had dialled, with the subscribers' names attached. There were several shops in the city and some names that didn't register any alarm bells. But right at the bottom of the list was an ex-directory number held by an E.A.Fraser. A coincidence? Surely not. Florence felt her stomach muscles tighten. She asked her assistant to check the address of the Fraser number and to get a tape of all the calls listed to Herson's phone. Then she hurried down the corridor to get permission from Keith Makuyana to re-assign a watcher to Mr Herson. And if this Mr Fraser was the Eugene

Fraser of Vitel, she would push very hard for an active tap on his and Herson's lines. She had a feeling that things were about to start moving at last.

❖

They picked up Craven easily enough. He opened the door of his flat in the Sunnyside district just south-east of the centre of Pretoria and two burly special branch men pushed past him.

They had Craven sized up from the beginning, and it wasn't difficult to break him.

They didn't use any violence. The two interrogators established a relationship with him over hours of conversation. One was hard, the other soft. They claimed to understand, even to sympathise with his point of view. They told him he was as much a victim of the system as they were; everyone was just playing out a role. They were simply doing their jobs, he had to understand that. After the first day, he was fairly disorientated by their friendliness. They even showed concern for his family, and how his reckless actions would affect his parents.

Then, having drawn him in, they produced pictures which they claimed were of ANC atrocities – pictures of burnt babies, of bodies mutilated by bombs – and, before the second day was out, he was beginning to confess.

He couldn't help himself. He hadn't been trained to resist. Well brought up individuals like him were naturally polite and automatically answered what appeared to be harmless questions, until they found themselves trapped in a web of incriminating little facts. He knew nothing about anti-interrogation techniques, such as remaining absolutely silent, refusing to face the interrogator by sitting head between legs, staring at a wall, climbing under the table or even exposing genitals to cause maximum embarrassment.

He felt so guilty – about himself, about deceiving his family. His parents had no inkling; they would be so ashamed, so angry at the loss of the family's good name. Then came the *coup de grâce*. His captors offered not to charge him, not to make public his arrest and detention, to help cover it up to his friends and relatives. After all, he hadn't taken a personal part in any atrocity or act of terrorism, had he? Why should they put a good Afrikaner boy like him in the dock where the opposition could take the mickey and the family's good name could be destroyed? If he helped them a little, he could help himself.

He didn't have much to confess. All his contact had been through dead letter drops or pick-ups from anonymous messages. There were some names from his university days, but they had long since been imprisoned, killed or had gone underground. However, there was one name that interested them enormously: George Peterson. He knew they were interested because one of them left the room almost as soon as he spoke it.

CHAPTER TEN

As Evans' Air Zimbabwe DC-10 took off from Gatwick airport, a man slipped away to call MI5's office in London's Curzon Street. And, within two hours, as the plane approached the Mediterranean coast of Africa, the phone rang in the Harare house owned by a Mr Paul Herson. Someone left a cryptic message to say that the fertiliser for his garden had been despatched as expected.

Swanepoel received the information non-commitally. He had already resigned himself to this additional task, but he wasn't very happy. He had quite enough on his plate.

❖

Wang Bi Nan wasn't briefed on the fresh information from London until his advance party booked into a three bedroom suite at Harare's Sheraton Hotel two days before Evan's departure.

He couldn't really blame anyone. Communications during the earlier part of the African trip had not been secure enough for his people in Peking to pass on such sensitive material. As far as he knew, it had originated in London, probably from British intelligence. Harold Williams might be involved, or possibly the CIA. He didn't know, and he didn't really care. What mattered was the new threat from Evans; the man was an infernal nuisance.

When Wang first learnt that the Englishman would be in Harare at the same time, he had resolved to have him put under routine surveillance, but at that stage there had been no reason to suspect he was there for anything other than a professional commitment. Now there was a real danger the whole operation could be blown. If Evans made contact with the ANC in Harare there was no telling what the consequences might be. Evans would have to be dealt with: this time, properly.

❖

It was one of those chance encounters. As Jenny walked into a political meeting about Northern Ireland, she heard a familiar voice.

'Jenny!'

'Lesley!' she returned the greeting warmly. 'It's ages since I saw you.'

'Yes – and you're a star now, I see,' her friend teased.

Jenny blushed. 'Only temporarily, I very much hope.' They hugged each other.

Jenny had always looked up to Lesley Stapleton. The two had been close friends at university. Afterwards they had been involved in various political campaigns together. Lesley was the more politically sophisticated of the two, always ready with a quote from a socialist thinker or a feminist writer to back up an argument. Her breadth of knowledge was a little intimidating. Tall and dark, she wore tinted glasses and travelled about London by bicycle.

'Look,' Lesley hesitated, as if uncertain, 'I was just thinking ... How long were you intending to stay at the meeting?'

'To the end, I suppose, but I'm easy. I came mainly to hear Sue.'

'So did I. How about slipping away after that? They'll only have loads of irrelevant questions and sectarian speeches from the floor.'

'Fine.'

Sue Brown, a backbench Labour MP, was unusual in that she managed to combine an enthusiastic following amongst Party activists with a growing reputation in Parliament. This had led some pundits to tip her for a top job, perhaps *the* top job, in the future. She was the third speaker and, from the warmth of the spontaneous clapping which broke out when she rose, most of the audience had come to listen to her.

Jenny noted not only what she was saying but how she said it. Her style was a mix of passion, logic and a gentleness, which made her most controversial case seem so reasonable and moderate. She didn't hector the meeting, she talked to people, rather than at them.

'We are now in the third decade of failed Government policies. The violence continues. The conflict continues. The bitterness continues. When will it all end? I'll tell you when. The day Britain admits it is a part of the problem. The day we create conditions in which the Irish people can themselves determine their own democratic structures and their own destiny. The day Britain declares its firm intention to withdraw. It won't be easy and there are many risks. The risk of violence. The risk that political obstinacy and prejudice will hijack the process of negotiating a settlement. But there are no easy solutions to the Irish crisis – only least worst ones. We should have the courage to make a start. Otherwise ...' she paused, holding the silent meeting in the palm of her hand, 'Otherwise the way things are going, Britain will be in the North forever.'

When the applause had died down, Jenny and Lesley slipped out and walked down the road to a wine bar.

As she poured out two glasses from a bottle of house red, Lesley explained that she had recently given up her job as a probation officer to work full-time for the Anti-Apartheid Movement in their Mandela Street headquarters.

'By the way, I thought you did really well to weather all those awful media attacks. Red Jen! God, what a joke. Except of course that it was a very effective smear job. But tell me about the Greenpeace business.'

It took about half an hour for Jenny to outline her experiences. 'If I'd known you were working for Anti-Apartheid, I'd have rung you up,' she said.

'Why?'

'It's a long story and I'm not sure what it all adds up to. But it seems possible that there might be some co-operation between Peking and Pretoria over nuclear weapons.'

'What? That's dynamite.' Her friend looked shocked – then thoughtful. 'Who else have you told.'

'I wanted someone reliable to get the information to the ANC. But it's all right, I managed to pass it on safely.'

Lesley looked relieved. Then she frowned. 'Who did you contact.'

'A friend put me in touch with John Howells of Azania Liberation. I can tell you, it took a load off my shoulders passing it on to him.'

'Howells! Azania Liberation! Fucking hell, Jenny you must be bonkers! What are you, a bloody political virgin or something?'

The uncharacteristic ferocity almost rocked Jenny back in her chair. Her face reddened visibly. 'What on earth do you mean?' she stammered.

Her friend reached out and touched her hand. 'I'm sorry. It's just that I've had a bellyful of the Azania Group. They have been such a headache. Always clashing with our London events. Supporting tiny Trotskyist sects within the liberation movement. A real problem. They are damaging our public image just at a time when the ANC are trying to get accepted into the political mainstream.'

'But they are so utterly dedicated. Their 24-hour picket ... I've never seen such motivated young activists ...'

'That's not the whole story, though, Jenny.' Lesley paused, weighing her words carefully. 'Do you know much about the CIA?'

'What's the CIA got to do with it?'

'A great deal. Listen, many on the left think that the CIA is only interested in fostering right-wing causes: the Contras in Nicaragua in the 1980s, the

Colonels' Coup in Greece in the 1960s, Atlanticist trade union front groups, and so on. But that's only part of the picture. Basically they are interested in getting a foot in the corridors of power, whichever group happens to be occupying them at the time, anything that helps them safeguard American business and military interests. In a situation like South Africa where it's not yet clear who will come out on top, they may back a number of different, sometimes competing, groups. They're hedging their bets.'

Jenny nodded, 'Doesn't surprise me.'

'Our information is that they are funding the Azania Liberation Committee as a direct alternative to the Anti-Apartheid Movement. It's pretty reliable information from foreign intelligence sources sympathetic to us, though of course we can't prove it. John Howells is on their payroll. So are a few others prominent in the Group. As for the rest – especially the young student activists – they are almost certainly unaware of the situation. The truth is that the Anti-Apartheid Movement can seem overly bureaucratic and cautious, especially to the radical young interested in direct action. The Azania Group offers them the opportunity for that direct action. Most of them are genuine and committed campaigners against apartheid.'

'So, in telling John Howells, I've told the CIA have I?' Jenny looked forlorn, cupping her glass in both hands. 'You'd better introduce me to a proper ANC person then.'

'That's not the problem. I can arrange a get-together easily. I'm much more worried about who else the CIA have told.'

'They are not going to be very interested in undermining the Peking Government, are they?' Jenny's question was rhetorical. 'It's doing pretty well by the West, opening up trade, lifting the bamboo curtain.'

'I agree. But I think we have to assume they've told British intelligence. And if the rightist faction in MI5 hasn't passed it on to the South Africans, the CIA might have done so themselves. They have had close links with Pretoria's agents in the past. In which case, Jenny, you and your friend could be in danger again.'

❖

When Makuyana arrived for his appointment at the President's office, he was surprised to be asked to wait for an audience with the man himself. He sat down in one of the outer offices gazing idly at the television in the corner.

Although the news was on, he hardly noticed what was being said. Suddenly, all his attention was on the screen. It was her! 'Red Jen', being interviewed in London. She looked better than in her newspaper picture, quite glamorous really. And she wasn't doing badly either. Though slightly nervous, she kept returning to her central message about the nuclear connection between Pretoria and Peking, fending off questions about her friendship with the murdered man. A natural Makuyana thought. The President's secretary interrupted his viewing. Robert Mugabe was a man of medium height, with shiny steel rimmed spectacles and piercing eyes. His rather austere, even severe, public manner concealed a warm personality. Mugabe had been an old comrade in the days of liberation. Although that was years ago now, Mugabe greeted Makuyana warmly, clasping both hands.

'Keith. Good to see you.'

'I was expecting to meet one of your aides.'

'Yes, yes, I know.' Mugabe looked impatient – a man with a lot on his mind, 'but I wanted to talk to you alone. I don't like the smell of this, Keith. Not one little bit. China is an old ally. Without her help, who knows whether ZANU would have triumphed. Nkomo and ZAPU might well have got into power with the backing of western capital. I find it difficult to accept that there is a link between Peking and Pretoria. In a few days we have the Leader's delegation visiting us. It is a very important visit. Perhaps the most important since independence. Our economy needs supporting and Peking can help us. It is a critical time. I don't want anything going wrong.'

Makuyana briefed him fully. Half an hour later, he was shown out, bearing a certificate with Robert Mugabe's personal authority to take extra powers and commandeer extra resources where necessary. He left a grim-looking President who waved aside complaints from his personal staff that the meeting had over-run its time and that his subsequent appointments for the day would cascade into each other. To hell with the other appointments. If something wasn't done about this situation they wouldn't be worth a candle anyway.

❖

Jenny was alone. Although it was nearly four miles to her flat she had decided to walk the full distance. She needed to think. Her mind was in turmoil. She felt bitter with herself: sheer incompetence. Jim couldn't have made a bigger mess of it if he'd tried.

The rain had stopped. She loved the cool, fresh smell of the city, washed clean and glistening in the dark. The streets resounded with the swish of vehicle tyres in the wet. The pavements were deserted, light reflecting from puddles into the corners of the night. It was late. She knew she shouldn't really be out on her own like this. But, she had to clear her mind. For the first time since the affair had begun, she felt beaten. It was as if all the adrenalin that had kept her going through the Greenpeace publicity had drained away. The wine hadn't helped. She was quite sober now, but she knew she shouldn't have drunk half a bottle without any food.

Nobody took any interest in her as she trudged through the night.She walked across Waterloo Bridge, St Paul's looming gracefully to her left and the Houses of Parliament to her right. London could be spectacular at night, especially along the Thames. Unless of course you were homeless in which case it was cold and desolate. She looked over towards the concrete arches alongside the Royal Festival Hall where people were lined up in their cardboard boxes sleeping off another weary day of begging.

She walked on, down through Vauxhall, towards Clapham and her flat in Balham. Her mind was clearing now. She would ring Jim when she got home. He had to be warned. They might even try again to kill him. Jenny shuddered, it was like a bad nightmare returning to plague her. All the elements present in the China trip were re-appearing: once more he was caught outside his familiar surroundings with unseen forces closing in on him, an innocent amidst the professionals. The more she thought about it, the more she wanted to be with him. She was just an amateur herself, but if she was there beside him, maybe she could give some protection. As she walked down along Clapham Common, its shadows licking at her feet, she was consumed by guilt. It was all her fault. She had put him in danger. How could she ever forgive herself?

When she reached her flat she went straight to the phone. International directory inquiries produced the number of the Sheraton Hotel with astonishing speed, but reception refused to put her through to Jim's room. None of the conference delegates were to be disturbed. They were tired after a long flight. However she could leave a message. But what could she say? Phone me back? How frustrating, how utterly puny.

It was well after midnight when she gathered up all her spare change and left her flat for a call box down the road; it was not worth taking a chance on her own phone since it might be monitored. She rang through to airline bookings at Gatwick and discovered there was a seat available on the next day's Air Zimbabwe flight to Harare. Without hesitation, she reserved it on her credit card.

She didn't know how she would afford it, nor how her boss would take her request for immediate leave. But at least she would be *doing something*, instead of waiting idly nearly 5,000 miles away in the comparative safety of London.

Before she left, the next day, having convinced her boss to grant her immediate compassionate leave from work, Jenny made two other calls. The first was to the Sheraton in Harare again; still no luck. She decided not to warn Jim that she was coming, that might alert their opponents. *Their* opponents. She was already being swept back into the twilight world of suspicion and fear.

Her second call was to her Aunt Ruth who nipped next door to call her neice back from a neighbour's house; the two had arranged this precautionary measure before she had left Burton Bradstock with the copy of Sewell's documents. Their conversation was brief. Jenny told her where she was going and why: somebody had to know in case anything went wrong. And who better than her Aunt? She trusted Ruth implicitly. Her parents certainly wouldn't understand.

Then she caught a cab home, packed hurriedly and took the train for Gatwick Airport. It was not until Sussex disappeared and the English Channel lay nestling far below that it fully hit her: she had taken an irrevocable step, a foolhardy, costly and futile one at that. She was off to a strange country on an even stranger mission – and without anywhere to stay. Was it for love or out of guilt? Both perhaps, she reasoned – though she had to admit love might just have the upper hand.

❖

Venter and Coetzee returned from their trip, bronzed and considerably the wiser about Zimbabwe's archeological heritage.

They caught a cab to the safe house and, despite having a front door key, entered it gingerly. It had been rented for a year and the owners had left it fully furnished. There was a grandfather clock ticking away in the hall. It reminded them of a timer: the countdown had begun.

In another part of the city, Swanepoel was driving down the street toward his home. He suddenly found himself on full alert. He didn't know why. There appeared to be nothing out of the ordinary. Nevertheless, he found himself sweeping the vicinity like a radar on the look-out for something out of place.

People talked about having a 'sixth sense' in a casual way that Swanepoel found hard to accept. His had always stood him in good stead. He didn't pretend to understand what it was. There were all sorts of fancy theories about it. But the plain fact was it had saved him from bother time after time. Like now.

Suddenly he knew he was being watched. If anybody had stopped him and said 'prove it', he wouldn't have been able to do so. He didn't have to. The tell-tale tingling up his spine was quite sufficient.

There were less than five seconds for him to decide what to do. Were they onto him? How serious was it? Did he have time to make an exit gracefully or should he just run now?

He pulled into his drive and parked. As he climbed out he noticed a car in the driveway of a house on the opposite side of the road. Although it was an unfamiliar car, there was a man working on the engine, for all the world as if it was his own house. To someone else it would have looked a perfectly innocent scene. To Swanepoel it signalled danger.

From the moment he had moved in he had planned for such an eventuality. There wasn't anything incriminating in the house, though he wouldn't care to trust his luck if they brought in sniffer dogs: the weapons and the explosives he had stored there were long since gone, but they might still pick up the smell.

He looked out the window. Nothing different. The man still appeared to be fixing his car. There was no-one else in sight. His house had not been searched: it was just as he had left it but he had made up his mind. He grabbed some personal belongings. Still no action outside. He made a brief phone call to a direct line in the city centre. The man at the other end would recognise the real meaning of the otherwise innocuous query about share prices: Swanepoel was moving out – and this time there was no coming back.

The man bending over his car engine didn't rushed to follow the target

Herson. That was the beauty of a homing device: you could follow at a distance. It wasn't as good in a real chase, because you were never near enough to respond to any smart dodges. But in these circumstances it was ideal.

Half an hour after the target had stopped, the agent located Herson's car parked outside a house on the other side of the city. He radioed through to Florence Sithole who noted the address down carefully. It was time she took over the surveillance herself she thought. Something was about to break. She didn't know what exactly, but she sensed things were coming to a head.

Makuyana picked up the phone on his desk – an action that would never be quite the same again for him after the way Robert Temba had died six weeks before. Now he always lifted the receiver with involuntary apprehension.

It was Selby Mngadi calling. 'Some news Keith. Don't bother any more about questioning my aides. George Peterson has skipped.'

'What!'

'Yes. Done a bunk. He disappeared yesterday without a trace. None of our people can locate him. If your outfit can keep a look-out that would be very helpful, though I don't think you'll find him.'

'That's a real setback.' Makuyana knew he sounded downbeat. There was no point pretending: Peterson would have been an invaluable conduit into the enemy – if they had managed to get to him in time.

'Anyway, it's not all bad news, Keith. At least we know who the nigger in the woodpile was.' Mngadi laughed uproariously.

'I suppose so.'

While they made small talk for a minute, Makuyana's mind was racing ahead. So Craven had been genuine after all. He felt guilty at having doubted the man. What had happened to the young Afrikaner? And how had they found out about Peterson's cover being blown?

Swanepoel was confident he hadn't been followed. He had taken the usual precautions to shake off a tail and he had been too long at the game to make a mistake. The only real worry was that he didn't know how they had rumbled him. What about his controller in the City? If Zimbabwe security was onto him, they would probably have tapped his phone and that could have led to his controller.

The new house was fine. More spacious than his bungalow – just as well because he now had a lodger. The informant Peterson was about to be transferred into his care. It was a pain. Having a Coloured on your side was one thing, expecting you to look after the bugger was something else again. Surely he wasn't expected to treat the guy as a buddy? First Evans, now Peterson. How did they expect him to concentrate on the main task in hand, the thing they had all been working towards? It was just as well Venter and Coetzee were so good. Otherwise he would have been in real trouble.

Evans' itinerary had been supplied to him by British intelligence. Why couldn't *they* take him out? Despite his irritation, the question answered itself. Too risky for the Brits. Even he had to admit that.

Tomorrow Evans was due to give a paper at the conference and Swanepoel had managed to acquire a ticket. He would try to size the man up. And after that? He knew his days in Harare were numbered. In a way it was a relief. Whatever KJ said, he knew he was getting too old for this sort of caper. It was time to go home.

❖

Wang's meeting with Venter and Coetzee was a strained affair. He didn't care for racists. His alliance with South Africa was one of pure convenience. As for these two, they were an arrogant pair. Not cocky – they were too professional for that sort of self-indulgence – just plain bloody arrogant: supremely confident of their physical prowess and, he suspected, of their racial superiority too.

He spent two hours going over all the details with them, checking and re-checking, clarifying and re-clarifying. Nothing could be left to chance.

But as Wang departed and made his way back to the Sheraton, he had a curious sense of emptiness. After all the months of intrigue, the pressure and the strain, there was little he could do now. Just wait. And hope it all went to plan.

❖

As the limousines wound their way in a cavalcade through the streets of

Harare the Old Man watched from the windows. Africa had a special feeling, almost a rhythm to it.

The Zimbabwe top brass had all been present to greet them on their arrival. Mugabe himself had led the welcome as the Leader came down the steps from the Air China Boeing: a sign of the importance and respect attached to the visitors.

As the countryside around the airport receded and the city began to swallow them, the Old Man found himself thinking ahead. If all went according to plan, in a little over 72 hours he would be making those phone calls to the army leadership in Peking and key Party bosses in the cities of Shanghai, Chengtu and Nanking. The calls to the Generals would be the most important. The garrison stationed at Peking would move fast to surround strategic buildings and place most members of the Politburo under arrest. At least one of the Generals was known to be reluctant, so the Old Man had to ensure the others moved first, producing a *fait accompli*.

There was bound to be a period of unrest and uncertainty. Party officials and middle-ranking army officers would want to see which way the wind was blowing before they committed themselves. That was why the Old Man knew he would have to cut short his stay in Zimbabwe and fly home to take personal command. In a way it was a pity he could not have organised things so as to be on the spot at home; but at least this way he would be free from suspicions of involvement in a conspiracy. He could be seen to return to Peking with clean hands, a saviour for his country at a time of crisis.

❖

Sitting on the platform of the Sheraton's smaller conference hall, waiting to begin his lecture, Evans was feeling refreshed. He had enjoyed a deep sleep after the long flight. And the hotel was astonishing: a towering cream complex just to the west of the city centre, five-star luxury. Besides the usual restaurants, bars and shopping arcade, it had a swimming pool, tennis courts and a gymnasium.

His brief forays into the city had been like leafing through a history book. Up Julius Nyerere Way, left down Stanley Avenue, along Kenneth Kaunda Avenue and Park Lane: a nice juxtaposition of the modern face of Africa and its colonial antecedents.

The only slightly niggling concern was the message from Jenny. Why was she calling him from London? Was something the matter? He had not been able to get hold of her either at home or at work. But for the moment he cleared these thoughts from his head, concentrating on the talk before him.

While he waited for the introductory remarks from the chair to end he had assessed his audience. Mostly academics mixed in with a fair proportion of government scientists, it was a thoroughly professional group. He was at home among his peers, save for a handful of outsiders to whom tickets had been allocated by local embassy officials and half a dozen journalists. There were delegates from all over the world. Many spoke English, albeit as a second language, but a third needed interpreter facilities and wore earphones. He wondered how much of what he had to say would be conveyed accurately by the translators; the irony was nobody would ever know.

His lecture was delivered with rather more passion than normal, partly because of the subject, but also because, since his experiences in China, he felt a new sense of social responsibility and an urgency about communicating what he knew. However, his analysis was cool and factual. Though he could admire polemic from other speakers – Jenny came to mind, for example – he felt uncomfortable with it himself. His was the business of objective, scientific inquiry, he could not afford to toy with the speculative, the value-ridden.

'By the turn of the century,' he began, 'a total of 2,000 tonnes of plutonium will have been produced by the world's civilian nuclear reactors, and production will be running at around 160 tonnes a year.' He paused, letting the enormity of the facts sink in. 'To give you a comparison, today the world contains about 700 tonnes of civilian plutonium and production is running at nearly 80 tonnes a year. So, in under ten years, output will have more than doubled.'

'Now the danger is this. As against these huge quantities, just a minute 35 kilograms of plutonium oxide is sufficient to generate a nuclear explosive. And, if the plutonium oxide is converted to plutonium metal – a fairly straightforward chemical process – even less is needed for a nuclear explosive: just 10 kilograms.'

Evans deliberately paused to drink some water. It was always difficult plying an audience, even a highly informed one, with such large slabs of data. They needed time to absorb what he had said.

'This poses an enormous, and I would suggest impossible, security problem. We do not have (and nor is it conceivable we are likely to obtain) the kind of sophisticated technology to detect the theft of such relatively tiny quantities of plutonium when thousands of kilograms are separated each year. The risks of theft are very high indeed.'

Evans continued talking for forty-five minutes, covering each angle, backing up each fact by referring to the appropriate sources. The essential argument was simple enough, but the scientists he was addressing traded in scepticism; that was in the nature of their discipline.

In his conclusion he departed completely from his written paper. 'If we are serious about meeting the threat I have described, there is only one way we can significantly reduce, if not eliminate, it. That is by banning reprocessing. Instead, spent reactor fuel elements should be permanently disposed of; the risk of theft of these elements is non-existent for they are so highly radioactive that they effectively shield themselves from being stolen.'

Evans gatherered up his notes and sat down to applause which he noted seemed to rise above the conventionally courteous. The lecture had clearly made an impact. As he listened to the vote of thanks and the concluding comments from the chair, he wished Jenny had been there to hear it. I must try and ring her again, he thought, and he found himself longing to hear her voice again. He couldn't get her out of his mind. He thought so frequently and intensely about her, it was almost becoming a distraction from his work. He had never been in this situation before. Until now, his work had been almost the entire focus of his adult life. The surprising truth was he didn't really mind the distraction. He was finding out things about himself that he never knew.

❖

Although Makuyana had put out an alert to trace the ANC defector, George Peterson, he shared Mngadi's pessimism about finding the man. He might already be out of the country.

For the moment his priority was the Chinese leadership's visit. So far everything had gone smoothly. The arrival had gone like clockwork. The visitors, safely ensconsed in the Chinese Embassy, had already attended their first meeting and reception. Makuyana had been a guest at the latter too, partly duty, partly social. He hadn't felt relaxed there. Wearing a collar and tie was bad enough, but making small talk got him down. It was little comfort that many of the other guests appeared to be similarly tense, especially the wives dragged about behind their important husbands. Did *anybody* really enjoy such occasions?

He did, however, have the honour of being introduced by the President to the Chinese Leader and his Ministers. It was hard to assess them. They shook hands and bowed politely, courteous and impassive. If anything went wrong they knew who to blame, Mugabe had joked.

The Leader was a small bespectacled man shaped rather like a cone, his body widening out steadily from his guant narrow head. His two accompanying Ministers were very different. One, the Trade Minister, was young and fully at ease in the cosmopolitan gathering – clearly a man of the new reformist era, Makuyana guessed. The other was considerably older, with an almost imperious air; he must be one of the old guard.

Their security people were quite easy to get on with and Makuyana's staff had reported a good working relationship. That was a relief. Often there could be real tension as visiting and domestic personnel inevitably strayed onto what each felt was their own patch. Florence Sithole had checked through the list of aides on the party and reported that she had made contact with all except several attached to one of the Ministers who had arrived early and were staying at the Sheraton. Wherever the Delegation went, there would be an advance party of police and his staff sweeping the route, checking on buildings, monitoring surroundings. Nothing special, the sort of thing you usually laid on for foreign leaders. He had been over the details again and again to the point where his staff had clearly become resentful. There was nothing he could point to, nothing he could put into words, but he was on edge; something didn't smell right.

❖

Evans mixed with the delegates at the rear of the hall, chatting about various aspects of his lecture over coffee. Some probed the detail of his argument, others wanted to chat socially. They had half an hour before the next session, the final one of the afternoon.

The lecture seemed to have gone down well; a good omen for the talk he had to deliver on radiation two days later. After the initial cluster of academics had made their points, someone hovering on the edge of the crowd stepped forward. She was a local reporter, notebook in hand, eyes shining keenly as she sought clarification. Had any of this material been published before, she wanted to know? How new a story was it? He told her that much of the evidence had been published, mostly in scientific journals, but as far as he knew nobody else had drawn it all together and pointed out the global implications.

'It's a nightmare. My news editor will go big on this. I must rush. Deadline to meet.' She smiled and thanked him for his assistance and quickly left the hall.

Evans turned, almost bumping into an elderly man. 'Sorry! I didn't see you there.'

'No problem, sir,' the man spoke with a thick accent, 'I wonder if I might ask a favour?' He didn't wait for Evan's response. 'I am a local photographer. Your lecture seems to have stirred up a heck of a lot of interest. Could I have a picture outside in front of the conference centre?'

Evans looked at his watch. 'There's only five minutes to go until we begin again. I can't be late. Will it take long?'

'Just a couple of minutes. I need some decent light. Also, the background will make a more interesting picture for our readers.'

As they hurried out, Evans was preoccupied. What was the man's accent? It was a lot stronger than that of the white Zimbabweans he had met around the conference. He blinked into the bright sunlight.

'Just over there please,' the man pointed to a van parked by the kerbside, 'My camera's in the back. I can get a nice wide-angle portrait from there with the Sheraton behind you.'

Evans followed obligingly. The man opened the back door and reached inside. The engine was running. Odd, Evans thought. Then the man turned, the expression on his face quite different: hard and businesslike. He was carrying a gun.

'Quick! Inside!'

Almost before he knew it, Evans found himself half pushed half-clambering into the back of the van. The doors were slammed and in the next instant the van drove off. His head banged against the offside wheel arch. He was dazed. What was happening to him? Everything was a blur. He couldn't think straight.

Jenny hardly noticed the countryside around Harare as her taxi sped towards the Conference Centre. She had told the airport immigration official that she was here on holiday. Where was she staying? With a friend, Jim Evans, at the Sheraton Hotel; her answer had come quite spontaneously. She had changed some money at the airport. It was ridiculous. She had come with one hundred pounds sterling in cash drawn from a dispenser at Heathrow. She had no time to get the local currency before she left and no idea whether her credit card would be accepted out here. But at least she was here. She could think only about reaching Jim as soon as possible. She was almost certain he was in danger. He must be warned. He must be protected. For now, the absolute priority was to get to Jim. It was late afternoon and the light was beginning to fade.

The cab stopped in front of the hotel and she fumbled for the fare, unfamiliar with the new currency. Grabbing her case, she rushed in and asked for the conference hall. Which one? The receptionist explained patiently that there were five conferences going on.

'I don't know what it's called.' She sounded feeble, she felt feeble, realising she didn't even know the title of the bloody thing. 'Lots of international scientists are attending', she blurted out.

'The World Academy of Environmental Physics? Could that be it?'

'Yes – I suppose so.' It sounded august enough.

'Down there,' the receptionist pointed to a notice leading the way to the conference centre. You want Hall number 3.'

'Thank you. Can I leave my baggage, please?'

'Are you staying?'

'Yes,' she replied involuntarily.

'Your name, please.'

'Evans, Jennifer Evans. My husband's already booked in. I was to follow.' She found herself making it all up as she went along. Mrs Evans! Despite the tension, she had a smile at her own expense. Long ago, she had decided never to give up her maiden name.

The receptionist checked a list, frowning. 'I'm sorry, Mrs Evans, only your husband has been booked in.'

'There must be a mistake. Look, can you keep my things while I get hold of him. Then we can sort it out.' Christ! All this trivia. She was screaming inside to get to him. She half ran, half walked, through the plush corridors to the conference hall, conscious of people watching her, a hurrying figure, out of place in these leisurely surroundings.

There was a desk outside the entrance to the hall. 'Are you registered, dear?'

The woman at the desk stopped her going inside.

'I'm afraid I'm not. But my husband Jim Evans is giving a lecture and I need to talk to him urgently.'

'Ah, yes, Mr Evans,' she glanced down at some papers, 'He gave his lecture earlier in the afternoon. They are nearing the end of the following session now. Do you want to wait for him. It'll be over in ten minutes.'

'No. Please. It's an emergency. Can I go in and find him?'

Perhaps the woman noticed how distraught she was, perhaps she was just being sympathetic. 'Well, I have strict instructions to admit only those with passes. But why don't you just slip in and see if you can spot him.'

Jenny found herself at the side of the hall. A large number of delegates turned to watch her as the door swung shut. It reminded her of the many other conferences she had attended. Any to-ing and fro-ing had a disruptive effect; people couldn't help turning to see what the distraction was. But there the comparison ended. This gathering had a studious, heavy air about it, more formal than anything she was used to.

She scanned the rows of seats. No sign of Jim. She supposed he might have spotted her coming in. Virtually everybody else seemed to have done so. Mind you, he would probably be concentrating so deeply that nothing else would impinge on his little world. Typical.

Somebody from the floor was droning on monotonously. She didn't know what he was talking about. She felt a fool, just standing there. To hell with Jim. Where was he? She wandered quietly round to a seat in the back row. At least she could be inconspicuous there. Still no sign of him. Just rows of mostly male heads stretching in front of her.

Eventually – it seemed like a long time, though in fact she realised it was only about fifteen minutes – the conference adjourned, the delegates rose and began milling about. She made her way to the front and approached the chair, a grey-haired man with a bow tie.

'Where can I find Professor Evans, please?'

He scanned the hall, his brow creasing. 'Can't see him my dear. Hang on, I'll make an announcement.' He moved across the platform and leant towards the main microphone. 'Will Professor Evans please come to the front?'

At the interruption, all the delegates looked round briefly, then returned to their conversations. 'That's odd. He was here earlier all right. He gave the early afternoon lecture. Bit rude of him to skip the following one. Sorry, dear, I suggest you leave a message at the desk outside, or try reception. He may have slipped back to his room.'

But he couldn't have done so, Jenny thought, unless he had been in his room when I arrived.

She checked again with the woman on the desk and with reception. Jim's key was there, so he wasn't in his room. Then a porter came up, carrying a briefcase.

'This was left in conference hall 3.' Jenny glanced over at the briefcase.

'That's my husband's!'

'Are you sure?' The receptionist started to look suspicious.

'Yes. Absolutely sure.' A feeling of total despair washed over her. She knew that something was badly wrong. Jim wasn't the sort to disappear from a conference like this. Even if he had gone for a walk, he wouldn't have left his briefcase lying around. He wouldn't even leave it locked up in a car when they had gone out together after work. It stuck to him like a leech.

'I want to speak to the security services,' she found herself saying in a shaky voice.

❖

Venter and Coetzee felt good about the job. It was so unusual having someone on the inside, feeding all the details. They could plan their operation with absolute precision.

In the last two days they had staged two rehearsals, even to the extent of diving into the get-away car and timing the dash to the airport, so that they would be just in time to catch the flight out to Paris. They would have checked in their baggage well beforehand, to ensure it would just be a question of walking through, a quick body search, clearing passports and then onto the plane. The timing was perfect. Enough leeway to allow for traffic problems, but not too much for the shutters to come down at the airport.

Their equipment had been checked again and again. The stun grenades were to stage a decoy, the rifles for the assassination. The only slight problem was their visibility. A shame, since it was never comfortable operating out in the open, but that's the way it would have to be. Two days to go. They would relax, play some cards, watch lots of videos. They had enough food and drink; they had better stay inside, safely out of sight.

Florence Sithole was doing a spell on watch duty herself when the action began. Suddenly a Ford transit van had driven out of the garage attached to the side of the house where Herson was holed up. She hardly caught a sight of the driver; whoever he was, he seemed to be alone. She couldn't tell whether there was anybody in the back. She radioed back for a check to be done on the registration number. A pity they didn't have more resources so that she could tail the van while someone else maintained a watch on the house. But they were badly stretched just at the moment, what with the Chinese visit on top of everything else.

A few hours later the dark blue van had returned and backed into the garage, and Florence had watched as the driver closed the door: one that folded down from the inside, concertina style. The people who had designed and built these houses with a connecting door straight into the garage obviously hadn't considered the problems of external surveillance. Forty minutes later a minicab had arrived and dropped off a man who looked like an Asian. He might be a local, he might be foreign. She couldn't tell.

After that everything was quiet again, almost eerily so. Florence had reported the activity and sat back to wait again. It was dark now. She would find it increasingly difficult to see what was going on.

❖

Swanepoel knew he was taking a chance, but there was no time to do anything else. He phoned his man in the city centre company with the curt message: 'NOSLEN One Exit.' Back at home they would know he was having to get out in a hurry and they would be ready near the border to take him over.

It was too risky to stay in Harare now, especially with Evans on board. What was the point anyway? The boys were all set. He couldn't do anything more. His instructions were to get Evans and Peterson out as quickly as possible, the former for interrogation, the latter for de-briefing. He would have preferred to kill them himself, but they both had to be questioned.

Evans was obviously in a deep state of shock. He seemed totally confused: such a contrast with the confident professor lecturing from the rostrum only a few hours earlier. Wang, the Chinaman, had arrived to question him, but Evans kept repeating that he was simply an academic attending a conference.

He seemed to be telling the truth. Frankly, he looked completely out of his depth. But you never could tell. Swanepoel would know the answer when he went to work on him over the border.

❖

Not more aggro. Surely not. Makuyana couldn't believe something else was being dumped on his lap. A visiting English Professor had disappeared shortly after giving a lecture at the Sheraton, and now his wife was making all sorts of allegations, having insisted on seeing the security services rather than talking to the police. He would talk to her briefly and then get rid of her – delegate responsibility to a subordinate. He couldn't head up the missing people's bureau on top of all his other responsibilities.

There was a knock on the door.

'Mrs Evans for you, Sir.'

Makuyana looked up, without enthusiasm. Then he frowned. Her face was vaguely familiar. He had been only half concentrating when she arrived. Now he looked closely, all his attention focused, his initial mood of irritation subsiding. Who was she? He knew – surely? Yes – bugger me, it was the woman in the paper and on TV, the one involved in the China nuclear episode. What did they call her – 'Red Jen' wasn't it? What on earth was she doing here?

❖

Jenny entered Makuyana's office feeling psychologically bruised and emotionally drained. The security people hadn't shown much faith in the urgency of her story. They had resented her pushiness in demanding to see the top man. Why, they hardly ever got to see him themselves.

Now expecting to be given the brush-off again, she was surprised to see the man's face change from an expression of neutral indifference to one of startled interest. He pulled over a seat for her.

'Your husband has disappeared, I understand. How can I help? Surely this is a police matter?' he said, but his tone was sympathetic, even supportive. He had a striking face, deep and strong – though she didn't know what to make of the dark glasses: rather intimidating, though perhaps out of tune with his manner?

'To begin with, Professor Evans is not really my husband. We are just good friends.' How embarrassing to trot out that old cliché. 'I don't really know where to begin.' She had got this far, all the way from London, all the way to this man, and now she couldn't get herself together! Her self-confidence had gone just when she needed it most.

He took her by surprise again. 'You are the one they call "Red Jen", aren't you?'

'How on earth do you know that?' She was dumbfounded.

'I happened to see an English newspaper with a story about you. Then I saw you interviewed on TV. The subject was close to my heart.'

'Greenpeace?'

'No, China and the nuclear connection.'

A confusion of thoughts tumbled through Jenny's mind. It was uncanny, as if this man had suddenly unlocked the door and switched the light on. There was someone to talk to at last. Someone who might understand. Someone who had the power to act. She was so relieved, she felt almost tearful. It had suddenly become very tiring playing the game on her own.

'It's a long story,' he was saying. 'But leave that aside for a moment. Tell me why you are here and what you think has happened to Professor Evans.'

Jenny told him about the visit to China, about Dick Sewell, about the mistake she had made in passing on the South African angle, about her reasons for flying out.

She saw from his expression that, strange as it was, her story was making some kind of sense to this man. As soon as she mentioned the South African link he reached for the phone and gave an instruction for someone called Florence to be contacted.

❖

No, it wasn't really happening. It couldn't be. For Evans, the events of the last few hours had blurred into each other. First the abduction straight from his academic ivory tower to the brutal world which he had briefly inhabited back in China. Then Wang's unexpected appearance. Wang? What the hell was *he* doing out here?

The man had been his old self: arrogant, accusatory, nasty. He kept demanding to know what Evans was *really* doing in Harare. Evans kept telling him he was attending a bona fide academic conference.

'You are lying again,' Wang screamed, 'Lying again as you did in China. We should have finished you off then.'

He disappeared as suddenly as he had arrived, and Evans could hear him talking to his abductor in muffled tones in the next room while a guard watched over him. The guard, who didn't say anything, was a tall man of mixed race. He didn't seem that hostile, more the brooding type.

There was a sound, first of a door shutting, then of receding steps. His abductor walked back into the room and gestured to the guard. Both left the room. He was on his own again. He looked out the window. Nobody in sight. Just a garden and what was presumably a back fence. He felt more alone than ever before in his life. Perhaps this was how Sewell had felt in Hong Kong. Perhaps he would suffer the same fate.

❖

Makuyana had been going over Jenny's story in detail, making the odd note. The English professor had been seen talking to an elderly man just before he disappeared from the Sheraton, a man who fitted the description of the suspect in the Robert Temba case. And that man Herson fitted both descriptions. Could it be that they were dealing with the same person? What was the connection?

The phone rang.

'Yes, what is it?' He sounded impatient.

'Sorry to interrupt Sir, but this has priority. The tap on the company's direct line threw up a word we have flagged. NOSLEN, Sir.'

'NOSLEN?' Makuyana was concentrating on nothing else now.

'The exact message was NOSLEN One Exit.'

NOSLEN! It was the code the ANC had discovered. Events must be moving fast. It sounded like somebody or something was getting out of Harare.

Makuyana put a call through to alert surveillance on the border. No, he couldn't tell them what to expect, just maintain extra vigilance – and report back if there was anything unusual: like someone trying to cross into the Transvaal illegally. And if a certain Mr Herson tried to cross legally he must be detained at all cost.

Evans had been sedated without too much difficulty. He was dead to the world.

Swanepoel couldn't take a chance with the van. It might well have been identified and if so they would be looking for it. He ordered that it be moved out onto the road temporarily and replaced by his own car so they could load it in the privacy of the garage. They propped Evans up next to Peterson on the back seat. Another agent would drive. In the circumstances, Swanepoel needed as much rest as he could get. He settled into the passenger seat as the garage door opened. Then the car eased out into the road and sped off into the evening. The van quickly replaced it.

As they drove out, Florence Sithole reached for her radio and called in the details. Then she switched on her monitor. To her relief the bleeper was operating loud and clear. She would have to stay fairly close through the city streets. Only if they hit an open road would she be able to drop back.

She hadn't been able to see who was in the car since the light was bad. But she had an impression that the driver was not alone. For the last few hours she had felt lethargic, repeatedly catching herself dozing off. Now she was on full alert.

CHAPTER ELEVEN

The Nimrod cruised comfortably at an altitude of 24,000 feet, watching and listening to the world down below. Back and forth along the Zimbabwe-South Africa border, that was its regular route. From Mozambique on the east to Rhodes drift on the west – and sometimes North-West up the Botswana border to the Caprivi Strip which bordered also on Angola, Zambia and Namibia – its sophisticated surveillance equipment missed very little of note.

By now, Captain Peter Geffen was familiar with the aircraft. Bought from Britain six months earlier after a surprising concession to Zimbabwe's Government – the word was London had started hedging its bets after decades of tacit support for Pretoria – the Nimrod had been fully operational for nine weeks. Geffen and his crew had been intensively trained in England, but it was never the same on your own. For a start the terrain was so different. Wide open spaces covering thousands of square miles with nothing much happening – then sudden, concentrated bursts of movement on both sides of the border.

Apart from radar, the plane had video equipment developed from satellite technology, enabling remarkably clear pictures of the ground which could be relayed back to base. The crew were learning to distinguish between the routine and the unusual, between a small herd of wildebeest and several military vehicles. They maintained a particular watch on the airbase at Louis Trichardt, because if there was ever any serious aerial threat that was probably where it would come from. Already, the Nimrod had got used to the South Africans popping up in their Cheetah jets to have a look. There was almost a cameraderie in the air, as the Cheetahs sometimes zoomed up alongside and both sides played with each other, daring, testing how far they could go before one or the other got serious.

Nothing much had happened during the day and in such routine circumstances they were cruising, using only two of the plane's four engines. Night was closing in quickly and Geffen had just taken over from his co-pilot after a couple of hours of very welcome kip. Then a message came through from control. Someone high-up in security at Harare wanted them to maintain a special watch. There was suspicion about a possible illicit border crossing in the region of the main road southward. If Geffen spotted anything he was instructed to contact a Major Keith Makuyana direct. The request for surveillance was to take absolute priority; the President had endorsed it.

The name Makuyana was familiar enough. Although they hadn't met, Geffen knew him by repute. Tough, straight, a man who didn't mess about. A man after his own heart, Geffen thought – even though, over a decade earlier, they had been fighting on different sides in a different war. Now they were together, old adversaries turned comrades in the same struggle to protect the land of their birth.

In the early days, after ZANU had eclipsed white minority rule in 1980 and Robert Mugabe had been transformed almost overnight from the feared 'black Hitler' of white propaganda to a national statesman, Geffen's small world had been turned on its head. Initially, the switch in roles had played tricks with his sense of self-identity and certainty, but no longer. Although blacks were in power, his children had continued at the same exclusive schools, his wife had continued to work as a senior nurse, his standard of living had been maintained. Above all, he was the same professional he had always been. There was a job to be done and he would do it well, not least because he had grown to respect the dedicated people who now ran the country.

❖

The little screen fixed to the dashboard flickered in the gloom as Florence Sithole kept a close eye on the movement of the flashing dot which represented the car a mile or so ahead of her on the open road. She wished she had a colleague with her to navigate: it hadn't been easy trying to drive out in the rush-hour traffic while half-concentrating on the screen as she anxiously followed the driver's left and right turns.

At least she was on the main road now, with Harare's traffic an hour behind. Herson's vehicle showed no sign of deviating from the long drive south. Makuyana had just come on the radio to brief her on the intercepted NOSLEN message. It appeared someone was about to leave the country, and it could well be the car she was following. He told her briefly about the English woman and the information she had brought. It could be the car ahead was carrying the Professor: pure speculation of course, but it fitted the otherwise confusing picture.

Makuyana's men had raided both Herson's house and the one she had been watching. Both were clean, though sniffer dogs had located a cupboard in Herson's place where explosives and ammunition had been stored. Forensics were checking it out now. However, there was one positive lead. The blue

Ford transit parked outside had been spotted at the conference centre at about the time when Evans must have disappeared.

Despite these new dimensions, her instructions remained the same: tail at enough of a distance to avoid detection but close enough to ensure she kept in touch. They couldn't risk alerting police in Bulawayo to make an interception, because they wanted to see where the target was heading. The destination could be another safe house, in which case Makuyana wanted the address. He had a helicopter standing by with some extra operatives so that he could follow her down when things started to get lively. Meanwhile, everything was down to her. He didn't need to add that if she messed up this one, she would not be forgiven: she knew that only too well.

❖

The tension was starting to get to the Old Man. Unusually for him, he had not been eating well. It wasn't the seminar for top military strategists he was about to lead – that wouldn't tax him too much. It was the knowledge that within twenty-four hours events would reach a climax and the course of international relations would be transformed.

Nevertheless he forced his attention back to the task in hand. The thirty men sitting in a half circle before him were all senior figures in Zimbabwe's armed forces, and they were expecting to hear about the modernisation of the People's Liberation Army. Mostly re-trained at Sandhurst after spells in Peking or Pretoria, according to whether they were black or white, they appeared sharp and assertive. He wondered how much of the Chinese stamp remained on the ex-ZANU men.

His notes had been prepared by the Leader's office which had insisted on a common, modernising and reformist slant to public or semi-public pronouncements from any member of the Delegation. It was typical of the new regime, the Old Man snorted to himself: public relations came before ideology. Although he had been a Politburo accomplice to the reforms, he hadn't agreed with all of them. Yet he had to sound enthusiastic, espousing the Leader's line with no hint of deviation.He began with the famous quotation from Chairman Mao: 'Political power grows out of the barrel of a gun.' During Mao's leadership of the Party, the Peoples Liberation Army played a central role in his political strategy, the Old Man explained.

'However, in the last decade or so the PLA has changed dramatically. It has ceased to play such a major role in political and Party life. Many features of western armies have been adopted. For example, we have restored the ranking system abolished in 1965 during the cultural revolution. We now consider it has an important part to play in the modernisation process.'

He didn't add – though he would have liked to – that the old egalitarian spirit of the PLA had been extinguished, that its former status as a revered institution in Chinese society had plummeted, and that the strict enforcement of retirement age limits had meant replacing the ideological veterans of Liberation with a younger generation schooled as technocrats rather than political leaders.

'The PLA has also formed several elite rapid reaction forces, known as "First Battalions". Highly trained, with about 700 men each, they compare with anti-terrorist groups or special forces in the West, like Britain's SAS, for example.'

Again, he refrained from saying that these elite groups offended against the spirit of egalitarianism in which the PLA had been founded over 60 years ago. In the past all army units were meant to be equal. But now the elite forces received better pay, extra rations and the best equipment. Neither did the Old Man tell his attentive audience that, when about one million soldiers had been demobilised and retired in the mid-1980s, he had resisted the pressure to step down himself. He had used his influence to thwart *that* particular manoeuvre of the new Party leadership.

The Old Man spoke for about twenty minutes. He didn't need an interpreter because he was fluent in English. When he had finished, it was time for the Zimbabwe military to ask questions about the exact details of modernisation. Several officers wanted to know how the old peasant army of liberation had been transformed into an instrument of the state. Were there disciplinary problems? Had there been any resistance by the former guerrillas to bringing in and depositing their arms? The Zimbabweans were interested because they had been gone through a similar process, and it had been fraught with problems. Even now, there were still marauding bands unwilling to relinquish their relative autonomy and creating havoc in some rural areas.

'The Party ensured that the transition was smooth. The Party must be strong.' The intimidating tone of the Old Man's reply left much to the officers' imagination. But although he answered their questions dutifully and efficiently, he couldn't prevent his mind straying to the next momentous day.

❖

The blip on the screen stopped very suddenly, startling Florence Sithole into alertness despite the almost soporific warmth of her heated car. She pressed her foot down and accelerated hard.

As she came up over the brow of a hill, she realised with some relief that there was a filling station ahead. Just as well. She needed to put in more petrol too.

She eased her car into the garage fore-court, pulling up behind Herson's vehicle. It was a good opportunity to have a closer look inside. There were three passengers; the driver was dealing with the petrol attendant. She couldn't see their faces properly, but one seemed to be slumped over or asleep in the back.

As she waited for her tank to be topped up, the driver came back and the target car sped off. She didn't recognise him. Herson was probably the large one in the front passenger seat.

They had travelled a hundred miles already and were a couple of hundred miles from the border – three hours drive at the speed they had been going. Florence used the opportunity of the stop for a welcome visit to the toilet. Then she drove off the fore-court to the edge of the road where there were no buildings to interfere with reception on her radio link to Makuyana.

'Keith,' she spoke urgently into the little microphone concealed in the sun visor above her head, 'I just got a closer look when they stopped for petrol. There are four of them, one apparently asleep in the back. Herson seems to be in the passenger seat. They will hit the border in about three hours. I think you should come down now with reinforcements and alert security ahead.'

There was a pregnant pause and the line crackled, as if in anticipation. Then Makuyana responded: 'Okay. I haven't been able to get away so far because of security checks on the bloody Chinese visit. But I will board the chopper in fifteen minutes. We should be with you before they hit the border. I don't want to come too close because it might alert the enemy. On the other hand we don't want them to get over the border. It's a problem. Are they armed?'

'I couldn't see.'

'We have to assume they are. Stay in contact – and for Chrissake don't do anything dangerous.'

Jenny was aching with exhaustion, frustrated at her inability to do anything decisive. She had asked for permission to stay in Makuyana's room, watching and listening as communications and instructions came and went.

The chair was uncomfortable and it was a very long time since she had slept. But it was re-assuring to see him in action, an authoritative figure in whom she had a growing confidence. She tried to doze now and then, but her mind kept racing ahead. She snatched yet another glance at her wrist-watch: God, didn't time drag when you wanted it to go quickly.

A secretary brought in a tray of food at one point. There wasn't anything on it she should really be eating, but, partly out of politeness, partly out of sheer hunger and anxiety, Jenny consumed it all. She had been offered a bed elsewhere to rest on, but she wanted to stick closely to Makuyana for one simple reason: he didn't know it yet, but when he went after these people she was determined to go too.

His phone rang and she heard him talking to his deputy who was tailing a car southward. Why this game of cat and mouse? Why couldn't they just stop the car and rescue Jim? From what they had told her she felt almost certain that he was on board. She had listened to Makuyana's reasoning. No point in a premature interception when the car might lead you to catch bigger fish. But that wasn't much consolation to her. She just wanted Jim back in one piece.

Makuyana was giving instructions for the helicopter to be made ready to leave and for his car to be brought round immediately.

Now was the moment. She leapt to her feet, her voice urgent: 'I want to come with you please.'

He swivelled round in his chair. 'Sorry. Not possible.' A final statement. No argument. But Jenny couldn't allow herself to hear that.

'I have to come. It's the whole reason that I travelled out here from London. I put him in this mess after all. Anyway' – she added, almost as an afterthought – 'you don't know what he looks like. If you close in on the group and there is shooting, you might shoot the wrong person. Only I can identify him with absolute certainty.'

Makuyana glanced at his watch, then back at the young woman in front of him. She was determined, not just a hanger-on. He remembered that type from the anti-racist demonstrations of his student days in London in the late

1960s: the sort who would slip into a mainstream career once they left university and shift quickly rightward thereafter. She was different; a person of substance. It was against all the rules, but then this was a very unusual case. What the hell, he thought. She might even be useful.

'All right. On one condition. You do exactly what you are told.'

❖

The Nimrod's eyes had spotted something that needed further investigation. Captain Peter Geffen strained to make sense of the pictures and signals he was receiving.

There had been nothing of note since he was asked to maintain extra vigilance. But now something was happening in the direction of Louis Trichardt air base, sixty miles across the border. There was an aircraft of some sort flying very low, probably under radar level, towards Zimbabwe. It was travelling too slowly for a fighter; that meant it had to be a light civilian-type plane or a helicopter. It would probably reach the Limpopo in ten to fifteen minutes.

Geffen put in a call to Makuyana's helicopter and the security chief came straight on the line. 'We have identified a low flying aircraft – probably a chopper – heading for the border from Louis Trichardt.' He read over details of the flight path.

At the other end, Makuyana paused as he quickly translated the co-ordinates onto the pilot's map. Then he extended the line over the border. That was it! The Chopper was on course to intersect with the main road on which Herson's vehicle was travelling. They were going to lift them out of the country.

'Any more details needed?' Geffen's voice crackled in his headset.

'Not for the minute, thanks. Please keep us posted.' Makuyana needed a little time to think. The South African chopper would be armed to the teeth, that was certain. So there were two options. Either take them on when they landed which meant a potentially bloody clash, or play a waiting game, let the party be lifted out, and then move in. The latter was equally risky: the party might be taken too deep into the Transvaal to be rescued. Alternatively, could the car be intercepted? Probably not – it was too far away and the chopper might pursue them even if they managed it.

He called Geffen back. 'Tell me, if their chopper crosses the border, do you think they will return to Trichardt?'

'Hard to say. Depends how open they are prepared to be. If this is a covert operation, they are unlikely to return to the airbase because they know we monitor it closely. If they don't care who knows and aren't worried about international flak, then they will shoot straight back there.'

Makuyana weighed the options. Evans would be on board. That meant the South Africans were kidnapping a British subject. Not even they could get away with brazening that one out. It had to be covert. He was also driven by the need to understand the whole picture. He decided to take the chance.

'Okay. We are going to let the chopper return. We will hang back and keep a safe distance for a while. Please monitor its flight and tell me where it lands,' he told Geffen.

I hope you are right man, I hope you are right, Makuyana said to himself. If not, he might just have blown it completely.

Once their car had turned off the main road to Beitbridge, Swanepoel identified the track to the right just in time for them to bump along it towards a farmhouse silhouetted in the distance.

They were a little early for the rendezvous, but that was better than being late. The car stopped in the shadow of a shed and he got out to stretch his legs and urinate in the bushes. The others followed suit – except for Evans who was still out cold.

Everyone was tired, hungry and irritable after the long journey. Still, it shouldn't be too long now. He was looking forward to being back in the Transvaal again, back at home where cheeky kaffirs were dealt with properly instead of being permitted to run the bloody country. All his time in Harare he had resented being polite to blacks, treating them as equals, on occasion even allowing them to order you about. It was part of his cover, but that didn't mean he had to like it. He had suffered in silence.

Swanepoel looked at his watch. Assuming everything was on time, the helicopter should be landing in the clearing alongside the farmhouse in about ten minutes. They had timed it to a tee. Everything was working out just fine. He lit a cigarette and began to relax.

❖

Florence Sithole noticed a sudden deviation in the path of the dot on the screen. She radioed Makuyana:

'Target has done a sudden right. Can't tell where to.' She gave the approximate location and slowed down, straining to see a signpost in the dark. Then she shut off her lights. She didn't want to fall victim to some trick to identify or shake off a tail. But where had they gone?

The moon was high and visibility was quite good. The flashing screen indicated that the vehicle had pushed ahead quite a distance off the main road. That suggested nobody was lying in wait for her. A signpost loomed up: 'Bubye Farm'. That could be it, must be named after the river to the east. She turned slowly rightward and bumped onto a rutted track. The signal was getting stronger now. They were straight ahead. She cut the engine and coasted to a halt, winding down her window to listen. The monotonous vibrations of crickets and the the tell-tale sounds of the bush greeted her: the howl of a prowling hyena, the whistle of a bird, the ubiquitous crackling of life and movement.

For a moment which felt like a day she sat absolutely still, listening, smelling, wondering. Then she climbed out, grabbed her Kalashnikov and slipped slowly down the track, eyes scanning the scene in front of her. Suddenly in the distance, came a regular throb. Gradually, it got louder. There, hovering above, a few hundred yards in front, was a helicopter, spotlights shining down like a UFO in the dark. It hung, as if suspended in time, then settled down out of sight.

Florence ran forward to see the helicopter, guns glinting with menace, as it stood in a clearing with a farm in the background. Four people, one of them apparently unconscious and being carried, hurried over and climbed aboard. It was tantalising. They were so near, yet so far. With a bit of luck, she might have been able to gun it down from where she stood, but these were not her orders: a relief really, because if she opened fire and missed the gunship would have turned and blasted her to oblivion.

As it lifted off, she turned and sprinted back to her car, grabbing her microphone, giving her exact position from the map she had recently unfolded. 'A helicopter has just arrived and lifted all four of them out. One seems unconscious: injured or sedated, I can't tell which.'

She walked back. The farm looked deserted. A quick search of Herson's car showed it to be clean, save for a few sweet wrappers and empty beer bottles on the floor. The key had been left in the ignition. She took it out and locked the car to protect it for fingerprinting. Then she waited, gun slung over her shoulder.

The Nimrod watched as the helicopter lifted off and headed back across the border towards Louis Trichardt. It skidded across the tree tops, terrifying the wildlife and the villagers sheltering in their shacks and mud huts below. Then it suddenly veered to the left and, about ten miles south of the Limpopo, it disappeared from sight. Geffen peered at the pictures more closely. No movement, no presence anymore.

Just half an hour before he had been toying with the thought that a combination of spy satellites and surveillance aircraft like his Nimrod were making undercover work almost impossible. Gone was the time when secret agents could operate in comparative freedom, James Bond figures vulnerable only to the wit and skill of their opponents. Now you could observe even a single human being from eyes miles up. It was almost as if the fun had been removed: the intelligence world had trapped itself into a straitjacket. Soon spying would all be conducted through fibre optic cables and cameras in space by people sitting in front of computer screens.

Except that there was always an element beyond the control of technology. Like now. The chopper had disappeared. Geffen knew where it had landed, just across the border in the foothills north of the Magato Mountains, but he couldn't tell what was happening around it.

Tensely, he spoke into his microphone, crisply relaying the position of the landing. He had performed his part. Now it was all up to Makuyana.

Evans blocked his ears against the deafening sound of the engine twirling the rotor blades above him. He felt nauseous, half-conscious, helpless as he realised there was nothing he could do to stop them transferring him bodily from the car into the back of the helicopter.

As he was dumped unceremoniously on a metal floor, he strained to overcome the disabling effect of the sedative. Then the engine revved and he was aware that the great bird was lifting off. Every bone in his body jangled. His brains shook about as if suspended in the cavern of his head. His stomach was taut, as if undecided whether it needed food or couldn't stand the stuff. He didn't know the time, how long he had been travelling, where he was being taken, or what was happening to him. He closed his eyes again, trying to shut out his misery.

They weren't in the air for much more than five minutes before the gunship sank gently to the earth again. A couple of figures ran toward it from some low buildings. Swanepoel gave instructions for Evans to be pulled out and taken away as the rotor blades whirred above, creating a small dust storm on the ground around it.

The shouts of Swanepoel's men were drowned in the din. Even once inside the building they could hardly hear themselves talk. Then, abruptly, the chopper revved up and lifted off again. Within a couple of minutes the noise had disappeared and all that remained was windswept grass and clouds of dust hanging in the vicinity of the landing.

Swanepoel rubbed his hands in the cold. The exit had gone perfectly. Everything at the deserted farmhouse, long since commandeered by SA security, was as he had expected; plenty of provisions – thank God, because he could eat a horse. Beds, even some liquor. His people had thought of everything. There were several cars for subsequent transportation. The helicopter shot back to the airbase, leaving no evidence that this had been anything but a routine border patrol, even the incursion into Zimbabwe could be passed off as an error.

It was midnight. He would get some sleep in a while, but first they would interrogate Evans. There was nothing to beat going for the knock-out when your target was reeling and disorientated. He beckoned to Jan Viljoen, the agent sent from Pretoria earlier in the day to prepare for their arrival. Young and lean where Swanepoel was old and paunchy, Viljoen was the perfect foil. Together they had broken many tough men. This one should be a piece of cake.

❖

Makuyana's helicopter landed in the clearing Florence had marked with her car headlights. Even though she had a pilot's licence herself and had often flown choppers, Florence remained in awe of the machines. They were so adaptable. How had people ever coped without them?

She waited as he climbed down and ran blinking across the beams toward her. She was delighted to see him, but Makuyana wasted no time in greetings.

'They landed just across the border. We are going in after them,' he said abruptly.

'What? Will the President sanction that?'

A frown creased his forehead. 'It's risky, but the kidnapping and Herson's terrorism give us justification. Now this is what we will do…'

He outlined the plan, then they ran back under the blades and up into the cockpit. Just three minutes after it had touched down, the chopper took off and swung round toward the Limpopo, leaving the two cars parked forlornly in the bush.

❖

Jenny hunched in the back. It was incredibly noisy and cold. There were six armed men sitting with her on the bare metal floor in the back, AK-47 assault rifles glinting menacingly, grenades clipped to their combat jackets. The men didn't say much. It wasn't the occasion for small talk and you had to shout to be heard.

Makuyana sat up at the front with the pilot, headphones on, presumably for permanent communication with others involved in the operation. His deputy, the woman who they'd just picked up, remained with him for some time, then she made her way back to where Jenny sat.

'My name is Florence Sithole.' Jenny looked up at the attractive woman standing above her, holding out her hand as she munched a sandwich. 'Sorry about eating while I talk. My mother would never approve!' Florence smiled, breaking the ice, 'I haven't had any food since lunchtime.'

She was a woman, similar in age to herself, Jenny judged. It was nice to have another female in the group. The soldiers were cocooned from a civilian like her and Makuyana had seemed more and more aloof; she wondered if he was regretting bringing her.

Mind you, apart from age, she and Florence were hardly alike. With a Kalashnikov propped up casually at her side, Makuyana's deputy reminded Jenny of the women guerrillas involved in liberation movements. She looked like the kind of picture Jenny would have collected at university. She remembered the intense debates at that time in the local women's socialist collective. Some had argued feminism was intrinsically non-violent, that there would be fewer wars if women were in charge. Whilst accepting that men were more aggressive, Jenny had always insisted that the main problem was one of a sexist political *culture* rather than *maleness*. Slotted into different roles in the same systems, women could, out of necessity, perfectly easily act violently too. Momentarily, she wondered how this striking woman now briefing her would act in the heat of battle. From what Florence was saying, she would find the answer to her question sooner rather than later.

❖

Evans wasn't proving to be the pushover Swanepoel had anticipated. Not that the man was deliberately resisting their interrogation, if anything he seemed completely confused. He kept denying any ulterior motive for his visit to Harare. He was a Professor, not a political activist, still less some kind of secret agent.

He looked pathetic, huddled on the floor when they had switched on the light from the outside and entered the bare room. He was evidently near breaking point. All Swanepoel's experience told him that. But still no admissions. There was a puzzling innocence about the man.

They pummelled him with questions, Viljoen being the hard man, Swanepoel periodically acting as his 'friend', almost apologising for Viljoen's aggression. When Evans eventually collapsed on the floor, Swanepoel decided they weren't getting anywhere. Let him rot for a while. They would catch some much-needed sleep themselves and return in several hours. By then whatever was left of his inner defences would have crumbled and he would sing like a canary.

And when they had broken him, they would start to de-brief Peterson. The Coloured had been pretty uncommunicative so far, sullenly keeping himself to himself. Such a good source whilst inside the ANC, he seemed uncomfortable now he had come out and openly joined the side he had been assisting. As Swanepoel's eyes shut, he made a mental note to keep a special eye on Peterson.

❖

The Zimbabwe army helicopter touched down after its short flight across the river, and figures tumbled out. Jenny's long blonde hair sprayed up around her head. She stuck closely by Florence Sithole as the group melted into the darkness and the chopper lifted off again exactly a minute after its descent, to slip back over the border and wait for a signal.

There had been a fierce, tense argument as Makuyana instructed her to stay with the chopper. But then he had relented, perhaps realising she could be useful after all. 'Look after this –' he handed her a walkie-talkie type handset – 'As soon as you hear shooting, press the red button. It will send a signal to the helicopter to come and get us. Don't press it early, but not too late either. We may need to get out fast.'

The journey by foot to the spot where Herson's party had stopped would take around three hours. That meant they would arrive at daybreak; a pity, Makuyana would have preferred the cover of total darkness, but they couldn't risk landing any nearer. Fortunately, according to the map, the terrain looked relatively unbroken.

Two of the soldiers had remained in the chopper. The other four fanned out, with Makuyana in the lead and the women in the middle. Jenny was terrified. Walking across the veld, the full enormity of the situation hit her. A few days earlier she had been going about her life in London. Now she was in enemy territory, an illegal on a secret mission which would assuredly not be accomplished without at least some violence. She hoped she wouldn't get in the way: that would be disastrous. She hadn't anticipated the bitter cold and was not properly dressed for it. Yet the hope that Jim was ahead of her and the companionship of the woman at her side kept her going. She was determined not to be deflected by any personal failings now.

They marched on at a brisk pace, stopping every so often to listen and observe, checking that they could proceed in safety. All around them were the sounds of the veld: owls, crickets, the scream of bats, and the rustle of small animals. Jenny was astonished at how noisy it could be in the middle of nowhere during the dead of night. It was quite unlike the long walks through the Dorset countryside which she enjoyed so much with her Aunt: hours of gentle tranquility, literally a world apart from the tension which now gripped her every step over this rugged country.

Just as light started to peek hesitantly over the horizon, Florence Sithole tugged at her arm. Makuyana had gone ahead and now he was heading back, motioning them to stand still.

'We are nearly there. They are inside some farm buildings clustered at the bottom of a small depression. So far as we can tell, there are only two guards. Apart from one lighted room, the buildings are in darkness.'

Florence took Jenny by the arm. 'We have instructions not to shoot anybody who is unarmed. That should protect your man. Stay here, out of sight. Remember the red button.' She gave her a small hug. 'There's something else. You won't need to use it, I very much hope, but just in case anything goes badly wrong, take this. It is loaded and the safety catch is off. All you have to do is point and pull the trigger.'

Before the full implications of what Florence was saying had sunk in, Jenny found an automatic pistol nestling in her hand, menacingly heavy and cold.

❖

It was after 4 a.m. at Trichardt when the Major in charge of the night shift manning the control tower pondered the information he had just received.

The report was a routine one, typical of the kind he routinely sifted. Some time after midnight, there had been signs of helicopter activity on the border in the area from where their own chopper had returned several hours ago after a hush-hush mission. He didn't know the details, except that it was security, not military. He flicked back a few pages from the print-out, reminding himself of an earlier report of a helicopter journey south from Harare; he had scanned it when he came on duty. Then he moved across to a large map on the wall, above the row of consols and screens in the control room. Interesting: the chopper's flight south ended in the vicinity of the reported border activity.

What was the significance of that? He stared at the map. It was frustrating not knowing the detail of the mission; security guarded their territory jealously. But there was no harm in being careful He would get a Cheetah to go and take a look. Just in case.

❖

Outside, dawn had broken and the sun was sending fingers of gold shooting across the veld. But inside Evans had lost all sense of night and day.

The bright light burning constantly had seen to that. Whichever way he turned his head, however tightly he closed his eyes, the light found him, piercing through, blurring consciousness into semi-consciousness.

'We'll leave it on to keep you company. So you don't get lonely.' The thick

Afrikaner accent made the sneer more biting, the mirthless laughter more sinister.

They had left him sometime after midnight, with a promise to 'come and talk again' in the morning. As the door banged shut and was locked, he felt utterly alone and afraid, his mind numbed.

The interrogators had forced him to stand at an angle to the wall, his feet a yard from it, his fingers resting against its whitewashed surface taking the weight of his body: simple, yet devastating. When he slumped, a strategic kick sent him back into position.

After just ten minutes he had to concentrate to stop himself screaming. After several hours his senses were so deadened he could barely produce a grunt in answer to their endless questions. Eventually, he slid down the wall, collapsing on the concrete floor, too exhausted even to groan.

As their voices died away, he tried to get a grip on himself. The room was bare, save for some old sacks in a corner; he staggered over to them. He was aware for the first time of the bitter cold, adding to his disorientation. Surely South Africa was a warm country? Not now. Not at night in the winter anyway. Not here in this remote building in the country's far north. He didn't know exactly where. But he knew he was across the border: they had told him that much.

Ever since he had been snatched from the Sheraton he had tried to question them. What did they want? What had he done to deserve such treatment? Where were they taking him? Who were they? But they ignored his pleas, pounding him with a barrage of questions and accusations of their own: What did he know about the China operation? Who was he really working for? Simply on an academic visit? Who did he think he was kidding? They seemed to know an awful lot, in fact most of what Jenny had told the anti-apartheid activist in London. After a while he had begun to wonder whether they might not indeed be correct? His own, brief, bumbling Peking experience and the allegation that he was some sort of agent began to blur into a confused kind of sense in his tired brain. But what had it all to do with Zimbabwe?

As they fired their questions, he kept repeating: 'You are making a terrible mistake. I don't know what you are talking about. I know nothing. Nothing. Nothing.' Even now, hours later, the denials bounced round in his aching head.

He closed his eyes again, thinking: I can't believe this is really happening to me. Then, as silence was broken by the call of a bird outside, a sudden, even more bewildering, thought gripped him. They wouldn't go to all this trouble for nothing. Perhaps I am guilty of something after all. If only they would tell me what I am supposed to have done.

❖

Jenny watched from the rim of the depression as the soldiers skirted round in a circle. From where she sat she could see everything. It was almost exhilarating. Two dark figures – Florence and Makuyana? – slipped across the yard and slid up against the whitewashed walls of the buildings which were becoming increasingly visible as dawn broke. It seemed like a farmhouse and yet it wasn't. She noticed that everything looked unnaturally clean and tidy. There were no signs of animals and yet the place was obviously being looked after: fences in good order, the bush cut back.

She felt tense and expectant. Anytime now, surely the action would start. It brought to mind the films she had seen as a kid. But real life was a lot messier – and a great deal less predictable. Where was Jim? All her instincts told her he was in there. But could she trust her feelings or was she simply trying to justify her decision to make this long crazy journey?

Suddenly, catching her quite off guard, was a loud crashing noise followed by the sound of gunfire and screams. Theirs or ours? She couldn't tell, but she pressed the red button on her handset as instructed.

❖

Makuyana had spotted the guard at the front door half an hour earlier. His cigarette glowed in the dark as he stamped his feet in the cold. Another was permanently circling the complex: that one needed taking out first. There were three cars in the courtyard, which implied a maximum of around twelve people inside. In which case his party was in a distinct minority. But they had the advantage of surprise.

They had slipped into position: he in readiness for the guard on the move about to come round the corner, she concentrating on the one at the front door. All he could think of was Robert Temba and Ed Tombe: valuable, vital lives blown away. It was time to settle some scores. In a curious way he was grateful for the excuse to avenge their murders: it made what he had to do all the easier.

A shadow fell across the corner of the outhouse and dawdled there as if the owner couldn't decide whether to commit himself. He was probably scanning the perimeter of the farmyard. Makuyana could hear him breathing and shuffling in the sand. Then the shadow became a man, eyes focussing on something quite unexpected. In the split second the guard took to start raising his gun, Makuyana was upon him, stainless steel knife slashing viciously at his adam's apple. The gun clattered to the ground, echoing loudly. The expression in the man's eyes switched from amazement to a dull glaze and he fell to the ground.

At that precise moment, Florence Sithole pumped two shots into the other guard. One exploded in his brain, transforming it instantly into a tangle of useless matter; the other drilled through his heart. He had presented a perfect target for her night sights and she found the clinical manner of his execution deeply satisfying – not a sensation within herself which she cared to explore further. She rushed for the door and twisted it open.

A man was sitting in front of her, on a chair, in what must have been the main living room. A fire glowed in the background. Unlike the others, he wasn't white. He had a sub machine gun pointed right at her. She froze and started to level her Kalash. But she knew her number had come up at last. The man would splatter her against the doorframe before she had time to fire. The fact that she had recognised him instantly as the traitor George Peterson was no consolation.

❖

Swanepoel jerked awake at the sound of firing. Jesus! It wasn't possible. Had Evans escaped? What the hell was going on?

As he switched on the bedside lamp and made to grab his pistol, the window shattered and a figure tumbled into the room, rolling across the bed, half on top of him, involuntarily knocking his gun to the floor. As if in a slow motion movie, the figure banged against the far wall and righted itself. Swanepoel saw a tall black man. He couldn't tell whether he was blinking as his pupils contracted rapidly to the sudden change in light, because he was wearing dark glasses.

He knew him! He knew him! This was the man they had snapped at Harare airport. The one they'd never been able to identify had come back to haunt him again.

In a vague kind of way Evans became aware of chaos and commotion around him, of unfamiliar sounds: screams, bangs, the clatter of gunfire. The loud noises compounded his dilirium. Then the door was flung open and one of the interrogators, Viljoen, burst in and pulled him roughly to his feet.

'Commaan Mister. You my ticket to safety.' His rasping Afrikaner accent cut through Evans' confusion. He had ceased trying to make sense of what was going on. But he got the message loud and clear and stumbled out into the darkened corridor.

❖

Jenny watched, transfixed, as two Zimbabwean solidiers approached the building. Suddenly a window swung open and the vicious rattle of a machine gun cut them down. They writhed in agony until, almost simultaneously, they both shuddered and lay still on the ground. She gasped. Two human beings had just died in front of her, no more than fifty yards away.

Then she spotted a third Zimbabwean crawling along the wall towards the open window. He crouched low, lobbed something inside and scampered away. There was a thunderous explosion and the inside of the room seemed to spill out.

On the other side of the building there was some more firing. She saw a figure fall from a tree and hit the ground with a dreadful thud. Then a burst of fire was returned from elsewhere. A figure cut across at the far corner of her view. More shots, followed by a deathly silence. Were they all killing each other? Would she be left here on her own?

❖

After the longest, most terrifying moment in her life, Florence realised Peterson wasn't firing at her; nor would he. His gun was real enough and his advantage was unquestionable. But he seemed unable to move. Gradually he let his arms sag.

'Shoot me if you want,' he blurted out, falling onto an armchair. The gun slipped from his hands. 'I can't kill you.'

She was stunned at this unexpected behaviour, but there was no time to ask questions.

'Where is Evans?'

'Through a connecting corridor to the neighbouring building. He is locked in a special cell.'

'Take me there.' She looked at his drawn and troubled face. There was a sound of gunfire, followed by an almighty explosion which shook the whole house.

'How many South Africans are there in here?'

'Four inside, two others outside.'

They headed out of the room, Peterson leading the way, his posture and her machine gun implying he was a prisoner. Perhaps he wanted it that way in case they bumped into any of his 'colleagues'. Florence didn't care as long as they kept moving: time was of the essence now.

The recognition was mutual. Makuyana knew instantly that this was Herson and he drew back from pulling the trigger to finish him off.

'Mr Herson. Not your real name I suppose.'

'Mr Inkala. Not your real name either.' Even in adversity, caught off guard, Swanepoel retained his composure. It was not the first jam he had been in nor was it the first time he had faced possible death, though he couldn't understand how this had happened. He was desperately trying to fathom how they had been followed. It couldn't have happened, or rather it *shouldn't* have. 'I am Captain Swanepoel of the South African security services.' He wanted the other man to know who he was dealing with, whose patch he was trespassing upon.

Makuyana absorbed the information without responding. 'Where is Evans?'

'Who is Evans?' Swanepoel shrugged nonchalantly.

There was no time to waste. Makuyana hit him in the teeth with the barrel of his Kalash, drawing a spurt of blood. 'Don't piss me about you bastard. You killed Robert Temba and you've probably killed many others. You will die yourself if you don't co-operate.'

Swanepoel felt curiously detached from the situation. He realised he didn't care anymore. He was at the end of his career, probably in the twilight of his life. He could view the situation perfectly objectively. And he knew that the black man menacing him didn't have the time for a proper interrogation.

'Fock yourself,' he spluttered.

Makuyana hit him again. This time the butt of the gun, crashed into his jaw. Then he kicked him deliberately in the balls, provoking a scream of pain. He didn't enjoy what he was doing, but he didn't mind either. It was as if someone else was at work, coldly and methodically doing what had to be done.

'Where is Evans?'

'Fock yourself.'

Again Makuyana didn't lose his temper. He had heard the firing around him. He needed to move. This one would be too hard to crack in the time available. He shot Swanepoel deliberately in both knees with the South African's own pistol and searched the room quickly to ensure there were no other weapons. Then he turned and left the room. Swanepoel lay in agony amidst a growing pool of his own blood and mangled flesh: a job accomplished with maximum efficiency.

Evans found himself being manoeuvered outside into the fresh sharpness of the dawn, Viljoen's revolver poking at his side. Grotesquely, he imagined the scene must be classic western.

They edged slowly away from the building, Viljoen revolving constantly to place Evans between him and any gunfire, sounds of which had periodically interrupted their progress.

Visibility was good. For the first time Evans was able to take in the surroundings: dry, flattish terrain with only patches of bushes, shrubs and scattered trees with flat tops. He felt so very far away from everything familiar, geographically, physically, emotionally. He wasn't capable of making sense of this anymore. He was stunned into sullen submission.

Viljoen had been aiming for one of the cars parked outside, but they had come out at the opposite end of the buildings and couldn't risk moving there directly. He would climb up onto the rim of the depression and move round. There was someone crouched down near the cars, gun poking out; so it wouldn't be easy to get there. He was right up to his neck in shit. There wasn't an obvious exit. He didn't know how many of his side were still around to fight back.

The pair shuffled awkwardly up a path and crouched behind some bushes. 'If you so much as fart, you a dead man,' Viljoen grunted at Evans.

❖

Makuyana found two dead South Africans in the room which had been blown apart. He grabbed their guns and headed through the rest of the single storey house, a plain dwelling with minimal furniture. It had an un-lived in, temporary air.

Then he spotted Florence and Peterson turning back from the empty cell where Evans had been detained.

'He's not there,' she muttered. 'Are you sure that was where they kept him?' She rounded on Peterson, who nodded.

Makuyana watched the other man closely, noting that he was unarmed and seemed to be co-operating. But the former ANC man wouldn't return his stare. His eyes were fixed to the ground.

'Florence, have a quick look at the other outhouse. You must find Evans.' Makuyana jerked his head towards Peterson. 'What's he playing at?'

'He could have killed me, but he didn't. Says he wants to help.' She shrugged, then turned to go; let the boss make sense of this one if he could.

Makuyana was unable and unwilling to disguise his contempt for Peterson. 'What's going on here?'

'They didn't tell me much. Swanepoel was their main field agent in Harare. He was responsible for most of the explosions and killings.'

'What about Evans? Why did they kidnap him?'

'I don't know. Except…' Peterson hesitated.

'Yes? Come on. We haven't much time left.'

'It's to do with the Chinese. Swanepoel kept hinting about something big. Some operation. They have their people in place. It must be very soon.'

'Is that all you have to tell me?' Makuyana wasn't alerting the other man to how keen his interest was.

'They were playing it close to their chest. Wouldn't tell me much at all. After they brought Evans back to their safe house, a Chinaman appeared. He had a go at Evans, then left again.'

'What did he look like.'

'Horn-rimmed spectacles. Not old, not young. Nothing very distinctive about him.'

'And why should I believe all this from a man like you? A traitor to your people!' The abrupt harshness of Makuyana's voice startled the other man.

'I had no choice.'

'No choice?' Makuyana spat the words out. 'I wish all those who died because of you had the choice to keep living.'

'They were after my family in the Cape. They would have killed them if I hadn't co-operated.' Peterson's voice was firm now, even confident, where previously he had been defensive and diffident. 'You can't understand. I should never have left them behind. I should have brought my wife and children out with me into exile.'

Makuyana's face was expressionless, apparently without sympathy – though he understood the man's anguish better than Peterson could possibly have suspected.

'Come with me,' he snapped. He headed back to find Swanepoel again.

❖

Florence was desperate. Where was Evans? The carnage had been dreadful. Only one surviving Zimbabwean soldier and most of the South Africans dead or captured; only one was unaccounted for as far as she could make out. He could be anywhere.

She searched for movement. Nothing. What about up on the rim, toward the open veld? She ducked involuntarily as a South African Air Force jet shot low overhead. Shit! Had they been blown? Where was their chopper? Had the Englishwoman sent for it yet?

Florence began to climb urgently to where they had left Jenny. She *had* to find Evans. They must get out before it was too late.

❖

The Cheetah's pilot spotted the Zimbabwean helicopter flying low over the Limpopo, clear as a bell in the early morning sunshine, its shadow skirting the bush. He radioed back to base and then dived straight towards it.

The chopper pilot was nearly a mile into the Transvaal before he became aware of the threat. Immediately, he banked away and then turned quickly, racing back, switching to and fro so as not to offer a clear target.

On the ground below, Viljoen looked up in relief as he heard the distinctive whine of the plane's Snecma engines. Were they sending some help? He had to get to safety, but he wasn't covering much ground; Evans was proving a nuisance. The man had gone limp and was in a complete daze. Was he really that bad or was he faking? He banged the gun in the Englishman's back but that had no palpable effect. Viljoen let him sag to the ground. He was a liability at this rate; better to make a run for it on his own.

Viljoen looked around. There wasn't much cover up here, but he had to get to a car before they came looking for him. He would have to skirt round, climb down and creep up on the black soldier guarding the vehicles. It should be possible. He could get to one of the cars via the shed which would protect him from view. He began to move round, crouching low amidst the long grass on the rim.

He was concentrating so hard on the buildings below, he almost stepped on the girl.

❖

Jenny heard the grass rustle, but then she was distracted by the roar of the jet above. So when a man almost fell on top of her she was caught off guard.

The pistol in her hand, was resting uselessly on the earth. What would she have done with it anyway? The man straightened up as if to get a proper fix on her. His machine gun levelled itself. She was no longer a spectator; she was about to become part of the action. This was it. She was going to die. She was not so much terrified as numb.

'And who'err you then?'

If she had had any doubt, the slur on the r's in the Afrikaner accent identified the man as one of *them*.

'Jennifer Stuart,' she stuttered, 'of London.'

'Of London'. It sounded so pretentious. Or so pathetic.

'Bitch!'

Instead of squeezing the trigger, he reversed the gun and lifted it, butt in the air to bring it crashing down on her head. She screamed. And then, in the split second as he rocked back to put his weight into the swing, the world about her all but exploded. The man was lifted bodily in the air as a grotesque cavern appeared in his head, the gun clattering down, grazing her shoulder.

There was a sound of running feet and Florence Sithole appeared, crouching with her Kalash ready, eyes darting like a sleek black cat. 'Are you okay?'

'I think so. Thank you...' Jenny's voice tailed off feebly. She felt utterly useless beside this formidable woman: one second a clinical killer, the next a supportive sister, giving her a quick, reassuring hug – and then grabbing the handset to signal the chopper.

'Come on, come on – what's the hold up?'

Jenny couldn't hear the reply, just a crackle of sound.

'Going back? What the hell do you mean you are going back?'

Florence stared into the distance. Then she spoke firmly: 'Carry on retreating, but come back in about twenty minutes and hover just across the river. We will drive towards you down the nearest road or track. Pick us up this side if possible.'

'Come on,' she said to Jenny, 'Where is Evans? That jet is bad news.'

❖

Makuyana wasted no time with Swanepoel. 'Answer my questions and we will leave you to be rescued. Say nothing and I kill you.'

Swanepoel didn't believe he had a choice. They would kill him anyway. In some ways it would be a relief because the pain was appalling; he would never walk properly again. The black bastard could get knotted.

'What is the China operation? We know something is planned. What is it?'

Swanepoel ignored him and kept holding his legs as he slumped, eyes closed, almost passing out, warm urine dribbling down his pants.

'Tell me your plan. We know the outline and we know it's going to happen soon. We are prepared.' The last bit was bluff and the South African probably knew it, Makuyana realised. He felt sick with frustration. If only he had more time, he could have broken the man. But he had no time. The sound of the jet and the additional gunfire underlined that point.

Swanepoel didn't rise to the bait. Makuyana kicked one of his legs and the man screeched in agony. 'One last chance. Answer the question.'

'What question?' Swanepoel was grinning in spite of the pain.

It was pointless. Makuyana knew he wasn't going to get anywhere. And sparing the enemy was for Hollywood. Better to cut your losses and remove all witnesses. He brought up the Kalash and fired into Swanepoel's heart, the report almost piercing his eardrums as it echoed around the room.

❖

The man was trying to drag him to his feet again, but Evans wasn't having it. Going limp was about the only card he had to play. He wasn't going another step.

The man was saying something. 'Jim, Jim, wake up.' It wasn't the same Afrikaner voice. Different. Yes, very different. 'Jim': familiar, too. He jerked himself out of his dazed state, forcing himself to concentrate on what was happening to him. His mind must have gone totally this time. This was Jenny's voice, but it couldn't be. It couldn't possibly be. He blinked in the glare of the sun. But it was!

'Jenny,' he began to tremble uncontrollably. What on earth was Jenny doing here? Truly, nothing made sense anymore.

❖

Makuyana didn't know that the Cheetah had radioed back to Trichardt for a support gunship to come straight up, but he sensed they didn't have much time.

The six of them piled into two cars, the only surviving soldier with Peterson, the others together, with Florence driving so Makuyana could talk to Evans. The man was clearly in a state and had to be treated gently. Makuyana recognised the shock symptoms.

'I need to ask you some questions. Urgently. You could help us prevent a disaster. Who was the Chinaman who came to question you at the house in Harare?'

'How do you know about that?' Evans looked dazed.

'Peterson told me?'

'Who is Peterson?'

'The coloured guy in the other car. He was with you in the house. Never mind why for the moment. He said a Chinese man tried to interrogate you. Who was he?'

Evans looked at Jenny who sat in the front passenger seat. She had turned around to face them. 'His name is Wang Bi Nan,' he said.

'Wang?' she gasped. 'Out in Harare?'

'Who is he?' Makuyana sensed something important.

'The man who was behind the attempts on Jim's life during our China visit,' Jenny replied. 'If he is out here that spells trouble.'

'What sort of trouble?'

'Who knows,' she said wearily, 'but he has good connections. Even with British intelligence.'

'There was the photo,' Evans murmured.

'Photo?'

'Oh, yes', Jenny interjected, 'I snapped Wang accidentally on the Great Wall – a tourist shot.'

Makuyana looked quizzical, trying hard not to lose his patience.

'Jim's home was searched when the Greenpeace story first broke. Nothing was taken – except for that particular picture, one of about a hundred.'

He must be important, Makuyana thought. But could they get to him in time?

❖

Florence Sithole was sure the Fiat's suspension had gone. The steering wheel jarred up to her shoulder blades as she drove down a dusty, bumpy track that was little more than a cattle path.

Although the sun shone brightly now, it was still cold and would remain that way until mid-morning. They were less than a mile from the river, she judged. Not long now, though the going was painfully slow.

She was trying to listen to the conversation between the other three, but it was difficult because the driving needed such concentration. How did she keep going? By not stopping to think: not about the killing nor the danger nor about how desperately tired she was. She just had to keep going. It was almost unreal being on South African territory.

They came suddenly up to the end of the track. There was no gate, no way through the fence standing the other side of a ditch which the cars could not possibly cross.

'We will have to make a run for it,' she called urgently.

They jumped out and started moving across the ditch and into the field. But Peterson tapped Makuyana on the shoulder.

'I am not coming,' he said simply.

'What do you mean? We are in danger. We have to *move*.' Makuyana was angry at the hold up. He gestured to the others to keep going.

'There is no future for me back in Harare. You will have to try me for espionage – if the ANC don't execute me first. I don't want the humiliation. My family will never recover. The township comrades could come into our coloured district and kill them. I am not coming.' Peterson sat down on the ground.

Makuyana thought about forcing him on, but he could see that it was pointless.

'What will you do then?'

'Try and get away, maybe start a new life. Leave me those spare guns and ammunition from the dead soldiers. If there is any problem getting across the river I will try to cover you.'

Makuyana thought for an instant. Was he trustworthy? The guy might pump bullets into their backs the moment they turned, but he didn't think so. Once again, Makuyana decided to back his instinct. He hoped it was right this time as it had so often been before.

'Okay,' he shrugged.

'Amandla!' Peterson called. Makuyana heard the ANC's rallying call as he hurried away, but he couldn't bring himself to return it. Not that Peterson cared about the lack of a response. He was at peace with himself for the first time in years.

❖

The throbbing sound of the gunship engines pierced the morning stillness. Makuyana realised it wasn't theirs: it was coming from behind. The party was half way across the field which led down to the Limpopo. Florence had stopped and was speaking urgently into the handset.

As he came in, sweeping the area for any sign of activity, the South African pilot spotted the running figures. Before he could swoop and take a closer look, he noticed two parked cars. Familiar unmarked security service cars, probably the same ones from the farmyard when he had dropped the party off. A man was standing by the side gesticulating, apparently waving him down. The pilot looked ahead. He might just have time to drop a rope ladder, haul the man up inside and still get to the running figures before they reached the border. The problem was he didn't know who was on their side. The call-out had been vague, very little more than 'go and take a look'. He had stopped at the farmhouse for a few minutes – long enough to confirm it was deserted after a bloody battle – but he was still very much in the dark.

The rope was unfolding as it tumbled down to the man below. The pilot couldn't see him now: he was under the fuselage. Suddenly the crew started shouting in alarm. The pilot pulled sideways and began to lift. Then he spotted the man, still on the ground, with a gun, its barrel pointing upwards.

Shots crashed into the cockpit, gashing the pilot's leg, drilling a neat hole in the head of his co-pilot. He pulled desperately at the controls, trying to get the gunship away and at the same time to turn so they could gun the bastard down.

'Chopper ahead! Chopper ahead!' The voice of his navigator burst through the intercom and he glanced up to see a helicopter hanging over the running figures, down near the river, no more than two hundred yards away. His men were firing at the man on the ground now, but they couldn't get a decent sight as the gunship twisted in the sky. Bullets still assailed them from below. It was a matter of time before one hit home somewhere vital.

Searing pain in his legs; he kept climbing, then threw the gunship round to face the enemy chopper, firing off a rocket. He hadn't time to steady properly and the missile sailed harmlessly overhead. But it was a sitting duck, settling on the ground now. He began to accelerate towards it, but another bullet from below crashed into the cockpit, hitting him in the stomach. He jerked in his harness, shock sweeping his body as he grappled with controls.

'Got him sir,' the triumphant voice came through his headphones. Too bloody late, he thought bitterly, too bloody late. No it wasn't! He had a clear sight of the enemy helicopter sitting right in the middle of his view-finder as he raced forward. One hundred yards away and closing fast. No mistake this time. He fired some tracer bullets which tore into the brute. The pain flamed through him, blood bursting from his shattered body. He positioned his index finger over the trigger to fire the other rocket. But as he tried to press it, the gunship fell sharply to one side. There was nothing he could do. He had lost control, and the rocket swept away into the distance.

His Sparks just had time to put out a distress signal before they crashed in a sheet of raging orange flames. The whole field seemed to shudder with the impact.

A beautiful sight. Peterson's last thought was a happy one as his bullet-ridden form rolled back and slumped to rest on the grass.

CHAPTER TWELVE

Although the city had not yet awoken, the Leader had been hard at work for over an hour, putting the final touches on the speech he was due to deliver that evening at the Parliament building.

It was unusual for a visiting Head of State to be permitted the privilege of addressing Parliament. This special gathering in the old building erected by Cecil Rhodes and, until independence in 1980 dominated by whites, reflected the importance with which Zimbabwe viewed its links with China and the debt owed to Peking's consistent support for ZANU's liberation struggle. The leader wanted to honour the occasion with a major speech about socialist fundamentals in the modern age. Gorbachev had done it in style for the Soviet Union. He was in the same modernising tradition which had gathered momentum throughout the Communist Bloc. Socialism was no longer full of certainties. It was in a state of flux, and sometimes crisis, throughout the world.

In China, he was being pulled in all directions. Centralised economic planning of all production, distribution and exchange simply did not work. To modernise the economy and secure the massive growth it needed, the door was being thrown wide open to western capital, but there was still an important role for planning. The market economy was incredibly wasteful and inefficient. Besides, it created huge injustices and inequalities.

Ownership had to be spread, not concentrated in either the hands of the state or a few privileged individuals who made up an elite class. Democratic rights had to be properly established by law and extended. He knew the Old Guard were vehemently opposed to this. They wanted power to be closely controlled by the Party. But their arguments against it – that Chinese culture lacked a strong democratic tradition, that the masses would not know how to exercise democratic rights – these were fallacious. Democracy should be allowed to grow and develop at its own pace. This would be his theme. It would be a watershed speech. The world's press had already been briefed. At home, the media would give it saturation coverage – one of the advantages of state control, he had to admit.

❖

Venter and Coetzee were also early risers. They showered and ate a light breakfast. After the weeks of waiting and then the days of detailed planning, they felt relieved that it would soon be over: the big day had arrived.

Fit and fresh, their bronzed bodies tuned to perfection, they felt completely confident. Nothing had been left to chance. They would pick up the special van at midday and load it. Then they would drive to the chosen position and place some temporary bollards by the kerbside to reserve the spot which had been officially cleared for their use, before returning to their rented house. At two o'clock, the make-up artist would arrive to transform Venter into a black inspector of the Zimbabwe police. She would need two hours for a proper job to have him ready for the matinée performance at the theatre which, she had been informed, was the purpose of the exercise. Afterwards Venter and Coetzee would drive in the van to their spot in the city centre. All being well, they would be flying out a little under two hours later.

❖

KJ didn't wake early by choice. His emergency phone jerked him out of a deep sleep at around 8 a.m. As he sat and listened, his mood changed abruptly from one of half-awake irritability to pure, concentrated anger. The *debâcle* near the border was an absolute disaster. How the hell had it been allowed to happen? There was no explanation. It was incredible. A massacre. Some of his best people wiped out on their own patch. Two crucial detainees snatched back from under their noses. A chopper shot down – again on South African territory. Was it the ANC or the Zimbabweans? Nobody was able to say for certain. But a Zimbabwean helicopter had been detected crossing the border some hours beforehand; it sounded suspiciously like an operation sanctioned by Harare.

How had a wily old bird like Maritz allowed it to occur? Ah ... Maritz. As he put the phone down, memories of his old friend flooded back. Of the great times they had enjoyed together during the days when to be a white security policeman was to be immortal, when you ruled the world: nobody could touch you, certainly no black. Now it was different. You had to fight for your very existence. And sometimes you lost.

The old counter-measures were not sufficient any more. Tit-for-tat killings no longer seemed to work. Bumping off ANC sympathisers, harassing the opposition, letting his boys loose in the principal townships for an hour or two. These were no longer sufficient. The enemy needed to be taught a real lesson before things got completely out of hand: a nuke. Not a big one. A short range weapon would do nicely, one that could be fixed to the chassis of an armoured vehicle. They already had nuclear shells for their tanks, but these had severe limitations. They needed something like NATO's Lance missile, or, even better, the Pentagon's new Multiple Launch Rocket System which was more accurate and had a longer range than the Lance's 75 miles. That would be enough to shake the very foundations of Zimbabwe and to ensure that it put a block on any more ANC activity on its territory. The problem was that the military didn't have the necessary technology. Delivery depended upon Peking.

Of course these weapons had their dangers: they might wipe out some of your own forces, the fall-out could drift back across onto your own territory. But so what? It was a small price to pay for the bigger prize: security for the *volk*; security to maintain control; security to maintain privilege. No, dammit, not privilege – God-given rights.

❖

They clung to each other after the helicopter landed and they were pulled swiftly aboard. It swept away and back over the border, racing northward in the bright sunshine, sweeping up and over the hills.

The pace of events had been so quick, the killings so shocking, and the sheer noise so mind-boggling, that Evans was numbed into silence. The glimpse of the enemy chopper exploding in flames was the final straw: it could so easily have been them. He mumbled a few endearments to Jenny, but mostly just stared ahead. His eyes closed to try and escape the terror of the last seven hours, but it wouldn't leave him.

It was Jenny who kept him going. Jenny: her sudden appearance on the scene had added to his disorientation. Like one of those classic adventures, she had appeared right on cue, a saviour in the morning light. He wanted to cuddle her, to comfort her, so they could draw on each other's drained resources. But, somehow, he couldn't offer her anything. He had no emotions left, nothing to give, only to take. The shock had left him flat, remote and detached from her. There was nothing to say. Just let him rest for now. In time he would make it up. But at the moment he couldn't imagine when that might be.

Makuyana reported over the scrambled line both to his headquarters and direct to the President's duty officer. The man wasn't exactly thrilled with the news. Makuyana could almost hear his mind ticking over as he thought ahead about the diplomatic and possibly military consequences of the invasion of South African territory – for that was the word that would surely be used: invasion. Ever since independence they had lived with the nightmare of a border incident or an ANC incursion escalating into open warfare. This one could be portrayed as a blatant act of aggression. The bloody bodies left behind – including those of Zimbabweans – would be hard to explain away, even with the alibi of a rescue operation.

But Makuyana had no time to concern himself with such matters. He was more worried about the Chinese visit. That must be the target. But in what way? The fragments of evidence he had gathered together all implied an imminent climax. But what was it about? The main breakthrough was Evans' identification of the Chinese, Wang. When talking to his own staff, he had asked for the man's whereabouts to be pinpointed and covert surveillance to be set in motion. He had come tantalisingly close to cracking the whole business. Yet each time it came within sight, another door closed, the latest being Swanepoel's capture and death. When he shot him he was angry – not with the man himself, but with the necessity to blow away another vital source, perhaps even the most vital one of all.

He was reluctant to disturb the English couple. They looked absolutely shattered, the man completely out of his depth. Nevertheless, he had to talk it all through again, to make sure he hadn't missed anything. He left the flight deck and went to the main cabin. For the next hour the three of them sat, huddled uncomfortably on metal seats, engrossed in discussion.

❖

During the night and through the daybreak, Major Peter Geffen had watched the to-ing and fro-ing in the airspace along the border. He saw one of their own choppers escape homeward. He had made contact with Makuyana's people and been briefed on the situation. Then things had returned to normal.

But now it was as if there had been a short circuit on the Nimrod's screens. Blips all over the show, flashes too, and darting flickers. Pictures showed the whole world down below had erupted into a frenzy of activity. Inside South Africa, the airspace around Trichardt was becoming more and more like Heathrow in the summer. Fighters taking off, transport planes coming in from the South, and on the ground vehicles moving toward the Zimbabwean border. Some of them fast – probably trucks and jeeps. Others slower – maybe Casspir APCs. Still others, crawling along – probably tanks.

Grim-faced, Geffen signalled to Makuyana and back to Harare. It looked mighty like the country was going to be invaded before the day was out.

❖

Just as the party was touching down at Harare, there was a knock on Wang's door. One of the Sheraton's porters handed him a sealed envelope. It contained a phone number which he was instructed to ring in exactly five minutes. He had already bathed and changed and was about to go down for breakfast.

Within minutes of dialling the designated number, Wang had learned all he really needed to know about the disaster at the border. The aspect which caused him to freeze and grip the phone until his knuckles whitened was the fact that Evans had been sprung. That meant his cover had probably been blown. Not for the first time, he cursed the English Professor.

He grabbed some essentials, took the lift down and left the hotel, skipping breakfast and climbing into one of the taxis waiting for customers outside. If the opposition, tipped off by Evans, caught up with him, he would claim diplomatic immunity. Meanwhile he had important things to do. The Old Man had to be warned. And he still had a meeting to attend: a meeting with one of Pretoria's illicit representatives in the city.

He was so engrossed in re-arranging his plans for the day that he failed to notice the unmarked car following the cab at a comfortable distance.

❖

It was remarkable how you could keep going on sheer adrenaline. Makuyana hadn't slept for well over twenty-four hours and he had been on the move all that time, under intense pressure, both before and during the border affair. Yet, after a quick wash and shave at the office, he felt fine. A little brittle perhaps, but fine. He knew everything would catch up with him before the day was out, but he could get by until then. Florence Sithole was in much the

– 246 –

same state. She looked unreasonably bright and cheery, having showered and changed from denims into a skirt and jumper. Once again, he found himself admiring her stamina, her guts and her sheer ability. She had acted with almost brutal efficiency at the farmhouse, and now he was calling upon her once more.

Evans and Jenny had gone back to his room at the Sheraton with strict instructions to rest. A watcher was tailing Wang. Soon they would have to pick him up, but not before they had found out what he was up to. He asked Florence to join the watcher outside the Chinese embassy which Wang had reportedly entered half an hour ago.

The news from the Nimrod of South African military movements was disturbing, but there was nothing he could do about that. He forced himself to concentrate upon the Chinese delegation. Who was in it? What were its movements? What was the master plan? What the hell was he looking for?

Systematically, he went back over the picture he had constructed for himself, an outline, recently coloured in by the English couple. Through all the intrigue and complexity, he clung to a core deduction: a faction in the Chinese ruling elite seemed to be co-operating with Pretoria over nuclear weaponry. So, why had the action shifted to Harare? He stared at the ceiling, noticing a spider's web in one of the corners. A faction. In Peking's ruling elite. The top brass in that elite were all right here in Harare. His thoughts strayed to the details of the day's itinerary. Then he jerked them back. Here in Harare. The Chinese leadership. And perhaps members of the faction too? What were they planning? And who exactly did Wang work for?

Makuyana rang through for an aide to bring him the names of the full delegation with a breakdown of the back-up staff and who they were attached to. The names would be no problem. He could have them in a couple of minutes. But the relationship between the leaders and the staff would have to be checked, either with the President's office or possibly the Embassy itself.

❖

As overall head of the country's armed forces, General Gert Strijdom hadn't wasted much time with consultations. Ever since the military had been eased sideways from the central power position they had enjoyed in the heyday of President P.W. Botha's rule over South Africa, the General had been waiting for an opportunity like this.

As soon as the hotline buzzed at his bedside he sprang into action like a steel coil. Immediately alert, his six foot frame silhouetted naked against the morning light, he listened impassively to the briefing. It was just the excuse he needed.

After the initial call, he made a few of his own. He asked to be put through, first to the Army chief and then to his counterpart in the Air Force. They had anticipated his instructions and troop and aircraft movements were already being put in train. But both were shocked by an additional instruction: to replace conventional shells and bombs with nuclear warheads in a selection of Oliphant 2B tanks and Cheetah aircraft. Was there Presidential authority for this, they both asked independently? Yes, Strijdom had lied. He would get the necessary clearance retrospectively.

The first tank regiments should cross the border in about five hours.

❖

The news of the successful Zimbabwean attack in the Northern Transvaal spread like wildfire through the unofficial networks in the townships. Black pupils heard about it during their mid-morning breaks and there was a concerted move from the playgrounds into the surrounding streets. Spontaneous black demonstrations started to break out all over the country, the young comrades in the vanguard.

And within the ranks of Umkhonto we Sizwe, ANC cadres began to activate plans which had lain dormant for years in readiness for the right moment. Arms and ammunition were gradually retrieved from ingenious secret stores. Guns and bombs were moved in old cars and dustcarts, grenades and pistols in the nappies of babies on their mothers' backs. By midday KJ would start to get reports from informers of the biggest black mobilisation for armed struggle they could ever have imagined.

As news of the troop movements towards the border began to leak out, there was panic selling of shares in Johannesburg and the Rand took a sharp tumble on the foreign exchanges. White mothers looked anxiously at their black maids as they continued to iron and clean, obediently performing their duties. White schools called emergency assemblies and headteachers told ranks of scrubbed faces in hushed tones about the development. Parents started jamming school switchboards with messages to say their little ones would be picked up after lessons rather than left to walk home as usual. Amongst leisured whites, the chatter at coffee mornings and on bowling greens was about nothing else. In offices and workplaces, the news spread fast too. During lunchbreaks there was a buzz of debate and speculation in canteens and restaurants.

By early afternoon it was clear that wildcat strikes were breaking out across the country. Groups of black miners walked out. So did car workers. Construction workers downed tools and left sites. If the momentum continued, the Chamber of Commerce reported, production would be at a virtual standstill by the next day.

❖

In Harare, activity throughout the morning was becoming almost as feverish. Mugabe had ordered the armed forces to stand by, Pretoria's far superior strength and fire-power meant it would be difficult to halt any invasion. All they could do was to stand in its way at strategic points and force the South Africans to show their hand: either retreat or attack.

The President had informed Zimbabwe Television and radio that he intended to make a live broadcast that evening, shortly after the state ceremony with the Chinese Leader. Despite everything, the ceremony would go ahead; Pretoria would not be allowed to disrupt important diplomatic and political business.

Meanwhile Makuyana had discovered that Wang was attached to the staff of Mr Hua Zhi Yang, a veteran Minister in the Chinese Politburo, and that he had flown in a few days ahead of the main party. Interesting, that. Had it given Wang more time to plan and prepare? If so, for what? Makuyana kept coming back to the central question: what and when?

He called political intelligence for a quick telephone briefing on the politics of the Chinese ruling group. Then he called an aide: 'I want an appointment with the Chinese Leader. Urgently. On the President's direct authority. I have the necessary documentation giving authorisation.'

❖

Save for Florence Sithole, watching from the surveillance vehicle outside the Embassy's grounds, nobody took much notice when the Harare businessman, Mr Eugene Fraser, presented himself at reception for a pre-arranged appointment. Florence immediately requested identification through his car registration number, but it was normal for business people to have contact with delegations like these. Some people maintained they were really more about fostering trade than better diplomatic relations, others that there was no difference between the two: diplomacy, one way or another, was usually a lubricant for better business.

Mr Fraser was shown in to a small room occupied by just two men: an old one, diminutive, formal (that must be the Minister) and a younger colleague with horn-rimmed glasses (that must be Mr Wang).

There was no interpreter present: the two Chinese spoke fluent English. They got down to the discussion right away, much of it technical: about the delivery of more warheads and a target date for after the new weapons had been properly tested. Under an hour later, Fraser departed, climbing into his white Porsche.

As he sped out of the gates back to his office, an anonymous car swept in and Major Keith Makuyana, smartly turned out in a dark suit, asked for his pre-arranged audience with the Leader. While he waited, he inquired casually who the previous visitor had been to see.

'Mr Hua.' The receptionist smiled at the courteous, handsome man before her, quite unaware that she had added yet another vital piece to his jigsaw puzzle.

❖

The meeting with the Leader didn't take long. Makuyana had decided not to tell him about his suspicions of Hua and Wang. He didn't want to risk alerting the pair, nor to promote speculation within the delegation. He said simply that he had good reason to believe there might be an assassination attempt. As to timing, he couldn't be certain. But the Leader would be most vulnerable during the major public appearance of the visit when he addressed Parliament this evening.

The Leader absorbed the information without noticeable shock. A cool customer. Did Makuyana have any idea who the assassins might be? No, the security chief replied quite truthfully, relieved that he hadn't been asked a more general question about the source of the attempt. Could the Leader speculate himself? No, he hadn't a clue.

Makuyana made two requests. First, that the Leader told only his personal security team and not the rest of the delegation. That did provoke a break in the Leader's characteristic inscrutability, indicated by a raised eyebrow. But Makuyana was insistent about the need for confidentiality. His second request was granted more swiftly. He wanted to travel with the Leader in his armour-plated car when he left the Embassy and be with him at all times.

Then he departed, leaving behind a very thoughtful and somewhat subdued Leader to get ready for an official luncheon at the Embassy.

❖

The two of them had dozed through the morning and into the early afternoon, squeezed together in Evans' single bed. Makuyana had insisted there was nothing more they could do and had them driven to the hotel, leaving a guard posted on their door.

Despite their exhaustion, they had slept fitfully. Jenny was troubled by Jim's remoteness. Her attempts to approach him had not been so much rebuffed as ignored. He had withdrawn into himself, apologising that he was too tired to cuddle. They lay in bed back to back, and Jenny felt truly miserable, overcome by a great sense of anti-climax.

Eventually she rose and rang down for some sandwiches and salads. Evans continued to lie with his face to the wall, barely able to grunt his thanks at the idea of some food. Television didn't start transmission until the late afternoon, so she switched on the radio, at the start of a special bulletin. Suddenly she found herself jerking to attention, as a grim-voiced newscaster reported the threat of an invasion after a border clash. No details of the clash were given but it was clear to her that they were talking about the battle at the farmhouse.

'Jim,' she called, 'listen to this!'

He turned slowly, blinking from under the bedsheets. Then he seemed to collect himself. It was as if a mask had been pulled from his face. Suddenly, he was alert and functioning properly again as they both digested the news.

❖

Although Wang didn't know it at the time, he made his first major mistake just after lunch. He had wrestled with himself all morning. Should he make one final check with the two South Africans, just in case they had been put off by news of the border incident and the threat of an invasion? Never before had he been so dependent for such a crucial task on people outside his direct control.

The absence of callboxes in the city was frustrating. Eventually he decided to leave the Embassy for a nearby hotel where he could make a call. He let the phone ring twice, replaced the receiver, repeated the action, then rang properly. The voice at the other end was curt, but Wang didn't let that deflect him. He was simply seeking reassurance that all was satisfactory and confirming that the itinerary had remained unchanged.

What sort of a call was that, Venter wondered? The man must be jittery, because he hadn't said anything new. The two Afrikaners hadn't listened to the news all day; they knew nothing of developments on the border.

Wang left to walk back to the Embassy. But, just outside the hotel entrance, here was a young woman blocking his way. He hadn't noticed her arrive. He made an excuse to step aside.

'Mr Wang Bi Nan?'

'Yes.' The fact that it was a woman was probably the reason why he was caught so completely off guard when she addressed him.

'You are under arrest.' She took him by the arm, her other hand remaining in her jacket pocket.

'Nonsense. There must be a mistake. Who are you?' He pulled back, frightened now, realising that she was much stronger than he would have thought.

'No mistake, Mr Wang. You are wanted for questioning by the security police.'

'Then I claim diplomatic immunity. My Embassy is nearby,' he pointed in its direction. 'I am returning there now.'

'No you are not,' she replied firmly. Half dazed, he realised there was no point in arguing: she had pulled a gun on him.

❖

The unanimous resolution of protest from the United Nations Security Council fell on deaf ears. So did the cool diplomatic pressure from Washington and London. Pretoria was on its own and that gave the beleaguered white ruling elite a certain sense of reassurance. Deep down, they had always known they were on their own, like Jacob in Egypt. Come the crunch, their fairweather friends were always going to desert them. Nobody had ever understood them.

So the military momentum northward continued apace, the engineering corp in the vanguard, with portable steel bridges specially designed to drop into position at locations across the Limpopo selected a decade earlier. Scattered across the border at strategic spots, the white farmers, businessmen and pensioners who had been sleepers all this time were activated. The South African army needed advance intelligence on Zimbabwe's response. As the reports started to dribble back, the generals realised that there was no mass mobilisation. Harare was on full alert, there were signs of military activity, but there was no apparent push south. The Zimbabweans were seemingly playing a waiting game.

When the first Oliphant 2B clattered across the steel girders and strained up the other side and onto the plain, it stopped and its turret swept slowly round in an arc, the long barrel menacing the landscape before it. A grazing herd of Zebra galloped off in panic and as the shock-waves spread through the earth other wildlife went to ground, but otherwise, nothing. The tank crawled forward cautiously. Still nothing. Soon, other vehicles followed.

Four hundred yards away, hidden behind some rocks on the slope of a small *kopje*, a young soldier passed his binoculars to a colleague and reached for his transmitter. He would be the first to report hard confirmation of the news: the invasion had begun.

❖

They made love as they showered together, washing away the scars of the previous twenty-four hours. Afterwards they stood panting with the water continuing to flow over them. For her it was not so much a sense of release as of exhilaration at the power she had roused in him. As they dressed, she felt a wave of relief that he was still the same after all – his distant, cold manner of the morning replaced by a new drive and purpose.

But something was nagging at Evans: Wang. The image of his petulant questioning the previous day kept returning. What was the man doing here in Harare? Why was he so obsessed with Evans' own presence in the city?

He opened the door to their room and asked the bored-looking guard in the corridor where he could get hold of Makuyana. That was impossible he was told, the security chief was away from his office in charge of protection for the

Chinese Leader's state address.

It was the first Evans knew of the Chinese visit. The Peking Connection, yet again. There was something nasty afoot. He could feel it. He turned back to Jenny in the hotel room, alive with tension again.

❖

Wang wasn't giving anything away. He had been taken, protesting loudly at the breach of diplomatic protocol, to a room in a building which he had not been allowed to see because a bag was forced over his head as soon as they had him in the back of their car.

Once he saw his protests would simply be ignored, he refused to say a word. Florence Sithole had tried to interrogate him, then Makuyana joined her. They clearly knew something about his irregular activities – Evans had obviously told them about his presence in the city – but it was equally clear they didn't know the exact plan. Except that Makuyana kept returning to questions about the Leader. Did he support the Leader? Did his boss Hua support him? The questions were uncomfortably relevant.

Years ago his training had instilled in him that the best policy was to say nothing. Once you started talking, you couldn't stop. And he knew they were in a dilemma. It would be too risky for them to use physical force. He simply had to remain silent for the next four hours. Then the Old Man would secure his release. For by then, the Old Man would be in power.

❖

Makuyana left with Florence Sithole, frustrated at Wang's obduracy. As with Swanepoel, they were so near and yet so far. He needed time to break the Chinaman, and time was the one thing he didn't have. He was due at the Embassy soon to join the Leader's entourage.

The sense of crisis was heightened by the reports of convoys crossing the border. How far was Pretoria prepared to go? Was it a frightner in retaliation for the farmhouse clash? Normally they retaliated against an ANC incursion by hitting a village or attacking ANC officials. This was something bigger, much bigger.

As the other Generals studied developments, Strijdom paced the floor, pausing periodically to peer at the map electronically displayed in a sweeping curve which dominated the wall of the control room. It showed the steady advance of his forces as the computers fed in new data.

The President hadn't been happy at the way they had forced his hand. But Strijdom had brushed aside the lack of consultation with a polite reference to the contingency plans which the Head of State had himself authorised two years before. In any case, it was a *fait accompli* by now. Meanwhile the President could rest assured that he would be closely consulted until the war cabinet convened under his chairmanship at the end of the afternoon.

The puzzle was the lack of any obvious military response from Harare. Mugabe seemed to be lying back and waiting, almost daring him on. It was maddening; Strijdom needed a confrontation. He needed the Zimbabweans to attack – even just to get in the way – so that his forces could claim justification for a clash. Once he had a real battle he could produce his ace.

Not even white South Africa, for all its ruthlessness, could deploy a tactical nuclear weapon without some sort of half-presentable excuse. The doctrine of 'flexible response' allowed for a nuclear deployment in a conventional war if circumstances required it. An excuse, that was all they needed.

❖

The first trouble started, predictably enough, in Soweto. Demonstrating school pupils, the comrades in the lead, attacked and burnt down the home of a black councillor, denouncing him as a collaborator.

Within minutes, police had opened fire, first with tear gas, then with bullets. The crowd scattered, carrying their dead and wounded. Then they regrouped, their mood angry and defiant, police chiefs sensing a new and terrifying determination in their faces. Cars were overturned. Fires started. Smoke filled the air. Then, from behind the crowd – at first the police crouched in their Casspirs couldn't quite see where exactly – there came the sound of bullets whipping in a new direction: into the police lines for a change. Suddenly the sound of sniper fire was everywhere. The crowd roared its approval, surging forward again, the tense young faces almost manic and uncaring about their fate. A grenade burst underneath one of the Land Rovers, disabling it.

The police chief called for reinforcements, but another unit was under attack a mile across the township. And the army was pre-occupied with the invasion, though some help could be sent. Didn't they understand, he shouted down the line? He had already lost a dozen men, shot down dead. Others were wounded. White blood was being spilled right in front of his very eyes, man! This had never happened before. The fury in the crowd, the well-organised sniping, all of this was without precedent in the five years he had policed Soweto. There was no alternative: he ordered a retreat.

The people surged forward, triumphant, when they realised that they were winning. Excited chatter swept through their ranks. For the first time they had beaten the police. As the snipers melted away into the alleys and small boxes that passed for homes, the comrades went on the rampage.

❖

Rows of people lined the approach to Harare's Parliament Building, straining to catch a glimpse of President Mugabe when he appeared at the entrance to welcome the Chinese Leader.

Evans had come with Jenny, not so much to see the spectacle as from a gut feeling that he ought to be there. Florence had phoned through the news of Wang's detention. That was encouraging. But he still had an uneasy feeling about the situation. Anyway, he wanted to see what the Leader looked like.

Florence Sithole scanned the faces in the crowd, her eyes sweeping the scene systematically. The most dangerous moment would be when the Leader climbed out and walked the short distance to the entrance. They had cordoned off the crowd so that it was well back from the spot where his car would stop.

Everything seemed in order. Nearby buildings had been searched in case there was a gunman holed up. There were police everywhere. The mood was jolly. You wouldn't have thought the country was being invaded at this very moment. Why was Mugabe playing it so cool? She hadn't had a chance to discuss the situation with Keith.

She walked away from the Parliament building, surveying the approach. She had passed the stage of feeling tired: she was on automatic pilot now. On the other side of the road a Telecom van was parked in a spot which had been cordoned off by cones. A police officer appeared to be checking the van, watched by the white driver who had his back to her. One white worker, one black policeman talking together. A nice reversal of roles from pre-independence days. She smiled at the image. Then the tall white got into the driving seat and the officer stood nearby, looking at the crowd. She crossed the road to have one last check of the other side, glancing at her watch. The cars should be leaving the Embassy shortly. They would arrive in about five minutes. Everything seemed to be normal, everything under control.

❖

For the first time, the Old Man was worried. He could not locate Wang. His aide seemed simply to have vanished. Then there was the presence of the Zimbabwe security chief in the entourage. A new development and one that nobody had mentioned to him, which he also found troubling. He knew nothing about it until he spotted the man climbing into the limousine.

Makuyana pressed into the back seat alongside the Leader and his interpreter, apologising for the squeeze. As the cars swept out of the Embassy gate, he pulled out a pistol, cradling it on his lap. The Leader looked nervous and perhaps irritated at his intrusive presence.

Nothing was said during the journey. Makuyana kept his eyes fixed ahead. If anything was going to happen it would probably be out in front, though side roads had been closed off so that traffic could not intercept the procession. Once everyone was inside the Parliament building it would be much easier to tighten security. It was like travelling in a capsule. No traffic to worry about. No red lights to stop at. With outriders, their sirens screaming, the cavalcade swept along the empty roads and past pedestrians straining in curiosity to catch a glimpse of the Leader who had been much featured in the local media since his arrival.

Gun in hand now, Makuyana leant forward to try and make himself more comfortable.

❖

Florence Sithole wandered across the road, making another check of the other side, when a murmur went thought the crowd and she turned see the cars appear from round the corner. Four hundred yards away. She was distracted by the sound of an engine starting up. Three hundred yards away. It was the Telecom van. She started to walk toward it, reassured that the police officer

– he looked a senior man, probably an inspector – was standing alongside unconcerned. Two hundred yards. The officer had a familiar bearing. One hundred yards. But there was something not quite right about his face. Fifty yards. As the police motorbikes in front swept past, the van suddenly roared into life and accelerated out into the road right in front of the Leader's car.

The chauffeur screeched to a halt but he couldn't stop the car sliding into the side of the van and skewing to a halt. As the police officer ran over to the car, she saw the van driver climb out. He was familiar as well. A tall young white man. Yes! She recognised him! The killer she had seen in her office and the hospital. She was already moving forward when she saw him lob a stun grenade into the crowd to clear a path through.

As she ran after him, the police inspector rattled on the passenger door and the driver, relieved that there was hardly any damage, leaned across to wind down the window. In the second between recovering from being jerked forward by the emergency stop and looking around for an attack, Makuyana became aware of the policeman peering in and was vaguely troubled by the man's face. There was something about his eyes and his complexion that just wasn't right. The officer seemed to rock back as his hand came up. In the split second that an ugly looking pistol was levelled straight at the Leader, Makuyana had aimed his own revolver and squeezed the trigger.

There was a deafening roar. The policeman fell back, a neat hole drilled in his forehead, his face twisted in astonished agony.

'Get us out of here! There might be others.' Makuyana shouted at the shocked chauffeur.

❖

Standing a little way from where the telecom van had been parked, the two of them had a ringside seat. The sound of the gun and the grenade exploding seemed to crack their eardrums.

Evans saw a running man burst through the crowd followed by the sprinting figure of Florence Sithole. He was tall and strong. She seemed to be wilting. She would never catch him, he could see that. Without thinking Evans joined the pursuit, leaving Jenny to wait.

Florence Sithole was about two hundred feet ahead, the man the same again. He saw her stop and fire a shot. It seemed to hit the man in the shoulder and he stumbled, then ran on, disappearing round a corner. Florence seemed to

falter and Evans caught her up. She was panting with exhaustion and was startled at his sudden appearance on the scene.

'Chase him,' she gasped with exhaustion. 'I'll follow. But be careful.'

Evans sprinted off almost before he had time to think about it. The strain of the past day seemed to lift. He felt fine, grateful for his fitness. The man came into view again, half-way down a side road lined by offices. He looked injured and had slowed right down. Evans slowed too. What would he do if he caught him? He had no idea, but still he kept running.

❖

Coetzee staggered. The bitch: she had hurt him badly, he was losing blood fast. It was his right shoulder too. He would find it difficult to use his gun.

Where was Venter? He had heard the gunshot and assumed his friend would be following him. The car was parked just ahead, unlocked where he had left it for a quick get-away, their hand luggage in the boot. He might not be able to wait for Venter. Some bastard was following him. Blood was soaking through his overalls. He felt dizzy. Would they let him on the plane in such a state?

❖

Evans could see him clearly now. He hesitated, looking back. Florence was staggering along, catching up again. The man had stopped beside a Fiat Tipo and was opening the door. He might reach the car before the man had time to drive off. But what should he do?

The engine roared. Florence was just behind him now. But as he turned, she slipped, her gun clattering onto the road. It slid towards him. Involuntarily Evans bent to pick it up. The gun was strange and heavy in his hand, making him feel lopsided. Florence was still not back on her feet yet. Evans lifted the gun, holding it with both hands as he remembered seeing policemen do on TV, pointing it and squeezing the trigger. It jerked upward, jolting his frame, a bullet shattering the back window as the car began to move. The engine roared and the Fiat pulled out. Evans pointed the gun again and fired. This time the bullet went straight through the driver's window and shattered the windscreen.

The bullets missed Coetzee, but fragments of glass splintered into his face

– 259 –

like pellets, half blinding him. He had his foot down on the accelerator and the Tipo lurched across the road, mounting the pavement and smashing into a building. Evans stared transfixed at the results of his clumsy shots, feeling suddenly very frightened. If the man was still alive, he could turn and shoot him down. He shrank into a nearby doorway, peering out.

'Well done.' Florence Sithole startled him with a pat on the shoulder as she struggled up, grabbing her gun. He felt almost guilty.

She crept towards the car, poised to shoot. But Coetzee was slumped on the wheel in a daze, blood streaming down his face.

❖

Despite a fifty minute delay, the Leader's address went ahead as planned.

He was shaky at first, the shock of the assassination attempt still with him. The warmth of his reception owed more to the obvious relief and politeness of his hosts than the content of the speech, about which there was some ambivalence. ZANU's more fundamentalist left-wingers saw it as a revisionist departure from Marxist principles.

The Old Man would have agreed but, although he sat at the Leader's side, he did not hear a word that was spoken. His mind was in turmoil. The plot had failed. There was no point in phoning the Generals at home. All those years of planning had been in vain. His own future would probably be in question. Despite that, he felt not so much afraid as utterly defeated. There was no point in anything now.

❖

With the Chinese contingent safely returned to the Embassy, Makuyana confronted the badly injured Coetzee. He was in no state to resist once Makuyana had made it clear he would get no hospital treatment unless he co-operated. But the South African agent knew little about the background to the assignment; he was a technician, not a politician.

Makuyana kept Coetzee, blood still trickling from his shoulder, slumped in a chair. Then he had Wang brought in. The Chinaman's insolent facade dissolved immediately he realised that their plan had ended in failure. Makuyana put it to him bluntly: either he talked and was allowed to return home, or he would be detained and prosecuted. He talked.

Wang explained how the South Africans had acquired their battlefield nuclear weapons, but needed to upgrade their equipment for them to be deployed effectively. As the details spilled out under Makuyana's merciless probing, the full enormity of the threat shook the Zimbabwean. It was most unlike him, but he couldn't stop himself shivering. A new urgency gripped him. He had to get to Robert Mugabe right away. Major changes would be needed in the prepared script for his television address about the South African invasion.

❖

Still no fighting. Strijdom was intensely puzzled. His forces now had control over a section of territory up to fifty miles deep. All the border posts had been seized and Zimbabwean guards and officials taken prisoner without a shot being fired.

It was almost uncanny. His intelligence showed the enemy army retreating. If things continued like this, they could take Bulawayo before the night was out. But did they *want* to? The intention was to teach Zimbabwe a lesson, not to occupy the whole sodding country.

Meanwhile, the Cabinet was growing restless. Shares on the Johannesburg Stock Exchange were plummeting. The business community which had made so much profit out of apartheid was up in arms, with foreign companies and financiers threatening to pull out. The International Monetary Fund was demanding instant settlement of the country's debt. The gold price had plummeted and dealings had been suspended. Requests for military assistance in suppressing township uprisings were coming in thick and fast, a tone of panic in the calls from police chiefs.

Strijdom deliberated for several minutes. Then he consulted with military colleagues before ordering a halt to the advance.

❖

The staff lounge at security headquarters in Harare was crowded and silent as all eyes were glued to the television in the corner. Evans sat on a sofa, Jenny squashed in beside him. A grim-faced President came on the screen, a sheaf of notes before him. The media had received embargoed copies of the text an hour before, but at the last minute the word went round of substantial changes.

Robert Mugabe looked up from his desk as the camera closed in. 'My friends', he began, hands poised over the notes. 'Normally when I address you I have what is called an autocue there in front of me.' He pointed at the camera. 'It contains the full text of what I have to say. I had prepared just such an address about the South African invasion of our country. But within the last half hour, I have received disturbing new information which makes the crisis even more serious than I had supposed. I want to share that information with you because it threatens the very existence of life in our subcontinent of Africa.'

Evans felt tears welling up in his eyes. He knew what Mugabe was going to say. He knew it. And he felt proud. Nearly 600 miles south in Pretoria, Cabinet Ministers were watching too, their attention gripped by Mugabe's arresting opening.

'Some of you may have heard the news of the attempted assassination of the Leader of China whom we have been honoured to receive as a guest. The attempt was made while he drove to address our Parliament in Harare. Fortunately, our security services were alert and intervened to save his life. Fortunately as well, we caught one of the assassins. I have to tell you that they were both South African agents.' He paused to let the point sink in.

'Today we face naked aggression from South Africa. Pretoria has now taken over a great stretch of our country. *And* it has organised an act of terrorism in our own capital. We will not give in to such barbarism. We will fight if necessary.'

He paused again, rocking back slightly in his chair. 'Why, then, you may wonder, have our forces not engaged the South Africans already? They have been on our soil for over seven hours. I will tell you why. It is not out of weakness, though in all frankness they have a much more powerful military machine. No, it is not out of weakness. Every man, woman and child will fight to the last if we need to. We will not allow our country to be occupied. We will defend our right to be free.

'The reason I have not yet ordered our forces to fight is that I will not be provoked. I have learnt today what I have suspected for some time. Pretoria wants the excuse to unleash the terror of nuclear war upon our people and our beautiful land. Their forces are equipped with nuclear warheads. In exactly what quantities I do not know. Certainly some of their aircraft are carrying these warheads and probably some tanks too. It does not seem to worry their

leaders that their own troops could suffer the devastation of fall-out and radio-activity, whilst they destroy our country. It does not seem to bother them that prevailing winds could contaminate the Northern Transvaal too.

'I appeal to the people of the world, including white South Africans, to prevent such a catastrophe. I say to Pretoria: you have nothing to fear from Zimbabwe. I reject their assertion that last night's clash on South African territory could possibly justify military mobilisation on the scale we now see. The clash was at a spot ten miles across the border. Zimbabwean forces were indeed involved and I regret that. However, the truth about the clash has not yet been told.'

He paused again, looking at his notes. Across the country, millions of people watched and listened anxiously. Across the world, journalists scribbled and waited for his next words. In the security staff room, there was hushed silence.

'A small party of security agents and soldiers were lifted across the border by helicopter to rescue a British Professor who had been kidnapped by the South African National Intelligence Service under the direction of Captain Maritz Swanepoel. We accomplished the rescue and we retreated immediately. We were on South African territory for only a few hours. In the clash which took place there were casualties on both sides.

'I say this to the President of South Africa. If your forces continue to advance into Zimbabwe, we will have no alternative but to defend ourselves. However, I appeal to you to withdraw before such a catastrophe strikes. And, above all, I appeal to you to instruct your armed forces *not* to deploy nuclear weapons. The horrific consequences of such an action would disfigure our land for generations.'

As his picture faded out at the end of the address, there was a still silence. In the staff room, the tension was broken with a burst of spontaneous clapping. In tens of thousands of homes in the big cities and mud huts in villages throughout the country, there were tears of fear mixed with tears of pride.

❖

The General in charge of the Peking Garrison was ready by his special phone when it rang three hours after the stipulated time. He picked it up, half-eager, half-apprehensive at the instruction he was expecting.

The familiar boom of the Leader's voice caught him completely off guard. He was so surprised that he could barely concentrate on their conversation. The Leader quietly informed him about the assassination attempt. Everything was now under control. There was no reason to worry. That message should be transmitted down the line in order that the People's Liberation Army could be reassured and protected from the spread of unsubstantiated rumours and fears.

At the end of the call, the Leader added casually, almost as an afterthought, that there was some additional news about their trusted colleague Hua. Sadly it had to be said that age had finally started to catch up with him. His retirement would be announced shortly after the Delegation returned. A fine man. A dedicated servant of the people. The last of the Long March veterans. He would be irreplaceable. Such a pity.

As he contacted his fellow military chiefs and Party confidantes to break the bad news, the General's initial depression gradually shifted to a spirit of cautious optimism. There was too much turmoil in the country for the Leader to survive. The student activists were increasing the tempo of agitation. The workers were stirring too. He and his fellow conspirators need only bide their time, the General thought; one day soon, the call would come for them act.

❖

The four had slept like logs and they were bright and eager when they arrived for their appointment with the President in his office. During the night, the premises of the company headed by Eugene Fraser were raided and at the same time members of Makuyana's security department had taken him from a dinner party with business colleagues and detained him after a cursory search of his house.

It was remarkable how resilient the human constitution could be, Florence mused as she stood, refreshed and ready for the meeting with Mugabe. It was just as remarkable that the Head of State had found time to see them amidst the pressure caused by the continued presence of South African troops on Zimbabwe's territory. But the man was in a reflective mood, perfectly cool in the moment of crisis.

'Thank you for coming,' he began, as if they were doing a big favour by gracing him with their presence. 'I wanted to express my supreme gratitude at the determination and courage you have all shown. Had the assassination been successful, I dread to imagine the consequences, for the people of China, ourselves and indeed world security. We are indebted to you all.

'However, I had another reason to ask you over.' He paused, standing up and looking thoughtfully out of the window. 'I want to hear at first hand your story Mr Evans, and yours too Miss Stuart. Keith – perhaps you can intervene and clarify where necessary. And you too Miss Sithole.'

For the next hour – interrupted by just two brief phone calls – Mugabe listened and questioned, a secretary taking furious shorthand. Two of his aides took notes as well. Then he nodded, as if satisfied and began to usher them out, repeating his thanks.

The door was beginning to close behind the four, when he called them back. 'One other matter', he said seriously, looking at Makuyana, 'That special letter of authority allowing you to invoke Presidential power. Do you still have it?'

'Of course,' Makuyana looked defensive, expecting a reprimand.

'Good. Keep it for another day. And then I want you to go to the restaurant of your choice and celebrate with a good meal. Use the letter to get them to send me the bill.' He chuckled broadly as he saw their anxious faces crease into uneasy smiles as they wondered what had come over this man with the severe, puritanical reputation.

'It will be a good test of how far my decree runs!'

❖

Pretoria's public response to Mugabe's dramatic broadcast had been an immediate denunciation of his 'wild allegations' and a flat denial that they had ever contemplated using nuclear weapons.

Troops had been sent over the border as a warning that any further transgressions by Zimbabwe would not be tolerated. There was never any intention to advance further, a Government spokesman lied, but they would not back down: the troops would stay until Pretoria was satisfied that no 'further aggression' was contemplated by Harare.

Privately, however, the broadcast rocked the Government and the white population in South Africa. Its accuracy had stunned the few Cabinet Ministers and military leaders in the know. Even whites loyal to the Government began to believe there was something in what Mugabe had said. As the implications of deploying even battlefield nuclear weapons sank in, there was unprecedented pressure on the State President. A meeting of the Nationalist parliamentary Caucus was demanded by MPs previously so compliant as to be virtually on the leadership's payroll. Rumours of a motion of no confidence in the President – unheard of in the Party – swept through political circles.

The Government was also buffeted by international pressure. The Washington-based Gold Institute, representing bullion dealers and refiners, issued a 'member alert' notice, warning that a freeze on dealing in South African gold was imminent. Even prominent figures in the Italian jewellery business, which for decades had bought most of its 200 tons of gold from South Africa, announced they were investigating alternative sources of supply, notably Russia. From Geneva, the World Gold Council, a public relations agency for the South African mining industry, issued a statement expressing alarm that unspecified 'recent developments' could knock the bottom out of the country's market in gold exports.

Virtually alone, a backbench British Conservative MP, known colloquially as 'the Member for Pretoria', said that he fully backed the military intervention. 'You can only answer force with force,' he insisted in an interview on the BBC morning programme *Today*. The incredulous interviewer omitted to ask whether the Honourable Member's opinion might have been influenced by his many free trips to the country. The latest was two weeks of luxury in the famed Kruger National Park in the agreeable company of a mystery blonde half his age.

❖

Quietly, even unobtrusively, the retreat began. The supply vehicles were first to slip back over the border, followed by troop carriers, then tanks. There was no announcement and no admission, but, two days after it had begun, the occupation was over and the military turned their attensions to more pressing business at home.

In an unprecedented gesture of defiance, the green, yellow and black flag of the ANC had been draped over the statue of the old Afrikaner hero, Paul Kruger, in Pretoria's main Church Square. It had been illegal to display the flag for decades.

KJ spoke darkly about a 'nationwide conspiracy mounted by the ANC'. His forces moved to suppress it. But privately he wondered whether the white state still had the political will to fight on. He was tired. They were all tired.

But tiredness was the last thing another 'Old Man' felt. Down at the tip of Africa, he looked out from the comfortable cottage in his prison compound through the vineyards at the beauty of the Franshoek Valley. He looked up to the surrounding mountains: the Groot, the Klein Drakenstein, the Simonstown. Their majesty inspired him, just as he inspired millions across the world. He sensed his time was coming. He had prepared long and hard – the careful diet, the daily keep fit sessions, the studying, the reading, the thinking, the discussions with the powerful who had increasingly come to him. They had locked him up for over a quarter of a century, but they had not broken him. He was stronger than them. Soon they would need him to save his country.

❖

The world's press were waiting as Evans, Jenny at his side, returned to the Sheraton. Photographers clicked away and reporters gathered round while TV camera crews jostled to get a decent position. As if it had been pre-arranged amongst the scribes, the BBC's Southern Africa correspondent pushed to the front and thrust a microphone forward. 'Mr Evans, do you have any knowledge of nuclear weapons deployed by the South African army?'

The question was neat. Not, 'have the invading South Africans got nuclear weapons?' (to which Evans, being an academic rather than a politician, would have been obliged to reply he didn't know).

It was as if he had been waiting for this moment through all the troubles of the past few months. At last he could have *his* say. At last he could pay some debts: to Hu, his father, and the brave students in Peking; to Dick Sewell; to the Zimbabweans; and also to Jenny.

'The South Africans have battlefield nuclear warheads developed in co-operation with several other countries, especially China. The Government of Pretoria must come clean and Peking must deal with the faction responsible for trading nuclear know-how and weapons with South Africa.'

The journalist did not interrupt. He could already see a perfect clip for that evening's news bulletins. The questioning went on for another twenty minutes. Jenny was pressed for an eye-witness account of the battle at the farmhouse. She could already envisage a resurgence of 'Red Jen' stories in the London pop papers.

Afterwards, correspondents from the London *Guardian*, *Independent* and Reuters News Agency asked her for some background. How had she come to be out here so soon after the Greenpeace story had broken in London? She told them: about her suspicions of the CIA, her fears about the duplicitous role of British Intelligence. She was sceptical about how much of it would be printed, but she wanted the truth to be told.

As she talked, she glanced across to see what had happened to Jim. Most of the reporters had hurried off to file their copy or dispatch their tapes. But there were several TV teams who still wanted individual interviews. He was surrounded by a camera crew and someone was fixing a microphone to his shirt.

At that moment, he looked up, smiling as he caught her eye. The journalists had expressed considerable interest in the lecture he was still due to give the next day on the ubiquitous character of nuclear radiation. They wanted to attend. He realised he could use it as a platform.

As their eyes held, he wondered whether he would ever be able to retreat again into the relative anonymity of apolitical academia. Or, with Jenny there, whether he would even want to.